THE CLIFF HOUSE STRANGLER

ALSO BY SHIRLEY TALLMAN

Murder on Nob Hill
The Russian Hill Murders

THE CLIFF HOUSE STRANGLER

SHIRLEY TALLMAN

 St. Martin's Minotaur ⚑ New York

This is a work of fiction. All of the characters, organizations, and events portrayed in this novel are either products of the author's imagination or are used fictitiously.

www.minotaurbooks.com

Library of Congress Cataloging-in-Publication Data

Tallman, Shirley.
    The Cliff House strangler : a Sarah Woolson mystery / Shirley Tallman.—1st ed.
    p. cm.
    ISBN-13: 978-0-312-35756-6
    ISBN-10: 0-312-35756-7
    1. Women lawyers—Fiction. 2. Cliff House (San Francisco, Calif.)—Fiction. 3. San Francisco (Calif.)—Fiction. 4. Seances—Fiction. 5. Domestic fiction. I. Title.

PS3620.A54C55 2007
813'.6—dc22

                                                        2007011274

First Edition: July 2007

10 9 8 7 6 5 4 3 2 1

To Carol, with love always.

And in memory of Kate Fleming, an enormous talent and a wonderful human being. In her performance as Anna Fields, Kate's delightful reading style created the perfect voice for Sarah Woolson in the first two audio books in the series. She will be sorely missed, both as a gifted reader and as a friend.

Last, but never least, to H. P.

ACKNOWLEDGMENTS

I want to express my sincere thanks to the San Francisco Sheriff's Office, and particularly to Sheriff Michael Hennessey, for introducing me to the jails and penal system of 1880s San Francisco.

Many thanks as well to my good friend Val Nasedkin for helping me with my mostly nonexistent Russian vocabulary. *Bol 'shoe spasibo,* Val!

I also owe a debt of gratitude to Alexandra Sechrest, who kindly allowed me to borrow her lovely name for this novel.

As always, heartfelt thanks to my writing buddy, JoAnn Wendt, for the many hours she spent critiquing this book. Your help is invaluable.

AUTHOR'S NOTE

Perhaps some of you have noted that the Cliff House pictured on the jacket of this book is not the edifice that actually stood at the northwest tip of San Francisco in 1881. That earlier building, often referred to as the "second" Cliff House, had a rather lackluster appearance, even after Captain Foster (who leased the property in the early 1860s) tripled the size of the building by adding two wings and a long balcony.

After much thought, my editors and I decided that it would be far more interesting to feature the famous Cliff House erected by Adolph Sutro in 1896, some fifteen years after fictional events portrayed in *The Cliff House Strangler* took place.

Although we apologize for taking this creative, if historically incorrect, liberty, we cannot regret the decision. The depiction of Sutro's Cliff House—towering in stately majesty over the Pacific Ocean, the night sky lit by jagged streaks of lightning—perfectly sets the stage for Madame Karpova's séance and the tragic events that followed.

THE CLIFF HOUSE STRANGLER

CHAPTER ONE

I can't believe I let you talk me into this!" Robert Campbell grumbled.

As if to punctuate this complaint, jagged bolts of lightning flashed across the night sky, followed by a resounding clap of thunder. That brief burst of light revealed my companion's tense face as the cabbie's frightened horse nearly ran our brougham off the road. Eddie Cooper—the young lad I'd met several months ago during the Russian Hill murders—quickly brought the dappled gray under control. Unfortunately, he seemed disinclined to lessen his horse's pace as the first heavy drops of rain splashed onto the roof of the carriage.

My tall, brusque colleague—until recently one of my coworkers at the prestigious San Francisco law firm of Shepard, Shepard, McNaughton and Hall—pressed his face against the window to glare outside at what was rapidly turning into a downpour.

"I told you we were in for a storm. But no, nothing would do but that you drag me out to Land's End in the middle of a hurricane. And for a séance, of all the bizarre—"

"Oh, for the love of heaven!" I sighed, fighting to retain my patience. Robert Campbell, who had proved to be a loyal ally in several past adventures, nonetheless could exhaust the fortitude of a saint. "Hurricanes occur in the tropics. This is nothing more than a rainstorm. Do stop being so melodramatic."

Naturally, he ignored me. "If your brother Samuel is so het up to write an article about ghosts and goblins, why didn't he make this ridiculous trip himself?"

"For the dozenth time, Samuel had to leave for Sacramento this morning. And as he has not as yet acquired the ability to be in two places at once, he asked me to go in his stead." I was forced to grip the seat, as our carriage wheels bounced over a deep pothole, resulting in a fresh mumble of curses from my disgruntled companion. "Robert, be honest. Aren't you the least bit curious about Madame Karpova? The city has talked of little else for weeks. From what I've heard, her European tour earlier this year was a huge success."

He gave a low grunt. "I don't have any patience for gullible people who believe that this—this charlatan can actually communicate with the dead."

He jerked as another flash of lightning threw the bleak countryside into stark illumination. "And why in God's name does she have to perform her parlor tricks all the way out at the Cliff House, instead of some decently dry room in the city?" He ran his fingers through his unruly mop of red hair, causing it to stick up in small irregular patches. I also noted that his Scottish *r*'s were rolling along nicely, becoming ever more pronounced as the storm intensified.

Not wishing to encourage Robert's bad temper with a response, I silently busied myself straightening the folds of my dark lavender skirt, particularly the horizontal pleating, which had become tangled with my boots during the uneven ride. My unhappy colleague did not take the hint.

"It's a mystery to me why Junius Foster agreed to this crazy idea in the first place. Lieutenant Foster has been managing the

Cliff House for fifteen years, and damn profitably, too. What do you suppose possessed him to turn the place over to a Russian tea-leaf reader, of all people?"

"Apparently, Madame Karpova has some very influential admirers in San Francisco society," I replied, determined not to be pulled into another one of Robert's pointless arguments. "I've never been to the Cliff House myself, but Madame Karpova evidently claims the place possesses a unique atmosphere conducive to ethereal vibrations."

"Good lord, Sarah! Do you hear yourself?"

"Oh, do calm down, Robert. I'm merely repeating what Madame Karpova is reported to have said. I suggest you put away your preconceptions for the evening and approach the experience with an open mind."

He muttered something largely unintelligible by way of a reply, then once again came an inch out of his seat when another flash of lightning lit the carriage. It was quickly followed by a clash of thunder.

"Try to relax," I said, steadfastly ignoring the frayed state of my own nerves. "I'm sure this bit of weather will soon play itself out."

Half an hour later, I was forced to eat these words. Not only had the "bit of weather" not dissipated by the time we reached our destination; it had developed into a full-fledged deluge, made worse by erratically gusting winds.

Successfully negotiating the last rugged stretch of muddy road leading up the cliff, Eddie reined up in front of what had become popularly known as the "Second Cliff House." It had acquired this name some ten years earlier when Lt. Junius Foster added two large wings to the original structure, which, heretofore, had primarily consisted of a saloon and dining establishment. This ambitious remodeling provided hotel accommodations for moneyed guests who, after an overpriced dinner, chose to postpone their long trek back to the city until the following morning. From rumors I'd heard, these rooms were just as frequently occupied by politicians and gamblers, or by gentlemen seeking a convenient trysting place to bring their paramours.

I looked out the carriage window at the single-storied edifice perched high above the northwest tip of San Francisco. One of the reasons for the Cliff House's burgeoning popularity was the spectacular view it afforded of the entrance to the Golden Gate—at least on a clear day. Tonight, the churning black sea crashed against Seal Rocks, as if determined to crush them into sand. And for once, there was no sign of the sea lions, otters, and seals responsible for naming the famous rocks, even though they commonly cavorted upon the sandstone cliffs at night. Perhaps Robert is right, I thought, looking out at driving sheets of rain; most sensible mammals would not venture out on a night like this.

Descending from his perch at the front of the brougham, Eddie Cooper opened the carriage door and handed me an umbrella. I nodded gratefully, although I feared it would do little to protect us from the torrent, which, at the moment, was pouring almost horizontally down upon us from the west.

"Take the brougham around to the carriage sheds, Eddie," I shouted, attempting to be heard above the howling wind. "After you've wiped the horse down, go to the kitchen. I've made arrangements for you to be given food and something hot to drink."

"Righto, miss," Eddie replied, his youthful enthusiasm not in the least diminished by the storm. He looked furtively around, then pulled a heavy brown stocking from his coat pocket. By the way it jangled as he whacked the sock into his palm, I guessed he'd filled the toe with a goodly number of coins, making it into an effective, if somewhat primitive, cosh. "If you or Mr. Campbell need me, miss, just call out."

I wasn't sure whether to smile or frown at this improvised, if serious-looking, weapon. "I'm sure that won't prove necessary, Eddie. But it's good to know you've come prepared."

With a conspiratorial wink, Eddie helped me out of the carriage and I opened the umbrella. As Robert and I danced about
trying to avoid the larger mud puddles, the boy leapt back onto his
seat at the front of the brougham and clicked the horse off in the
direction of the carriage sheds. True to my fears, the umbrella was
next to useless as Robert and I hurried up the wooden stairs to the
Cliff House entrance.

Before we reached the front door, it was flung open by a tall,
rangy-looking man with a riotous black beard set off by vivid
streaks of white, shaggy black eyebrows, and equally forbidding
black eyes. The stranger's appearance was startling enough to take
anyone by surprise, but the way his towering frame filled the doorway certainly created a chilling enough atmosphere for the upcoming séance.

I must say he was well suited for the role. The deep lines on his
craggy face had been uniquely chiseled, having the curious effect
of making him appear menacing one moment and devoid of emotion the next, depending upon the angle in which he was viewed.
He was dressed entirely in black from head to foot, which produced the brief but startling illusion that his head floated through
the air independent of a physical body. I guessed him to be in his
fifties, but his deeply lined skin made age difficult to judge.

After several moments of awkward silence, the man stood back
from the door, allowing us to enter. Although he uttered not one
word of introduction—or, indeed, of welcome—I knew from
Samuel's description that this must be Dmitry Serkov, Madame
Karpova's brother. Stone-faced and mute, the gloomy Russian
reached out his hand and inclined his head at our wet coats. Just as
silently, we handed them over, then followed him as he led us to
what I assumed must be the Cliff House dining room.

When we reached the door, I stopped so abruptly that Robert
collided with me, bumping into my back. Even then, I made no
move to go any farther. Call it my imagination, but the atmosphere
in that room was so palpable, I felt goose bumps rise on my arms.

For a dazed moment, I thought I had somehow stumbled upon Aladdin's cave!

All around us, dozens of candles sparkled like glittering jewels, darting about this way and that as they were caught in a confluence of small drafts caused by the storm outside. While my eyes adjusted to this optical extravaganza, I spied a large, beautifully rendered Japanese screen standing against the wall to my right. I blinked as the flickering candlelight made the daintily painted birds and butterflies on the screen appear to flap their wings and fly.

Feeling Robert's none too gentle nudge upon my shoulder, I mentally chided myself on being fanciful. Gathering my scattered wits, along with my sadly dampened skirts, I stepped through the door and into the dining chamber.

It was immediately apparent that the room had been considerably rearranged, in honor, I supposed, of tonight's séance. Most of the dining tables had been moved to either side of the room, creating an empty space before an expanse of windows overlooking Seal Rocks. There, three or four tables had been pushed together to form one long rectangular surface, totally bare except for a large white candle glittering in its center. Normally, this location would have been ideal for viewing the popular rocks below. Tonight, however, the famous boulders were visible only when lightning illuminated them with stark streaks of light and shadow, making them loom up before us like some kind of demonic sea monster.

So taken was I by nature's frenzied display that it was only when someone coughed that I realized a group of people were already seated at the improvised table. Recalling myself to tonight's task, I noted that nine guests sat before the window, five women and four men. All of them were dressed in fashionable, if dark-colored, clothes. Are they afraid, I wondered a bit giddily, that the sight of brighter tones might offend the spirits?

Everyone sat in awkward silence, as if not sure what to expect and therefore unwilling to let down their guard. A few people regarded

Robert and me with fleeting curiosity, then immediately shifted their eyes elsewhere.

Before we reached the group, a tall, exotic-looking woman seemed to materialize out of nowhere. Since the only visible door was the one through which Robert and I had just entered, I concluded the woman must have stepped out from behind the Japanese screen. For effect? If so, it had certainly succeeded. Almost surely the partition must conceal a second entrance into the dining room, I realized, perhaps from the kitchen, or even from the saloon.

The four gentlemen at the table rose to their feet as the distinctive-looking woman swept majestically to the table. From her regal bearing, I was certain this must be the famous—or should I say infamous—Madame Olga Karpova, the self-proclaimed Russian aristocrat and psychic who had successfully conquered Europe and who now seemed determined to triumph over North America, as well.

Sinking gracefully into the vacant chair at the head of the table, Madame Karpova motioned for the gentlemen to take their seats, then beckoned Robert and me toward the last two unoccupied places at the far left-hand side of the table. Our company now numbered an even dozen, but the tension I'd originally sensed in the room had increased exponentially with the clairvoyant's entrance. The drama was about to begin, and I felt a brief shiver of anticipation. Looking at the expectant faces watching her from around the table, I was sure I wasn't the only person eager to see what Madame Karpova had in store for us.

While those around the table resettled themselves, some sharing whispered comments with their neighbors, others darting inquisitive looks at Madame Karpova, I, too, took the opportunity to study the psychic. She presented a singular appearance, both in her manner of dress as well as in her demeanor, which, like her brother's, was decidedly theatrical. Perched straight-backed in her chair, hands placed palms down on the table before her, Madame Karpova resembled nothing so much as an enthroned queen surveying her subjects. She had yet to utter a single word, yet she easily dominated the room. Even those individuals in our company who numbered among the cream of San Francisco society were regarding her with expressions of uneasy yet undeniable deference.

There was no doubt that Madame Karpova gave the impression of a woman accustomed to being in control; every movement of her slim body exuded self-confidence and absolute faith in her own powers. As was her brother, she was dressed completely in black, her gown constructed from some sort of diaphanous material and decorated with astrological signs, some rendered in gold and some in silver. The flowing long-sleeved dress was fastened at her throat by an onyx broach. The dangling silver and gold bangles that hung from her ears were also shaped into astrological signs, although the light was too dim, and I was too far down the table, to identify which ones they represented.

Madame Karpova's face was long and boldly sculpted, with high cheekbones and a thin patrician nose. Her light olive-colored skin was very smooth and surprisingly free of wrinkles for a woman who had to be approaching fifty. Full, beautifully shaped black eyebrows arched elegantly across a high forehead, and her lips were dark and somewhat severe, as if they rarely curved into a smile. The woman's hair color was a mystery, since she had wrapped her head in a black turban. This, too, was fastened with an onyx broach.

Despite her unorthodox costume, the psychic's most distinctive features were her dark brown—almost black—eyes. The heavy kohl she had applied to outline them was obviously for dramatic effect, but there was a deeper, almost magnetic quality about them that transcended artificial enhancement. To say that they were penetrating would be an understatement; I found them absolutely compelling.

Madame Karpova was effectively using them now to capture her guests' attention. One by one, every eye at the table fixed upon her. Except for the uneasy shuffle of Robert's feet and the sound of rain beating upon the roof and windows, the room was eerily silent. Like an actor milking every ounce of drama from a scene, she waited several long moments before speaking.

"Welcome, my friends," she said at last. "I am Madame Olga Karpova." She paused, as if to give this pronouncement the significance it deserved, then gestured to the beautiful young girl in her mid- to late teens seated to her right. "This is my daughter, Yelena." Turning to the dour man who had let us in, and who was now seated directly to Robert's right, she added, "And this is my brother, Dmitry Serkov. It is my practice to dispense with further introductions to protect the privacy of my clients. Be assured that those spirits beyond the pale require no introductions. They come to us in peace, bringing comfort and enlightenment to those loved ones who have been left behind."

The clairvoyant's voice was deep and richly textured. Although I detected a Russian accent, her command of the English language was surprisingly good. It was so exceptional, in fact, that I questioned her insistence that she had only left her native Russia three years earlier.

Once again, she paused, taking us all in with that darkly intense gaze. "I have one implacable rule. Those entities who choose to join us this evening are to be treated with the utmost respect and deference. Is that understood?"

This was answered by a surprised nod of heads and a general, albeit hushed, murmur of agreement.

Seemingly satisfied, Madame Karpova turned to her brother. "If you please, Dmitry."

Silently, the tall man stood and, with a lumbering gate, made his way around the room snuffing out candles. As he slowly but methodically set about this task, Madame Karpova explained what we might expect to see that night.

"Unlike many spiritualists, I disdain the use of cabinets, curtains, or other such props. They are for those pretending to possess *the gift,* that rare ability to communicate with those souls who inhabit the nether world beyond our own."

She spread her arms to indicate the empty space surrounding the table, and particularly the area around and behind her chair.

"I, Madame Karpova," she went on with histrionic self-importance, "have no need to hide behind such artifice. I will remain in your sight throughout tonight's reading." Her dark eyes captured those of each of us in turn. "Even when I am no longer in possession of my body."

This last bit was said in a voice so pregnant with implications that it precipitated another low, nervous murmur around the table. She quickly squelched the response.

"There are some of you in this room who scoff, who doubt not only my powers but the very existence of life beyond the dark portals of death. Oh, yes, I know who you are." Her voice rose to a crescendo, drowning out even the storm. I felt Robert stiffen beside me, and could not deny my own quick intake of breath. If nothing else, Madame Karpova certainly knew how to mesmerize an audience.

"Yes," she went on. "I tell you the world is filled with disbelievers. But cynics beware. The spirits have been known to exact a terrible vengeance upon those foolish enough to deny their existence."

She paused, and such was the sheer magnetism of the woman that not a single sound filled the sudden void.

"I must also caution you," she resumed in low, compelling tones, "I have no control over which entities will choose to join us tonight. My primary control—the spirit I will allow to inhabit my body during tonight's reading—is Tizoc, an Aztec priest. But even a spirit over a thousand years old has limited influence over those who have traveled beyond our earthly plane."

As she droned on about the world on the "other side," Robert leaned close to my ear and asked what I knew about the others seated at the table.

Thanks to my brother Samuel, who had somehow managed to obtain a list of tonight's attendees, I was able to identify most of the guests. I required no list, however, to recognize the distinguished-looking man sitting directly to my left, at the opposite end of the table from Madame Karpova.

"That's state senator Percival Gaylord," I informed Robert quietly. My elder, sadly narrow-minded brother Frederick was also a member of the California senate. Since I had been forced to listen to him gush ad infinitum about Gaylord, who, for reasons best known to himself, had become Frederick's mentor, I'd been more than a little surprised to learn he would be present tonight. What would my brother think, I wondered, if he knew his revered adviser was taking part in a séance?

"That's the senator's wife, Maurilla Gaylord, seated to his left," I went on in a hushed whisper.

Robert gave a derisive grunt, then nodded toward the young man seated to Mrs. Gaylord's left. "What about the boy? He looks too young to be taken in by this spirit nonsense."

Unobtrusively, I peered down at Samuel's notes, which I'd placed in my lap. My brother's horrible handwriting and the dim light made them difficult to read. Yet because of the young man's age, there could hardly be a mistake.

"That must be Nicholas Bramwell," I told my companion. "He's the younger son of Edgar Bramwell—you know, the San Francisco contractor. Samuel says he recently graduated from Yale University's School of Law. That must be his mother, Philippa Bramwell, seated to his left."

I nodded toward a plump middle-aged woman stylishly dressed in a burgundy silk gown, the long cuirass bodice decorated with narrow satin stripes that gleamed in the candlelight as her breath moved in and out of her ample bosom. Atop her perfectly coiffed brown hair perched a small but elaborate burgundy hat, trimmed in feathers, jewels, and the same satin material.

"The elderly widow next to her is Mrs. Theodora Reade. Apparently, she and Mrs. Bramwell are devotees of spiritualism and rarely miss one of these events."

"Then we have Yelena, Madame Karpova's daughter," Robert murmured, admiring the lovely dark-haired girl sitting to Madame Karpova's right. "By the silly look on the Bramwell boy's face, he's clearly taken a fancy to the lass."

I had also noticed the admiring looks the young man was bestowing upon the medium's daughter. Although Yelena pretended to be unaware of young Bramwell's attention, the occasional sidelong glances she gave him from beneath long, thick black lashes told me she was very conscious of him indeed.

Seated directly to Madame Karpova's left was another unlikely attendee: Lt. Frank Ahern of the San Francisco Police Department. Ahern was a short, rather burly middle-aged Irishman with a ruddy, good-natured face and sandy-colored hair liberally sprinkled with gray. His eyes were a vivid blue, and seemed to gleam with ill-disguised skepticism as he regarded the Russian clairvoyant. To his left was his wife, Nora, a small, pleasant-looking woman who was watching Madame Karpova with single-minded intensity.

"By the horn spoons!" Robert exclaimed after I'd identified the Aherns, his so-called whisper loud enough for Madame Karpova's penetrating eyes to fasten on us in silent disapproval. "A state senator and a police lieutenant. You'd think they'd be the first ones to escort this Karpova woman and her bag of tricks out of town."

"Shh," I hissed, as other faces at the table frowned in our direction.

With a final disapproving glare at Robert and myself, Madame Karpova's attention went to her brother. In that same ponderous pace, Dmitry Serkov extinguished the last candle—save for the white pillar positioned in the middle of our table—then once again took his seat between Robert and Mrs. Ahern. The light cast by this sole remaining candle barely penetrated beyond the twelve of us, leaving the rest of the room in virtual darkness.

Madame Karpova cleared her throat and solemnly announced that we were ready to begin. "I would ask each of you to relax and concentrate on the entity you wish to contact," she instructed.

CLIFF HOUSE DINING ROOM *Seating for Séance*

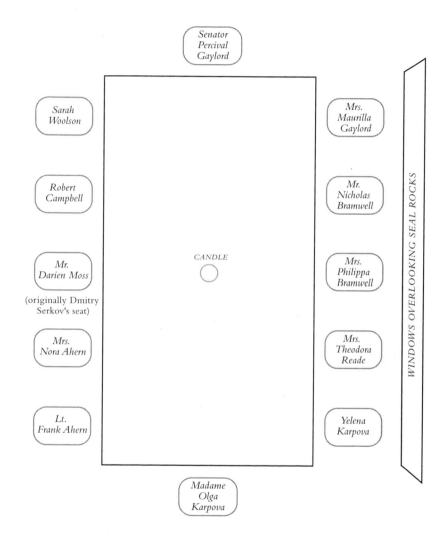

Senator Percival Gaylord

Sarah Woolson

Mrs. Maurilla Gaylord

Robert Campbell

Mr. Nicholas Bramwell

CANDLE

Mr. Darien Moss

(originally Dmitry Serkov's seat)

Mrs. Philippa Bramwell

Mrs. Nora Ahern

Mrs. Theodora Reade

Lt. Frank Ahern

Yelena Karpova

Madame Olga Karpova

WINDOWS OVERLOOKING SEAL ROCKS

"Please remember, once I have entered into a trance, I will be in an altered state, delicately balanced between this world and the next. While I am out of my body, it is vital that no one make any sudden sounds or movements, or attempt to—"

Her words abruptly cut off as the dining room door swung open with a bang, and the room was vividly lit by another flash of lightning. Startled, we all turned to see a large man standing framed in the doorway. At least I supposed the intruder was comprised of flesh and blood. In truth, he was so bizarrely dressed in a long black cape and matching cowl pulled low over his eyes that for a wild moment I thought he might actually be one of Madame Karpova's spirits.

Since he was illuminated for only a fleeting moment, I had to question whether the figure had truly been there at all. But when a second bolt of lightning quickly followed the first, I knew the stranger had been no figment of my imagination.

With a muttered oath, Lieutenant Ahern rose halfway out of his chair. By the light of the table's flickering candle, I could see that his expression was a cross between anger and barely suppressed fear.

"Darien Moss!" the police lieutenant hissed. "What in the name of all the saints are you doing here?"

CHAPTER TWO

For a long moment, the stranger didn't move. Then, as if he were the long-awaited guest of honor, he threw back his rain-soaked cowl and walked boldly into the room. To my left, Senator Gaylord cursed softly, and his wife stifled a gasp. Looking toward the head of the table, I saw Madame Karpova's body stiffen; then, glancing to my right, I noticed a look of outright malevolence cross her brother Dmitry Serkov's scarred face.

The newcomer was well over six feet tall and on the brawny side. Despite Moss's long cape, it was apparent that his youthful muscles were beginning to lean toward flab as he approached his middle years. It was too dark to see his features clearly, but I knew from the way he swaggered toward us that he was enjoying every minute of our stunned reaction to his appearance. The man had obviously timed his entrance to create the utmost drama. And it had worked.

"Who's Darien Moss?" Robert asked in a whisper I was sure could be heard around the room.

"He's that nasty tell-all reporter from the *San Francisco Informer*," I told him with distaste.

Robert chuckled. "You mean the one who called you a silly,

empty-headed society girl pretending to be an attorney, when she should have been home playing with her dolls?"

I was not pleased by the humor in his tone. "Yes, that one," I replied tightly.

As if he had overheard our conversation—which he very well might have, given Robert's version of a whisper—Darien Moss glanced in our direction.

"Ah, Miss Woolson. Fancy finding you here. Does this mean you've given up your"—he gave a rude chuckle—"*law practice* in favor of more esoteric pursuits?"

Not only was the reporter insulting but his high-pitched voice had an annoying whine to it. Considering the man's venomous pen, it seemed distinctly ill-suited to his persona. I was trying to come up with a stinging rejoinder, when I realized the man's small gray eyes had already moved farther down the table.

"Well, well. Senator Gaylord, and Lieutenant Ahern. I hardly expected to see two of our city's most noted public servants seeking advice from the spirit world." Both men turned red in the face, but Moss gave them no chance to object.

"Mrs. Bramwell," he said, nodding his head at the woman sitting bolt upright in her chair, a disapproving frown on her haughty face. "I should have known that San Francisco society would be represented at this little soiree. I suppose an empty mind must find something to fill the void, no matter how ludicrous."

The matron's green eyes turned hard as nails as she fixed the reporter with an icy glare. A satisfied smile curled the corners of Moss's mouth, as if he was pleased that his barb had once again found its mark, and he turned to the young man seated to the woman's right.

"And this must be your younger son," he said in that thin, strident voice. "Janus, is it? No, sorry, I believe I have the boy confused with a god from Roman mythology." For some reason, he seemed to find this mistake vastly amusing. "Ah, yes, I remember now. It's Nicholas. I heard you'd passed the bar, young man. I'm sure your father will find your legal expertise a valuable asset to his company." His smile turned nasty. "Given his penchant for cutting corners and padding his pockets on certain government projects."

Heat rushed up Nicholas Bramwell's neck, suffusing his face and turning it a dark red. He was halfway out of his chair before Philippa Bramwell took hold of his arm and forced him back down.

"Do not waste your breath, Nicholas," she told him with a dismissive sniff of her oversized nose. "The man is a reprobate, an unscrupulous boor. He is totally lacking in ethics or the basic principles of civil behavior. Darien Moss is the worst-possible example of modern journalism run amok."

Moss laughed out loud, slapping his thigh as if greatly amused. "Well, that puts me in my place, doesn't it? I'm gratified to know that one of the most supercilious citizens of our city deigns to read my modest paper."

Philippa Bramwell seemed about to suffer an apoplectic fit. Her distorted face broke out in ugly red blotches, and she sputtered more or less inarticulately as she flailed about in an effort to find words to express her outrage.

Moss turned with satisfaction to our hostess. "Madame Karpova, we meet at last. I've heard some remarkable stories concerning your"—again, the nasty smile appeared, making his face resemble that of a mischievous satyr—"accomplishments. This evening, I finally have an opportunity to view these feats firsthand. I'm sure my readers will be most interested in my observations. Judging from the distinguished company you've assembled, I believe I've underestimated your resources, or should I say your ability to hoodwink individuals all too eager to reveal themselves as fools?"

There was a collective gasp around the table as Moss swept off his wet cape and tossed it carelessly onto a table against the nearest wall. "I apologize for being late, but the roads are very nearly washed out in some areas." He gave Madame Karpova a sardonic little bow. "I'm relieved to see you have not yet begun. I would hate to miss any part of the show."

No longer able to contain himself, Lieutenant Ahern came out of his chair, fists clenched, his face beet red. "Watch your mouth, Moss!" he spat out. "If you've come here tonight to gloat or gather material for that filthy rag of yours, you can turn right around and march back out that door. And I'd better not see any of our names in tomorrow's paper, or by God I'll—"

"You'll do what, Lieutenant?" Moss's smile had become an outright sneer. "Arrest me for employing my First Amendment right to print the truth? For educating the people of San Francisco about their so-called leaders? To let them know how they're being robbed and hoodwinked—"

"That is enough!" Madame Karpova's low voice cut through Moss's diatribe like a knife slicing through butter. She had not risen from her chair, yet the power of her personality was enough to stop both men in their tracks. "If you cannot behave in a civilized manner, gentlemen, I will ask you to leave."

Lieutenant Ahern's blue eyes remained fixed on Moss with a look of profound hatred. I was afraid he was about to challenge the reporter physically, when his wife took him by the sleeve and urged him back into his seat.

Frank Ahern hesitated, clearly itching to put Darien Moss in his place. Then, looking around, he realized everyone at the table was watching him. His face turned an even deeper shade of red as he sank reluctantly back into his chair.

Instead of returning Ahern's anger, Moss again seemed to have found the entire exchange amusing. "Very sensible, Lieutenant. I'm sure you wouldn't want to do anything to frighten off Madame Karpova's spirits—that is, if any of them actually make an appearance tonight."

For the first time, Moss seemed to realize there was no room for him at the table. With a shrug, he started toward one of the chairs that had been pushed to the side of the room. "I see I shall have to make my own place."

Theodora Reade looked about in alarm. "But that will make thirteen at the table," she protested. "Thirteen people is—"

"Out of the question," said Mrs. Bramwell, interrupting her. She shot the reporter a look of profound dislike. "You are quite right, my dear," she added, giving the elderly woman a friendly pat on the arm. "Thirteen people at a séance will never do."

This caused a general murmur, but before anyone else could voice an opinion, Dmitry Serkov rose to his feet. Giving Darien Moss a last contemptuous look, the Russian stalked heavily, and silently, from the room.

"It appears you have a place after all, Mr. Moss," Madame Karpova said. Although her exotic face displayed no emotion, I could tell by the stiff set of her shoulders that she was not pleased by this addition to her table.

I understood her uneasiness. Yet, what else could the woman do? If she sent Darien Moss packing, she would undeniably pay dearly for the slight in tomorrow's *Informer*. Of course, she might well pay the same price if she allowed him to stay. It seemed glaringly clear that there wasn't one person at the table who didn't shudder at what he or she might read in Moss's next column. Including me, I admitted ruefully. The reporter had made it obvious that finding me at a séance would do nothing to improve his poor opinion of San Francisco's newest female attorney. It was also true that since I had opened my own law office, his power to cause me grief had increased immeasurably.

Eleven sets of wary eyes followed Moss as he settled himself in Serkov's vacated chair between Robert and Mrs. Ahern. He made himself comfortable, then reached into a pocket and removed a small black leather notebook and a pencil.

"Mr. Moss," Madame Karpova pronounced coolly. "You may not take notes. The spirits are easily disturbed."

Moss's expression was mocking. "My apologies, Madame Karpova," he said with a sardonic nod of his head. "By all means, we must endeavor to keep the spirits happy." His face twisted into an obnoxious smile as he put away the tools of his trade. My father, the Honorable Horace T. Woolson, superior court judge for the County of San Francisco, had no use for newspaper reporters, considering them to be social scavengers who make their living exploiting gratuitous violence and private scandal. I shuddered to contemplate Papa's reaction when he finally learned that his youngest son, Samuel, was an enthusiastic member of this fellowship. Although I didn't generally share my father's prejudice, at that moment I perfectly understood his feelings in the matter.

"It's of little consequence," Moss went on pleasantly. "As some of you have reason to know, I am blessed with a keen memory."

This comment precipitated yet another uncomfortable murmur about the table, as well as an angry grunt from Lieutenant Ahern. Madame Karpova once again cleared her throat in an obvious effort to reestablish the proper mood for the séance. For Darien Moss's sake, she briefly repeated her earlier instructions concerning correct behavior during the reading, then requested that everyone take hold of their neighbors' hands. Matching her actions to her words, the medium took her daughter's left hand in her right, then reached for Lieutenant Ahern's right hand and clasped it with her left. Finally, she directed everyone to close their eyes and attempt to relax.

Considering the aftermath of Darien Moss's surprise entrance, this was a difficult order to follow. Other tense movements around the table told me I was not the only one finding it difficult to calm my mind, much less my body. From across the table, I heard Mrs. Gaylord and Mrs. Reade take in deep breaths of air, followed by similar sounds from Mrs. Ahern and Mrs. Bramwell. Partially opening my eyes, I was amused to note that Senator Gaylord and Lieutenant Ahern were also peering around the table through slits in their own eyes. I was sure neither man had any intention of letting down his guard even for a moment, especially with Darien Moss in their midst.

After one last nervous murmur, everyone grew quiet. Slowly squinting about the table, I saw the room's sole candle waver fitfully in the draft, throwing the room and its inhabitants into sinister relief. Outside, rain pounded against the windows and the wind rose until it sounded like a wailing child. Once again, I felt tiny chills run down my spine. Had Madame Karpova planned it, she could not have created a more unnerving atmosphere in which to communicate with the dead.

The medium herself sat as still as a statue at the far end of the table, her proud chin slightly raised, her dark eyes closed, hands held fast to her daughter on her right and Frank Ahern to her left. Well, I thought, if she wants to establish her veracity, she couldn't choose anyone better to hold hands with than a lieutenant on the police force!

The seconds slowly ticked by, each one seeming to last longer than the one that had preceded it. When nothing occurred after what I judged to be a full five minutes, people began to grow restless. To my left, Senator Gaylord cleared his throat, and I heard Darien Moss mumble something about hocus pocus beneath his breath. One of the women gave a nervous giggle—I suspected it was Mrs. Ahern—but a stern "Shh" from Mrs. Bramwell's direction quickly stilled the lieutenant's wife.

I began to wonder if Darien Moss's unexpected, and clearly unwelcome, presence at the séance had somehow intimidated Madame Karpova and her spirits, but just then the woman gave a soft moan and dropped her head onto her chest. I felt a shiver of excitement, as it seemed something was at last about to happen. To my left, Senator Gaylord's hand tightened on mine, as did Robert's to my right. My own breathing had grown shallow. From the complete silence around the table, I realized no one wanted to break the spell that had settled around the medium like an otherworldly cocoon. Or, more practically, perhaps we were all simply tired of sitting there like a pack of gullible fools waiting for the performance to begin.

I caught Robert's dubious eye as Madame Karpova began mumbling words in tones too low to decipher. Then she flinched and her entire body commenced trembling. I know it sounds fanciful, but by the light of the single candle flickering in the middle of the table, I could have sworn the clairvoyant's pupils were spinning in their sockets before curving up until only the whites were visible. Blinking, I leaned forward, trying to see more closely into those strange colorless orbs.

In my transfixed state, the clairvoyant's eyes seemed to grow steadily larger, until her entire face filled my vision. Everyone else at the table faded into the background; it was as if Madame Karpova and I were the only two people in the room. With an effort, I tried to force my gaze away, but I was dismayed to discover that I couldn't tear my eyes off that spellbinding face. The experience was at once unsettling and strangely fascinating. Either the woman was a first-rate actress or she really was going into some kind of trance. Is it possible, I wondered, to will yourself into that state? And, if so, can you take others with you?

"Tizoc," the medium groaned. "Tizoc, is that you?"

The men to either side of me sucked in their breath as Madame Karpova rose halfway out of her chair, then sank down again, eyes closed now, body rigid. Moaning softly, her turbaned head rolled from side to side as an almost translucent white smoke seemed to appear out of nowhere. It swirled about the psychic's head, then spun down to enter her open mouth. As it did, her whimpering began to change. There were stifled murmurs as her natural voice, already deeply resonant, took on a much huskier timbre, slightly wheezy and hoarse, like that of a very old man.

"I am Tizoc, high priest of the Tenochcas," the new voice informed us in raspy tones. "Why have you summoned me?"

Tenochca, I repeated to myself. Where had I heard that name before? Then I remembered. As a young girl, I had read that the Aztecs—one of the most important Indian groups of the North American continent—were also known as the Tenochcas, a name derived from one of their ancient patriarchs, Tenoch. So, this was Madame Karpova's spirit control. An interesting choice for a Russian medium, I thought wryly.

"Is it your desire to communicate with entities on the astral plane?" the voice demanded.

Across from me, Mrs. Gaylord whispered, "Oh, please, yes. Dorothy. My baby."

Madame Karpova was silent for several moments; then once again she began speaking in that strange ancient voice.

"There is a child here," it announced. "A small girl of seven or eight with pale yellow hair. She is wearing a white pinafore with pink ribbons, and she is standing there"—eyes still tightly closed, the medium nodded toward the Gaylords—"between her parents."

Maurilla Gaylord gave a sob, staring at the psychic with wide, tearful eyes. "Oh, dear Lord," she cried plaintively. "Is it Dorothy? Has she really come back?"

"Yes," Tizoc's hoarse voice went on. "The child's name is Dorothy. She is kissing her mother's cheek. She wants her parents to know that she misses them both but that she is happy and at peace now."

"I felt it!" Mrs. Gaylord cried out, her hand flying to her cheek. "Percival, she kissed me! Oh, my darling baby. You really *are* here!"

"Oh, for the love of God!" Robert muttered. "What kind of cruel hoax is this to play on a poor woman who has just lost her child?"

I did not reply. My entire attention was taken up with Mrs. Gaylord. Her slender shoulders shook as she cried into a handkerchief. Senator Gaylord awkwardly patted her shoulder, obviously not having the faintest idea how to comfort his distraught wife.

"She's fine now, Maurilla," I heard him whisper, trying for her sake, I was sure, to mask his cynicism over this whole affair. "You heard what that, ah, priest said. Please, Maurilla, stop crying."

I couldn't hear the grieving mother's response because her mouth was buried in the handkerchief, but I clearly caught Senator

Gaylord's frustrated sigh. He looked up from her, and even in the dim light I saw his consternation as every eye at the table was focused on him and his wife. Embarrassment quickly overcame any sympathy he might have felt for the inconsolable woman.

"Maurilla, pull yourself together," he said, looking as if he dearly wished he could climb into a hole and pull it closed over his head. "Dorothy's at peace now. We should be happy for her. For God sake, stop crying!"

There was a soft snicker off to my right, and I turned, to see Darien Moss shaking his head, as if this was all too much for him. Madame Karpova (or should I say the high priest, Tizoc?) turned her face briefly in the reporter's direction, then went on in the Aztec's voice.

"Another entity is present—a woman," the voice droned on in a scratchy monotone. "I think it is—yes, it is an old woman. She is wearing a black dress with white lace at the neck and there is a gold pin shaped like a bird on the bodice. The bird has a sapphire eye."

"That's Mama's pin!" Nora Ahern cried out, staring expectantly at Madame Karpova. "Mama, is it really you? I'm so sorry I couldn't be with you when you—" She stopped, swallowing hard to fight away the tears that glistened in her eyes. "When you passed over."

Madame Karpova tilted her head, listening, it seemed, to a voice only she could hear. In the old priest's voice, she said, "Yes, yes, I will tell her." The clairvoyant's closed eyes turned to Mrs. Ahern. "Your mother does not wish for you to be distressed, my dear. She is with your father, and wants you to know that they love you and will always be with you in spirit."

Darien Moss grunted loudly in bored disgust. "Oh, please, enough of this trite nonsense. A dead child and an old woman— how very creative. Even on a bad day, any two-bit circus charlatan could put on a better act than this. Is that the best your so-called Aztec priest can come up with, Madame Karpova? Let's give old Tizoc a real challenge. Why doesn't he tell us why Lieutenant

Ahern here has been spending so much time with a lady—and I use that term loosely—who keeps a certain *business* on Sloan Street?"

Once again, Ahern came out of his seat, his face an ugly mask of rage. "Why you bloody good-for-nothing bastard—"

"Or can this so-called high priest of yours tell us why Senator Gaylord has consistently voted to levy taxes on small independent businesses in the city," Moss went on, ignoring the policeman's outburst, "while at the same time glad-handing those same businessmen and promising them low-interest loans? And can Tizoc tell us how," he continued before Percival Gaylord could retort, "the good senator has suddenly found the funds to construct a multimillion-dollar country estate in the Palo Alto hills?"

"How dare you, Moss!" the senator exclaimed, his right hand balled into a fist. "It's just like you to crash in here and bandy about your lies and innuendos. Have you no shame, man? Has the newspaper world sunk so low that it must resort to fabrications and character assassination in order to sell copies?"

Before Moss could come out with the explosive retort I saw forming on his lips, the Tizoc voice shouted, "Silence! Your childish bickering is driving away the spirits. They have—Ahhh—"

There was a collective gasp as a trumpet suddenly appeared above the psychic's turbaned head and began to float about the table. Although I had half-expected this rather mundane manifestation—after all, what psychic worthy of the name could not produce a trumpet or two some time during a trance?—I found it interesting to note that the instrument remained beyond anyone's reach, unless someone were bold enough to stand on the table. My eyes strained through the dim light to locate a string or a rod attached to the horn, but I could find nothing. I was forced to admit that, whatever it was, the so-called manifestation had been cleverly camouflaged.

As suddenly as it appeared, the trumpet vanished, and an unusual three-stringed instrument took its place, floating above our heads much as the trumpet had, well above everyone's reach.

I must concede that even I was momentarily startled when music suddenly began issuing from the interior of the instrument. As far as I could see—and believe me, I was doing my utmost to examine the apparatus through the flickering candlelight—there was no one remotely close to the stringed device as it drifted above the table. I did not recognize the tune it was playing, although I guessed it was a Russian folk song of some kind.

"Now that's a good trick." Robert chuckled softly, eyeing the illusion with a dispassionate eye. "How do you suppose they manage it?"

"I wonder if it plays 'Home on the Range'?" Darien Moss asked mockingly, picking up on Robert's comment. "Or perhaps 'The Last Rose of Summer'? That would be appropriate, don't you think, considering the sorry old bag of tricks this fraud is subjecting us to?"

Nora Ahern gasped at this, causing her husband to glare at the reporter who was seated to his wife's left, "That's enough, Moss," he hissed. "Either keep your damn comments to yourself or leave."

"It is a balalaika," Theodora Reade said to no one in particular, her voice—as is common with the hard of hearing—loud enough to drown out even Lieutenant Ahern and Darien Moss. "It is from Russia. Madame Karpova produced a similar manifestation at the last sitting I attended."

A chorus of shushing noises caused Mrs. Reade to flutter in embarrassment. "Oh, dear, I'm sorry. I didn't mean to disrupt the reading."

Even as she spoke, the balalaika seemed to vanish into thin air, much as the trumpet had disappeared before it. Madame Karpova stirred restlessly in her seat, head thrashing from side to side as if in considerable distress.

"Another spirit wishes to come through," the Aztec's voice intoned. "An angry, disturbed spirit. Who are you?" Tizoc demanded. "Whom do you wish to address?"

Outside, a particularly fierce gust of wind set the windows rattling, surprising us all and prompting several people to jerk nervously in their seats. The resulting draft caused the single candle on the table to sputter fitfully and go out, casting the room into total darkness.

To my right, Robert whispered sarcastically, "Nice effect, don't you think? A storm, a darkened room, an old Indian? This psychic of yours doesn't miss a trick, I'll give her—"

His works halted abruptly as a wraithlike figure—all in white and faintly gleaming with an eerie light of its own—rose up from behind Madame Karpova to stand between the clairvoyant and Lieutenant Ahern to her left. Mrs. Gaylord and Mrs. Bramwell cried out and I heard Frank Ahern mutter, "What the hell?"

Illuminated by this shimmering glow, I stared in fascination as the ghostly specter floated higher, until it towered over the medium's still figure. Try as I might, I was unable to detect the exact shape hidden beneath what looked to be some kind of white netting. It was impossible to tell if it was a man or a woman, much less how the thing had materialized.

"Why have you come?" Madame Karpova asked in Tizoc's voice.

Silently, the figure raised unearthly arms and began gliding slightly farther to the medium's left, until it hovered directly behind Lieutenant Ahern. It gave a low sigh and seemed about to speak, but when the room was lit by a brilliant flash of lightning. Several women at the table squealed in fright, and I heard the medium gasp as she was startled out of her trance. Then, as suddenly as the trumpet and balalaika had disappeared, the ethereal apparition was gone. Without the candle, or the strange glow that had accompanied the specter, the room was once again thrown into total darkness.

Although I could no longer see her, I heard Madame Karpova moaning softly. "Someone, please," she murmured, once again speaking in her own voice, "light the candle."

To either side of me, I felt Robert and Senator Gaylord rummaging through their pockets for a match. Across the table, Nicholas Bramwell beat them both to it. I heard the strike of a match and saw him lean forward. Once again, a pale, flickering light illuminated the table.

There was a general murmur of relief, followed by a few nervous giggles, when Mrs. Bramwell suddenly screamed. She was on her feet, one hand clutched to her heart, the other pointing across the table in horror. Mrs. Reade followed her gaze with bulging eyes, then with a shocked gasp, she silently crumbled into a dead faint. Luckily, Nicholas Bramwell was able to reach around his mother and catch the elderly widow before she struck her head on the floor. Next to Lieutenant Ahern, Nora Ahern's chair crashed over as she, too, jumped up and backed hastily away from the table.

All eyes followed Mrs. Bramwell's pointing finger. To the left of Mrs. Ahern's fallen chair, his thick body sprawled back in the seat, lay Darien Moss. The reporter's head had dropped onto his chest, and for a moment it seemed as if he had merely fallen asleep. The stream of blood flowing from beneath the reporter's chin onto his starched white shirt and brown woolen jacket, however, quickly shattered this illusion.

Carefully, Lieutenant Ahern lifted Moss's chin, revealing the victim's grotesque and darkened face. The eyes, which had exuded such arrogance and contempt only moments before, now bulged from their sockets in a blank, unseeing stare. A trickle of blood dripped slowly from his nose, and below this his tongue protruded through swollen lips. A deep red gash ringed the dead man's neck. I could just make out the glitter of wire embedded inside the wound. Evidently, this had been employed to snuff out the reporter's life.

On the floor behind Moss's chair lay the balalaika. One of its three strings was missing.

CHAPTER THREE

I t took Lieutenant Ahern an hour to deal with the aftermath of
our gruesome discovery. Theodora Reade had been carried
into the saloon and settled on a sofa. Nora Ahern, who had
recently nursed her own mother through a long illness, kindly offered to stay with the elderly woman until she recovered.

Additional candles were lit, along with some kerosene lanterns,
and the police lieutenant performed a cursory examination of the
body and the balalaika. Outside, the wind continued to howl and a
torrent of rain beat upon the roof. Ahern ordered the Japanese
screen I'd noticed earlier to be placed in front of the séance table,
blocking our view of the body. As several men moved the screen
from its place by the wall, I saw that it had indeed concealed a second door—which opened into the dining room—one that I
guessed led to the kitchen.

Eddie Cooper, the Cliff House cook, and Dmitry Serkov were
summoned to join us, after which we were directed to take seats in
chairs placed along the wall farthermost from the body.

"Cook told me a feller was killed by a ghost," Eddie said
breathlessly, taking a seat between Robert and myself. "Is that him
behind the screen? Was there lots of blood? Do they know who

done it? Dad-blame it! I wish I'd been here when the bloke made a die of it!"

"Eddie!" I admonished, drawing breath to give the lad a brief lecture on the evils of cursing. Then, noting the glare Lieutenant Ahern was directing toward us, I quietly informed the boy that we would discuss the matter later.

But before the police officer could take control of the gathering, Madame Karpova rose from her chair with an air of regal self-importance.

"If you think to find the villain in this gathering, Lieutenant, you are doomed to fail," she announced in sonorous tones. "The spirits recognized Darien Moss as a man of great evil. He was a malicious, disruptive force. I warned you that those who have gone beyond the pale do not take kindly to skeptics. Unfortunately, Mr. Moss ignored me." She swept an arm out toward the screen. "Now see what has happened."

Lieutenant Ahern looked confused, as if he wasn't sure whether to laugh at the woman or to order her back into her seat. "Are you implying, madam," he asked in a controlled voice, "that Mr. Moss was strangled by one of your so-called *specters*?"

Madame Karpova regarded the policeman levelly. "You, too, tempt fate by making light of such matters, Lieutenant. Of course the physical instrument used to extract punishment was of this earthly plane. But the spirits guiding that instrument cannot be found in this room."

"What's she goin' on about?" Eddie asked, eyeing the clairvoyant as if she'd just escaped from Bedlam. "I ain't never heard of any kind of whiskey what could strangle a man."

"She's not referring to that sort of spirit," I told the boy, hard-pressed, even under these grim circumstances, to suppress a grin.

"The lad's right," Robert muttered with a snort. "The woman is mad as a March hare."

Purposefully ignoring Madame Karpova, who sank back onto

her chair as if washing her hands of the proceedings, Lieutenant Ahern turned his attention to Senator Gaylord and his wife, Maurilla.

"Mrs. Gaylord," he said in a more conciliatory tone. "You were seated across the table from Mr. Moss. Did you see or hear anything out of the ordinary when the candle went out?"

"Good heavens, man," Senator Gaylord exploded before his wife could answer. "This entire evening has been out of the ordinary. Floating trumpets, phantoms, ghouls—white smoke billowing out of this charlatan's dress. Everything we've witnessed here tonight has been nothing but a blatant attempt to lighten our pocketbooks and deceive the gullible into believing in ghost stories!"

Ahern flushed in anger, and I noticed his Irish brogue had become more pronounced. "We're not here to be judging Madame Karpova, Senator, but to find out who's behind the killing of Darien Moss." He sucked in a deep breath, then went on in a calmer tone. "Listen to me, all of you. There's no way anyone's going to leave here tonight, what with the storm going on the way it is. Now, we'll get to the bottom of this business a good deal faster if you answer my questions honestly and to the best of your recollection."

Senator Gaylord's face darkened, but he managed to answer more or less civilly, "Yes, all right, I understand the severity of the situation. But why must you involve the ladies? Forcing them to remain in the same room with *that*"—he pointed an arm toward the screen—"is obscene!"

"Begging your pardon, Senator," Ahern replied with strained courtesy, "but it seems to me that the fairer sex often sees things that we men miss."

There was a titter of nervous laughter at this comment. Senator Gaylord looked about him, tight-lipped, then, muttering under his breath, fell resentfully silent.

Ahern waited until the room was again quiet, then turned back to the senator's wife. "All right, then, Mrs. Gaylord. Think hard now. Did you hear or see anything when the room went dark?"

Maurilla Gaylord darted quick, frightened eyes at her husband, but when he merely gave an irritated shrug, she replied in a small voice, "No, Lieutenant. I was—I'm afraid I was looking at Madame Karpova. I heard the noise of the storm outside, of course, but that's all."

Looking disappointed but not surprised, Ahern turned to Nicholas Bramwell. "Mr. Bramwell, you were also sitting across from Moss. Are you sure you didn't see anyone go near the man during that last flash of lightning?"

"I wish I had, Lieutenant," the young man replied. "Unfortunately, as with Mrs. Gaylord, my attention was focused on Madame Karpova." He gave her a self-conscious smile. "It was a remarkable experience."

Madame Karpova nodded at him graciously, as if such acclaim were no more than her due.

"And you, Mrs. Bramwell?" Ahern asked the young man's mother. He did not look as if he expected a helpful response, which was just as well, since the matron answered him with a decisive shake of her stiffly coiffed head.

"I hope I know my duty, Lieutenant," she replied, not bothering to hide a note of disdain in her carefully modulated voice. "If I had noticed anything unusual, you may rest assured I would have mentioned it forthwith."

I sensed Ahern's irritation as he turned to Robert, repeating the same question he had asked the others. As he'd been sitting to Moss's left, Robert said he thought he'd heard the reporter give a little gasp when the candle went out, but he had thought little of it. For my part, I was embarrassed to admit I, too, had been watching Madame Karpova and the specter she'd been conjuring, so, unfortunately, I could offer nothing new to the investigation.

With a look of mounting frustration, the lieutenant addressed Yelena, Madame Karpova's daughter. "What about you, miss? You must be used to these, er, get-togethers. Did you notice anything strange?"

The young girl lowered her lovely chocolate brown eyes. Her voice, though tremulous and bearing a strong Russian accent, was sweet and pleasant to the ear. "I am sorry, sir, I see nothing."

"Come now, miss. Seems to me you'd be curious how the others might be reacting to your mother's, er, conjuring act."

An uncomfortable murmur rippled through the room. Over it, Madame Karpova could be heard saying something in rapid Russian. By the tone of her voice, I was sure the words were not meant to compliment Lieutenant Ahern, nor his loosely veiled criticism of her psychic abilities.

Ignoring her outburst, Ahern doggedly continued, this time trying a different tact. "We were told to hold hands during the séance, Miss Karpova. Tell me now, can you say for sure you held tight to your mother's hand throughout the entire, er, performance?"

The girl looked startled. "Yes." Her wide eyes turned to her mother, then shifted quickly—and a bit guiltily, I thought—back to the lieutenant. "Yes, entire time."

"Oh, for the love of—" Ahern looked us over in irritation. "Can each of you swear you didn't let go of your neighbors' hands, not even once throughout the entire séance?"

I was surprised when everyone began shaking their heads. I knew for a fact that both Senator and Mrs. Gaylord broke the circle when the woman began sobbing about her lost child. I, too, had broken off holding Robert's hand when the candle went out.

Before I could admit to this, however, Robert said, "By the horn spoons! I'd forgotten all about that silly business of holding hands." His broad forehead creased in concentration. "As a matter of fact, we did let go, at least toward the end of the séance. That Moss fellow had hold of my right hand, but when the candle went out, he jerked it free. All of a sudden, too, as if my skin had suddenly caught on fire and was burning his fingers." He turned to me. "You released my left hand at the same time, Sarah. Remember?"

"You're right, Robert, I do remember." From the stir of those seated around me, I gathered that just about everyone else at the table had broken the chain of hands at roughly the same time. Even Senator and Mrs. Gaylord were nodding their heads now in the affirmative.

Ahern turned back to Yelena, his voice conveying a note of scorn. "Now then, young lady, are you asking me to believe that you and your mother were the only ones at that table who kept hold of each other's hands without once breaking contact?"

"The girl has already answered you, Lieutenant," Nicholas Bramwell interjected. "Stop badgering her."

His mother gave him a warning look. "Nicholas, you must allow Lieutenant Ahern to do his job. I'm sure Miss Karpova understands." She gave the girl a thin smile, then addressed her as if she were speaking to a simpleminded child. "You do understand the seriousness of the situation, don't you, my dear? This is not Russia. In America, you must respect your betters and tell the truth when asked to do so."

The girl's face colored. Her wide eyes, which had been regarding Nicholas Bramwell, as if she was unsure why he had come to her defense, dropped back down to stare at her lap.

"Well, Miss Karpova?" Ahern asked yet again, his eyes fixing on the Bramwells lest either of them should once again decide to interrupt.

"I—I maybe break off hand when light go out," the girl responded in a small voice. She did not raise her eyes to look at the policeman.

"Finally, the truth!" Ahern said, throwing up his arms in satisfaction. "Now, is there anyone here who *did not* let go of his neighbors' hands when that white ghost thing appeared?"

From the general response, it seemed no one had remained holding hands. Ahern sighed. "That's what I thought. So it seems anyone could have left his seat during that time, with no one else being the wiser."

His voice took on a harder edge as he turned to Madame Karpova's brother. "Now, Mr. Serkov, where did you go after Darien Moss arrived? Mind now, I want the truth."

Like his niece, the Russian did not meet the lieutenant's eyes, but instead stared down at the floor. I wondered if, as a foreigner, he automatically distrusted the American police, or if he had something to hide and feared it might be read on his weathered face.

"I go to kitchen," he replied tersely, and I realized this was the first time I'd heard the man speak. His voice was deep and coarse, not at all pleasant. His speech was also heavily accented. "I have cup of pitiful drink you call coffee." The man pursed scornful lips, as if he were about to spit, then seemed to think better of it and fell silent.

"You stayed in the kitchen the entire time?" Ahern persisted. "Until you were called back to the dining room?"

"I go outside, have smoke," Serkov admitted. His rough face stretched into a sarcastic sneer as he glanced balefully at the cook—a stocky man with a balding head, a thick, bushy mustache, and a well-chewed, unlit cigar clamped between his teeth. "*Durak!* He not let me smoke in kitchen. Say it make filthy smell. As if cigar not stink bad enough."

Lieutenant Ahern looked at the man incredulously. "You're telling me you went *outside* to smoke a cigarette? In this storm?"

"What you call storm not bother me. In Russia get real rain, not few weak drops like this."

The policeman continued to look skeptical. "How long did you stay out there, then, in our California *drizzle?*"

There was a scattering of uneasy amusement at this. Serkov merely shrugged, his face as harsh and unyielding as ever. "Few minutes, half hour, who knows. I no have clock for wrist."

Ahern turned to the cook. "Can you tell me how long Serkov was gone before he came back to the kitchen?"

The cook shifted the cigar stump in his mouth and gave the Russian a disgusted look. Clearly, there was no love lost between the two men.

"He was gone at least thirty minutes," he told Ahern. "Most likely, longer than that. The boy here," he said, nodding to Eddie, who immediately sat up straighter as all eyes fell upon him, "had just finished his dinner when this Russian bugger comes slinkin' back in, lookin' as if he'd been up to no good."

Serkov half-rose to his feet at this, but Ahern motioned him back into his seat.

Without prompting, Eddie chimed in, "What Cook says is true enough, Lieutenant. Never said a word neither, that Russki feller. Just sat there in the kitchen, glarin' at us like we done him some mischief, though I swear I ain't never so much as set eyes on the bloke before."

"Watch your language, boy-o," Ahern cautioned, albeit more or less perfunctorily. He stared at us for several minutes, then shook his head. "All right, then, I'm ready enough to give up the fiddle, at least for tonight. The bunch of you think over what you might have seen tonight, and we'll have another go of it in the morning. He nodded toward Madame Karpova, her daughter, and Dmitry Serkov. "The three of you stay behind. The rest of you can leave. Cook here will show you to your rooms."

There was a collective groan at this reminder that we would be forced to spend the night in the expanded hotel wing. We all started when the sky was suddenly filled with brilliant shafts of lightning, followed moments later by a boom of thunder. The rain had once again intensified, crashing solid sheets of water against the windows and battering onto the roof.

Ahern gave a half smile, as if nature had effectively proved his point. "As you can see, there's no use complaining. With this storm, the police can't get in and we can't get out. I suggest everyone make the best of it. Remember," he added as people rose, "no one leaves in the morning until the police arrive."

There was another low grumble, but it was halfhearted at best. By now, most of my fellow guests seemed more or less resigned to their fate. In truth, some of them appeared so fatigued, I was sure they were beyond arguing. As for me, I was very glad I'd had the foresight to warn my parents that I might not be returning home until the following afternoon.

Madame Karpova's dark eyes narrowed into black slits. "Why do you keep us here?" she demanded. "We have told you everything we know. My brother was outside. Yelena did not leave her seat. And I was in full sight the entire time. None of us could have strangled that horrible man, even if he deserved it."

Ahern practically pounced on this. "So, Madame Karpova, you admit you had a motive for doing away with Moss."

"That man had many enemies," she insisted frostily. "He told lies in his newspaper. He was ignorant, yet he scorned the spirits and the world beyond our own. I warned Mr. Moss, as I did all of you, that an attitude like that was dangerous, but he would not listen."

"You threatened Moss?" Ahern asked with growing interest.

The medium made a dismissive motion with her bejeweled hand. "There was no need to make threats. I, Madame Karpova, see all. I knew what lay ahead in his future. For all his—how do you say?—arrogance, he could not hide his black soul from me. Why should I threaten him, when his death was already written in the pages of time?"

"I don't care what you think you saw in Moss's future, madam," Lieutenant Ahern told her firmly. "You'll stay here until I say you can go."

I had followed the others toward the door. However, when I passed near the screen, which was blocking our view of the body, I pretended to stumble. Bending as if to check my bootlaces, I unobtrusively tarried, hoping to overhear more of Ahern's conversation with the Russians. I was not well pleased when Robert took my arm and hauled me unceremoniously to my feet.

"This is none of your business, Sarah. The police are trained to deal with murder investigations. You are not." Naturally, he made no attempt to lower his voice, and not surprisingly, it caught Lieutenant Ahern's attention. I knew there would be no more questions directed at the Russians until we had left the room. "Besides," Robert persisted, "it's after midnight and I'm done in."

"Then by all means, retire to your bed," I told him, calmly straightening my skirts. "I'll see you in the morning."

Robert eyed me suspiciously. "You've got that look on your face, Sarah. What the blazes are you planning now?"

"Once again, you are making mountains out of molehills," I retorted. "I simply mean to visit Mrs. Reade and ascertain how she is recovering. The poor woman appeared quite unwell earlier."

Robert studied me warily, but even he could hardly fault me for performing what was, after all, no more than my Christian duty.

My colleague's patience had apparently given out, for instead of offering further argument, he merely shrugged his broad shoulders. "Well, it's not my funeral. Just don't bombard her with endless questions. The poor soul's been through enough for one night."

I found the two women in the saloon, where we had left them earlier. Mrs. Reade reclined on the sofa, a light wool blanket covering her frail body up to the neck. She lay so still, eyes shut, her face dangerously pale, that I was tempted to hold a mirror to her mouth to ensure that she was still breathing. Nora Ahern, who sat on a chair beside the widow, glanced up expectantly at my entrance.

"Miss Woolson, I'm that glad to see you. Mrs. Reade's hardly stirred. If it wasn't for this storm, I'd ask one of the men to fetch a doctor."

"Yes, I agree it would be best if she could be examined by a physician." I crouched down beside the sofa and removed Theodora Reade's hands from beneath the blanket. They felt dry and brittle, the bones slight, the skin transparently thin; I could make out every raised vein and every swollen arthritic joint beneath the paper-thin flesh. The widow groaned softly as I attempted to take her pulse, then slowly opened her eyes. She stared at me in confusion.

"What—what's wrong? Where am I?" she asked weakly, her pale gray eyes going from me to Nora Ahern.

"You fainted, Mrs. Reade," I replied, gently rubbing her hands in an effort to increase circulation. "You're lying on a sofa in the Cliff House saloon. I fear you've suffered a terrible shock."

She continued to look at me blankly; then I watched as the awful memory came flooding back. Her already-pale face blanched nearly white. "Oh dear! I remember now. That nasty newspaper man. He was—he was—" Nervously, she licked her dry lips. "You'll think me a foolish old woman, but I have to know. That Moss person—is he really dead?"

"Yes, I'm afraid he is," I replied, gently squeezing her hands. "Try not to think about it, Mrs. Reade. Everything is being taken care of. There's no need to distress yourself."

I doubted she heard my words. Her eyes remained contracted and unfocused. Then she shook her head, as if trying to clear her mind. "It's all such a muddle, like a bad dream. And of course my eyes aren't as good as they used to be. I just cannot make sense of it."

"That's hardly surprising, dear," Mrs. Ahern said, kneeling beside me. "It gave us all a terrible fright, I can tell you."

It was clear by the strained look on Nora's face that this was nothing short of the truth. The lieutenant's wife appeared as if she, too, was finding Moss's death difficult to take in. The freckles liberally sprinkled across her nose stood out in stark contrast to her pale skin.

"I've never seen the likes of what went on here tonight," Mrs. Ahern continued, closing her eyes with a little shiver.

"Have you attended other séances given by Madame Karpova?" I asked.

She hesitated, then nodded, as if the need to share these experiences overcame her natural reticence. "I have indeed, Miss Woolson. And they weren't anything like this! I'd been suffering something fearful from dyspepsia during Mam's last illness. One or two sittings with Madame Karpova, and my stomach felt right as rain again. She seemed to have a knack for making me sleep better at night, too. I'd leave her rooms feeling so relaxed, like I was floating on air. She had a real knack for making my troubles just seem to disappear."

"Was anyone else ever present at those private readings, Mrs. Ahern?" I asked.

She thought for a moment. "The senator's wife, Mrs. Gaylord, was there once or twice. And Mrs. Reade here. Oh, and I remember Mrs. Bramwell attended a few times. Always very comforting the readings were, for whoever was present."

"I gather from tonight's séance that your mother recently passed away," I said gently. "I'm very sorry for your loss."

Her blue eyes filled with tears. "Yes, last month it was. And me not there when it happened! I only went to the market, but when I came back, she was gone." She paused to dab at her eyes with a plain white handkerchief. "Madame Karpova said it might make me feel better if I came here tonight. She said I could say good-bye to Mam, you know, proper like. And it did help. I truly felt as if she were here. But I should have known better than to bring my husband along. He doesn't take to such things." She dried her face and blew her nose. "Although I suppose with that reporter's death and all, it's as well Frank was here. I wonder, has he learned anything about who killed that dreadful man?"

"He's conducted a cursory interview," I told her. "Unfortunately, it's unearthed few hard facts. Everyone claims to have had their eyes fixed on Madame Karpova when Mr. Moss was attacked."

"That was when Madame Karpova conjured up the spirit, wasn't it?" Mrs. Reade asked in a small voice. The elderly widow had been so quiet, I had nearly forgotten she was there.

"Oh, wasn't that something?" Nora Ahern put in before I could respond. "I remember wondering if it was gonna speak." She gave a nervous giggle. "I don't mind telling you I was hoping it wouldn't."

The laughter quickly died away and her eyes once again grew serious. "Then that lightning flashed and made everything so bright, and Mrs. Bramwell screamed." She blinked her eyes. "Mr. Moss wasn't a nice man. Still, he didn't deserve to end his days like that."

"It must have been awful for you, Mrs. Ahern," I said. "You were seated directly next to Mr. Moss. Did he say anything before he, ah, before the candle was relit?"

For the first time since I'd entered the saloon, Nora Ahern's expression became guarded. "No, I don't think so. But then, like everyone else, I was busy watching Madame Karpova. Besides, Mr. Ahern and I hardly knew Mr. Moss, so I didn't pay him much mind."

Nora Ahern was a terrible liar. I watched the color creep back into her pale cheeks as she diverted her eyes.

"Oh?" I said, allowing my skepticism to be reflected in my voice. "When you said Mr. Moss wasn't a nice man, I thought perhaps you knew him personally. He did write a popular newspaper column. Surely you must have seen it."

"Mr. Ahern says that paper is nothing but trash and he won't allow it in the house," she said in a rush, then looked down at her hands, which she was twisting and untwisting in her lap. As if realizing this uneasy movement revealed the state of her nerves more than was prudent, she hastily folded her hands and held them still. Raising her eyes to meet mine, she even attempted a wan smile. "Now that you mention it, I believe I have seen Mr. Moss's paper once or twice."

"But you didn't know him personally?"

"Oh my, no. Mr. Ahern doesn't hold with reporters. Always getting hold of the wrong end of the stick, he says. Making the police look like a pack of idiots."

"Lieutenant Ahern didn't seem pleased to see Mr. Moss."

Nora laughed nervously. "Trust me, Miss Woolson, it was nothing personal. Just Mr. Moss's work and all." She looked toward the door, clearly anxious to leave the saloon—and, I thought, to escape my questions. "Now that you're here to watch Mrs. Reade, I'll just go and find Mr. Ahern. That is, if you don't mind."

"Yes, of course I'll be happy to—" I began. But with a rustle of skirts, Nora Ahern had already swept hastily out of the room.

I should have known I'd get no sleep until you had rehashed the entire evening," Robert lamented as Eddie Cooper and I crowded into his small bedroom.

I seated myself in the room's only chair, while Eddie sank onto the bed, which took up most of the limited space. A small table— upon which had been placed a kerosene lamp, a towel, and a washbowl filled with water—and a black-walnut wardrobe cabinet completed the room's simple decor. All the essentials, I thought, without any frills.

I'd waited in the saloon until Robert and the cook had assisted Mrs. Reade to her room, which was located next to the Aherns', in case she required assistance during the night. Afterward, Eddie and I—for of course the lad was determined not to be left out—had followed the Scot to his room.

"I'm sorry to disturb you, Robert, but there are one or two things I'd like to discuss while they're fresh in my mind." I hurried on before he could voice another objection. "To begin with, I'm sure you realize Dmitry Serkov was lying about going outside for a cigarette. His clothing was hardly damp. He may have gone out-side, but he could not have remained there for more than a few minutes, or he would have been drenched."

"Then, dash it all, where was he the rest of the—" Robert's face lit with sudden comprehension. "Of course. He must have slipped back into the dining room to help his sister with the séance. And since I didn't hear the main door open, he must have used the sec-ond entrance, the one hidden behind the Japanese screen."

"I was sure you'd noticed it," I said, pleased with his perception.

"If you recall, Mr. Serkov was dressed entirely in black. It would have been simplicity itself for a dark figure to avoid detection in the dim light."

Robert sank down next to Eddie, who was still sprawled on the bed, eagerly soaking in every word of our conversation. "Which would account for that strange-looking guitar—the balalaika, wasn't it?—apparently playing music on its own."

"A guitar what plays all by itself?" Eddie sat up straight, his eyes wide in amazement. "Dang it all, I'd 'ave traded my best shootin' aggie to see that!"

I gave the boy a look but refrained from correcting his language. "It was meant to appear as if it was playing on its own, Eddie. But I rather think Madame Karpova achieved that effect by attaching a small music box to the inside of the instrument. Her brother undoubtedly wound up the mechanism and 'floated' the balalaika around the room on the end of a black pole, or reaching rod. Of course, he must have donned a black mask and gloves to complete his camouflage. Since our attention was on the instrument, Serkov ran little risk of being seen."

Robert's brow creased. "But Lieutenant Ahern examined the balalaika. There was no sign of a music box inside."

"By then, I'm sure it had been removed," I said. "Either by Serkov or by Madame Karpova herself. Yelena admitted she released her mother's hand when the candle went out, although I suspect she'd let go of it long before then."

"You mean when that white smoke started to come out of her dress?" Robert asked.

I wouldn't have thought it possible, but Eddie's eyes grew even larger at the mention of this incredible feat of magic. "Man alive! How in tarnation did that medium lady go and make smoke come out of her dress? Was she on fire?"

"It's called ectoplasm. Some magicians achieve the effect by using dry ice," I explained to the boy, then remarked to Robert,

"That's undoubtedly why Yelena sat to her mother's right. I noticed that Madame Karpova is right-handed."

Robert's blue-green eyes narrowed. "Wait a minute. I thought you bought into all this spiritualist nonsense."

"I merely said I was attending tonight's séance with an open mind. And so I did. However, that did not preclude me from researching some of the more obvious tricks of the trade beforehand."

Naturally, my colleague did not hesitate to pounce on this innocent disclosure. "So you admit it's all a bunch of hocus-pocus."

"At least part of it is, yes," I replied. "But that's hardly the point. Obviously, no spirit or psychic phenomenon tightened the wire around Darien Moss's neck. A very real flesh and blood individual is responsible. The question is, which one?"

"If we're right and Serkov did sneak back into the dining room, then he must be the killer," Robert theorized. "After all, he wasn't holding anyone's hand. And as you pointed out, he'd be free to move unseen about the room. If Moss wrote an article exposing Karpova as a fraud, that would pretty much finish her in this town."

"Yes, it probably would. The problem is, just about everyone at that table had an equally valid reason for not wanting to see their names in Darien Moss's column. Including me, I'm ashamed to say."

"I can understand that. But surely no one was desperate enough to commit murder in order to stop him."

"Hmmm. I wonder." I removed Samuel's list of names from my reticule and smoothed it out on my lap. I was silently considering it when a loud scream shattered the quiet of Robert's room.

"What the hell?" Robert exclaimed, jumping up from the bed.

"I think it came from down the hall." Without waiting for a reply, I grabbed the kerosene lamp off the table and rushed to the door, Robert on my heels.

"Wait for me," Eddie cried, springing out into the corridor behind us.

I was right: The scream had come from the last room at the end of the hall. As I ran, I saw Madame Karpova dart into the room ahead of me. From the spill of light from the hall, I could make out the psychic as she gathered her daughter into her arms. The girl was sobbing uncontrollably, her small hands frantically rubbing at her throat.

"What is it?" I asked the girl, placing my kerosene lamp down and hurrying to her side. "Are you all right?"

"O, *bozche!* There was—man in room," she stammered. "I come in, he—he jump, knock me down, try to choke me. I scream and he run." Yelena started to cough through her tears. In a few moments, she was gasping for breath.

"Shh, *moya malenkaya.* Don't try to talk," Olga Karpova said, gently removing her daughter's hands from her throat.

I came closer, and was dismayed to see a dark red contusion ringing the girl's slender neck. In several places, it had broken the skin.

Robert stepped through the crowd of onlookers who were anxiously gathering at the door. Several had thrown coats over their undergarments, which, I assumed, they planned to sleep in. Every face appeared white with shock and horror at the sight of the stricken girl. Even Dmitry Serkov's dark expression had changed to one of alarm.

Striking a match, Robert lit the kerosene lamp that had been provided for Yelena's room, then held it closer to the girl so that we might better examine her wounds. "Who did this to you, Miss Karpova? Did you get a look at his face?"

Yelena had begun to shake violently. "Room dark," she managed to say through clattering teeth. "I not see."

As Robert and Madame Karpova helped the hysterical girl to a chair, I surveyed the room. Holding my lamp lower, I spotted something glittering, half-hidden beneath the bed.

Raising the comforter, I picked up the object. It was a length of wire. Turning it over in my hand, I saw that it was identical to the one that had snuffed out the reporter's life earlier that evening.

It seemed as though Darien Moss's murderer had struck again.

CHAPTER FOUR

The storm raged throughout the better part of the night, then finally subsided into a light drizzle, allowing the police access to the Cliff House by nine o'clock the following morning.

I was not surprised when neither Yelena nor her mother appeared for breakfast in the saloon, chosen over the dining room because the latter still held the remains of Darien Moss. Naturally, there was a good deal of speculation about the reporter's murder, but most of the sympathy, and apprehension, was reserved for the young Russian girl. It was hardly a secret that just about everyone disliked the tell-all journalist, and for good reason. But none of us could comprehend why would anyone would attack the sweet and innocent Yelena Karpova! The poor girl could not possibly pose a threat to anyone. Or could she? I asked myself.

After breakfast, Lieutenant Ahern checked on the injured girl, then appropriated the manager's office and set about interrogating everyone who had been present at the séance, this time interviewing the participants individually.

The first person to be taken in was Mrs. Theodora Reade, who insisted she was quite recovered from her faint the previous night.

I did not believe she was being completely honest about her condition. Before she was settled into a hired carriage for the ride home, I was able to speak to her briefly, and I thought she still appeared troubled and unnaturally pale.

"Please, my dear, don't fuss," she told me when I tried to persuade her to wait until I could drive her back to the city in Eddie's brougham. "I will be perfectly all right when I am in my own house." She patted my hand as I assisted her into the hansom cab.

"You're Judge Horace Woolson's daughter, aren't you, dear?" she asked.

"Yes, as a matter of fact, I am. Do you know him?"

"For years, my late husband and your father belonged to the same social club. They used to enjoy playing chess together." She chuckled at the memory. "Very competitive they were, too." She leaned closer in order to better study my face. "Yes, I see something of your father in you. The same strong chin and bright, intelligent eyes. And now you've followed him into the law. My, my, women lawyers. Who would have thought?" She sat back, looking very tired. "Well, I'd best be on my way. It has been a distressing affair. One cannot deny that. Simply horrible. I just wish . . ."

Her thin voice trailed off, and she wore the same faraway expression I'd noticed the previous night in the saloon.

"What is it you wish, Mrs. Reade?" I asked. "Is there something I can get you? A glass of water, perhaps, or another blanket for your lap? It's chilly this morning."

The old woman sighed and gave me a wan smile. "No, my dear, I require nothing more than to be away from here. I never thought to see such wickedness. And as I mentioned, my eyesight is not what it used to be. It is difficult to know what to make of it all."

"You're quite right. The sort of evil we witnessed last night is very hard to understand." I bade the widow good-bye, then stood back as the driver closed the folding carriage door and climbed up to his elevated seat at the rear of the vehicle. "Take care of yourself, Mrs. Reade," I called out as the man clicked his horse forward. She waved her hand at me, then leaned back in her seat for the long drive home.

As I watched one person after another come out of Lieutenant Ahern's temporary office, I saw that Mrs. Reade was not the only one who carried the signs of last night's tragedy. I doubted that anyone had slept well; I knew I certainly hadn't, and judging by the dark circles under Robert's eyes, neither had he. Senator Gaylord appeared to be in a foul mood, and his wife looked as if she, too, had spent a restless night. Mrs. Philippa Bramwell and her son Nicholas were somber and barely spoke a dozen words between them as they departed from the Cliff House in their cabriolet.

After our own interrogations, Robert and I were allowed to leave, but it was midafternoon before Eddie's brougham reined up in front of my Sutter Street office. We had dropped Robert off at his rooms so that he might freshen up before going to Joseph Shepard's law firm. Since I had no clients scheduled for that day, I decided to go on as I was, without bothering to change from the gown I had been wearing the previous evening.

Fanny Goodman, the plump middle-aged widow who ran the ladies' millinery shop downstairs, was outside washing her storm-muddied windows when I arrived. As soon as she saw me, she dropped her rags into a pail of vinegar water and dried her hands on the starched white apron protecting her dress. Tucking a few strands of graying hair into the knot at the nape of her neck, she greeted me with a warm smile.

"So there you are, Miss Woolson. When you didn't come in this morning, I feared you might have taken ill. Seems like half the city is suffering from catarrh. I declare it's all this wet weather we've been having. Seeps right through a body and into the chest."

"My health is excellent, thank you, Mrs. Goodman," I said, returning her smile. "I'm afraid I was unavoidably detained."

It was obvious that Mrs. Goodman was dying to know what had been important enough to keep me from my law practice, such as it was. Although I'd grown to like and respect my downstairs neighbor since establishing my Sutter Street practice two months earlier, I was loath to relate last night's adventure, lest I open myself to a flood of questions. It was a relief when Eddie joined us, thus diverting the good woman's ever keen curiosity.

"Good day, ma'am," the lad said, tipping his cap courteously. His bright brown eyes gleamed mischievously. "I wonder, has it been a busy day for you, then, Mrs. Goodman?"

Mrs. Goodman shook her head in mock disapproval, all the while grinning fondly at the boy. The milliner had no children of her own, and she had taken an immediate liking to my young hackman from the day he and Robert had helped me move into the two upstairs rooms. Lately, she'd begun spoiling Eddie with treats from her homey kitchen, unaccustomed delicacies he had come to eagerly anticipate. Like several other tradespeople who kept shops along the street, Fanny Goodman occupied small living quarters behind the store. Since I had opened my law office upstairs, I'd found it a warm, cheery haven offering hot tea, fresh baked goods, and surprisingly stimulating conversation.

Mrs. Goodman might look like a typical old-fashioned grandmother, but in reality she was a shrewd businesswoman and a great advocate of women's suffrage. Ten years earlier, she had been one of the organizers behind the first annual meeting of the California Women's Suffrage Society here in San Francisco. It was a cause she continued to support with great energy and fervor. I could count on Mrs. Goodman to supply me with the latest letters and essays from the brave women championing this worthy movement.

"You've a nerve, Eddie Cooper," she scolded good-naturedly. "What you mean is, have I had time to bake today."

Eddie grinned a bit sheepishly but made no effort to deny the accusation. "Well, you do make the best pudding and cherry pie in the city, Mrs. Goodman. And that's the gospel truth."

"Listen to the boy," Fanny tittered, looking enormously pleased. "You're shameless, that's what you are, Eddie Cooper. As a matter of fact, I found a few minutes this morning to make up some brown Betty. You wouldn't be interested in a bit of that now, would you?"

At the boy's eager response, she led the way through her shop and into the tidy kitchen that comprised one of the three rooms—along with a bedroom and a sitting room—located behind the store. Eddie's eyes grew very wide at the tray of apple dumplings cooling on the windowsill. With a brisk nod, Fanny Goodman motioned for him to take a seat at the kitchen table, where she promptly served up several pockets of dough filled with delicious-smelling baked apples with a dash of cinnamon. Lastly, she poured him a glass of fresh milk from the icebox.

"There now," she pronounced. "That ought to fill even your stomach, Master Cooper." Waiting only long enough to see his enraptured expression upon biting into the first dumpling, Fanny motioned me back into the millinery shop.

"There was a woman asking for you this morning," she informed me, straightening a perfectly orderly line of gloves displayed on one of the counters. "She seemed to be a timid sort. Looked real disappointed to find you were out, like it had taken all her nerve to come here in the first place."

My interest was immediately piqued. I'd had few enough clients—at least those who could afford to pay for my services—since leaving Joseph Shepard's law firm. To have missed being here to greet my first real client was disheartening. "Did the woman leave her name?" I asked. "What did she look like?"

"She wouldn't leave her name, though I asked. But she was attractive and looked respectable enough." Fanny sniffed as her trained eye surveyed the hats, bonnets, scarves, gloves, and other ladies' accessories that were tastefully displayed throughout the tidy shop. "Her gown was plain but clean and neat, although her hat was from last season, and not a style I fancied, even when it was new. Still and all, she seemed nice. I told her to come back later this afternoon." She gave me a conspiratorial wink. "I let on that you were out on an important case. Oh, I almost forgot. Your brother Samuel is waiting for you upstairs."

She rolled her eyes and smiled. "I swear that young man could charm the angels out of the heavens if he had a mind. I let him in with that spare key you gave me for safekeeping." Her face grew suddenly worried. "I hope that was all right."

"Yes, of course. Thank you, Mrs. Goodman."

Leaving Eddie to enjoy his feast, I hurried upstairs to tell Samuel of the surprising happenings at the Cliff House the previous night. Expecting to find my brother waiting impatiently for my report, I was surprised to find him ensconced in my office chair, legs resting comfortably upon my desk, perusing the latest issue of the *Police Gazette.*

"So, Lieutenant Ahern finally let you go," he said, smiling at me from over a lurid picture of a female corpse, her scantily clad body drenched in blood, a long dagger protruding from her well-endowed chest.

"You know about Darien Moss's murder?" Once again, I was amazed by my brother's apparently countless news sources. "Lieutenant Ahern wasn't able to get a message out to the police until early this morning. I didn't see George among the officers who responded." I referred of course to George Lewis, Samuel's good friend and fellow pugilist, who was a sergeant on the San Francisco police force.

"No, he hasn't been assigned to the case. But he managed to get word to me in time to get a few lines in this evening's *Chronicle.* Now," he went on, taking out his notebook and a pencil, "why don't you give me all the gory details so that I can do a proper job of it."

I pulled a face at him, then moved one of the room's two side chairs until I sat opposite him. This chair, I might add, was a good deal less comfortable than the generously padded cherry-wood armchair I had selected to go with my desk, and which Samuel currently occupied.

"George tells me Moss was strangled?" Samuel's bright blue eyes were alight with interest; nothing fascinated him more than the smell of a good story. Which was why he had chosen to become a journalist, rather than follow the law career our father had had his heart set on since his youngest son was a small boy.

"Yes, he was. With a wire string from a balalaika."

He looked up from the notes he'd begun to scribble on his pad. "A what?"

I described the unusual instrument Madame Karpova had "materialized" at the séance. Then, at his insistence, I proceeded to relate the evening's events, starting with our arrival at the Cliff House. When I finished, he settled back in the armchair, regarding me speculatively.

"You say you found another string, identical to the one used to garrote Moss, in Yelena Karpova's room after she was attacked? Did you have an opportunity to examine the—what did you call that instrument again?"

"A balalaika."

"Hmmm, yes. I'm just wondering if you had a chance to look at the balalaika again before you left the Cliff House this afternoon."

"I managed a quick glance as a police officer carried it out to the patrol wagon," I told him. "Only one string remained out of the original three. I'm almost positive the second missing wire was the one I found in Yelena Karpova's room."

"And that second string was still attached to the balalaika after the murder?"

"Yes, I'm sure it was."

"So presumably the killer returned to the dining room after everyone else had left, and cut another string from the instrument. Which means Yelena's attack was premeditated." He tapped the end of his pencil against the desktop, lost in thought. "But why would anyone want to kill Madame Karpova's daughter?"

"Why indeed?" I replied. "I spent half the night asking myself the same question. I can think of any number of reasons why someone might want to do away with Darien Moss, but what could anyone possibly have against a young Russian girl who's been in San Francisco less than a month?"

Samuel shook his head. "Perhaps the murderer thought that by killing Yelena he could hurt the girl's mother, or her uncle."

"You think someone attacked Yelena because he didn't approve of Olga Karpova's so-called spirit manifestations? That seems far-fetched."

"Yes, put that way, I suppose it does." Samuel drew a few meaningless squiggles on his paper. "Tell me more about the people who were at the séance. You said Lieutenant Ahern and Senator Gaylord were upset when Moss turned up. Given Moss's tattle sheet, that's hardly surprising. But did anyone look especially disturbed— enough to kill the man, I mean? Let's face it, Sarah, whoever tightened the wire around Moss's neck was desperate enough to chance it with eleven other people in the room. Unless the killer is an accomplished actor, I have to believe hatred that intense would be difficult to hide."

I thought back to the night before, trying to remember everyone's reaction when Darien Moss made his melodramatic appearance. I'd seen surprise, dismay, and anger. And something else, I realized. Fear! In fact, now that I put my mind to it, I decided fear had been the pervading emotion.

"Have you read Moss's columns lately?" I asked. "I was wondering if there was any particular person or issue he's been focusing on over the past few weeks."

Samuel considered this. "I don't remember any specific issue. Of course, he's written one or two derogatory articles about spiritualism in general and Madame Karpova in particular. Let me see, what were his exact words? Oh, yes, he accused her of being a 'self-proclaimed Russian aristocrat who performed circus tricks any child could see through.' He went on to promise that he would personally expose her tomfoolery in an upcoming column." He laughed. "I can see why Madame Karpova might have wanted to slit his throat."

"Or her brother, Dmitry Serkov," I said thoughtfully. "He's quite a character, by the way. He was dressed entirely in black, and looked like one of those villains pictured in your *Police Gazettes*. Robert is convinced Serkov is the culprit, and I have to admit the Russian certainly possessed motive and opportunity. Remember, he left the room when Moss arrived, and was free to move around the place pretty much at will. Yet, why in the world would he want to kill his niece?"

"You're assuming that whoever killed Moss also attacked Yelena."

"It seems a bit much to assume there were two murderers present last night," I replied dryly. "By the way, what do you know about Madame Karpova and her family? You must have done some background work for this article you're writing."

A look of frustration crossed my brother's handsome face. "I tried to dig up information on them, but I didn't have much luck. Following their trail since they arrived in the States six months ago was easy enough. And it appears they spent the previous three years traveling through England and Europe. Piecing together their earlier lives in Russia was another matter. I ran into one dead end after another." He grinned. "Let me put it this way, Sarah, if those three are members of the Russian aristocracy, I'll eat my hat."

"Moss certainly seemed to consider Madame Karpova a fake. But I'm not yet ready to place the blame on the Russians. Almost everyone at that séance had a motive to kill Moss."

"Popular fellow," Samuel put in with a derisive smile. "As a matter of fact, I'd be hard-pressed to name one person who actually liked Darien Moss, and that includes his coworkers at the newspaper."

"There are ghosts in everyone's closet, Samuel. That's why journalists like Moss are so feared. As Rosencrantz says in *Hamlet,* 'many wearing rapiers are afraid of goose-quills.'"

"Yes, their pens wield an enormous amount of power. Perhaps too much power. Still, it took a lot of temerity to murder the man in front of so many potential witnesses. And since you claim no one knew Moss was going to attend the séance, his murder had to have been a crime of opportunity."

"I think you're right. The problem, of course, is figuring out which one took advantage of the situation." I thought for a moment, then asked, "Samuel, would you see what information you can find on Darien Moss? I've read his column a few times, but I know next to nothing about the man himself."

He smiled. "I've already started. As soon as George told me what happened last night, I did a quick search through the newspapers files. I didn't find much, but then, I haven't dug very far yet. I do know that Moss moved here from New Jersey about fifteen years ago. I'll make a better job of it next week. If I have time, I'll also see what I can find out about the other people who were at the séance."

"Good. In the meantime, I'll do a little snooping myself, especially about Madame Karpova and her brother. Someone must know where—"

I was interrupted mid-sentence by the door banging open and Eddie Cooper charging headlong into the room. His bright, lively eyes immediately fastened on my brother. The lad had taken quite a fancy to Samuel when he'd discovered, quite by accident, that my youngest sibling was the popular crime writer Ian Fearless. Since then, Eddie's ambition to become a private-inquiry agent had waned considerably, and he'd begun to lean more toward a career in crime journalism. The fact that the lad had never attended school, or learned to read and write, was an obstacle he refused to let daunt him, and which Samuel and I were determined to rectify.

"Mr. Samuel!" the boy exclaimed, skidding to a halt in front of my desk. "I just heard you was here. Are you workin' on a new story, then?"

"A good newspaperman is always working on a new story, Eddie," Samuel told him, clearly enjoying his newfound celebrity, at least as seen through the worshiping eyes of a fifteen-year-old boy.

"Speaking of which, it's high time I was about my business. Thanks to you, little sister, Ian Fearless's latest submission may make tomorrow's front page."

As he gathered up his things, he picked a children's storybook off the desk. "By the way, Sarah, where did you find this old copy of *Rollo Learning to Read*? I thought I got rid of all those old Rollo books when I was ten."

"I'm using it to teach Eddie his letters," I explained. "Mama found it stored in a box in the attic, along with some of your old toys and copybooks from school. It seemed a logical choice."

"It is if you want to bore the lad to death. Sarah, have you ever actually read any of the Rollo books? They may be fine for a five- or six-year-old, but for a boy of fifteen?" He chuckled as he opened the book. " 'Tick, tick, tick, I wonder what o'clock it is?' " he read. Then: " 'Oh it is a fine thing to be a cow.' " With a "What were you thinking?" look, he tossed the book back onto the desk.

Eddie, a foolish grin on his thin face, was nodding his head in joyful agreement. Then, catching my expression, he muttered, "I'm sure Miss Sarah was just tryin' to help me, Mr. Samuel. And the story about that Rollo fellow climbin' up the mountain weren't so bad."

"Yes, that does sound exciting," Samuel replied, not bothering to hide his sarcasm. He picked up his copy of the *Police Gazette* and, before I could object, handed it to Eddie. "See if you don't find this a bit more interesting than little Rollo Holiday wondering what it's like to be a cow."

"Samuel, he can't read well enough yet to attempt a newspaper," I protested. "Even a rag like the *Police Gazette*."

"You'll be surprised by how fast he'll learn," my brother countered with a chuckle.

Eddie beamed, as if he'd been given all the ice cream he could eat. It wasn't just the reading challenge the paper presented that concerned me; it was also its content. Aware that the *Police Gazette* spent far more time covering brutal murders, boxing matches, and houses of ill repute—including coarse engravings and photographs of barely clad women—than it did on everyday police affairs, I felt obliged to object. Which, of course, did not the slightest good.

As if deaf to my protestations, the boy settled himself in the straight chair by the window, buried his nose in the tawdry tabloid, and began to read—*avidly*. Which brought me up short. Upset as I was about Samuel's choice of reading material, I had never seen Eddie exhibit even a fraction as much interest in the Rollo books, despite their popularity. In fact, coaxing him to read the Jacob Abbott series was becoming a decidedly unpleasant chore.

"If you want to teach someone to read, Sarah," Samuel said with maddening superiority, "you must first capture their interest."

Directing a jaunty salute at Eddie, my brother gave me a wink and sauntered cheerfully out the door.

I confess I spent the remainder of the afternoon creating busy-work for myself, trying to keep alive the fading dream that I could make a go of my own law firm. Two months earlier, I had marched into the office of Joseph Shepard, senior partner of Shepard, Shepard, McNaughton and Hall, and with profound delight had tendered my resignation. My erstwhile employer had turned very red in the face, torn between relief that I would be out of his life and disbelief that I would relinquish my position in his prestigious law firm. He'd sputtered that no reputable law firm in the city would hire a woman attorney, a warning that caused me little concern, since I planned on establishing my own law practice.

Famous last words, you might say, and if you did, you would be correct. Seven weeks after opening my Sutter Street law office, I had yet to entertain one client—one *paying* client, that is. So far, the only business I'd conducted had been for several of Eddie's friends (who had paid for my services with pennies, a deck of playing cards minus all four aces—which, I feared, might still be lodged up the boy's sleeve—and some moldy cheese), along with a drunken derelict who was determined to sue a local saloon for refusing to serve him any more whiskey until he paid his bill. If it were not for the money generously given to me by Li Ying, an infamous and mysterious Chinese tong lord, following the Russian Hill murders, I would have been forced to close my office door weeks ago.

As it was, my remaining funds would last but four more months, and then only with the most rigid budgeting. But what bothered me the most about failing was proving all the naysayers correct. My eldest brother, Frederick, was the most vocal of my critics, predicting not only my social ruin if I continued to act upon this insane idea, but also the end to any expectation I might entertain of contracting a suitable marriage. Since I had no desire to marry—a state that, even in 1881, places a woman firmly under her husband's control—I'd ignored Frederick's pessimistic ranting. So, too, had I disregarded Robert Campbell's protests that only a fool would leave the premiere law firm in San Francisco to open her own office. Especially a woman attorney!

The very thought of being forced to eat crow before either of these detractors was enough to make me see red. Which, of course, got me nowhere. Heaving a deep sigh of frustration, I berated myself for wasting valuable time and energy worrying about what might or might not happen four months from now. "Sufficient unto the Day" must become my motto, I vowed. *Defeat* was a word I could not and would not allow to enter my vocabulary!

And so I spent the remainder of the afternoon reading the latest issue of the *San Francisco Law Journal,* an informative periodical that had commenced publication some three years previous. So immersed was I in an article concerning the law of negligence that I started half out of my chair when I was interrupted by a knock on my door. Opening the gold timepiece pinned to the bodice of my dress, I was taken aback to see that it was going on six o'clock. Assuming it was Fanny Goodman inviting me downstairs for a pot of tea before I left for the day, I called for her to enter.

To my surprise, it wasn't my neighbor who timidly entered the room, but a woman I had never seen before. She appeared to be in her early thirties, and was becomingly slender and of average height. Her dark blue day dress was simply cut, with a very small bustle, and her thick chestnut hair had been wound into braids and tucked beneath a stylish brown hat. Her thin oval face might have been considered pretty, if it were not for several fading bruises on her forehead and cheeks. Her right eye was also discolored and slightly puffy. My temper flared at the sight of these contusions, and it was all I could do to stop myself from asking outright who had subjected her to such violence. The poor woman appeared so frightened and ill at ease, however, I decided that for the time being at least I would hold my tongue.

"Good afternoon," I said, rising from my chair. I had been practicing law for less than a year, yet I understood the courage it required for most women to visit an attorney, especially those who were married and used to their husbands making all the decisions in their lives. Indeed, my visitor fitted this description to a tee; she looked so nervous, I feared that at any moment she might bolt back out the door.

Hoping to ease her anxiety, I gave her a welcoming smile. "Please, take a seat," I said, motioning her to the chair in front of my desk. "How may I help you, Mrs. . . ."

"Sechrest, Mrs. Luther Sechrest." Her voice was timorous and uncertain. After a brief hesitation, she sank tentatively into the chair I had indicated. "I—that is, I came here to ask you—" The woman's lovely face colored a pale pink. "I was here earlier today, you see, but the lady downstairs informed me you were out. I—it took me the rest of the afternoon to muster the courage to return." Her face grew even more flushed. "You must think me a terrible coward, but—well, I had no idea consulting an attorney would prove so difficult."

"I understand," I told her with genuine sympathy. "It's an undertaking most people would prefer to avoid entirely. Unfortunately, there are times when dealing with the law cannot be avoided, and it can be a difficult road to navigate on one's own. Now, Mrs. Sechrest, why don't you try to relax and tell me what brought you to my office this afternoon."

Biting her bottom lip, Mrs. Sechrest leaned back farther in her chair and opened her reticule. Withdrawing a small white envelope, she handed it to me across the desk. "Perhaps this will help explain matters."

I accepted the envelope and slit it open. Inside, I discovered a brief letter written in a neat, familiar hand. Dropping my gaze to the signature, I was surprised to see that it was from my very first client at Shepard, Shepard, McNaughton and Hall, Annjenett Hanaford, the young widow I had represented when she was accused of murdering her wealthy husband, Cornelius Hanaford. She had since remarried and was now known as Mrs. Peter Fowler.

I scanned the brief missive and was pleased to see that Annjenett, who had been shamefully ill-treated by her first husband, had used the fortune she'd inherited from him to establish a home here in San Francisco for abused women. According to Annjenett, Alexandra Sechrest had fled to the safe house, seeking shelter from her drunken and violent husband. So that is who had so cruelly mistreated the poor woman, I thought, grateful that because of Annjenett's largesse, women such as Mrs. Sechrest now had a secure haven where they might be out of harm's way.

"Mrs. Fowler tells me that you're interested in obtaining a divorce from your husband," I said.

"It's not what I want," she protested. "I never thought to bring such shame upon myself and my family. But I feel I have no other choice. It's my boys, you see. Johnny is ten and Harry eight. If I don't remove them from their father's house, I'm afraid he'll begin to mistreat them as he has mistreated me. Luther drinks and—" Her blue eyes filled with tears. "I cannot allow that to happen to them, Miss Woolson." Burying her face in her hands, she began to cry.

I removed a clean handkerchief from a pocket hidden in the folds of my skirt—I always have one or two of these handy appendages added to all my working clothes—and, walking around the desk, handed it to Mrs. Sechrest.

"Then we must ensure it does not happen," I said firmly. It was true that I had not yet heard the details of the case, but already my heart went out to this unfortunate woman, not to mention her sons. "Where are your boys now, Mrs. Sechrest? Did you take them with you to Mrs. Fowler's safe house?"

Her face was a mask of hopelessness. "I had them with me for the first week, but Luther, my husband, sent two of his men to take them away from me."

"You mean they grabbed your children by force?"

She nodded, too lost in misery to speak. I waited while she brought her emotions under control. I only wished there was some way to comfort the poor woman. The idea that a husband would snatch his young children from their mother's arms appalled me. Even worse was the fact that in most cases the law permitted such behavior from a father.

"Mrs. Fowler was kind enough to contact Mr. Sechrest on my behalf, but he refuses to return the boys to my care. He even threatened—" Once again she stopped as a fresh rush of tears interrupted her narrative. "He told Mrs. Fowler that if I did not return to his house and resume my wifely duties, he would—he would make certain I never saw my sons again."

Once again, the poor woman buried her face in the handkerchief, her shoulders shaking with silent sobs. I could not watch her misery any longer without offering some kind of comfort, even one whose benefits would be fleeting.

Assuring my visitor that I would be right back, I hastened into the small room adjoining my office proper. This space was to serve as my law library and file room—at least it would once I accumulated files and books to store there. Since clients were hardly beating a path to my door, it currently provided me with a relaxing place to sit and read, or to enjoy a hot cup of tea and some light refreshments.

Striking a match, I lit the spirit lamp I kept on a side table, then scooped a generous spoonful of tea leaves into two strainers and settled them into the cups standing ready for this purpose. Fortunately, the water in the kettle was still warm from tea I'd brewed earlier, and it was not long before I returned to the front room carrying the two steaming cups, as well as a plate of gingersnaps and Sarasota chips I kept stored in tins.

"There now," I said, laying the refreshments out on my desk. "Why don't you tell me everything, starting with when and where you and Mr. Sechrest were married."

Alexandra Sechrest gave me a quick smile and gratefully sipped her tea. Placing the cup back in its saucer, she took a deep breath and commenced her story.

"Mr. Sechrest and I were married twelve years ago. He is the foreman of the Leighton Mining Company here in the city. Actually, he is much more than that. Mr. Leighton is getting on in years and has no sons to run the company after he's gone. Although he hasn't actually promised to leave the business to my husband, for the past seven years Luther has taken over the day-to-day operation of the plant."

Her face clouded. "My father favored our marriage. My mother did not. She felt I was marrying below my station, which was probably true, but my family had fallen upon hard times and Papa could offer little dowry. And he has two younger daughters to settle in marriage. It seemed a godsend when Luther promised to provide my family with a monthly allowance. And to give him his due, he has kept his promise, at least the one he made to my father. As for me—" She shuddered. "My husband began to change soon after we were married. He was no longer the man I had come to know and respect."

I waited while my guest once again regained control of her emotions. Unfortunately, the story she related was far from uncommon; tragically, it was Annjenett Hanaford's tale, as well. Mr. Hanaford, like Mr. Sechrest, had appeared to possess a genial nature before marriage. It was not until the union had been consummated that he began to show his true colors.

"I beg your pardon, Miss Woolson." Alexandra dabbed at her damp eyes, then managed another weak smile. "I'm truly embarrassed. I don't seem to be handling this very well."

"To the contrary, you're doing just fine. Matters of this nature are always distressful, especially when there are children involved." I reached for a pad and pencil and sought to established the facts concerning the divorce. "You say your husband physically abused you. Did anyone witness this abuse? Say your personal maid, or other servants?"

She shook her head. "I was always careful to hide it from the household staff. My lady's maid probably saw some of the bruises, but she never remarked on them. Then there's my sister Emily. Last year, she paid a surprise visit, and was actually shown in by the maid no more than a minute or two after Luther had struck me across the face. She must have seen the mark of his hand, yet she has never questioned me about his behavior."

I was not surprised. Convention dictated that what went on between a husband and wife in the privacy of their own home was no one else's concern. The law went to great lengths to ensure that a man's home remained his castle. Unfortunately, spousal abuse was all too often met with a blind eye—by servants, by families, and, regrettably, by the law.

"If it becomes necessary, do you think your sister or your maid would testify in court on your behalf?"

She blanched. "Surely it won't come to that."

"I appreciate your distress, Mrs. Sechrest, but in divorce actions such as this, a court appearance is almost a certainty. Your case will be best served if we are prepared for any eventuality."

Alexandra's face remained pale, but she could hardly find fault with this sensible precaution. "Yes, undoubtedly you are right, Miss Woolson. It's just that I did not anticipate airing our private problems in public."

"Of course not. No one does. However, allowing Mr. Sechrest to continue this destructive behavior might well result in serious injury." I watched her reaction to this statement, trying to gauge the extent of her commitment to the action she proposed. If she went ahead with the divorce, the process would be anything but smooth. If I was to act as her attorney, it was my duty to warn her of what lay ahead.

That she had taken my words to heart was obvious by the frown lines on her smooth forehead, and by the way her bosom rose and fell beneath her dark blue bodice. For the first time since she had entered my office, I sensed that Alexandra Sechrest was questioning her decision to dissolve her marriage.

"I appreciate your honesty, Miss Woolson," she said at length. "I confess I feel very naïve. The divorce procedure sounds perfectly dreadful." She paused, then stared directly into my eyes. "Despite the possible consequences, however, I am determined to see the matter through, not so much for my sake, but for my sons'. I would never forgive myself if their father mistreated them in any way. Nor could I bear it if they grew up imitating his wretched behavior."

"If that is your final decision, Mrs. Sechrest, I suggest we meet here again next week and draw up a plan of action. We will need to discuss gaining custody of your sons, as well as formulating a strategy in the event your husband contests your petition of divorce."

Despite her newfound bravery, my client's shoulders drooped perceptibly. "I am certain Luther will contest my request for a divorce, Miss Woolson. Not because he loves me, but because he is fiercely protective of his possessions. And that is all I have meant to him for many years now. You were right when you said we must be prepared for any eventuality."

She heaved a sigh of what I took to be resignation. "I fear we must brace ourselves for a bitter battle."

CHAPTER FIVE

I was not looking forward to dinner Saturday evening. I knew the food would be excellent and the wine carefully chosen to complement each course in what I feared would be a far too drawn-out meal. The servants would be in full livery—although heaven alone knew why, since only the immediate family would be present—padding noiselessly about the candlelit dining room like so many well-trained penguins. In brief, everything would be perfect. The only fly in the ointment was that the party was to be held at my eldest brother Frederick's monstrosity of a house on Nob Hill. And because the dinner was in honor of Papa's sixty-fifth birthday, there wasn't a thing I could do to get out of attending!

Since everyone in the family, excluding Frederick and Henrietta, still lived at our Rincon Hill home, Papa had hired two cabriolets for the occasion. Mama, Papa, and my middle brother, Charles, would travel in one, while Charles's wife, Celia, my youngest brother, Samuel, and I would go in the second.

Despite my lack of enthusiasm for the evening, I had to admit that we arrived at Frederick and his wife Henrietta's house in grand style.

"This house never fails to amaze me," Charles said as we waited for everyone to alight from the carriages. Although my brother Charles would never say anything derogatory about someone's house—particularly his own brother's—I knew from past visits that he found it a bit of a monstrosity.

"That isn't precisely the word I would use," I said. "But yes, it's something all right."

As always, the sight of their overblown residence caused me to cringe. Frederick's determination to erect a home that would compete with the railroad and Nevada silver mine moguls' multimillion-dollar feudal castles was an ambition doomed to failure, given his modest budget. The end result was a hodgepodge of French and Italian styles, with columns, balustrades, gingerbread trim, and even a dome thrown in for good measure. These conflicting designs seemed to have been added without the slightest regard to aesthetic beauty or architectural harmony. Not only was the edifice an eyesore, but the money Frederick had been forced to borrow to erect it would ensure his continuing indebtedness for years to come.

We were met at the door by Woodbury, Frederick's stodgy and very proper butler, who showed us into the front parlor. I will not bore you with a description of the interior of the house. Suffice it to say that the rooms reflected the same unabashed disregard for eye-pleasing symmetry as did the exterior. The objective in furnishing the rooms had been to demonstrate my brother's success and personal worth (even if most of it was owed to the bank), rather than to provide a pleasant and comfortable haven in which to live.

Opening the parlor door, Woodbury announced our arrival as if he were presenting us to European royalty. We were, I saw, just in time for an aperitif and the dreary discourse that invariably accompanied these dinner parties. For some reason I had yet to fathom, my eldest brother and his brittle, rail-thin wife, Henrietta, disdained any verbal exchange that involved conflict or unpleasantness of any kind, or that required more than the most minuscule intellect.

These conversational restrictions, I need hardly point out, made for extremely dull evenings.

I eschewed the glass of sherry Frederick automatically served my mother, Celia, and I, opting instead for the whiskey mix meted out to the men. This was not my usual predinner drink, but given the long, dismal evening stretching before me, I decided that I required all the help I could get.

Frederick's eyebrows lifted until they nearly collided with his slicked-back and rapidly receding hair. Sensing that I was about to be broadsided by one of his tiresome lectures, I gratefully accepted the whiskey and soda Samuel handed me, a broad grin on his face.

"Don't bother, Frederick," he said before our host could protest. "I'll just help myself to another."

Samuel had already taken a glass from the side table and was proceeding to fill it with far more of the amber liquid than Frederick's initial allotment. He added a meager splash of soda, then held it aloft.

"To Father on his sixty-fifth birthday," he toasted. "May he be blessed with many more."

"Yes, to Papa," Celia said, beaming at the in-law who had become more like a father to her than the man who, in 1862, had marched off to join the Confederate army in its first invasion of the North. Celia had been eight years old at the time. She never saw her father again.

"To Father," the rest of us exclaimed in chorus, even Frederick and Henrietta, although judging by their sour expressions, you'd have thought their glasses contained unsweetened lemon juice.

"I see that Rudolph Hardin's been talking to the newspapers again," Samuel said to Frederick. "This time, he's accusing you of buying your victory in the last election."

Samuel was referring, of course, to my eldest brother's major political opponent and archenemy. The two had started out as rivals in law school, and the hostility between them had increased exponentially over the years. Lately, it seemed as if Hardin's primary goal was to usurp Frederick's seat in the state senate.

"The man is an imbecile!" Frederick snapped, growing red in the face. "Every time I open a paper, I find that he's concocted yet another outrageous story about me. What I don't understand is why reporters even listen to him. He's nothing more than a duplicitous windbag."

"It sells copies," Papa put in, warming to one of his favorite subjects. "That's all these damn reporters care about, glorifying violence and blackening someone's good name. All in the interest of increased circulation."

I gazed guardedly at Samuel, who, as a covert reporter himself, was squirming in his seat. Well, I thought, appreciating the irony of the situation, that's what he gets for broaching such a volatile subject around Papa.

Thankfully, dinner was announced before the discussion could grow any more heated, and we were shown into the dining room—a commodious space furnished with a carved Italian walnut table and chairs, a matching buffet and credenza. Some quite lovely murals of Parisian scenes had been painted on the walls. I admit I found this one of the more pleasing rooms in the otherwise-pretentious house.

We had completed the soup and salad courses, and a platter of steamed oysters (Papa's favorite) had been deposited on the table, when I decided it was time to introduce a more interesting subject than the latest society scandals and the best way to prepare wild duck.

"I ran into your friend Senator Gaylord a few days ago, Frederick," I said, passing the oysters to Samuel, who sat to my left.

Frederick squinted at me suspiciously. "Oh? And where was that?"

So, I thought, my brother had not yet learned of his mentor's presence at Madame Karpova's séance. This did not unduly surprise me. When I had failed to find his name in any of the newspapers covering Moss's death, I realized that the Senator must have exerted considerable influence to retain his anonymity. Lieutenant Ahern and his wife had also escaped mention.

Regrettably, Robert and I, along with Theodora Reade, Philippa and Nicholas Bramwell, and, of course, Madame Karpova and her family, had not been as fortunate. Our names had been bandied about in every newspaper, not only as devotees of the occult—an accusation that particularly incensed Robert—but also as murder suspects. This coverage had certainly not endeared the Scot to his employer. And since Robert could hardly take out his anger on Joseph Shepard, I had become the target of his considerable wrath.

"Senator Gaylord and his wife were at the Cliff House séance Robert and I attended," I told Frederick, ashamed to experience such childish delight in dropping this bombshell. "You know, where Darien Moss was murdered?" I pretended not to notice Frederick's and Henrietta's shocked reactions.

"I don't believe it!" Frederick exclaimed. "Senator Gaylord would never be taken in by such foolishness. Good Lord, Sarah, a séance? Never!"

"I believe he and Mrs. Gaylord were hoping to communicate with their deceased daughter," I told him, serenely spooning out a second helping of oysters. They really were quite excellent. Glancing at the chair to my left, I could sense Samuel fighting not to laugh.

"It's preposterous," Henrietta proclaimed indignantly. "Out of sisterly affection, Frederick and I have put up with your increasingly wild flights of fancy, Sarah. But to malign the good name of one of San Francisco's most beloved and self-sacrificing citizens is not to be tolerated!"

To my right, Papa chuckled as he heaped his own plate with more oysters. "So, my girl, it seems you were in good company," he said, ignoring Henrietta's outraged sputters. "I don't blame Percival Gaylord for not wanting word of this to get out." He slapped the table, as if struck by a hilarious thought. "Just imagine if he were accused of governing the state based on the position of the stars"—by now, he was laughing so hard that he could scarcely speak—"or with the help of otherworldly beings."

Frederick, whose face had turned a blotchy red, was not amused. "I fail to see what is so amusing, Father. We are discussing a California state senator, a man who surely deserves our respect."

"Yes, son, you're right, of course," Papa admitted, wiping tears of laughter from his eyes. "It's just that Gaylord is one of the most dreary and unimaginative men I know. The very idea of him attending a séance is—" Once again, he was overcome with mirth. "Well, you have to admit it's damned ironic."

"Horace, please, your language," Mama put in, then looked embarrassed for having corrected her husband in front of his children.

"You are entirely correct, Mama Woolson," said Henrietta, darting daggers at me. "This conversation is entirely unsuitable for the dinner table. I have gone to considerable effort to celebrate Papa Woolson's birthday. I think it is best if we speak of happier matters."

"Oh, but I find the present conversation quite stimulating," Papa said cheerfully. "And as you pointed out, Henrietta, it *is* my birthday."

Henrietta flushed. I could practically hear her teeth grinding as she forced her thin lips into a none-too-convincing smile. "If that is what you wish, Papa Woolson. Although I shudder to think of the ill effects such a conversation will have on our digestions."

Papa's eyes twinkled at this concession, knowing what it had cost his daughter-in-law. "Thank you, Henrietta. Now, Sarah, tell us more about this séance. Who else was there besides Percival Gaylord and his wife?"

"Let me see." I mentally pictured the people seated around the table that fateful night. "Mrs. Philippa Bramwell came with her son Nicholas, and a Mrs. Theodora Reade was also there. Their names were in the paper, along with those of Madame Olga Karpova, her daughter, Yelena, and her brother, Dmitry Serkov. Oh, and Lieutenant Frank Ahern and his wife, Nora, also attended."

Papa coughed on some food he was chewing and stared at me in surprise. "Frank Ahern was at a séance? Well, now I really have seen the elephant! What in tarnation was he doing there?"

"Mrs. Ahern's mother died recently," I replied. "I believe she was hoping to make contact with her."

Frederick made a disparaging sound, as if this was just the escape hatch he had been seeking. "That explains it, then. The unfortunate man was dragged to see this charlatan by a gullible wife. As was Senator Gaylord, I dare say."

Henrietta sniffed. "I regret having to say this, but Maurilla Gaylord has always been far too whimsical for her own good. Now she may have irreparably damaged her husband's political future. The Cliff House is acquiring a most unseemly reputation. I can't imagine what she was thinking, forcing that unfortunate man to escort her to such a place."

"I expect she is so anguished over the death of her little girl that politics did not enter her mind," said Celia, herself the mother of two small children and expecting a third child in less than two months. Of late, she'd fairly glowed with happy expectation. "Regardless of my personal feelings about clairvoyants and communicating with the dead," she went on, "I cannot help but pity the poor woman."

"As do we all," said Mama, perhaps remembering the death of her first daughter, my elder sister, Kat, when the child was but five years old.

"You say Mrs. Bramwell was there with her son," Papa said, passing me a basket of freshly baked bread. "If I'm not mistaken, Nicholas Bramwell recently passed the California Bar examination and has obtained a position as associate attorney at Riley and Taft." He referred, of course, to one of the more prominent law firms in the city.

"He has political aspirations," Samuel put in as the now-empty oyster plate was removed from the table. "Or rather, his mother does. His older brother is being groomed to take over their father's construction business, which leaves Nicholas free to pursue a seat in the senate."

Frederick regarded his younger brother. "And just how do you happen to know so much about Nicholas Bramwell?"

"We belong to the same club," Samuel replied, spearing a piece of roast chicken from the platter that had replaced the oysters. "I might add that Nicholas is very popular at the Bohemian Club, considering he's been a member for less than a year. I'd say he possesses the intelligence and personality necessary to get himself elected to public office."

It was clear that Frederick did not find this a particularly heartening thought. In the years to come, Nicholas Bramwell might well become his political rival. As I held no false illusions about Frederick's governing abilities, I found this prospect rather comforting. Frankly, it surprised me that California had thus far survived my brother's first year in the state senate. Still, I saw no reason to press our luck by reelecting my brother to a second term.

"It surprises me that no one at that séance saw or heard anything," Papa said speculatively, getting back to Moss's murder. "Seems to me it would be damn hard to kill a man with eleven other people in the room."

"It's all rather horrible, isn't it?" Celia put in with a little shudder. "Who could have wanted to see the poor man dead in the first place?"

Papa gave a little chuckle, which was quickly dashed by a disapproving look from Mama. "I'm afraid, my dear, that Darien Moss was not a very nice man," he said, very nearly parroting the words Nora Ahern had used to describe the reporter. "I'm sure he has made a great many enemies through that tell-all column of his."

"Perhaps," said Charles, who, as a physician, tended to measure death in medical terms. "But to hate him enough to commit murder?

It's sad enough when a man his age passes away of natural causes. But to die like that. It seems so unnecessary—and tragic.

Frederick was studying me, a questioning look on his broad face. "I would like to know what you were doing at that séance in the first place, Sarah. I've never known you to put much stock in the supernatural."

Samuel's foot nudged mine beneath the table, but I required no reminder to keep his name out of this affair. So far, I was the only member of our family who was aware of his secret profession as a freelance journalist. A *crime* journalist at that! Papa, who held most newspaper men in extremely low esteem, would have had a conniption fit. As it was, he was growing ever more frustrated that Samuel had not yet taken his California Bar examination.

"I, ah, was just curious," I said rather unconvincingly. I kept my eyes fixed on my plate, hoping no one would notice this slight departure from the absolute truth. I had, after all, been interested in meeting Madame Karpova and witnessing one of her famous séances. On the other hand, it was doubtful I would have traveled all the way out to Land's End—and in one of the worst storms of the year—had it not been for Samuel's persistence. "I'd heard so much about Madame Karpova, I thought it might be fun to see her for myself."

"I knew it!" Frederick exclaimed, his voice accusing. "I warned you this would happen, Father, if you continued to be so permissive with Sarah. First, she had the gall to call herself an attorney, meddling in affairs no decent woman should even know about. Then she disgraced the entire family by opening her own law practice. And now she's—she's—"

"She's taken to speaking to the dead," said Henrietta, finishing her husband's sentence. Her stern, angular face was red to the very roots of her mousy brown hair, and her gray eyes flashed with anger. "Really, Papa Woolson, you must do something to stop your daughter's irrational behavior. Now that Frederick is a senator, we have a social position to maintain. Sarah is making a laughingstock of us in front of Frederick's colleagues—indeed, in front of all our friends. Can no one control her?" Abruptly, she stopped speaking and looked around the table, embarrassed to find every eye fastened on her in varying degrees of alarm and distress.

Her face was flushed scarlet as she turned to me in a fury. "Just see where this conversation has led us, Sarah Woolson. As usual, you care nothing about your family, but only about your own irresponsible and selfish aims. I realize it is your birthday, Papa Woolson, but I must insist that we cease speaking of these dreadful matters before the evening is completely ruined."

Henrietta took a deep breath, attempting, I assumed, to calm her nerves after this outbreak. Gradually, her red face returned to its normal pasty color, and we went on to speak of mundane matters, which captured no one's interest and caused the remainder of the evening to pass in what felt like an eternity of boredom.

The following afternoon, as I attempted to catch up on some correspondence in the library, Mama entered the room carrying an armful of material.

"Ah, there you are, my dear. I would appreciate your help deciding which fabric to choose for the new dining room drapes."

Spreading the material across the backs of several chairs, she sat down next to me as I wrote at the escritoire.

Her request made me smile.

"Shouldn't you ask Celia, Mama? She's the one with an eye for this sort of thing. You haven't forgotten, have you, my attempt to remodel my bedroom several years ago? As I recall, you said the greens clashed so badly they made you seasick."

"Oh, dear, I remember now," she said, laughing. "Yes, perhaps I had better ask Celia to assist me." She started to get up, then spied an envelope lying atop some letters I had yet to answer. "I don't mean to pry, Sarah, but is that a letter from that nice young man, Pierce Godfrey?"

I groaned inwardly, certain that I was in for yet another lecture on matrimony. I had met Pierce Godfrey when I became involved in the Russian Hill murders several months ago, and Mama still had not recovered from my rejection of his offer of marriage. Shortly after his proposal, he had departed for Hong Kong, where he planned to open a new office for the shipping firm he owned with his brother Leonard.

"It's true that we still correspond, Mama, but nothing has changed between us. We continue to be nothing more than good friends."

"Ah, but that's one of the most important aspects in a successful marriage, dear," she said gently. "You'd be surprised at the number of couples who can barely tolerate being in the same room with each other, much less behave as if they're friends."

"I know, Mama." I reached out and squeezed her hand, realizing she only wished to see me happy. Remaining a spinster by choice was incomprehensible to her, consequently she couldn't imagine such a life could bring contentment and satisfaction.

"I'm exceedingly fond of Pierce," I went on, remembering the suave, handsome, and, yes, I admit, exciting man who had very nearly swept me off my feet. "But our lives are so dissimilar, I don't see how a union between us could survive. He's always sailing off to one exotic place after another, while I'm forever burying my nose in law tomes."

Mama shook her head and sighed. "You truly are hopeless, Sarah. You have so much to offer a husband: beauty, intelligence, sensitivity, a sense of humor. Ah, well, perhaps if you meet the right man one day, you'll change your mind."

"Perhaps," I agreed. The prospect was exceedingly unlikely, but I loved my mother too much to take away all her hope of seeing me settled and raising a family. With time, I prayed she would be able to accept, if not understand, the path I had chosen.

Leaning down, she kissed my cheek, then picked up the swaths of material she had spread out on the chairs. "I'd better find Celia, if I'm to place the order for these drapes tomorrow. I'd like to have them up in time for the holidays."

Monday morning an unusual September fog billowed in through the Golden Gate. The gray mist crossed the Embarcadero, then slithered up the hills in snakelike tendrils until it was finally dissipated by the sun.

I departed for my Sutter Street office before the fog had given up its hold on the city, and the streets were damp and colder than usual. I did not feel the chill. All weekend I had been formulating plans on how best to serve the first genuine client to find her way into my office. The weeks of doubt and worry about my increasingly dire financial situation were, like the fog, beginning to dissolve, leaving me energized and eager to commence work for Mrs. Sechrest.

Since Friday, I had spent hours sequestered in my father's library, searching California law books for appellate opinions and legislation pertaining to marriage and divorce. The information I found confirmed what I already suspected: Obtaining a divorce from Mrs. Sechrest's abusive husband would be relatively simple; gaining custody of her two young sons promised to be a great deal more difficult.

My downstairs neighbor, Fanny Goodman, was just opening the front door to her millinery shop when I arrived at my place of business. As was her custom, she asked me inside for a cup of coffee before I commenced work. Over the past two months I'd made it a habit of accepting these invitations and always found Fanny's company enjoyable and stimulating. This morning, however, I declined, pleading that I had only come by my office to pick up one or two necessary items before journeying to the Department of Records to conduct further research concerning the Sechrest case.

"Good for you, dear," she said, beaming when I told her of my new client. "I never doubted for one moment that you'd make a success of your practice. Mark my words, news will spread and soon you'll have more clients than you know what to do with."

It was impossible not to be cheered by Fanny's enthusiasm, although I knew it was overly optimistic. Yet how nice it felt to have such a steadfast ally.

As it turned out, my plan to leave posthaste for the Department of Records was delayed by the arrival of two unexpected visitors. I had been in my office for only a few minutes when, to my considerable surprise, I found Madame Karpova and her daughter Yelena standing outside my door. Actually, if I had not instantly recognized Yelena, I'm not at all certain I would have known her mother. The last time I'd seen the medium, she'd been dressed entirely in black, and her hair had been hidden by a black turban.

The change in her was extraordinary. This morning she wore a mauve silk dress with a small bustle and a skirt with horizontal pleating. A dark mauve hat with feathers sat becomingly over her thick, dark brown hair, which had been arranged in a neat chignon. Unlike the night of the séance, the psychic's eyes were not outlined in kohl, nor was her mouth colored, but instead was as nature intended. The effect was to make the woman look a good ten years younger and surprisingly attractive. Her haughty, self-confident bearing, however, remained the same, and she took the seat I offered as if she were honoring me with her presence.

Her daughter Yelena looked much recovered from the attack she'd suffered four days earlier at the Cliff House. She was dressed in a light green day dress that displayed her slim figure to good advantage but, because of its high collar, hid the neck wound that I was sure must still be noticeable as it healed. Her hat, which was a bit smaller than her mother's, was decorated with artificial flowers instead of feathers, and had been placed upon her head at a jaunty angle.

"Madame Karpova, Yelena," I said, once the two women were settled in their chairs. "What may I do for you?"

Yelena glanced at me nervously, then looked to her mother.

Madame Karpova sat ramrod straight, her handsome head held high, her unblinking eyes squarely meeting mine.

"We come, Miss Woolson," she began in that rich, deep voice, the slight Russian accent ironically making it even more captivating, "because I fear for my daughter's safety. Since her assault last Thursday night, the police have done little to apprehend her assailant. Because we are Russian, they do not care if we are attacked, or even murdered."

"I'm sure Lieutenant Ahern and his men are doing everything they can to find whoever did this to Yelena," I said, hoping this was truly the case. Unfortunately, she was correct; our police department did not always spend as much time on crimes committed against foreigners as they did to those perpetrated against their own citizens.

"Do not speak nonsense, Miss Woolson," the woman chided. "You know as well as I do that is not the case. The authorities regard us as villains. Even now, they waste valuable time treating my brother as if he is a murderer. All day they question him, then come back the next day and ask him the same questions again. If I could, I would take Yelena out of this city of violence. But your police will not let us go."

"I'm sorry to hear that, Madame Karpova," I said, feeling genuine sympathy for the woman and her brother. "Unfortunately, there's nothing I can do to put a stop to it. That's the way murder investigations are carried out in this country; people are questioned while the police attempt to discover the truth. In this case, everyone who was present at the séance will remain under suspicion until they do."

"Do they question *you?*" Madame Karpova asked bluntly. Her dark eyes fastened on me with steely resolve. How was it, I wondered, that she could go so long without blinking?

"I've been questioned," I said hedging, fully aware that my brief interrogation could not be compared with the grilling Dmitry was receiving. The fact that he was a foreigner—and truly did look and dress like a villain in a dime novel—only made his situation worse. "We've all been questioned."

She swept out a hand, as if brushing aside this pathetic answer. "Not like Dmitry. He is Russian, so they persecute him. You must make it stop!"

"I wish I had the power to do that," I told her. Despite her arrogant manner, she and her family were strangers in this country. Now they were involved in a homicide. They must feel very confused and frightened, I thought.

"The police won't listen to me, or to anyone else, until they identify the murderer," I went on. Her eyes did not move from my face; indeed, they appeared harder and more determined than before. I sighed and searched for a way to make her understand. "Madame Karpova, let me give you some advice. The best way for Mr. Serkov to convince the police of his innocence is for him to answer all their questions completely and honestly. It is very important that he hold nothing back, for it will all come out in the end and will look even worse for him if he's prevaricated."

The woman raised her chin so that she gave the appearance of looking down her nose at me. "What is this word, *prevaricated*?" she demanded.

"It means to evade or stray from the truth. That's the worst thing anyone can do in a murder investigation."

Once again, my guest made a dismissive gesture with her hand. "Dmitry does not trust your police. But he does not lie to them."

I watched her closely, but she was too much in control of her emotions to allow a facial expression to betray her inner feelings, or distress. "Then your brother has nothing to fear. Nor do you, Madame, if you've been equally candid with the police."

Out of the corner of my eye, I saw Yelena Karpova start in her chair. Giving the girl my complete attention, I saw her delicate nostrils flare slightly and noticed that she had turned a trifle pale around the mouth.

"What about you, my dear?" I asked. "Have the police been distressing you, as well?"

The girl looked at me in surprise, taken aback, it seemed, to be spoken to directly. Her lovely brown eyes had grown very large, and she was twisting her hands nervously in her lap.

Madame Karpova's expression softened as she regarded her daughter. "*Moyo malenkaya*, Miss Woolson is speaking to you. Please, try to answer." To me, she added, "Ever since the night she was attacked, she has been terrified. She still has night tremors and eats like a bird. It is impossible not to worry."

"I can certainly understand why she's upset, Madame Karpova," I said. "I'd be frightened, too, if someone suddenly jumped out at me and tried to pull a wire around my neck. It must have been horrible."

The clairvoyant nodded, then looked at her daughter with concern. "Yes, it was a dreadful experience. I should not have allowed that policeman to change her room. Mrs. Reade did not need to be directly next door to Mrs. Ahern. She is old, and old women faint. Besides," she added with a meaningful nod, "she does not have long to live." She tapped her right index finger against her temple. "I, Madame Karpova, know these things."

I stared at her, confounded by what she had just said. "Excuse me, Madame Karpova. What was that about changing rooms?"

"The policeman wanted the old woman closer to his wife, so he made Yelena change rooms. You know, in the event Mrs. Reade required assistance during the night."

I managed to keep my voice controlled. "So, what you're saying, Madame Karpova, is that the room Yelena occupied the night Darien Moss was killed was originally intended for Theodora Reade?"

"Yes, that is what I said. Yelena should have been in the room next to mine." Her face darkened and she hissed several words that sounded like a Russian oath. Then she exclaimed, "If Yelena had been attacked there, I would have taken care of the assassin—with my bare hands, if need be! I tell you, Miss Woolson, you must do something. I want to take my daughter and brother and leave this awful place."

I spent the next quarter hour trying to convince my over-wrought visitor that there was truly nothing I could do to stop the police department from questioning her brother. I could tell by her set expression that my words were making no impression. It was, therefore, a relief when Robert came bursting into my office (he rarely, if ever, knocked).

"Sarah, before you say no, I want you to think—" He stopped short when he saw the two women. "What are they doing here?" he added with his usual nonexistent tact.

The medium drew breath to put him in his place, but I managed to speak first. "Madame Karpova, Yelena, I think you remember my colleague, Mr. Robert Campbell, from the séance. Robert, we've been discussing how the police are coming along in their investigation of Darien Moss's death."

He eyed me warily. "Just discussing?"

"Of course." Rising from my chair, I addressed my guests. "I hope you will excuse me, ladies, but Mr. Campbell and I have urgent business to discuss."

Madame Karpova seemed about to object, then thought better of it. "Yelena, *nam pora idty*. It is time to go."

Without taking her frightened eyes off Robert, the girl rose from her chair and went to stand by the door.

"I expected better of your country," Madame Karpova told me tersely. Then, head held so high that I feared she might trip on the stairs leading down to the street, she sailed out of the room with her daughter.

When the door closed behind them, Robert sank into the chair Madame Karpova had just vacated, his turquoise eyes regarding me with suspicion. "So, what was that little visit *really* about? And don't tell me that woman came to see you just to discuss Darien Moss's death, because I don't believe it for one minute."

"I'll tell you about it on the way," I replied, reaching for my coat, which was hanging on the clothes rack behind the door.

"On our way where?" he asked with a scowl. "I only stopped by to offer you work—*paid* work, I might add. Joseph Shepard doesn't have to know that you were the one who actually did the job—"

"That will have to wait," I told him. "Did you happen to see Eddie and his brougham parked outside? He was supposed to have been here half an hour ago."

"Yes, he's down there. But where the devil are you going?"

"*We,* Robert," I announced, walking out the door. "I would very much appreciate it if you would go with me."

CHAPTER SIX

You think Mrs. Reade was the intended victim and not
Yelena?" Robert asked after we were seated in Eddie's
brougham and I had told him about the last-minute room
change.

"Don't you agree it makes a good deal more sense than someone attacking Madame Karpova's daughter?"

At that moment, Eddie took a corner too fast and I slid into my
companion, causing him to grab hold of me to prevent us both
from crashing into the door. Embarrassed to find my face all but
pressed against his, I started to apologize, only to find myself inex-
plicably breathless.

"Sarah!" he exclaimed, looking as self-conscious as I felt. "Er,
that is, I—" His words, such as they were, cut off and he sucked in
a quick gulp of air. The blue-green eyes staring into mine appeared
very large, or perhaps they seemed that way because they were a
mere inch or two from my own.

I was the first to blink, and that seemed to break the sudden tension between us, leaving me surprisingly winded. Extricating myself as gracefully as possible from Robert's embrace, I moved over
to my usual place on the seat, straightened my skirts, and tried to

recall what I had been saying. For some reason, my previous train of thought had become a bit muddled. Then, as Eddie narrowly avoided hitting a depot wagon driven by an angry man with a very red face, it came back to me.

"Ah, yes, about the room changes. If you remember, Robert, Mrs. Reade sat almost directly across from Moss during the séance. The most likely explanation is that in that brief flash of lightning, she saw whoever killed him. But, of course, she fainted before she could tell anyone. The murderer must have known, or at least suspected, he'd been seen, and set out to silence her. What he didn't realize was that Mrs. Reade's room had been switched with Yelena's, so that she might be closer to Mrs. Ahern."

Robert shifted in his seat and cleared his throat, but he did not reply. Glancing at him, I wondered if he were going out of his way to avoid looking at me. The thought crossed my mind that he might still be discomfited by our chance collision moments before; then common sense disabused me of that fanciful notion.

"Robert? Are you all right? You appear to be flushed."

"I'm fine," he replied rather brusquely, still not meeting my eyes.

"Well?" I prodded. "Don't you agree that is a likely hypothesis for what happened?"

"Yes, I suppose it is." He darted a quick look at me from the corner of his eye and once again cleared his throat before going on in a more normal tone of voice. "I admit I found it hard to believe that Serkov would attack his own niece."

"So you're still convinced Dmitry Serkov is the killer?" I asked, not bothering to hide my annoyance.

Mumbling beneath his breath, he finally turned to face me. "Of course I am. Think about it, Sarah, who else could it be?"

"There were twelve of us at that table, Robert," I reminded him. "And for several minutes, the room was in complete darkness. Anyone could have slipped out of their seat during that time."

"Of course that's possible, but he—"

"Or she," I said, interrupting.

He looked genuinely surprised. "A woman? That seems unlikely. It hardly seems the sort of crime a woman would commit."

"Not ordinarily," I agreed. "But as it was most likely a crime of opportunity, even a woman might jump at the chance to silence Moss. That is, if she feared him enough."

Grudgingly, Robert nodded his head. "All right, for the sake of argument, let's assume the killer could be a man *or* a woman. Either way, he or she was taking a terrible chance of being seen."

"I know. That's why I'm convinced the killer had to have been truly desperate. Moss must have known something extremely damaging about that individual. And the assailant knew, or at least suspected, that Moss was planning to print it in his column."

"That goes without saying. Discovering what that damaging information was is an entirely different matter. Moreover, it's a problem best left to the police to solve."

"Yes," I agreed evasively, "at least for the time being. What worries me at the moment is Mrs. Reade's safety. If we're right and she was the intended victim, then her life is in grave danger."

Before he could respond, Eddie reined up in front of a handsome Gothic-style redwood home on Pacific Street. The three-story dwelling was typical of houses erected in the 1860s, complete with an ornately carved bargeboard along the gabled roof, and a number of ornamental rooftop finials. It boasted a small garden in front—a vanishing luxury in a town seemingly determined to place as many houses as possible on increasingly limited land—and was enclosed by a black iron fence. Perhaps the dwelling's most prominent feature was its lack of bay windows, having been constructed prior to the advent of what was rapidly becoming a city-wide rage.

Eddie leapt easily down from the driver's seat and opened the carriage door with a flourish so overblown that I was—despite the seriousness of our visit—strongly tempted to laugh. It was touching how hard the boy worked to please us.

Robert and I passed through the gate and up the brick path to the front door. Our knock was answered by a tall white-haired man, who announced himself as Mrs. Reade's butler.

"We would like to see your mistress if she is receiving callers," I announced, handing the man my card. "I am Sarah Woolson and this is Robert Campbell."

The butler barely glanced at my card before placing it upon a silver salver that lay on a table by the door.

"I am sorry, Miss Woolson, Mr. Campbell, but I'm afraid Mrs. Reade is not at home." The man's voice was so somber, I felt it would have better suited an undertaker than a domestic servant. "I will inform madam of your visit as soon as she returns."

"When do you expect her?" I asked when he started to close the door.

The man seemed taken aback by my forwardness. "I really cannot say, miss. If you would care to call back tomorrow after lunch, I'm sure madam would be pleased to receive you."

Robert made an impatient sound. "See here Mr., er—"

"Fennel, sir," the butler said, beginning to look annoyed at our rude insistence.

"Yes. Well, Fennel, it is imperative that we see your mistress today, not tomorrow, not the next day. She may be in grave danger."

The butler's eyes grew large. He looked from Robert to me, then back to Robert. "Did you say, sir, that she is in danger?"

"That is exactly what I said," Robert replied. "Now, if you will be kind enough to tell us where your mistress has gone, we will depart and leave you in peace."

Once again, the man looked from one of us to the other. "I— that is, I really don't think I can reveal—"

"You can and you must," Robert told the man firmly. "That is, if you care about your employer's well-being. Come, man, there is no time to be lost!"

Fennel's somber face displayed his growing alarm. "Daniel—that is the footman—drove her to Washington Square about three-quarters of an hour ago. Madam enjoys visiting the park on fine days like—"

"Thank you, Fennel," I said, following Robert down the brick path toward the waiting brougham. "Washington Square, Eddie," I told the boy as he assisted me into the carriage. "And hurry."

I should have known by now that instructing Eddie to hurry was tantamount to thumbing your nose at fate. Naturally, he took my instructions literally, and pulled back onto Pacific Street as if we were racing to a fire. I tried to call up to him that I had not intended for him to risk life and limb, but my words were lost in the din of traffic and the rumble of our own wheels. I could see that Robert was trying to tell me something as he clutched the seat with white knuckles, but all I could make out were the words "insane speed" and "kill us yet!"

We had gone on in this manner for a few hair-raising blocks, when I heard bells clanging loudly behind us. Looking out my window, I spied a police wagon pulling up on us hell-bent for leather, as Papa was fond of saying. Of necessity, Eddie was forced to lessen the brougham's breakneck speed and pull over far enough to the side of the road so that the police wagon could pass. As it did, I was surprised to see that George Lewis was one of the uniformed men aboard the racing vehicle. Lowering my window, I waved my hand and called out to him, but he was far too engrossed in his mission either to see or hear me.

I was annoyed to realize that Eddie was following closely behind the police van—this was hardly the time for the boy to indulge his fascination with crime and police detection. Then as we pulled to a stop behind the vehicle, I realized its destination and ours were one and the same: Washington Square.

Apparently, I had spoken too soon about Eddie's developing skills as a chauffeur. Abandoning the etiquette I had spent weeks attempting to instill in my young hackman, the boy leapt off the driver's seat and, instead of opening the carriage door as he'd been taught, took off pell-mell after Sergeant Lewis and his band of policemen. Hastily deciding that this was hardly the time to recall the youth to his duties, Robert and I hurriedly exited the brougham and followed in the lad's wake.

Entering through a gate in the white picket fence that had been erected to prevent horseback riders from trampling the grass, we spied a group of people clustered around some park benches. As we made our way toward the center of the square (which, in reality, was a rectangle), the police were attempting to push back a curious group of onlookers—most notably a very excited Eddie, who kept slipping through their clutches like a slithery eel.

As the area was finally cleared, I spied Sergeant Lewis leaning over to examine what appeared to be a pile of rags heaped onto one of the wooden benches. Drawing closer, I realized that the object of George Lewis's attention was not a pile of rags at all, but the body of an elderly woman slumped over in her seat. My heart sank when I caught a clear view of the woman's face. It was Theodora Reade!

With Eddie practically hanging on to my skirt, I made short shrift of the uniformed men Sergeant Lewis had positioned to keep out idle spectators. I was no idle spectator. Moreover, I knew Samuel's pugilistic partner would be eager to learn the identity of the victim, not to mention my assessment of the crime. Brushing aside the more determined of the men guarding the murder scene, I approached George Lewis as he stooped down to examine Mrs. Reade's neck. Eddie, who was so close behind me that he was literally treading on my heels, cried out when he saw the woman's face and promptly moved back from me as well as from the bench.

Truth be told, even I was forced to repress a gasp at the sight of her darkened face, bulging eyes, and protruding tongue. Perhaps it was due to her advanced age, but Mrs. Reade made an even more macabre-looking corpse than had Darien Moss. Her appearance was so dreadful that it was several moments before I spied the wire digging into the poor woman's gaunt and wrinkled neck.

Taking my nerves in hand, I stooped down beside George in order to better examine the deep gauge marks made by the thin wire, a wire, I might add, which closely resembled the balalaika string used to strangle Moss. To my dismay, I felt tears well up in my eyes. It was true I hardly knew the woman, but to see her like this, crushed and motionless, the breath of life literally drained out of her slight body, touched upon a surprisingly raw nerve.

This initial emotion was quickly replaced by a tide of rising anger. The unfortunate woman never had a chance; she'd been so frail, it would have required minimal strength to overpower her. Moreover, it must have happened so quickly that she'd had no time, or breath, to call for help. Once again, I was struck by the killer's audacity. What a gamble he'd taken to strike like this, in broad daylight, and with at least a dozen potential witnesses present throughout the park.

"Miss Sarah?" For the first time, I realized George had been speaking to me. I'd been so engrossed in poor Mrs. Reade that I'd failed to hear him. "Please, Miss Sarah, what are you doing here?"

I lightly touched one of the elderly widow's paper-thin hands, then sighed and rose to my feet. "We came here to warn her, George. And we were too late. If only—"

"We got here as quickly as anyone could," a voice said from over my shoulder. Turning, I found Robert standing behind me, his aquamarine eyes fastened not on the body but on my face. "It makes no sense to blame yourself, Sarah." His normally gruff voice was surprisingly gentle. "You did everything possible to warn her."

"Mr. Campbell," George said. I was startled that George knew Robert's name; then I remembered they had met during the Russian Hill murders several months ago. "I take it you and Miss Sarah knew this woman?"

"Yes," Robert replied. soberly. "Her name is, or was, rather, Mrs. Theodora Reade."

"And what led you to believe Mrs. Reade's life was in danger?" George asked.

This time, I answered. "Because she may very well have seen the person who killed Darien Moss last week at the Cliff House."

George started; obviously, this was not the answer he'd expected. "You mean the reporter who was strangled during that séance?" As he spoke, he pulled a small notebook and pencil from his uniform pocket and began to take notes.

I nodded, then explained the happenings of the previous Thursday night. "So you see," I concluded, "Mrs. Reade was seated opposite Mr. Moss when the sole candle illuminating the room was extinguished by a draft from the storm. When the candle was relit, and we discovered Darien Moss had been strangled, the poor woman fainted dead away."

George rubbed his square, clean-shaven chin. "And you think she may have seen the killer during the flash of lightning?"

"Of course that's what we think," Robert said with annoyance, either because I had inadvertently left him out of the discussion describing Moss's death or because he believed George Lewis to be slightly dim-witted. "Why else would someone go to the bother of murdering a harmless old lady?"

George opened his mouth to reply to this reasonable statement but was prevented from doing so by one of his officers, the youngest one, I thought, and extremely eager to impress his sergeant. Behind him tailed a tall man in livery, appearing considerably distressed. He was staring wide-eyed at Mrs. Reade, a sickly look on his face.

"This here's the lady's driver, Mr. Daniel," the young officer said, indicating the man lagging behind him. "Says he drove her here about an hour ago, then went to run some errands. He just got back a few minutes ago, and was gonna take her back home."

George took one look at the footman's green-tinged face and told his officer to take the lad aside, that he'd talk to him later.

"And I been askin' everyone in the park if they saw anyone near the victim, just like you said," the policeman reported, nodding toward Mrs. Reade. "The lady and gent over there say they saw a man sitting next to her on the bench. Accordin' to them, he was dressed in black and had a big bushy black beard. They didn't pay him much mind, but the next time they happened to look over, the feller was gone and the old lady was slumped over on the bench, like she is now. They're the ones what sent someone to fetch the police."

Robert and I looked at each other, he in triumph at having his suspicions proved correct, I with misgivings. Could Dmitry Serkov be so obtuse that he would chose to kill Mrs. Reade in a public park, then wear such conspicuous clothes that he would be sure to be noticed? The man was surly and uncommunicative, but he hadn't struck me as stupid.

"Did you get their names and addresses, Perkins?" George was asking his young subordinate.

"That I did, sir. The lady's pretty upset by what happened, and the gent wants to know if they can leave now, so's he can take her home."

"Not just yet," George told him. "I want to speak to them first." He turned to Robert and me, his manner subtly getting across the message that it was time for us to take our leave, as well. "I'm sorry you weren't able to warn Mrs. Reade in time, Miss Sarah. But Mr. Campbell's right. There's no cause to be blaming yourself for the poor woman's death."

"Wait a minute, Lewis," Robert said. "The man those people saw sitting with Mrs. Reade, I think I know who—"

"Please, Robert, I, too, am distressed," I said, giving him a pointed glare and nodding toward the brougham. "Let's leave George to get on with his job."

Robert darted me a sour look, but I managed to stare him down. Rather grumpily, he bid George good day, then allowed me to lead him to the carriage, where Eddie was already waiting. The boy's face was very pale, and I knew he was mortified by his reaction to what had probably been his first encounter with a dead body. Without referring to the grizzly scene in the park, I instructed the lad to drive Robert to his office. Without a word, he nodded, climbed up to the driver's seat, and clicked his dependable dappled gray horse into the afternoon traffic.

"So, what's all this nonsense about you being distressed?" Robert asked, looking considerably annoyed. "You've got one of the strongest constitutions of anyone I know, man or woman."

"Of course I wasn't distressed, Robert, at least not in the way I meant it to sound. I deeply regret Mrs. Reade's death, but I wanted to get you away from George before you mentioned Dmitry Serkov."

"And why is that? You know as well as I do it must have been Serkov that couple saw with Mrs. Reade. He'd stand out in any crowd."

"Yes, I know. That's precisely why I find it so hard to believe it was really him."

He threw up both hands in exasperation. "Curse it, Sarah. You're making no sense whatsoever."

"I must say I'm disappointed in you, Robert." I maintained my calm, refusing to be drawn into an argument. "Unless Serkov is a total dolt, which I doubt he is, why would he go out of his way to be seen with his victim right before he killed her?"

"That's simple enough. Obviously, Serkov was trying to discover how much the old woman knew about Moss's death. When she realized he was the man she'd seen strangle the reporter, he had no choice but to silence her then and there. Another crime of opportunity. The man is becoming famous for them."

"Oh, really? And he just happened to have a length of wire in his pocket. How convenient."

"Good Lord, Sarah, he came prepared, that's all."

"With a woman as old and fragile as Mrs. Reade, the only weapon the killer required were his bare hands." When his expression remained skeptical, I grew frustrated. "Don't you see? I believe the whole thing was a deliberate attempt to place the blame on Serkov. The impostor contrived to be seen speaking to Mrs.

Reade, then strangled her with the same type of wire that had been used on Moss, thereby making it appear as if both victims had been killed by the same person."

"Which they had!" Robert exclaimed. "You're proving my point for me, Sarah. Serkov murdered Moss, then was forced to kill the old woman before she could tell the police what she had seen."

"That's certainly what we're intended to believe. And I agree that one person is likely responsible for both deaths. What I question is whether Serkov is that individual."

Robert ran a hand through his unruly mop of red hair. "You're making this too complicated, Sarah. I'll be the first one to admit you've been damn clever in the past routing out unlikely scoundrels. Perhaps that's what's bothering you now. This time, the most likely suspect is almost certainly the killer. Why can't you simply admit there's no mystery here for you to solve?"

I realized the fruitlessness of this conversation. I had no proof to bolster my theory that someone was trying to frame Serkov. And I was forced to admit that all the evidence we had obtained so far pointed directly to the Russian. Still, I could not rid myself of the conviction that the disagreeable man was being set up.

"We'll see," I replied noncommittally. "As it is written in Hebrews, chapter twelve, verse one: 'let us run with patience the race that is set before us.'" Really that was all I could do for the moment.

After Eddie dropped Robert off at Shepard, Shepard, Mc-Naughton and Hall, I directed the lad to take me to what was now coming to be know as San Francisco's "old" City Hall, located on Kearny between Washington and Merchant streets. There, I hoped I might complete the errand I had originally planned for that morning, gathering information in order to prepare for Alexandra Sechrest's divorce suit.

I had to admit that Mrs. Reade's murder had left me considerably shaken. Despite Robert's insistence that there was nothing I could have done to prevent the tragedy, I continued to berate myself for not recognizing the widow's danger earlier. From the beginning, I'd experienced a distinct uneasiness concerning the attack upon Yelena the night of the séance. If only I had trusted my instincts and made one or two simple inquiries concerning room assignments. If only I had taken a few more moments to ask this question of Mrs. Reade the following morning, or, indeed, of Yelena herself.

If, if, if! The humbling truth was that I had not seen fit to act upon my intuition, and subjecting myself to further self-flagellation would merely drain away energy I sorely needed if I were to represent Mrs. Sechrest and her two small sons successfully. No matter how badly I wished I could set back the clock, I had to accept that there was nothing I could do to breathe life back into Theodora Reade.

Entering the county supreme court building, I went to the second floor, where I spent the next few hours examining California's divorce and custody laws. Unfortunately, it appeared that the state wasn't altogether clear what its laws on these subjects encompassed. Even those few lawyers who thought they did understand had been uncertain how to interpret them.

For one thing, there was little consistency in the court rulings I scrutinized. The outcome of these proceedings depended almost entirely upon which courtroom the case had been assigned. While one judge might have construed the law to favor the wife, just as many, if not more, had decided in favor of the husband.

Child-custody rulings were even more arbitrary. After pouring over dozens of cases, it seemed to me that children were parceled out to whichever parent led the more "principled life," whatever that happened to mean to the presiding judge. This laissez-faire interpretation of the custody laws resulted in widely divergent decisions. What I found most incomprehensible was that the child's welfare rarely, if ever, influenced the final decision!

Temporarily giving up this frustrating quest, I requested and received the forms I would need to file for Alexandra Sechrest's divorce, them made my way out of the courthouse.

The sun was setting in a dazzling blaze of red, orange, and gold as I came out onto the street and walked the two or three blocks to the nearest cable car line. Not only was I weary from my efforts to strategize a plan for Mrs. Sechrest, but the full impact of Theodora Reade's murder once again overwhelmed me as I passed newsboys crying, "*Call, Chronicle, Examiner!* Read all about it! Shocking murder in Washington Square! Read all about it!"

The news hawkers were besieged by customers, mostly well-dressed gentlemen on their way home from offices and shops, eager to obtain all the gruesome details of the city's latest brutality. Hoping it might carry new information about Mrs. Reade's death, I, too, purchased a newspaper—the *Examiner*, to be exact—which I planned to read on the cable car.

Some minutes later, I opened the newspaper as the conveyance made its way northeast along Market Street. I did not have to search long for the story; Theodora Reade's brutal murder was splashed in bold black headlines across the front page.

But it was the subheadline that caught my attention. It read RUSSIAN ARRESTED FOR ELDERLY WIDOW'S DEATH! A surprisingly accurate and detailed account of the capture and arrest of this individual, along with his relationship to the famous Russian clairvoyant Madame Olga Karpova, followed.

How had the reporter managed to gather so many intimate details so quickly, I wondered as I scanned down three columns of text, not only about the murders of Darien Moss and Theodora Reade, but about the villain himself?

Then I noticed the familiar byline that appeared at the end of the piece, and I understood. The article, it appeared, had been written by none other than my brother, the inveterate crime reporter Ian Fearless!

CHAPTER SEVEN

I found Celia in the nursery when I arrived home, chatting with her two small children, Tom and Amanda, as they sat partaking of their evening meal.

"Where is everyone?" I asked, picking several books and toy soldiers off the nursery rocking chair and pulling it over to join the homey little group.

My sister-in-law fairly radiated good health and happiness. She'd had the same glow when carrying her older children and, as then, her inner joy had the power to light up every room she entered. I've never denied my critical opinions about the marital state, particularly as it affected women. However, my brother Charles and his lovely wife, Celia, were the exception that made up the rule. Remarkably, they gave every indication of being just as much in love now as they had been at their wedding nine years ago.

If I could have been assured of the same marital bliss they had achieved, I might have reconsidered my views on this perilous institution. Unfortunately, the great majority of women ran a far greater risk of being treated as chattel—a husband's property, to be dealt with as he saw fit—than becoming his helpmate and equal. Still . . . My thoughts drifted to the dashing and extremely handsome Pierce Godfrey, whom I'd met during the Russian Hill murders. Despite the grizzly killings, which had put even my own life in danger, we had enjoyed each other's company immensely. And he'd been one of the few men to truly believe in my abilities as an attorney. He had so impressed me that I'd even wondered, if only briefly, what it would be like to become his wife.

Much as I might take pleasure in having a husband and children, as well as a home of my own, however, the risk was simply too great. I had made my choice years earlier to do everything within my power to balance the scales of justice for women as well as for the downtrodden, be they male or female. I could not willingly do anything now that might countermand that vow.

Celia's lighthearted chuckle broke into my reverie. "You're miles away again, Sarah. I was saying that Mama and Papa are dining at the Watsons' house tonight. Charles is out on an emergency call, and I have no idea where Samuel is. Cook says dinner will be served in an hour. I hope you'll be here to share it with me. I hate to dine alone."

"Of course I will," I replied with a smile. Truly, it was impossible to remain dejected in Celia's presence. Ever since she and Charles had moved into our parents' home (a temporary arrangement extended indefinitely, due to my physician brother's refusal to turn anyone away from his door, whether or not they were able to pay), I'd looked upon her as the sister I'd never had. "I'm sorry to appear so distracted. It's been a difficult day."

Celia immediately sobered. Spying the newspaper tucked into the front pocket of my briefcase, she said, "I read about what happened to Mrs. Reade, Sarah. Wasn't she one of the people you met at the Cliff House?"

"Yes. Poor soul, she was the elderly woman who swooned after we found Mr. Moss had, er . . ." In deference to my young niece and nephew, I hesitated, not wishing to frighten them.

"Had departed?" their mother put in tactfully. She gave a little shiver. "It has all been rather horrible, hasn't it? Thank goodness they've arrested the man responsible."

I nodded without commenting, but Celia had always been able to sense when I was holding something back. "You don't believe this Serkov fellow did it, do you, Sarah?" she asked, wiping bits of potato off Mandy's face with a damp cloth.

"No, actually I don't, although nearly all the evidence supports his guilt. Just some silly notion I can't seem to shake."

Whatever Celia was about to say was cut short by the arrival of Mary Douglas, the children's nanny. "I'm sorry to interrupt you, Mrs. Woolson, Miss Woolson," she said with a smile. "I can take the children's dishes now, if they've finished. Cook has some fresh gingerbread just out of the oven, if Tom and Mandy would like to go downstairs."

"Yes, yes!" both children cried, jumping up from their chairs and running to the nursery door. Celia smiled fondly as they raced after their nanny. Gingerbread was a great favorite with the little ones, and Cook unashamedly used it to lure the children into her kitchen. There, she regaled them with stories from her childhood in County Cork, Ireland.

As Tom and Mandy went whooping down the stairs, Celia rose stiffly to her feet, placing both hands on her waist and stretching out her back. Now, late in the seventh month of her pregnancy, it seemed as if her protruding stomach grew larger with each passing day. Although Celia rarely complained, it was apparent that her lower back was protesting the ever-increasing burden it was forced to bear.

"Let's go to my boudoir," she said, smoothing the folds of her skirt across her extended abdomen. "I'll ask Ina to bring us a fresh pot of tea and perhaps one or two cookies. I know it's almost dinnertime, but I find myself ready to eat every hour or two these days. By the time I deliver this baby," she added ruefully, "I'll have become as big as a house!"

Celia was still chuckling when we reached the sitting room that led off the bedroom she shared with my brother. The room wasn't large, but it comfortably held several chairs and a cushioned chaise lounge, as well as a small oak bureau and matching tripod table, which always featured a fresh bouquet of seasonal flowers. I didn't know how she managed it, but my sister-in-law had taken a rather ordinary room and transformed it into a cheery, peaceful haven in which to read, embroider, or receive visitors.

In due course, our little Irish maid, Ina Corks, brought our refreshments, then left to help Cook with dinner preparations. Celia insisted on pouring the tea, then settled heavily into the padded armchair by the window. During the summer months, this window overlooked the colorful back garden my mother and Celia lovingly tended, and which supplied us with so many flowers and even a few homegrown fruits and vegetables during the summer months.

"Please, Sarah," she said once she was comfortable, "tell me more about this clairvoyant—Madame Karnova, is it?"

"Karpova," I replied, correcting her. I eyed her curiously. "I didn't realize you were interested in that sort of thing, Celia."

She flushed. "I'm not, really—well, actually I do think it might be interesting if someone really could tell the future, or communicate with those who have passed over. When I was ten or eleven, I saw a magician perform at a fair. He wore a bright blue turban on his head and told fortunes. He was really quite good." She smiled. "At least I thought so at the time."

"It sounds as if he impressed you."

"Yes, I admit he did. Nothing more than childish nonsense, I expect. The man in the turban was probably just playing silly tricks on us, and easily deceiving a gullible little girl."

"But if he had been a genuine psychic—assuming, of course, that there are such people—what would you have asked him?"

"When I was just a child, you mean? Oh, most likely I would have asked if I was going to get the new dress I wanted so badly for my birthday, or perhaps a much too expensive dollhouse I fancied. Something very mundane, I'm sure."

"And now?"

She shook her head, as if wishing she had never broached the subject. "This is absurd—really too fanciful of me."

"We all have our little fantasies, Celia. We'd be extremely dull people if we didn't." Taking a sip of tea, I asked, "Now, why don't you tell me what's behind all this?"

She set her cup on its saucer and leaned forward in her seat. "All right, Sarah, but promise you won't laugh. If I could consult with someone who truly possessed such a gift, I would ask him, or her, to . . . to communicate with my little Sophie." She gave a nervous laugh. "There now, I told you it was foolish."

I felt a catch in my throat. Sophie was Charles and Celia's first child, a little girl who had died of a fever when she was just two years old. Sophie had been a bright, angelic child, the image of her mother, with golden curls and a happy, easygoing personality. We had all felt her loss keenly. Belatedly, I realized that after six years, Celia still mourned the toddler's death.

"The desire to speak one last time with a loved one is never ridiculous," I told her gently. "It's the most natural thing in the world."

She looked at me with guarded hope. "You said there was a mother there, at the séance the other night, who wanted to speak to her child. Can you—would you tell me what happened?"

I was torn between fostering the hope I read on her face and honestly sharing my opinion of Madame Karpova's abilities. In the end, I simply described what I had seen without adding any embellishments or personal judgments.

"Mrs. Gaylord seemed certain her little girl was standing next to her," I concluded. "She even claimed she felt the child kiss her on the cheek. I'm afraid the rest of us saw nothing."

"But the mother sensed the child was there." She considered

this. "Yes, I can believe a mother might feel her child's presence, even if no one else did. There's such a strong bond between them. . . ." Her voice trailed off and with a sigh, she poured fresh tea into our cups. "Enough of this. I'm sure there isn't a mother in the world who wouldn't give anything to hold her child one last time, to feel her close and to kiss away her tears. Unfortunately, that is not how this world works."

She gave a little start and placed a hand on her stomach, and I knew she had just felt the baby kick. "This tiny one constantly reminds me that soon I'll be bringing a new life into the world to join little Tom and Mandy. I've been very blessed, Sarah. I must never forget that." She picked up her teacup and leaned back comfortably in her seat. "Now then, why don't you tell me everything that happened at the Cliff House that night, starting from the beginning."

Celia listened quietly as I described the séance. Although I tactfully omitted the more graphic details of Moss's death, I faithfully recounted all the other particulars, including the attack upon Yelena when she retired to the room that had originally been intended for Theodora Reade. Reaching in a pocket for my notepad, I even drew a quick sketch of where everyone sat at the séance table, the position of the lone candle, and where Madame Karpova's murky white specter appeared.

She sat quietly for several minutes after I had finished my narrative, seemingly digesting the facts of the case as I'd presented them. It was not until the downstairs bell rang for dinner that she stirred and finally spoke.

"Clearly, you were correct about Mrs. Reade being the intended victim and not Yelena Karpova. I'm sure you were also right that Mrs. Reade was killed because of what she saw when that bolt of lightning illuminated the room. Someone obviously possesses a very dark secret, one he is willing to go to any lengths to protect. I fear that discovering the truth will prove difficult, and dangerous."

She regarded me with fearful eyes. "Please, Sarah, promise me that you will be very careful. I sense a great evil at work here."

A s chance would have it, Robert was in my office the following afternoon when Madame Karpova and her daughter Yelena once again paid me a visit. My ex-employer, Joseph Shepard, had assigned Robert a new case, which required him to conduct research at the courthouse, much as I had done for Mrs. Sechrest the day before. He had come by to invite me to a late lunch, when the Russian women arrived.

"What are the two of you doing here again?" he rudely demanded, behaving for all the world as if this were his office and not mine.

Yelena blanched and drew back behind her mother, whose face had darkened. "Not that it is any of your concern, Mr. Campbell," the psychic informed him brusquely, "but I have come to ask Miss Woolson to represent my brother, who has been outrageously arrested for a murder he did not commit. It is because we are Russian that this has happened. We are treated by your authorities with suspicion and contempt."

Robert drew breath to give what I was sure would be a scathing response, but I managed to speak first. "Please, ladies, pay no attention to Mr. Campbell. His bark is a good deal worse than his bite. Besides, he was just about to leave."

"What about lunch?" Robert glared at the psychic as if she had deliberately set out to ruin his plans. "I don't have all day. Shepard expects me back at the office."

"Then by all means, you must return there at once," I told him, keeping my tone calm but firm. "As you can see, I must confer with my clients. Madame Karpova, Yelena, please take a seat while I see Mr. Campbell out."

"Your clients!" he exploded. "Good God, Sarah, don't tell me you're seriously considering taking that man's case. Dmitry Serkov is as guilty as sin. You haven't a prayer of convincing a jury that he isn't."

Yelena, who had seated herself in one of the straight-backed chairs, started nervously at this, while her mother's face grew even darker. In an effort to defuse the situation, I took my colleague by the arm and resolutely escorted him to the door.

"Perhaps we can have lunch tomorrow," I told him. "Why don't we meet down the street at the Jackson Hotel, say at one o'clock?"

"But I want to eat now," he protested as I all but pushed him out of my office.

"Good. I'm glad that meets with your approval. I'll see you tomorrow afternoon." I closed the door and set the lock before he could offer any further objections, then turned to my visitors. "Now then, Madame Karpova," I said, settling in the chair behind my desk. "I take it that Mr. Serkov concurs with your decision to engage me as his attorney?"

Olga Karpova hesitated. "I have not yet been allowed to speak with my brother. The police treat us shamefully. But I, Madame Karpova, know his mind. He wants you to represent him."

It was my turn to hesitate. "Actually, I'm afraid I cannot accept the case without first speaking to Mr. Serkov. This must be his decision."

Madame Karpova drew herself bolt upright in her chair. "I tell you *I* make the decision. And I have chosen you!"

I decided that a compromise was in order. "Why don't I visit your brother tomorrow morning, Madame Karpova. After we've discussed the charges against him, we can decide on how best to plan his defense."

"But you will act as his attorney," she persisted.

"Yes, if that's what he wishes," I replied.

"Good. It is what he desires. I tell you so." She reached into her reticule and took out a lovely gold medallion attached to what appeared to be a solid gold chain. "Here," she said, pushing it across my desk. "This belonged to my mother. Now you will take it to represent Dmitry."

I picked up the pendant. The piece was surprisingly heavy and appeared to be very old. The front was beautifully decorated with hand-engraved filigree, while the back had been inscribed with several words I did not recognize.

Noticing my confusion, the woman explained proudly, "It was a gift from Maria Alexandrovna, the wife of Czar Alexander, Lord have mercy upon his soul." Executing a hasty sign of the cross, she continued. "The czar was brutally murdered earlier this year by a student revolutionary. That is Alexandrovna's name on the back of the pendant, engraved in Russian." She beamed triumphantly. "You see, I am willing to pay very well to free my brother from prison."

"I'm afraid it's more complicated than that, Madame Karpova. Bail is almost never set in murder cases. And as I said, I will have to speak to Mr. Serkov before anything is settled." I tried to give her back the pendant, but she stood, indicating to her daughter that the interview was at an end.

"If you must speak to my brother before taking his case, you will please do so first thing tomorrow morning." She made this pronouncement as if issuing a royal command. "It is my wish that you keep the medallion. Dmitry will agree that you are the best attorney for him, and then it will be settled, as you say."

She rose to her feet, then suddenly paused, staring at the wall behind my desk as if in some sort of trance. "You will please tell your sister that her new child will be a boy," she unexpectedly proclaimed. "And that he will be healthy and very clever." She chuckled, as if she found this amusing. "Yes, just like his papa. Very clever and very generous."

With that, the psychic swept out of my office, pulling her daughter, who had not uttered a single word throughout the entire consultation, behind her.

The last visitor of the day walked through my office door just as I was about to depart for Rincon Hill, and what I hoped would be a quiet evening given to constructive contemplation of the day's surprising events.

"Samuel," I said with some surprise. "What are you doing here?"

"Good evening to you, too, little sister," he said, grinning as he helped me on with my wrap. "I have come to take you to Gobey's Oyster Parlor for dinner, and then to the theater."

Straightening my wrap evenly across my shoulders, I eyed my brother with fond amusement. "That can only mean one thing. Whatever lady you currently favor has canceled at the last moment, forcing you to beg the company of your spinster sister. What's the name of the play, by the way?"

"It's a revival of *Snowflake and the Seven Pigmies*," he said, holding the door open for me. "The reviews caution young ladies who are 'faint of heart' not to attend, as the 'tragic story will tear at the soul of all but the most stalwart.'"

"What? For God's sake, Samuel, tell me you're not serious."

"As a matter of fact, I'm not," he said, laughing that his joke had brought about such a splendid response. "Although that old saw really has been taken out of its well-deserved mothballs and is showing at the Tivoli Gardens. Actually, I have tickets to *Richard the Third* at the California Theatre. It's supposed to be an excellent production."

"Yes, that's what I've heard." I felt a thrill of excitement. Suddenly, a quiet evening at home had lost its appeal. I hadn't been to the theater in months, and, brother or not, Samuel was excellent company. "But look at me," I said, indicating my office attire. "I'm hardly dressed for the theater, especially the California Theatre."

He cast a critical eye over my dark green two-piece suit, one of several garments in varying styles and colors I'd had specially made to coincide with the opening of my new office.

"Hmmm. It's true you aren't going to set any fashion trends, but if you redo your hair a bit—and wash that ink off your fingers—I think you'll be passable. At any rate, there's no time to go home and change. As it is, we have to hurry if we're to have dinner before the performance. Unless you'd prefer to catch a late supper after the play."

I shook my head; I was far too hungry (having missed my lunch with Robert) to wait until nearly midnight to eat. "No, Gobey's it is. I'm famished!"

Dinner at Gobey's "Ladies and Gents Oyster Parlor" was always a treat, and my boiled terrapin was excellent. While we ate, I told Samuel about Madame Karpova's strange prediction that afternoon concerning Charles and Celia's new baby.

"Has she ever met either of them?" my brother asked, looking surprised.

"No, I'm sure she hasn't."

"Then where in the world did she—"

"I have no idea, Samuel. Frankly, I find it a little chilling—the way she just came out with it, I mean. We hadn't been talking about my family, or the baby, or anything of a personal nature. She just blurted it out, like it was the most natural thing in the world."

"Are you going to tell Celia?"

I thought about this. Everything Madame Karpova had said about the new baby was positive. Yet somehow I hesitated to say anything about it to our sister-in-law. Things had been going so smoothly during her pregnancy; I didn't want to risk upsetting her over something that might well turn out to be complete drivel, as Robert would say.

"I don't think so. At least not yet." I smiled at my brother, suddenly anxious to change the subject. "Why don't you tell me what you've been able to learn about Darien Moss."

My brother shook his head. "All I can say is that you live a very interesting life, Sarah, especially for a woman." He laughed and held up his hand to stave off my retort. "All right, all right, to business, then. I've wired several friends in New York about the fellow, but they're having a difficult time piecing together his background. It seems clear that at some point preceding his relocating to California, Moss must have changed his name. There's certainly no record of a Darien Moss being born in New Jersey within the time lines we've established. Of course, he may have been born in another state, or outside the United States, for that matter.

"However, I have a colleague who says Moss occasionally mentioned that his mother was a minor opera singer, and that his father was a minister. Using that information, one of my sources found a Daoud Moussa listed in the records of a New Jersey hospital at about the time Moss would have been born. Sure enough, Daoud's mother is listed as Irena Moussa, who used to sing with a second-rate opera company, and his father as the Reverend Pasek Moussa. Daoud was an only child, and apparently he had some sort of run-in with his father, which may be one of the reasons he left for California."

"Do you know if his family is still alive and residing in New Jersey? If they are, they should be notified of his death."

"I have someone looking into that. It seems that Moss—I'm having a hard time thinking of him as Daoud Moussa—worked at one or two newspapers before leaving the state, and we may find more information about him there."

"What about the articles he was working on before his death? Were you able to go through his office at the *San Francisco Informer?*"

"Unfortunately, I was too late. Someone broke into Moss's office the night after his death. His desk was ransacked, and according to one of his colleagues at the paper, several files were missing. None of the typesetters, or the handful of other people working that night, seems to remember seeing a stranger. No one even noticed the break-in until the police arrived the following morning. By then, George says there was little of interest to be found."

"Including, I take it, material for his upcoming exposés."

"I'm afraid so. Anything that even hinted at what he was planning to write was gone." His blue eyes teased me over the flickering candlelight. "However, I'm happy to report that all is not lost. Your ever-resourceful brother managed to discover that the colleague I spoke to was also one of Moss's few personal friends, and also a fellow member of the Bohemian Club. Consequently, in a selfless quest for knowledge, I spent last night in our club saloon, pumping the fellow for information and, I might add, buying him an astonishing amount of alcohol. The man must have a cast-iron stomach!"

"What did you learn?" I asked, unable to curb a fresh wave of hope.

"Actually, more than I expected. This fellow seemed perfectly content to toss back scotch whiskey and blabber on for hours about what a wonderful reporter Moss was, and how he had a way of digging up the most intimate details of people's lives. He proceeded to prove this to me by describing all the really important scandals Moss was planning to expose in his upcoming columns."

"Such as?"

"Patience, little sister, I'm getting there. Let's see, where was I? Oh, yes, it seems the most damaging story Moss was planning was an exposé on the new City Hall debacle. According to my by now-inebriated source, he intended to name names, as well as list the companies and city officials involved in the fiasco."

"Good heavens." My mind boggled at the repercussions this would almost certainly produce, possibly throughout the entire state! "The city's newspapers have been hinting at some sort of collusion since they broke ground on the building ten years ago."

"And for good reason." Samuel followed an oyster with a sip of really excellent chardonnay (as far as I'm concerned, my brother is one of the finest wine connoisseurs to be found in the whole of San Francisco). "Back in 1871, the project planners boasted that the new City Hall would be the largest, grandest, and most durable structure in San Francisco."

"Didn't they also promise that it would be completed in four years, and for under two million dollars?"

"One million five hundred thousand, actually," he replied. "As you say, it's now ten years later and the job is largely unfinished. And the cost has more than doubled, with no end in sight. Maurice Blake, Mayor Kalloch's chief opponent in this year's mayoral election, has made the new City Hall fiasco a major political issue. Pressure on city government to do something about the mess has been escalating every day, especially as the election grows closer."

"So, Moss's corruption charges may have some basis in fact." I paused as Samuel poured more wine into our glasses. "Presumably, he had evidence to back up these allegations, or he and his newspaper would run the risk of being sued for libel. I haven't heard of any other newspapers threatening to name names."

"According to Moss's friend, he had a boxful of documents, secret correspondence and even a few incriminating pictures. But don't forget, Sarah, the fellow was feeling very little pain by this juncture in our conversation."

"Where is this box now?" I asked, barely able to control my excitement. "Do you think the killer found it when he broke into Moss's office at the newspaper?"

"According to my talkative drinking companion, no. He insists Moss kept few documents of any importance at his office." He took a sip of wine and added with a dry chuckle, "Apparently, he didn't trust his colleagues at the newspaper not to steal his stories. My informant seemed to think he stored most of his more sensitive material in his lodgings at the Baldwin Hotel."

"The Baldwin!" I said in surprise. "That's one of the most expensive hotels in town. How could any journalist afford a room there?"

"Rooms, plural. Darien Moss rented a suite. And you're not the first person to ask that question. In fact, that's partly what fueled the speculation he might have been engaging in a little blackmailing on the side."

"You mean people paid him to keep their names out of his column?"

"That's the rumor," he said. "Mind you, it's just speculation. No one was ever able to prove that he took so much as five cents to protect someone's reputation."

Before I could question him further, my brother glanced at his watch and then said we'd better hurry if we wanted to be seated before the curtain went up. After using a piece of bread to soak up what was left of his oyster sauce, he finished his wine and called for our waiter.

While Samuel settled the bill, I excused myself and did what I could with my hair in the ladies' water closet. Smoothing my skirts, I regarded myself critically in the looking glass. Samuel was right, I decided: I would never be noted as a lady of fashion. Ah, well, I had done the best I could with what I had to work with. And as Mama was fond of saying, at least I would not shame myself or my family if, God forbid, I should have an accident and be taken to the hospital.

Samuel was waiting for me outside the restaurant, having just hailed a hansom cab for the short ride to the theater. Again, my questions had to wait until Samuel had paid the driver and we'd been shown to our seats in the theater. Once we were comfortably settled, I used what little time we had before the curtain rose to find out what else my brother had learned.

"Samuel, please, finish the story. Have the police searched Darien Moss's hotel rooms yet?"

My brother darted me an amused look, and I knew at once he'd anticipated this question. Of my three older brothers, I have always been closest to Samuel, not only in age but also in personality. Mama used to complain that between the two of us we caused more mischief than all four of her children put together, while Papa often marveled that our house was still standing by the time we'd reached our majority.

"Sorry, little sister, but if you hoped to get there first, you're too late. George and some of his men conducted a search of Moss's rooms over the weekend."

"That's all right. I don't see how we could have gained access to Moss's rooms anyway, at least legally. That's all I need right now, to be arrested for breaking and entering. My law practice would be finished before it ever really began." A woman seated in the row in front of us threw me a reproving look over her shoulder, and I lowered my voice. "So what did George find when he went through Moss's hotel rooms?"

"The killer apparently beat them there, as well. George couldn't go into details, of course, but I received the impression that what little evidence he did find in the reporter's hotel suite revealed that, as rumors indicated, Moss's new City Hall exposé was more than an idle threat. George also hinted that Moss planned even more derogatory articles on Madame Karpova and, as he put it in one of his recent columns, "her preposterous circus sideshow act." Unfortunately, that was about it, and neither of these stories come as much of a surprise."

"It looks as if the killer walked off with the most incriminating files." I was unable to mask my disappointment.

"Almost, but not quite. Evidently, Moss kept a few items in the hotel safe downstairs. At George's insistence, the manager opened it. Inside, they discovered a small fortune in women's jewelry, including two or three diamond rings, a ruby necklace and brooch, and several pairs of pearl and diamond earrings."

"Unless he was keeping those pieces for a relative or a lady friend, that seems to bear out the speculations that he was accepting bribes. At least now we know how he was able to afford to live at the Baldwin Hotel."

"That's what George thought. But the next part of the story is even more interesting. They also found a small black leather diary inside the box containing the jewelry. It seems to have been written in some kind of peculiar language or code, so George couldn't make head nor tail of it. However, because of the numbers listed next to some of the code words, he suspects, as do I, that it's a list of the individuals Moss was planning to expose in his column, and very likely people who were paying him blackmail money."

I fairly itched to get my hands on that book! "Samuel, where is that diary now?"

"It's in a locked room at the police station, where they keep all the other evidence they've collected over the past few years."

"Do you think George would allow me to have a look at it?" I asked with some excitement. "After all, I'm Dmitry Serkov's attorney, and that book could very well provide us with vital evidence in his case."

"I knew you were going to ask me that," he said with that superior "big brother" smile of his. "I've already spoken to George about it. He says if you drop by the Central Station some afternoon this week, he'll do his best to give you limited time alone with the diary. You won't be able to remove it from the station, of course."

"That's fine, as long as he allows me enough time to read through it and take notes. If you see him, please tell him I'll stop by the station in the next day or two." I thought of something else. "Oh, and if you can, would you please see if you can find out where everyone was yesterday afternoon around the time Mrs. Reade was killed?"

"Surely the police are looking into that."

"I sincerely doubt it. They're too convinced they have their murderer in custody to bother investigating anyone else. Since I suspect the same killer murdered both Moss and Mrs. Reade, it would be a great help to find out who *couldn't* have strangled the widow yesterday in the park. As it stands now, it could have been just about anybody. We need to narrow down our list of suspects."

"*We*," he repeated with a short laugh. "I might have known you'd find even more ways to rope me into this business. All right. No promises, mind you, but I'll see what I can find out."

"Samuel, thank you," I told him sincerely. "I know I'm asking a great deal of you, and I really do appreciate it."

"Oh, it's not all altruism," he said, giving me a cheerful wink. "Ian Fearless expects to get one hell of a story out of this. An *exclusive* story—a front-page, headline story."

I laughed; Samuel's good nature was contagious. "You know you will if I have anything to do with it," I promised.

The same woman in the row ahead of ours once again turned in her seat to dart us an annoyed look. When she showed no inclination of turning back around again, Samuel gave her one of his most ingratiating smiles.

"Good evening, madam," he said pleasantly. "Allow me to compliment you on your lovely hat. That shade of mauve seems to be all the rage this season, doesn't it? But not every woman can wear it with such panache. I must say that on you, madam, it is exceedingly becoming."

It was amusing to watch the woman—who must have been at least sixty—dissolve into girlish simpering in the wave of my brother's considerable charm. When she began coyly batting her eyelashes at him, I'd had about all I could stand of this stomach-turning display. I was about to say so to Samuel, when the words died on my lips.

As the lights in the theater dimmed, I glimpsed out of the corner of my eye an usher hurriedly guiding a couple to their seats across the aisle from ours. It was with some surprise that I recognized the man as Nicholas Bramwell, the young lawyer who had escorted his mother, Philippa, to the Cliff House séance.

But it was his companion who caused my mouth to open in unabashed astonishment. The lovely young lady holding fast to Nicholas's arm, and wearing a modest but exceedingly becoming green silk gown, was none other than Madame Olga Karpova's lovely daughter, Yelena!

CHAPTER EIGHT

Honoring my promise that I would speak to Madame Karpova's brother as soon as possible, I had Eddie drop me off at city jail the following morning. To my astonishment, I found Robert pacing back and forth in front of the building.

"What are you doing here?" I asked.

"I'm waiting for you, of course."

I darted him a suspicious look. "How did you know I'd be here this morning? I certainly didn't mention it to you."

He had the good grace to flush in what I took to be embarrassment. Stumbling to excuse his actions, he finally gave up and blurted, "I was several blocks away yesterday afternoon when I realized I'd left my briefcase just outside your office door. I walked back in time to see that Karpova woman and her daughter walk down the stairs to the street. I couldn't help but overhear you mention that you planned to visit Dmitry Serkov this morning."

"And you feared I was incapable of conducting this interview without your strong arm to lean upon?" I said with what I considered justifiable sarcasm.

"Don't be ridiculous. It's your safety that concerns me. This man has very probably killed two people within the past week, and God knows how many more he did away with back in Russia. If he were to attack you in his cell, you'd be dead before the guard could come to your defense."

I thought about this, then agreed that he should go with me. Not, of course, because I feared the Russian might accost me, but because I sensed I might get more out of the prisoner if I were accompanied by a man, especially a man of Robert's muscular proportions. On the night of the séance, I'd received the impression that Dmitry Serkov had little respect for women, excluding his sister, to whom he seemed steadfastly devoted. Whether or not he retained me as his attorney was of secondary importance. I was primarily concerned about how much information I might glean from him. For reasons best known to himself, I was convinced Serkov knew a great deal he was not divulging.

Lest Robert misunderstand my ready agreement to allow him to accompany me to interview Serkov, I explained my reasons as we entered the jailhouse.

"And you think he's going to open up to either of us?" He sounded scornful. "Sarah, the man is a cold-blooded murderer. He's not going to tell you anything incriminating, whether I'm with you or not."

"You may be right, Robert," I said as we reached the front desk in the cold, damp building I had grown to hate. "But we have to try."

I presented my credentials to a skeptical uniformed officer—no matter how often I was obliged to visit the dreadful place, I was forced to go through the same maddening exercise in order to convince the guards that I was an accredited attorney. After cooling our heels for a good quarter of an hour, a wiry jailer of medium height and in his mid-thirties arrived to escort us to Serkov's cell.

"You give a yell when you've had enough of this Russki," he told us, choosing a large key and placing it into the lock. "Mean as a mad dog this feller is, miss. If I was you, I wouldn't go within a mile of the bugger. Don't know why they let these foreigners into the country in the first place. The sooner he sees the end of a rope the better is what I say!" He turned the key and, accompanied by protesting squeaks, pushed open the door. "The name's Cecil Vere. When you've had enough of this nutter, just call out."

The door clanged shut behind us, and we could hear Vere whistling a popular dance-hall song as he walked back down the row of cells. In front of us, Dmitry Serkov sat tall and stiff on his cot. He paid scant attention to Robert or me as we entered, just continued to stare over our heads at the room's solitary barred window, which was located high up on one wall.

"Mr. Serkov," I said, flashing him a professional-looking smile. "Perhaps you remember us from Madame Karpova's séance last Thursday night. I'm Sarah Woolson, and this is my colleague, Mr. Robert Campbell. I have come here today at your sister's request. She indicated that you wished me to represent you against these murder charges."

The man's black eyes flickered over Robert's tall frame without expression, then went back to staring at the window. He did not look at me at all.

"Serkov!" Robert's voice boomed through the small cell, the sound so loud and unexpected that I gave a little jump. The prisoner, on the other hand, scarcely moved a muscle. "Miss Woolson is addressing you. Have you no manners, man? It's common courtesy to stand when a lady enters the room."

Dmitry Serkov apparently did not possess any manners, nor did he appear to be interested in acquiring any now. His dark eyes remained glued to the window, as if expecting something, or someone, to miraculously separate the bars and come floating in to save him.

"I'm going to call the guard," Robert uttered, sounding thoroughly annoyed. "We're wasting our time here."

I raised a hand to restrain my impatient companion. "Wait. Let me at least try to reason with him."

Robert grunted and threw up his hands in disgust. "Go ahead, for all the good it's likely to do. Personally, I wouldn't spend another minute on this oaf. He's nothing but a cold-blooded killer. It's written all over his face."

"*Ti idiot!* I not kill lady," Serkov declared, his booming voice startling us both. "Not kill reporter, too. Police lie!"

"Mr. Serkov," I said, searching for a way to reach this stubborn man. "You've been accused of committing two brutal murders. You claim you're not guilty of these charges. However, if you're to have any hope of proving your innocence, you're going to require an attorney. Your sister has asked me to represent you."

"Not need attorney!" He gestured around the cell with contempt. "Police know they lie. Let me out of here."

This statement was so outrageous, I was temporarily struck dumb. Robert suffered no such inability to voice his opinion.

"You're talking complete rubbish, Serkov," he bellowed, his Scottish *r*'s becoming ever more pronounced as his temper escalated. "Furthermore, you're in total ignorance of our laws if you think the authorities are going to smile and allow you to walk out of here a free man." He stepped forward, until he towered over the annoyingly self-assured man who sat unmoving on the cot. "Let me explain what's going to happen to you. You're going to be tried in a court of law, where you'll almost certainly be found guilty. You'll then be sentenced to hang for your crimes at the end of a rope."

Serkov dismissed Robert with a curt wave of his hand and what sounded like a rude Russian curse. "*Durak!* Go, both of you. I no need attorney. Police let me go." As if to punctuate this declaration, Serkov dredged back in his throat, harked up some phlegm, and spat it at Robert. The disgusting spittle stuck to Robert's coat, then began to run down his lapel.

"Why, you miserable, no-account—" Robert shouted, lunging at the Russian.

I hastily stepped between the two men, holding my irate companion back with two hands and a warning look. "Robert, stop!

He isn't worth the aggravation. You were right: We're wasting our time here." When I was certain he had his temper under control, I went to the cell door and called out for the jailer. "Mr. Vere, we're ready to leave now."

When I heard Vere's jaunty whistle coming toward the cell, I turned back to the prisoner. "Mr. Campbell's right: You're the fool, Mr. Serkov. You are in grave trouble, yet you choose to hide your head in the sand and hope that it will go away. I assure you, however, that much as you might wish it to be true, no one is going to allow you to walk out that door."

Behind me, I heard the scrape of a key in the lock, and once again the cell door clanged open.

"*Uydi ot suda.* Throw them out!" Serkov ordered the jailer. "And bring food. I eat now."

"Like hell you will," Vere told the Russian. "You'll get your food at noon, like everyone else."

"Right annoying yob he is," the guard said, ignoring Serkov's angry leer. "Orders us around like he was the Emperor Norton hisself, God rest his soul," he went on, referring to San Francisco's most beloved character, the self-proclaimed Emperor of the United States and Protector of Mexico, who had died the previous year. "What did you go and say to this here lady, you ornery varmint?" he snapped at Serkov. "You just sit there nice and quiet like and shut yer cussed trap—beggin' yer pardon, miss."

But Robert had already hustled me out of Serkov's cell. We heard the door bang shut behind us, and once again our loquacious guard kept up a steady stream of conversation as he led us back to the front of the jail.

"These damn foreigners—beggin' yer pardon, miss—think they can come over here and take over the place. Well, they're in fer a hell of a surprise, I'll tell ya that—beggin' yer pardon, miss. And that dad-blame sister of his—what calls herself a clair . . . clairvint or somethin' like that—ain't much better. Acts like she's the bloody queen of Sheba."

"Clairvoyant," I said, correcting him, but the jailer's capricious mind had already changed directions.

"And how about those crazy women who go around callin' themselves a temper somethin' or other?"

"Are you referring to the Woman's Christian Temperance Union?" I asked. The group had recently held their second annual convention at the Young Men's Christian Association Hall here in the city, and were beginning to make a name for themselves—a most unpopular name in some quarters, I'm sorry to say.

"That's right," Vere agreed with a wide grin. "Tryin' to stop a bloke from havin' a horn or two after a hard day's work. Mind you now, I ain't talkin' about gettin' corned or nothin' like that. Just a grog or two, or maybe some old orchard is all I'm sayin'. I ask you now, where's the harm in that? Now my Annie—that's the girl I'm gonna marry soon as I've saved enough to rent us a decent room— no, my Annie don't hold with all that temperance twaddle. A man deserves a taste of whiskey after workin' ten, twelve hours, that's what my Annie says. Finest, prettiest girl yer ever gonna find is my Annie." He turned to Robert. "Now then, you agree with me, don't you, sir? About havin' a nip or two now and again, I mean?"

Robert was about to answer (in support of Vere's opinions on this subject, I'm sure), when we were met by Lieutenant Ahern, who appeared to be on his way to one of the cells.

"Miss Woolson, Mr. Campbell." He looked taken aback to find us there. "And what sort of business brings you to our fair jail, may I ask?"

Before either Robert or I could answer, Cecil Vere piped up. "They been to see that worthless Russki. You know, the one what killed the old lady and the newspaper feller?"

Lieutenant Ahern could not hide his surprise and growing misgivings. "Dmitry Serkov? Now why would you be wanting to visit that nasty piece of work?"

I was in no mood to beat around the bush. The sooner Robert and I were out of this horrible place the better. "Are you quite certain that Dmitry Serkov is Darien Moss's killer, Lieutenant? Or that he murdered Mrs. Reade in the park two days ago?"

Lieutenant Ahern's bushy eyebrow's rose and he regarded me as if I'd suddenly gone mad. "Of course I'm sure. I wouldn't have arrested the sod if I didn't think he was guilty as sin!" He stopped and took a breath, obviously trying to contain his quick temper. When he continued, his voice took on a condescending tone. "You're a proper young lady, Miss Woolson. Be grateful you're not familiar with the seamier side of life that I'm forced to deal with every day. Believe me when I tell you that Serkov is as mean and ruthless a scoundrel as they come. But I'm giving you my word he'll be getting exactly what's coming to him. Oh, yes, he'll pay dearly for his crimes."

I caught Robert's eye and the obvious warning he was trying to send me. I chose to ignore it. "Does that mean you've closed the murder investigation, Lieutenant Ahern? You're no longer looking at other suspects for Mrs. Reade's and Mr. Moss's murders?"

"Now why in the name of all the saints should I be doing that?" he responded, once again showing signs of impatience. "Didn't I just tell you that Dmitry Serkov is our murderer, plain and simple?"

"He claims he's innocent," I said, unwilling to let the matter drop so easily. "In fact, Mr. Serkov seems convinced you'll soon realize your mistake and allow him to go free."

Ahern's face turned red. "Oh, he does, does he? Well, let me tell you that's just so much claptrap, girlie. Mark my word, that man will be swinging from the end of a rope before Christmastime. And that's a promise I mean to keep!"

Despite his growing agitation, I doggedly pressed on. "All right, Lieutenant, but tell me this. Why would Dmitry Serkov attack his own niece?"

"Sarah!" Robert protested. He took my arm and tried to nudge me toward the door. "We're taking up the lieutenant's time. I'm sure he has other matters to attend to."

"And not one of them having to do with the murders Dmitry

Serkov is accused of committing," I retorted. "I'll admit he's not a particularly agreeable man, but that doesn't necessarily make him a murderer."

Ahern was now thoroughly angry. I was standing in his domain, challenging his abilities as a police officer. That kind of audacity was too much for the man to endure without getting back some of his own.

"You'd best see to the dirt that's lying beneath your own prying nose, young lady," he spat out, his face now scarlet with rage. "Starting with that know-it-all brother of yours—Frederick, is it?—the one who somehow managed to get himself elected to the state senate."

It was my turn to look startled. "Frederick? What about Frederick? I didn't even realize you knew him?"

"I'm happy to say I've so far managed to avoid meeting him," Ahern shot back. "But I know *of* him, missy. And what I know can be summed up by saying the man's a first-class idiot. I'm warning you that if that brother of yours isn't more careful in his political dealings, he just may find himself a resident of city jail. Along with your good friend Dmitry Serkov!"

It was only then that I realized Cecil Vere was still in our company, taking in every word we said with eager curiosity.

"I swear you're the beatingest female I ever met, Miss Woolson," he declared as soon as Ahern was well out of hearing range. A broad grin extended across his jovial face. "Gosh dang it, you sure as hell settled his hash—beggin' yer pardon, miss. By God if you didn't!"

With a snort of delight, he slapped his side as he left us to follow the lieutenant back into the bowels of the jailhouse. We could still hear his laughter echoing back to us as we excited the building.

"What do you suppose Ahern meant by that remark about your brother Frederick?" Robert asked once we were outside. "Not that you didn't provoke the man beyond endurance."

"If by provoking you mean demanding that our police force be held accountable for their actions, then I plead guilty." I grew serious, unable to hide my concern about the lieutenant's inexplicable warning. "I have no idea what he meant about Frederick, though. I wish I did."

"I admit Frederick isn't my favorite member of your family, Sarah. Still, I find it hard to believe he'd be involved in anything criminal. To be honest, I've never considered him—"

"Bright enough?" I said, finishing for him. "I don't think there's anything wrong with Frederick's brain. It's just that his prejudices and consuming ambition all too often take precedence over good sense."

"So, what are you going to do about it?"

"I'm going to pay a visit to my brother's house tonight and ask him, of course."

R obert and I just had time for an early lunch before leaving for our respective offices, I for my second meeting with Mrs. Alexandra Sechrest, and Robert to work on the new case he'd been assigned. While we ate, I speculated aloud about Serkov's insistence that he had no need for an attorney. Even more inexplicable was his belief that he was going to be let out of jail without so much as a hearing.

"The man obviously has no idea about criminal procedure in this country," Robert said. "Believe me, he'll come to his senses quick enough when they handcuff him and lead him into the courtroom."

"Or maybe he just doesn't want a female attorney," I speculated dryly. "That certainly wouldn't surprise me."

"Who knows? As far as I'm concerned, you're damn lucky he turned you down. That's a case even the most experienced lawyer in San Francisco couldn't win, male or not."

Maybe Robert was right, I thought. I might not personally believe the disagreeable Russian was a murderer, but it might be impossible to convince a jury of his innocence. In any event, I didn't look forward to informing Madame Karpova that her brother had declined my services.

I decided to use what time we had left to update him on what Samuel had discovered about Darien Moss and his missing box of incriminating evidence.

"So, presumably Serkov has them now," Robert ventured over his second cup of coffee.

"Perhaps—*if* he's the murderer," I countered. "Don't forget, Samuel said no one noticed a stranger at the newspaper that night. I can't imagine Serkov sneaking in there without being seen. Or into the Baldwin Hotel, for that matter. As far as I'm concerned, this provides us with even more reason to question his guilt."

"Not necessarily. Maybe the killer didn't take them after all, but someone on the *Informer* staff. The papers Moss supposedly kept in that box would make for very interesting reading. I doubt there's a reporter at that newspaper who wouldn't pay a pretty price to step into Moss's shoes now that he's gone."

"You realize, of course, that information would also make for very profitable blackmail. On the other hand, anyone who attempted blackmail now, after two people have already been murdered, would have to be either very brave or very stupid." I pushed aside my plate and sipped at my own coffee. "No, I think it's more likely the killer got to that box first. The *real* killer, I mean. Not Serkov."

"Come on, Sarah, Sergeant Lewis hinted he'd found evidence suggesting that Moss planned a series of damaging articles about Madame Karpova and her family."

"Yes, among others. We have no idea how many victims he was preparing to expose." I leaned across the table and lowered my voice, although the restaurant was so crowded and noisy that it was doubtful anyone could have overheard our conversation. "Consider this. What if the killer stole any incriminating documents he found pertaining to himself, and deliberately left behind any evidence that pointed toward Dmitry as being the killer?"

"That doesn't sound very likely."

"Robert, admit it. It would be a very clever ploy to set the police off in the wrong direction."

"All right, I suppose it's possible, although I still say it's highly improbable.

I was delighted he was at least willing to consider my theory. "That's why I feel it's so important to keep an open mind about the investigation. If Serkov does turn out to be the killer, I'll be the first one to congratulate the police. If not—"

"Then you won't give up until you've found him. Or her," he added with a smile. To my surprise, the smile turned into outright laughter. "To borrow a phrase from one of your admirers, Sarah, you really are the beatingest."

I had no idea what to make of this curious comment. "If you're referring to Cecil Vere, I didn't understand half of what that man said."

"Don't be naïve. Cecil Vere heartily dislikes Serkov, but he finds you irresistible." He finished his coffee and reached for the bill before I could snatch it up first. "As a matter of fact, despite your obstinacy, your infernal prying, and the fact that you invariably blurt out whatever comes into your head, regardless of the consequences, I admit that there are times when I find you irresistible, too."

I stared in astonishment at Robert's back as he rose to pay the bill. What in heaven's name, I wondered, did he mean by that?

Mrs. Sechrest arrived at my office promptly at two o'clock. This time, I was ready to offer her fresh tea and a dish of assorted cookies and cakes. As she nibbled on a piece of peppermint cake, I took the opportunity to study my new client. I was not entirely happy with what I saw. For one thing, she appeared to have lost weight just in the few days since our last visit, and there were dark, puffy circles beneath her eyes. Her complexion was pale and drawn, and despite her efforts to cover them up with a brushing of powder, her right cheek and mouth showed unmistakable signs of recent bruising.

"Are you still determined to go through with the divorce, Mrs. Sechrest?" I asked when she had finished picking at her cake.

She hesitated, and I could see she was frightened. "Actually, I'm not sure. I just don't know if I can do it."

"And why is that? Has something happened since our last meeting?"

"Yes," she replied in a small voice. "I'm afraid it has." She rubbed a finger lightly across the purple discolorations on her face.

"Is that the extent of your injuries?" I asked.

Without answering, she undid the top four buttons on her shirtwaist. Pulling back the material, she exposed several dark red-and-purple bruises on her upper chest.

I was so unnerved by this display of violence that it was necessary to clear my throat before I could speak. "Mrs. Sechrest, when did this happen?"

"Two nights ago," she replied, her voice barely above a whisper. "There are more bruises on my stomach and upper thighs. Will you need to examine those, as well?"

"No, that won't be necessary." I tried to keep the revulsion out of my voice. How could any man inflict injuries like this on a woman? "You said you were staying at Mrs. Fowler's home for abused women. I assume you're still there?"

"Yes. I'd vowed never to see my husband alone again if I could possibly help it. But Luther sent a message to the safe house. It said he felt badly about taking the boys from me, and was willing to allow me to visit them." There was a catch in Alexandra's voice. "I tried to convince him to bring the children to see me at a nearby park, but he refused. In the end, I—" She looked up, as if willing me to understand. "I so longed to see them, Miss Woolson. In the end, I felt I must take the chance."

"And did Mr. Sechrest allow you to visit your boys?"

She shook her head, no longer able to hold back the tears. "No.

He just threatened me again that if I did not agree to remain at home, he'd ensure that I never saw my children again. When I refused, he—that's when he tore off my clothes and beat me. He—he did other things, as well. He claimed I was his wife and that he could use me in any way he wished."

"What happened after that?" I asked, controlling with great effort the anger boiling inside me.

"He got drunk, just like he always does. When he finally stumbled to bed, I waited until I was sure he was asleep; then I dressed and tried to sneak upstairs to my boys' room. I had made up my mind to take them with me back to Mrs. Fowler's shelter."

"I gather you were unable to accomplish this?"

She gave a deep sigh. "No, one of my husband's men was watching their room. I threw a chair at him and managed to run back downstairs and out the front door. One of my neighbors, Mrs. Hardy, heard my screams and allowed me to spend the remainder of the night in her house. I left just before dawn and made my way back to the safe house."

"Did Mrs. Hardy see your bruises?" I asked, hoping I had located a possible witness to Luther Sechrest's abuse.

Alexandra's face reflected her embarrassment. "I felt so stupid for believing Luther's promises. I didn't want her to see what he'd done to me. But the bruises were visible on my face, and I'm sure she guessed there were more."

"Do you think Mrs. Hardy would be willing to testify to seeing these abrasions?"

She leaned forward in her chair. "When you first told me we'd have to go to court, I thought I could endure anything to be free of my husband. Now I'm not sure I have the strength to face Luther again."

"Even for your children, Mrs. Sechrest?" I asked gently.

She stared at me, her bruises standing out starkly against her pale skin. How terrifying it must be, I thought, to challenge the monster who has brutally misused you for over eleven years. Perhaps even more damaging than the physical blows were the wounds he'd inflicted by attacking her self-respect and value as a person. Now I was asking the poor woman to meet the brute head-on, and in the always-intimidating arena of the courtroom.

At length, she sucked in a deep breath of air. "Yes, Miss Woolson. For my children's sake, I will do it."

I felt a surge of admiration for Alexandra, followed by a renewal of my anger that our laws made it so difficult for women in her situation to retain custody of their children. That I was forced to explain the details of these biased laws to my client made me wish more than ever that I had the means to change them. Until women were given the vote, however, I feared we would be bound by the laws men created and enforced. Most of these men, like Papa, Charles, and Samuel—yes, and even Robert, for all his bluster— were undoubtedly decent and well-meaning. That a mere one half of the population possessed the power to construct the edicts by which we were all forced to live, however, seemed unjust in the extreme.

Keeping it as simple as possible, I outlined to Mrs. Sechrest the procedure ahead of us, explaining that our first task would be to prove that Luther Sechrest had habitually beaten her.

"That's why Mrs. Hardy's testimony is so important," I concluded. "Also, I mentioned during our first meeting that your sister and perhaps your maid might appear in court on your behalf. Have you had an opportunity to speak to them about this possibility?"

"I haven't been in contact with my maid since I left Luther's house. As for my parents, they live in Sacramento, as does my sister and her family. I haven't seen any of them since last Christmas."

"Your husband continues to send monthly payments to your father?"

"Yes. That's another reason I haven't informed them of my circumstances. Papa has depended on that money for so long now, I don't know what they would do without it."

"You cannot allow this to become your concern," I told her. "I realize that sounds harsh, but you must put your life and that of your sons first. I'm sure your parents would agree if they understood your predicament."

"I haven't heard from my mother or father since I left Luther's house. If any letters have arrived there addressed to me, he hasn't seen fit to forward them to the shelter."

"In that case, the first thing you must do is write your parents and tell them what has been going on in your marriage, and that you plan to file for a divorce. If your mother has been a witness to the abuse, I think it very likely she'll agree to testify on your behalf." I watched as she wiped fresh tears from her eyes. "Why don't we put that issue aside for now and move on to the matter of child custody."

She looked surprised. "Surely there can be no difficulty there. I'm the boys' mother. And they're very young, only eight and ten. Any judge must appreciate they need their mother."

She was looking at me so full of hope, it wasn't easy to give her an honest answer. "Unfortunately, many factors are taken into account before child custody is assigned. In the past, the argument has been that just as a woman has no right to file suit or enter into a contract, she also has no separate custody rights of her own. The law has made custody dependent upon support, which few women can provide."

"But—" She started to interrupt, then stopped, as if unable to find a convincing argument with which to dispute this regrettable fact.

Hating the current custody practice as much as my client, I pressed on. "In practice, custody of a minor child has more often than not gone to the father, especially when the child is a boy. The law assumes that sons need a masculine domestic environment in order to train them for life, particularly when they're over the age of seven. Which yours are."

While I was speaking, Alexandra had flushed a bright red, and apparently she could no longer contain her fury. "But that is outrageous! I cannot think of a more detrimental influence on my sons than their father."

"Then that's what we must demonstrate in court. Despite these precedents, there has finally been some progress made in taking the children's good into consideration when deciding custody. However, given your children's ages and the fact that they are boys, we'll be forced to prove to the court's satisfaction that your husband is an unfit father."

She regarded me with fearful eyes. "But how am I to do that? To the best of my knowledge, Luther has never hit the boys without justification. I'm the only one he's abused."

"And we both know that may change when you're no longer around to play the scapegoat." I tried to infuse my words with an optimism I was far from feeling. "We'll have to prove that your husband's pattern of violence is escalating, and that you fear he may begin to mistreat your sons."

Having truthfully stated the worst we might expect, I decided it was time to insert a bit of encouragement.

"I agree that it won't be easy," I said, "but that doesn't mean it can't be done. We'll have to plan our strategy in such a way that, in the end, there can be no doubt your sons are better off in your care."

"Then you really believe we have a chance?"

"Yes, I do," I replied, praying I wasn't giving the poor woman false hope. However, there remained one final question which must be asked—the most difficult question.

"Mrs. Sechrest, this is very important, and I must insist upon an honest answer. Is there anything in your past that can possibly be construed as improper or immoral behavior?"

She seemed completely taken aback. "Certainly not! That is a terrible thing to suggest."

"Yes, but it's one your husband is very likely to bring up if he's determined to fight you for custody."

"But that is—it's appalling!"

"Yes, it is. That's why you must give this question serious thought. If there is anything you've said or done that your husband could hold against you, I must know."

"Really, Miss Woolson, I can think of nothing."

"I hope not, Mrs. Sechrest. We cannot afford any surprises once we get to court."

As I left my office that evening, I picked up a copy of the *Call Bulletin*. The headline spread across the front of the paper read INCREASED CLAMOR FOR NEW CITY HALL REFORM! Reading the story as I waited for a cable car, I learned that the latest financial audit had revealed thousands of dollars missing from tax funds set aside for the project. According to the article, there was an angry public outcry—primarily fueled by Maurice Blake, Mayor Kalloch's rival in the upcoming election—demanding an investigation into the irregularities.

Samuel was right, I thought. The new City Hall fiasco was turning into a major political issue.

CHAPTER NINE

Instead of heading directly home, I boarded a cable car to Nob Hill. As I'd told Robert, I had made up my mind to discover what lay behind the strange threat Lieutenant Ahern had made about Frederick that morning at the jail. I couldn't dismiss the fear that my brother might have inadvertently become involved in something illegal, or perhaps even dangerous. While it was true he was frequently pretentious and overbearing, he was still my brother. I didn't want to see him publicly disgraced because of some silly mistake he might have made. He should have an opportunity to explain himself. At the very least, I felt he should be warned.

I arrived at Frederick and Henrietta's house, to find them entertaining dinner guests. Needless to say, they were not well pleased to have me show up unannounced on their doorstep. I was about to offer a suitable apology and depart, when I was surprised to see that their guests were Philippa and Edgar Bramwell, along with their son Nicholas. Considering that Frederick and Henrietta avoided mingling with people in the building trades—individuals they not so subtly regard as below their social station—I was curious at how they had come to be friends. And since I had not yet met Edgar

Bramwell, I decided to break with the laws of decorum and extend my impromptu visit, at least for a little while.

I watched in silent, if guilty, amusement as Henrietta fumbled for words to explain my impromptu appearance. At best, my sister-in-law was an anxious and exacting hostess. To have the least-favorite, and most unpredictable, member of her husband's family descend upon her without warning must have taxed her already tenuous nerves to their limit. Certainly it reinforced her poor opinion of my social skills.

"Sarah, my dear, what a surprise," she managed to say, darting Frederick a look of barely concealed panic. "Yes, a surprise. You, er, will join us for dinner, won't you?" Henrietta's wide eyes pleaded with me to politely decline her invitation and leave.

Instead of responding to this unspoken appeal, I smiled and gracefully accepted the offer. "If it will not inconvenience you, Henrietta. I had no idea you had guests."

My sister-in-law had little choice but to introduce me to the group gathered in the parlor for predinner aperitifs. Pangs of conscience, however, prompted me to accept without protest the glass of sherry my brother proffered.

"Mrs. Bramwell and I have met," I said, smiling at the stout, fashionably gowned society matron. Tonight, she wore a hunter green silk gown with a deeply cuirass bodice and a skirt with horizontal pleating, causing me to wonder if she had any idea how many inches this unfortunate cut added to her already-ample girth. "I've also had the pleasure of meeting Nicholas, but, regretfully, not his father."

"Then allow me to introduce you to Mr. Edgar Bramwell," Henrietta went on. "He and Mrs. Bramwell were very generous contributors to Frederick's senatorial campaign."

Ah, I thought, so that's why the Bramwells had been permitted to circumvent Frederick and Henrietta's social standards and are being wined and dined here tonight. I smiled up at the tall, straight figure standing before me. "I'm pleased to meet you, Mr. Bramwell."

"How do you do, Miss Woolson?" Edgar Bramwell said a bit self-consciously. Indeed, the man appeared distinctly uncomfortable in Frederick and Henrietta's overcrowded parlor. Somewhere in his early fifties, Bramwell was solidly built, with broad shoulders, a thick, muscled neck, and large, calloused hands. He had a full head of dark hair, slowly turning to gray, and a mustache that displayed more white than brown. His face was burned to a dark tan, and a good many lines fanned out from his eyes. Although he looked respectable, even handsome in his well-tailored tuxedo, he seemed the sort of man who would be far more at ease out-of-doors, working with his hands. Studying both of the Bramwells in turn, I had to wonder how two people so utterly mismatched had ever managed to get together.

I was sipping my sherry and listening with feigned interest to the predictable conversation between Frederick and his guests when a young lady I had never met swept into the room. She could not be described as conventionally pretty—her nose was a shade too large and her mouth too narrow to qualify for that accolade—but she knew how to dress in order to display her slender figure to best advantage. Her silk gown, a delicate sky blue color, perfectly matched her eyes and set off her blond hair, which had been swept up onto her head and fastened with diamond combs and pins. The intricate diamond necklace and bracelet set she wore must have been worth a small fortune, and I was nearly blinded by the large six-prong Tiffany diamond ring that sparkled on the third finger of her left hand.

She swept majestically into the room and made directly for Nicholas. Taking him by the arm, she gazed lovingly up at him through eyelashes that were suspiciously dark for someone with such fair hair. "Nicky, darling, get me a sherry, will you?"

"I see you found your comb, my dear," Henrietta said, fairly fawning over the girl. "I am so relieved."

"Yes, silly me, I must have dropped it in the foyer when I took off my wrap." She smiled at the room in general, displaying straight but slightly protruding teeth.

"And who is this?" she asked, staring at me with almost rude curiosity. Her eyes traveled with obvious distaste over my gray business suit and practical black hat. "I don't believe we have met."

Returning with her sherry, Nicholas stepped into the breach before my brother or Henrietta could decide on an approach that would result in the least loss of face. The fact that his little sister had become an attorney was one of the banes of Frederick's existence, and he and Henrietta did everything possible to keep it a secret from their friends.

"Aldora, I'd like you to meet Miss Sarah Woolson, Mr. Woolson's sister," Nicholas said. "Miss Woolson, I'm delighted to introduce my fiancée, Miss Aldora Radburn."

To say that I was surprised by this pronouncement would be an understatement, given that the last time I'd seen the young man he'd been escorting Yelena Karpova to the theater. "How do you do, Miss Radburn?" I politely replied. I started to reach out my hand, then thought better of it. Aldora Radburn did not seem the type of person to shake hands with a woman she very probably mistook for a common shop girl.

"Nicholas and Miss Radburn are to be married next summer," Mrs. Bramwell informed me proudly, unaware of her husband's involuntary flinch as she made this announcement. Clearly, Mr. Bramwell was not as enamored of the match as was his wife.

"Aldora is the eldest daughter of Mr. and Mrs. Milford Radburn, who have recently taken up residence here in San Francisco," Mrs. Bramwell continued. "I'm sure you've heard of the Radburns, Miss Woolson. They are a very old and distinguished Boston family. Actually, the Radburns are distant relatives of Queen Victoria."

"How nice to be related to a queen," I said. "Have you ever met Her Majesty, Miss Radburn? I understand she is still in mourning for her late husband, Prince Albert."

"I have not yet been honored to meet Her Majesty," Aldora replied, displaying all the arrogance I might have expected from the old girl herself. "Nicholas and I plan to commence our honeymoon by sailing to England. My mother has arranged for us to be presented to the queen at that time. Mama is Her Majesty's third cousin."

"How nice," I repeated, finding it impossible to think of anything more original to say. Actually, I found myself feeling rather sorry for Nicholas, and I wondered how he felt about this marriage. He'd seemed so happy in Yelena Karpova's company the previous evening. I had a hard time imagining the handsome young man spending the rest of his life with this pretentiously vain younger version of my sister-in-law Henrietta!

I was well into my second glass of sherry, and wondering how I could unobtrusively draw my brother aside to ask him about Lieutenant Ahern's peculiar comment, when the mountain came to Muhammad, figuratively speaking, of course. Under the pretext of showing me a new painting he had recently acquired, Frederick led me into his library and demanded to know the real reason I had suddenly appeared at his door.

"And don't tell me it was because you just happened to be passing by, Sarah. I know well enough that Mama and Papa practically have to drag you over here. Now, what's going on?"

"All right, Freddie," I responded, addressing him by the nickname I knew he abhorred. "I'll come directly to the point. I happened to meet Lieutenant Ahern at city jail this morning, and he said something decidedly odd about you."

Frederick opened his mouth and stared at me. "Ahern? You mean that blustering little Irishman who couldn't put two ideas back-to-back to save his life? And what in heaven's name were you doing at city jail?"

"I was there to interview a prospective client," I replied coolly, ignoring his censoring look. "And yes, that is the Lieutenant Ahern I'm referring to, although I think you underestimate him."

"Never mind that, Sarah," he said brusquely. "What did that idiot say that was so important you had to barge over here and disrupt our dinner party?"

"That's interesting, Freddie. Lieutenant Ahern used the same word only this morning to describe you."

My brother's face puckered until it resembled a dried prune. Through clenched teeth, he said, "Damn it all, Sarah, spit it out or leave. You seem to go out of your way to cause trouble. And stop calling me Freddie!"

I'm ashamed to admit that I was beginning to enjoy this little discussion. Please believe me when I say that for years I'd tried to grow closer to my eldest brother. Sadly, it was becoming increasingly apparent that those particular twains were never destined to meet. In fact, as time passed, I found the unfortunate chasm between us growing into a substantial abyss.

"He said, and I quote, 'I'm warning you that if that brother of yours isn't more careful in his political dealings, he just may find himself a resident of city jail.' Now, why would Lieutenant Ahern say such a thing?"

My brother appeared to have no ready answer, but at least I had managed to capture his attention. "Are you certain that's what he told you? I find it exceedingly hard to believe. That annoying little weasel wouldn't have the nerve!"

"Well, apparently he does." I eyed him squarely. "Now, what have you been up to that Lieutenant Ahern would make such a threat?"

Frederick drew himself up, indignant and very angry. "I have been performing my duties as a California state senator, that's what I've been 'up to.'" He glared down at me. "I think you've made up this entire thing just to aggravate me."

"Why in the world would I do that? According to Ahern, you've been associating with people who are questionable, or who may be operating outside the law. I only came here to warn you."

"Next time, stay home," Frederick snapped. "And keep your nose out of affairs you know absolutely nothing about. You are a woman, Sarah, and, contrary to what Father has led you to believe, women are physically and emotionally incapable of comprehending such matters. Go home and knit something and leave business like this to your betters."

"Frederick," an angry voice interrupted. I looked over, to find Henrietta glaring at us from the doorway. "I have been searching all over for you. Dinner will be served in ten minutes and you are neglecting our guests."

"I'll be right there," Frederick replied. "Sarah is just leaving." Moving with unusual alacrity, my brother helped me on with my wrap and, while Henrietta returned to her company, walked me to the door—probably to ensure that I actually left. He had started back to the parlor, and I was halfway out the door, when Nicholas Bramwell hurried down the hall.

"Miss Woolson," he said softly. "Might I have a quick word with you before you leave?"

"Yes, of course," I replied curiously.

"I saw you at the theater last night," he began. "You must wonder why I was escorting Miss Karpova when I'm engaged to another woman."

"It's none of my business, Mr. Bramwell. However, I hope you won't do anything to hurt Miss Karpova. She's very young, and hardly sophisticated in matters of the heart."

The young man drew himself up, looking wounded that I would suggest such a thing. "Please believe me, Miss Woolson, that's the last thing I would ever do."

"Then you must be honest with both young women. Miss Radburn seems very fond of you. This kind of deception all too often leads to disaster."

He looked crestfallen. "Yes, I know. It's an awkward situation. You see, Mother has her heart set on my marrying Miss Radburn. She feels it would be an advantageous match—for my political career. The problem is that I care very deeply for Yelena and—"

"Nonsense! Of course you don't care for that girl. She is nothing more than a common Gypsy."

Nicholas and I turned, startled to find that Mrs. Bramwell had come upon us from behind. For such a large woman, I was amazed she could move so noiselessly.

"Mother, I—"

"Nicholas, come to your senses. Any alliance with that girl is out of the question. It would result in your political ruin. I have sacrificed far too much to allow such a catastrophe to happen."

"You misunderstood, Mother. I was merely telling Miss Woolson that I found the Karpova girl attractive. Nothing more."

"Of course there will be nothing more," his mother stated with finality. "I will see to that. Now you will return to the parlor at once. You must escort Miss Radburn in to dinner."

She turned to me, a spurious smile pasted on her fleshy face. "Miss Woolson, I wish you good night." And with that, she took her son by the arm and led him back to the parlor.

I hurriedly slipped out the door, grateful to be out of my brother's home and free to breathe deeply of the clean night air.

After a light supper Cook had kept warm for me in the kitchen, I joined my father in his study for an after-dinner coffee, which, as was his custom, he generously laced with brandy. Everyone else was out of the house except Charles and Celia's children, who were snugly tucked in their beds.

I treasured these rare evenings alone with Papa, both of us comfortably ensconced in front of the fire, sipping our coffee and chatting, or simply enjoying a companionable silence.

Tonight, however, Papa was not in a good mood. Slapping a copy of that morning's *San Francisco Chronicle* on the table between our chairs, he proceeded to describe yet another derogatory article that had been written about my brother Frederick.

"It's that Rudolph Hardin again," Papa said, showing me the story he'd circled in pencil. "Damn the man! Now he's accusing Frederick of catering to special-interest groups, at the expense of his own constituents. I happen to know that it's all a pack of lies.

Blast it all, anyway, I'd give my best putter if Frederick could sue the blackguard for slander."

I took the paper and glanced over the piece. True enough, my brother's old nemesis from law school had once again fabricated an accusation against Frederick which, as far as I could tell, seemed mainly comprised of supposition and innuendos. Unfortunately, Hardin had worded the statement very cleverly, ensuring that Frederick would have a difficult time suing him for liable.

I patiently listened while Papa raged on about the iniquities of the press in general and Rudolph Hardin in particular, until he finally wound down and seemed to tire of the subject. Appearing far more relaxed, he poured out the last of the coffee—naturally adding a generous allotment of brandy—and inquired how my new law practice was coming along.

Sipping my coffee, I told him about Mrs. Sechrest and her determination to divorce her abusive husband, after which we spent some time discussing the child-custody issues we were certain to face when the case came to court.

"It's all going to boil down to whether Mrs. Sechrest can prove her husband to be an unfit father," Papa said, filling his pipe and striking a match to the bowl. "You realize that won't be easy."

"Yes, that's what I tried to tell her. I don't think we'll have any difficulty proving Mr. Sechrest to be an abusive and drunken husband. But even Mrs. Sechrest admits that to date he hasn't illtreated their two young sons."

"Hmmm." Papa pulled contentedly on his pipe and considered the problem. "Is there any way your client can demonstrate that her husband's drinking or violent tendencies are escalating? So much so that she fears her boys may be in danger?"

"That's our plan," I said, "although I'm not sure it's going to work. The problem is that Sechrest surrounds himself with lackeys who will undoubtedly swear to anything he asks them to. It may well turn out to be her word against his." I drained the last of my coffee. "Then, too, the case is further complicated by the children's gender. If they were girls instead of boys, we might stand a better chance of gaining custody. But two boys, both of them over seven—" I let my words hang between us.

"You have your work cut out for you, my girl. No doubt about it."

Papa rang for our butler, Arthur Edis, and requested more coffee. I watched as our old retainer carried in a fresh pot and set it down on the table. Suddenly, I was struck by how much the man had aged over the past few years. It's funny, I thought, but when we see someone every day of our lives, we tend not to notice the graying hair, the stiffening gait, or even the new wrinkles. Edis had been with my parents since well before I was born, quietly seeing to the family's comfort and anticipating our needs. He must be over seventy by now, I thought, and with a little start, I realized how different the house would seem if he were not there anymore.

Papa regarded me after Edis had left the study, the old servant silently closing the door behind him, as always. He must have guessed my thoughts, for he said, "Edis is beginning to show his age, isn't he? Mind you, the man has only five or six years on me, so I suppose the same thing can be said in my case." He chuckled. "Of course, growing old is infinitely better than the alternative."

Papa freshened our coffee cups from the new pot, then added another generous dollop of brandy to each. "Now then, my girl, why don't you tell me all about that séance you and Robert attended. And how that journalist fellow happened to end up with a guitar string around his neck."

I had told the story so many times by now that I was surprised to realize Papa hadn't yet heard it, at least not with all the details. But then we'd had little time alone together for the past few weeks, and I was reluctant to go into it in front of Mama, who tended to take the subject of murder very much to heart. Taking my time— for I trusted my father's judgment and was eager to hear his opinion—I started the tale from our arrival at the Cliff House. I included Lieutenant Ahern's interrogation, both that night and the next morning, and finished by describing the attack on Yelena Karpova in the room I later learned had originally been assigned to Theodora Reade.

Papa did not immediately respond to my account. He seemed to be quietly contemplating my narrative as he repacked his pipe bowl and once again lit it with a match.

"A strange story," he said at length. "Sounds like something out of a dime novel. I gather you believe Mrs. Reade saw the killer during that flash of lightning before the candle was relit."

"Yes. I'm sure that's why she was murdered."

"I used to be good friends with her late husband, Ralph Reade. We played chess by the hour at our club. Got to be quite a competition between us."

"Yes, that's what she told me."

"I met Mrs. Reade only once or twice, but she seemed a nice woman, if a bit on the quiet side. Why do you suppose she didn't tell Lieutenant Ahern immediately what she'd seen? That is, if you're right and she really did witness the reporter's death."

"I've asked myself the same question," I replied, sipping my coffee. "She fainted almost immediately after we discovered Moss's body sprawled in his chair, and she appeared confused and disoriented when I spoke to her later that night. When she was leaving for home the next morning, she said something about her eyes not being as good as they used to be."

Papa thought about this. "It almost sounds as if she knew the killer. Perhaps it was someone she trusted. If she'd told Ahern what she thought she'd seen and it turned out she was wrong, she would have seriously maligned her friend."

"Exactly. Which means if our assumptions are correct—"

"Then it's unlikely that Russian fellow is the killer." Papa smiled at me over his pipe. "I doubt that Mrs. Reade would have been reluctant to tell the police about a sinister-looking foreigner."

I nodded. "That's one of the reasons I question Serkov's guilt."

"From what you've told me, there's a lot of evidence against the man, including motive and opportunity. And you say witnesses actually claim they saw him in Washington Square just before Mrs. Reade was killed?"

"That's what they say," I told him. "But I don't think they could have gotten a very good look at his face. It would be easy enough to wear an old black suit, glue on a black beard and wig, and cover your head with a hat. From a distance, the disguise would be pretty convincing."

"And just about everyone at the séance had a motive to kill that pesky reporter, not just the Russians." He reached for a pad and pencil. "I'll tell you what. Why don't you take me through the list of people who were at the Cliff House that night. Only go more slowly this time. Let's see if we can't fit a few more pieces into this puzzle."

I did as he asked, describing everyone at the table, starting with Senator Gaylord and his wife. As I did, Papa drew a rectangle on the page and jotted down names in the order of where they sat. When I was finished, he silently studied his diagram.

"Senator Gaylord," he said thoughtfully. "He's the one who's taken a shine to Frederick, isn't he?" I nodded but didn't speak, not wishing to disrupt his concentration. "I've never known a politician who didn't have at least one skeleton in his closet. On the other hand, I haven't heard anything specific about Gaylord." He looked down at the page and made a tiny check next to the senator's name. "Let's see, you say Nicholas Bramwell sat next to Mrs. Gaylord?"

I didn't even have to think about it; the seating at the séance table was etched in my mind. "That's right. And Nicholas's mother, Philippa, sat to his left."

"Bramwell," Papa repeated, tapping his pencil on the pad. "Is she by any chance married to Edgar Bramwell, of Bramwell and Sons Construction?"

"As a matter of fact, she is," I replied. "Can you tell me anything about the company? I've met Mr. Bramwell, but he seems to be a man of few words."

"But a man of decisive action," Papa said with a smile. "He started the company about twenty-five years ago, and built it up through hard work and shrewd management. He seems honest enough. At least the mayor seems to think so. Bramwell and Sons does a good deal of work for the city."

"Have you ever had business dealings with him, Papa? Or met with him socially?"

"Actually, I first met Edgar Bramwell and his elder son, Lyle, a couple of years ago when they added a new wing onto the courthouse. I gather it was the younger son, Nicholas, you met at the séance, the one who recently passed his bar examination?"

"Yes, I think Nicholas's mother is determined that he take up a career in politics. This is the first time I've heard the elder son's name mentioned." I thought over what my father had just said about their family business. "Papa, do you know if Edgar Bramwell's company is involved with the new City Hall project?"

"As a matter of fact, they're one of the major contractors the city's hired to put up the cursed thing. Why do you ask?"

"Samuel heard that Darien Moss was planning an exposé on the scandal surrounding the new City Hall—you know, who might be taking bribes or padding their pockets at the city's expense. He seemed certain that Moss was planning to name names." To protect my brother's journalistic anonymity, I did not mention that his source was Sergeant George Lewis.

Papa looked amused. "And you think Edgar Bramwell asked either his wife or his son to strangle Moss before he could write these articles?"

I felt a flush of embarrassment. When put like that, the possibility did sound far-fetched. "I don't know what to think," I admitted. "It's hard for me to believe that anyone at that table was desperate enough to risk killing Moss in front of eleven possible witnesses."

"I agree. Yet it seems someone did just that." Papa again studied his drawing, checking off both Bramwells. "All right then, to Mrs.

Bramwell's left was Mrs. Reade, with Yelena next to her. At the far end of the table, sat Madame Karpova herself." He looked at me. "Do you think it's possible the medium could have left her seat without being noticed?"

"You know, she seems to be the only person at the table who couldn't have gotten up without being seen. She'd just conjured up some kind of flimsy white apparition when the candle went out. Everyone claims they were staring at Madame Karpova and whatever it was she'd materialized. I know she was still in her seat when the candle was relit."

"Hmmm. That doesn't completely rule her out, though, does it?" Papa said thoughtfully. "It would have been damn tricky, but performing tricks is what the woman does for a living. What about the daughter, Yelena?"

"I suppose it's possible, but I'd say it's extremely unlikely. She's such a timid little creature. And Moss was very large. I don't see how Yelena could have put that wire around his neck without him overpowering her."

Papa sighed and checked off the two Karpova women. "At least for now," he said. "Let's see, Lieutenant and Mrs. Ahern were to the clairvoyant's left. Logistically speaking, they were closest to Moss— except for you and Robert, of course. I suppose Moss could have had something on one of the Aherns and had threatened to expose them in his paper."

"He'd written negative articles about the police before," I said. "But I don't believe any of them specifically targeted Lieutenant Ahern."

"There's always a first time, my girl. By the way, what about this Serkov fellow? You say he left the room when Moss arrived?"

"Yes, but I suspect he came back in later and helped his sister with her special effects, like the flying trumpet and balalaika, as well as that filmy apparition."

"Did Lieutenant Ahern check everyone there for signs of blood on their clothes or hands?" Papa asked.

"He didn't come right out and have everybody hold out their hands. But I noticed he was watching everyone closely during our interrogation. Besides, the murderer could have wiped any blood off his hands afterward, and no one would have been the wiser."

Papa put down his pad and pencil, gave a long sigh, and relit his pipe. By now, what was left of our coffee had turned cold, and neither of us wished to bother Edis by requesting yet another pot.

"Seems to me you've got a real mystery on your hands," Papa said. "Do you think Serkov will change his mind and ask you to represent him?"

"That's another mystery, Papa. For some reason, he seems convinced the police are going to let him go free without his having to step inside a courtroom. Ahern had a good laugh when I told him about that. He claims he hasn't a doubt that Serkov's their man." I thought back to the scene in the Russian's cell. "Serkov is a stubborn, feral-looking creature, but I don't think anyone would consider him fanciful. Yet he is utterly certain he has no need for an attorney."

"Because the police are going to realize he's innocent and just let him go?" Papa said. "Do you think he fully understands the gravity of his situation? You said he speaks broken English. Have the police called in an interpreter?"

"Not as far as I know. But I don't think language is the problem. Serkov seems to comprehend why he's been arrested, yet he honestly believes that the doors to the city jail are going to fly open at any moment and he's going to walk out of there a free man. It's—it's insane."

Papa regarded me kindly over his pipe. "You may have just solved your mystery, my girl. What if this Serkov fellow really is insane? It would go a long way toward explaining things."

When I failed to offer any argument to this sensible suggestion, Papa continued, his voice gentle. "I know from personal experience how difficult it can be establishing one's own law practice, Sarah. And I realize you're eager for clients willing and able to pay for your services. Having said that, I have to admit that I hope Serkov does not end up as your responsibility. Even if it turns out that he's not mad, the man is hostile and unpredictable. Frankly, it frightens me to think of you in his company."

"I know, Papa, but I can't turn anyone in his predicament away, even a man like Serkov. His life may depend on me."

My father leaned forward in his chair, using his pipe to emphasize his words. "You have a good heart, Sarah, but I think you're making a grave mistake. Regardless of what happens in the courtroom, I'm afraid Dmitry Serkov will bring nothing but grief into your life."

CHAPTER TEN

The following afternoon, I went to the county superior court building to file Mrs. Sechrest's divorce petition. Since I had filled out all the necessary paperwork in my office, I anticipated I would be there no longer than it would take to deliver the forms to the proper department. Unfortunately, I was quickly disabused of this assumption.

I had just located the correct office when I literally ran into Robert, who was exiting the same room I was about to enter. His tousled mop of red hair was bent over a booklet of some sort, and despite my efforts to move out of his way, we collided, causing the papers I was carrying to fly helter-skelter onto the floor.

"Robert, really!" I said, reaching out a hand to steady myself. "You should pay more attention to where you're going."

"I apologize, madam," he said, then looked up from his pamphlet to see whom he had very nearly crushed. "Sarah! What are you doing here?"

"I was about to turn in some forms when you crashed into me like a runaway train," I said, stooping to retrieve my scattered papers.

Before I could lay a hand on them, Robert knelt down and

quickly began stacking the papers together. He rose to return them to me, then happened to see the name I had entered on the petition.

"Mrs. Alexandra Sechrest!" he exclaimed in surprise. "But that's—that's impossible!"

Placing the papers back inside the folder, I said without looking up, "What do you mean it's impossible? Mrs. Sechrest is my client, and she's filing for divorce. It's really quite simple."

Robert startled me by taking hold of my arm and all but pushing me toward an empty bench in the lobby.

"Have you taken leave of your senses?" I demanded, trying unsuccessfully to wrench myself free of his grasp. "Robert, let go of me this instant. Whatever has gotten into you?"

"Sarah, did you say you're representing a Mrs. Alexandra Sechrest?" he asked, pulling me down to sit next to him.

"Yes, but what does it have to do with—"

"And your client is married to Luther Sechrest, who works as foreman for Leighton Mining Company?"

I started to get up, then abruptly sat down again. "How did you know that?"

"Because I'm representing her husband. I just filed divorce papers on his behalf."

"You mean against his wife?" I said, not immediately grasping what he was saying. "On what possible grounds?"

"On the grounds that his wife has deserted him and their two minor children."

"Deserted them?" I stared at him, my astonishment turning to anger. "How dare he make such a preposterous accusation? She was forced to flee from him and seek refuge in a house for abused women. And, for your information, she took her sons with her."

"That's interesting, because Luther Sechrest has the boys now. He maintains that she's refused his repeated pleas to return home and care for them."

"Of course she refuses. The man has been beating her for twelve years. Luther Sechrest sent his men to steal the children away from her at the safe house, Robert. She's terrified that if they remain in that house, he may begin to mistreat them, as well."

Robert guffawed. "That's ridiculous. Luther Sechrest is an honest, hardworking man—a deacon in his church, in fact. He cares deeply for his wife and children. He would love nothing more than to see his family whole again."

"Who told you all this? I assume you've interviewed Mr. Sechrest?"

"Of course I have. I also discussed the matter with Joseph Shepard when he assigned me to the case." He lowered his normally booming voice as two well-dressed men took seats on a nearby bench. "Even if Shepard hadn't vouched for him, I could judge from our first interview that Sechrest was an intelligent, thoughtful man who has been treated shamefully by an ungrateful wife."

"*He's* been shamefully treated!" I exclaimed, my temper commencing to boil at the injustice of this accusation. "I wish you could see the bruises your thoughtful and caring Mr. Sechrest has inflicted on his poor wife."

"You know my views on striking a woman," he said with disgusting virtuousness. "Unfortunately, there are some men who do not share my sensitivity and self-control, especially when they're consistently driven to the end of their patience. When you consider Alexandra Sechrest's drinking habits, and her inexcusable behavior toward her sons while under the influence, I would hesitate to judge Mr. Sechrest too harshly if I were you."

I was stunned by this outrageous assertion. "That is so reprehensible, it's beyond belief," I all but shouted, causing the gentlemen at the nearby bench to cast disapproving looks in our direction. "Mrs. Sechrest isn't the drunkard; her husband is! And when he's in that condition, he beats her unmercifully."

"My client warned me his wife might take that tact," Robert said, shaking his head sadly that she had chosen to stoop so low.

"For the sake of their marriage, he's attempted to make allowances for her behavior. Now, however, he must consider the well-being of his sons."

"Robert, that is complete nonsense! Luther Sechrest doesn't care a fig about those boys. He's using them to regain power over his wife. How can you be so gullible?"

"I might ask the same of you, Sarah," he continued with that same annoying air of self-righteousness. "However," he went on before I could interrupt, "Mr. Sechrest has directed me to inform Mrs. Sechrest's attorney, which I now find is you, that he's willing to accept his wife back without prejudice—under the condition that she return to him at once."

"How magnanimous of him! And what is she to do when she gets there? Turn her cheek so he can blacken the other side of her face? Didn't you hear what I said, Robert? This man is a drunkard. He's also a bald-faced liar and an habitual wife beater. The next time he turns violent, he might very well kill her."

Ignoring Robert's protestations not only that I was being unreasonable but that I was too biased even to attempt to appreciate the husband's side of the matter, I gathered up my papers and rose to my feet.

"I will see you in court," I threw out over my shoulder, and left him sputtering behind me as I walked off.

After successfully concluding my business at the courthouse, I returned to my office, to find that a note had been pushed beneath my door. It was from Madame Karpova, pleading with me to visit her brother, Dmitry once again at the city jail. Since I considered it unlikely that Serkov had changed his mind about hiring me to represent him, I delayed this errand until I had completed some necessary work on Mrs. Sechrest's divorce case.

As luck would have it, Eddie came bounding up the stairs for his reading lesson just as I was about to leave for the jail. After engaging him to drive me in his brougham, I handed the boy another Rollo book to read while I visited Serkov's cell.

"I don't suppose you have a copy of the *Police Gazette,* Miss Sarah?" he asked hopefully, helping me into the carriage.

"No, I do not, Eddie. I realize that Rollo's adventures seem a good deal less colorful than the *Gazette,* but they are far better suited to your reading level." At his disappointed look, I added, "Look, I'll strike you a bargain. Once you've mastered the Rollo books, I'll let you have *The Adventures of Tom Sawyer,* by Mark Twain, as your next challenge. I think I can safely promise that you'll find it every bit as exciting as that disgusting rag sheet."

Eddie did not appear convinced about this, but he said nothing more about the matter. Closing the carriage door, he leapt onto the driver's seat and clicked his horse into the late-afternoon traffic.

We reached the jail in good time, and I left Eddie sitting atop the brougham, rather unenthusiastically perusing his new Rollo book. By now, the guards were growing more accustomed to my periodic visits to the facility. Some of them still regarded me with obvious, if unspoken, disapproval, but for the most part I was greeted with smiles, tolerably good manners, and even an occasional joke or gossip about various prisoners. As on my last visit to the jail, Cecil Vere, chattering nonstop, escorted me to Serkov's cell.

"He's in a good mood today, miss," Vere announced as we started into the cold, dingy bowels of the detention center. "Not that he's crackin' jokes, mind, but at least he ain't bitchin'—beggin' yer pardon, miss—complainin' about the food or the other prisoners. Most of the men don't want no truck with Serkov, him bein' a foreigner and all. And it don't help matters any that he keeps cursin' at them in Russian, or at least it sure as hell—beggin' yer pardon, miss—sure as heck sounds like cursin'. Can't swear to it, of course, but judgin' by the look on the bugger's face when he's spoutin' off, he sure ain't sayin' nothin' nice."

"How is your fiancée, Mr. Vere?" I managed to ask as he was forced to stop talking long enough to draw in a breath of air.

The jailer beamed. "Nice of you to ask after her, miss. Right as rain is my Annie. Works in a shop durin' the day, then sews shirts at night. We're both savin' every penny so's we can get married next year. You'd like my Annie, miss. She's the prettiest little thing you ever did see." He grinned at me. "But then I suppose I already told you that."

I was about to answer that indeed he had, but we'd reached Serkov's cell, and Vere rather importantly pulled the large ring of keys from his belt and placed one in the lock. As usual, it scraped and scratched in protest, then finally gave way, allowing the cell door to be pulled open. Every time I went to the jail, I itched to take along a can of oil to grease the locks. How the guards and prisoners could stand the incessant squealing of locks and banging of doors was beyond me.

Unlike my last visit, this time Dmitry Serkov looked up as Vere held the door open so that I might enter. The Russian was sitting on his cot, staring at nothing in particular, but at least he wasn't rudely ordering me to leave.

"Call out if you need me, miss," Cecil Vere said cheerfully, then clanged the door shut and whistled his way down the hall.

"Good day, Mr. Serkov," I said, smiling politely, in the hope that today's visit would proceed more amicably than the one that had preceded it. Sadly, this was not to be.

Serkov nodded his craggy head but didn't speak.

Wishing to waste no more time on this surly man, I decided then and there upon a direct approach. "I have come to ask if you've changed your mind about my representing you on these murder charges."

"*Nyet,*" he said, a self-satisfied expression on his homely face. "Tomorrow, I am out this place."

"'Out this place'? You mean they're releasing you from jail?

Tomorrow?" I regarded him skeptically. "Who told you that, Mr. Serkov?"

"My business, no yours."

I was sorely tempted to take the disagreeable man at his word and be done with the entire affair. On the other hand, what if Papa was right and his poor understanding of the English language had led to this gross misinterpretation of his present circumstances?

"Mr. Serkov, you will not be allowed to leave the jail tomorrow, or any day in the near future," I explained. "I don't know who gave you that idea, but it is incorrect. The murder charges against you are not going to be withdrawn, and you will be forced to remain in this cell until you have been tried for the deaths of Darien Moss and Mrs. Theodora Reade. When you go to court, you're going to need an attorney—if not me, then someone else. If you'd like, I could arrange for you to speak to another lawyer."

"No need lawyer. *Uydi ot suda!* You go now."

"Mr. Serkov," I said, trying again. "I don't how they do these things in Russia, but in the United States, you must abide by our laws."

He started to say something else, when a key scraped in the cell door and Madame Karpova entered.

"Miss Woolson," she announced. "I am glad to see you. I have come to help you speak to Dmitry. His English is not good."

"Thank you, Madame Karpova, but I was about to leave. Your brother has once again declined my services."

"Nonsense, you misunderstood him. It is good that I am here."

I started to tell her that I had no difficulty understanding the words *no* and *get out,* but she had already turned to Dmitry and was speaking to him in rapid Russian.

After several minutes of this obvious harangue, he waved a hand at her and said, "*Uzamolchi.* All right, all right. Have your way. But I out tomorrow."

Madame Karpova flashed me a triumphant smile. "There, you

see? I told you he would see reason. Now, when can you get Dmitry out of this place?"

I had already explained the matter of bail money to her in my office, but clearly she still did not comprehend the system. Once again, I told her I had no control over when Mr. Serkov would be released. He would first have to be arraigned, and then very likely he'd be held over for trial.

Madame Karpova was not a woman to give up easily, and it required a further quarter hour before I finally convinced her that although I would do everything in my power to help her brother, I could not change the law.

I left brother and sister speaking to each other in heated Russian, and Cecil Vere led me out to the front of the jail. Taking advantage of a momentary lull in his nearly nonstop chatter, I asked the guard if anyone had been to visit Mr. Serkov other than his sister and myself.

"Not him, miss. No one wants to be near the feller." He gave a dry chuckle. "Truth be told, there's more than one of 'em would be happy enough to slit the Russki's throat, just to shut his trap."

"What about Lieutenant Ahern? Has he been to see Mr. Serkov?"

"I reckon he's questioned the bugger once or twice, but we always bring Serkov to the lieutenant, not the other ways around." He gave me a sidelong look. "If you think we've roughed him up, miss, we ain't. When he behaves hisself, we treat him just like any of the others prisoners."

"I didn't mean to imply that I thought Mr. Serkov was being mistreated," I assured him. "I was just curious if he'd had any other visitors. He still seems convinced he's going to be released tomorrow."

He laughed shortly. "Not a chance of that happenin', miss. The only way that Russki's gettin' outta here is when they take him to the gallows and put a noose around his scrawny neck."

I could hear Vere's cheerful whistle as I let myself out of the building. Remembering Sergeant George Lewis's promise to allow me to examine Darien Moss's diary, I instructed Eddie to take me to Central Station. When we arrived, I was pleased to learn that he was expected back at any minute, and that I was free to wait for him if I wished.

As it turned out, George walked into the station shortly after my own arrival. He smiled when he saw me and drew me aside.

"I guess you're here about Moss's diary," he said, keeping his voice low. "I haven't asked Lieutenant Davis yet if it's all right to show it to you. But since he's not in today, maybe I won't have to. You're not going to be too long at it, are you?"

"I'll require enough time to page through it, and take notes, of course." I tried to calculate how much time it would require, but it was impossible to guess until I'd actually seen the book. And eager as I was to examine Moss's diary, I didn't want to risk getting George into trouble with his superiors. "Perhaps an hour or so?"

"That should be all right," he agreed. He turned and led me down a narrow, poorly lit hallway, then opened one of the doors and motioned me inside. Lighting a kerosene lamp, he closed the door behind us.

The room we entered was dusty and filled with boxes and file cabinets. As far as I could see, there appeared to be little rhyme or reason to the way evidence was stored, but George seemed to know exactly what he was looking for. Placing the lamp atop one of the file cabinets, he lifted a box down from its shelf and placed it on a table.

"We put the jewelry we found in a safe—can't have that lying about. But Moss's diary and some of his other papers are in this box. Go ahead and take notes if you like, Miss Sarah. But please don't take anything from this room. It would mean my job if something went missing."

After George left, I set to work. I went through the loose papers first, and found that several contained rough drafts of columns Moss had planned to write in the near future, including an exposé on the unsavory practices of several local bankers. Another partially completed article was aimed at the scandal surrounding the new City Hall project.

The final page in the box—concerning Madame Karpova and Serkov—made me catch my breath. The previous articles he'd written about the Russians had been more sarcastic than rancorous. This one was a vicious attack. Moss not only accused Madame Karpova and her brother of being frauds but also went on to chronicle a long list of crimes Serkov supposedly had committed in Russia, including several brutal murders.

According to Moss, the pair were nothing but common Gypsies, traveling around the countryside in order to bilk gullible people out of their savings. He also cast doubts on their relationship, saying he'd been unable to find proof that the two were siblings. The piece came to an abrupt end with Moss promising to attend one of Madame Karpova's much-publicized séances and then report his findings to his many readers.

I jotted down a few notes from each of the proposed articles, then turned my attention to the diary, excited to see that it was a duplicate of the black leather notebook Moss had brought out at the séance. Was it possible I had at last found the key to identifying the person who had murdered the reporter?

Eagerly, I opened the book, only to feel my heart sink. It was crammed with flowing yet precise handwriting, which filled both sides of each page. Unfortunately, as Samuel had warned me, it was written in a language, or code, I didn't recognize. Some of the characters reminded me of the Greek alphabet, while others made no sense at all.

Since it was impossible to copy even a fraction of the diary in the time I'd been allotted, I turned to the last few pages, reasoning that these would be the ones most relevant to Moss's murder. I made no attempt to decipher the writing, merely copying as many entries as I could manage. I would worry about making sense of them later.

True to his word, George came to retrieve me a little over an hour later, and I promised to inform him if and when I managed to make rhyme or reason of the entries.

I had told Eddie he was free to leave, since I had no idea how long I'd be inside the station, but he was waiting for me when I exited the building, his new Rollo book beside him on the seat as he calmly reread his well-worn copy of the *Police Gazette*. I started to reprove him for this, then thought better of it. At least the boy is reading, I told myself. And in truth, he had probably seen a good deal more of the world in his brief fifteen years than I had in my nearly twenty-eight. There seemed nothing for it but to admit I was fighting a losing battle.

Upon reaching my Sutter Street office, Eddie announced that he was driving back to the jail to visit an old friend who, as he put it, had been bagged for being a pickpocket.

"He and his ma have let me sleep in their kitchen many a night when Pa's gone on a spree," he explained. Fishing around next to him on the seat, he held up his new Rollo book. "Do ya mind if we do my readin' lesson tomorrow?"

Assuring the boy that tomorrow would be fine, I started up the stairs, when Mrs. Goodman called out to me from the door of her millinery shop.

"You've someone here to see you," she informed me—needlessly, as it turned out, for Robert came out of the store to stand behind her. Since he was the last person I cared to see after our row that morning at the courthouse, I turned on my heel and continued up the stairs.

"Do you have time for a nice cup of tea?" my neighbor called up to me.

"I'm sorry, Mrs. Goodman, but I have a good deal of work to finish before I leave for the day. Perhaps tomorrow."

"I suppose this work you have to do concerns the Sechrest divorce," Robert said, following me up the stairs to my office.

"As a matter of fact, it does. Actually, I'd prefer that you leave now, so that I can get on with it in private."

Naturally, the stubborn man paid no attention. Entering the room behind me, he said, "This isn't a social call, Sarah. I've conferred with Mr. Sechrest and he has offered his wife a truly generous proposal. In lieu of her regrettable drinking problem, my client has promised to provide her with the finest medical care available. No matter how long the treatment lasts, he promises to welcome her home upon its completion."

He smiled, seemingly proud of Luther Sechrest's munificent proposal. "There now, Sarah, even you can't find fault with such a benevolent offer."

"Not only can I find fault with it," I replied, barely able to contain my temper, "but I heartily reject it as arrogant, self-serving, and entirely without merit. You disappoint me, Robert. I accept that you subscribe to some of the more prevalent male prejudices against women, but I always considered you to be honorable and fair-minded. Today, you have succeeded in dashing that perception. Without the slightest attempt to learn Mrs. Sechrest's side of this issue, you have summarily judged her and found her to be guilty. All on the say-so of the man who has violently mistreated the poor woman for the past twelve years."

I sat behind my desk and angrily picked up Mrs. Sechrest's divorce papers. "I've made an attempt to separate my personal life from my professional one and not allow a court case to affect our friendship. However, since, as you say, this is not a social call, I would appreciate it if you would leave. As Mr. Sechrest's counsel, it's highly unprofessional for you to be standing there while I work on my client's case."

"Sarah Woolson, you are the most stubborn, narrow-minded woman I have ever had occasion to meet. At least have the decency to put Mr. Sechrest's proposal to his wife. It is her decision to make, after all, not yours."

"Naturally, I will inform her of her husband's gracious offer to place her in an asylum, perhaps for the rest of her life, while he continues, unchallenged, to carry on with his drunken and violent behavior."

Robert's face turned very red. "Blast you," he snapped, then spun around on his heel and slammed out the door.

Finally, and thankfully, alone, I bent to my task. However, before I'd spent little more than an hour on Mrs. Sechrest's brief, the door to my office flew open and Eddie Cooper came running inside.

"You'll never guess what happened at the jail, Miss Sarah!" he exclaimed, trying to catch his breath. "The whole place is talkin' about it."

"Eddie, calm down," I said, trying not to show my own growing alarm. "What's happened?"

"It's that Russki feller, the one with the black beard and the shifty eyes. You know, the one what said he didn't need no lawyer."

"Mr. Serkov? What about him?"

"He's been attacked, miss," Eddie announced, his expression a mixture of horror and fascination. "That Serkov feller's gone and got hisself stabbed!"

CHAPTER ELEVEN

In his excitement, Eddie raced his brougham through crowded downtown streets, taking corners on two wheels, hitting every pothole, and generally tossing me about like a bowling pin in a ten-pin alley. In our chaotic wake, we left scores of angry drivers and pedestrians, most of them shouting unrepeatable expletives. When Eddie pulled his poor horse to a stop in front of the jail, I exited the carriage, skirts twisted, my hat and hair askew.

"Eddie, we're going to have to sit down and have a serious discussion about your driving habits," I told the boy, pushing my hat back onto my head and patting, probably futilely, at my mussed hair. "Before you kill us both!"

I entered the station but was informed by the officer on duty that it would be impossible for me to see my client.

After several minutes of fruitless argument, I asked if Lieutenant Ahern was there, hoping he might prove more reasonable.

"No, ma'am," the man replied. "The lieutenant left word he'd be at a meeting with the mayor and some other big shots."

"See here, Mr. . . ."

"Alston, ma'am, Paul Alston."

"Yes, Mr. Alston. I understand that my client has been injured.

Under the circumstances, I really must insist on seeing him immediately."

I thought the guard was once again going to refuse me admittance, but he shrugged and called out to a young jailer, "Tilbert, show this lady to that Russki's cell."

"You mean now?" the boy said, looking appalled. "Considerin' what just happened, I—"

"Now!" Alston ordered. "She says she's his lawyer. I think we gotta let her in."

The young man gave me a look heavy with surprise and curiosity. "A woman lawyer? Don't that beat all!" Then, catching sight of Alston's face, he hastily unlocked the door leading to the cell blocks. "This way, miss."

The jailer led me down the same hall I had left only hours before. Ahead of us, I could hear the sound of voices; then we turned a corner and I saw several uniformed men gathered around Serkov's open door. Inside, two men were standing over a man's prone body. The victim, whom I could not get close enough to identify, was lying facedown on the cot, his head turned toward the wall. It was only when one of the men moved away from the cot that I made out the riot of white-streaked black hair and beard. I stared in horror. The wounded man was Dmitry Serkov!

"Miss Woolson, what are you doing here?"

I whirled around, to find Cecil Vere standing behind me, his face pale and drawn.

"I heard about the attack on Mr. Serkov," I said breathlessly. "How is he, Cecil? Is he going to be all right?"

His Adam's apple moved up and down as he swallowed. "I don't think so, miss. The police surgeon's in with him now. But I'm pretty sure the Russki's dead."

My heart lurched, and for a dizzying moment I wondered if I had understood Vere correctly. "When did it happen?" I asked, my voice not entirely steady.

"He was stabbed, miss." Vere's own voice sounded strained and flat. "I don't rightly know when. He was lyin' on his cot when I come to let his sister out, but I didn't think nothin' about it. When I come back a few minutes later, I realized he weren't movin', so I went inside and pulled back the blanket." Once again, he swallowed hard and his face took on a pasty look. "It was then I seen the blood, and the dirk stickin' out of his back."

"But how is that possible? The man was locked in a jail cell. Of all places, he should have been safe in there!"

I realized that in my distress I was speaking more loudly than I'd intended. The men inside the cell turned to look at me, first in surprise, then in annoyance that I had been allowed to enter the cell block. Before they could order me to leave, I stepped away from the open door and out of their sight. Cecil followed, regarding me with concern. I had to admit my limbs seemed a bit wobbly, and I suddenly felt light-headed.

"You don't look so good, miss," Vere said, taking hold of my arm. "Why don't you come over here where you can sit down." Without waiting for me to agree, he led me to a room down the corridor from Dmitry's cell. It was furnished with a table and several chairs. The guard guided me to the nearest seat and gently lowered me into it. He perched on the edge of the table, still watching me, as if he feared that at any moment I might slip over and onto the floor.

When he finally decided I wasn't going to keel over after all, he said, "If you think you'll be all right for a minute, miss, I'll fetch you a glass of water."

"Yes, thank you," I told him weakly.

By the time he returned, I was feeling more like my old self. I was not proud of my momentary weakness—normally, I was made of sterner stuff. However, seeing the poor Russian lying there on his cot like that, a knife sticking out of his back, would be enough to unnerve anyone. It's the last thing I expected, I thought in growing fury, with my client supposedly locked safely inside a jail cell! Again I wondered how something like this could happen?

I inhaled a deep, bracing breath and slowly felt my head begin to clear. Anger, however justified, would have to wait. It was time to pull myself together, to think clearly, to decide how best to proceed. Certainly, Madame Karpova and her daughter would have to be notified, but what could I possibly tell them? How could one explain something that was utterly inexplicable?

The first thing I had to do, I decided, was learn as much about Dmitry's death as possible. Somehow I had to try to make sense of this tragedy.

"When I left the jail earlier this afternoon," I said, placing my empty water glass on the table, "Madame Karpova was in the cell talking with her brother. Did Mr. Serkov receive any other visitors after that?"

Vere shook his head. "I didn't bring no one else in, miss. After you left, the Russki and his sister started fightin' pretty good. She was yellin' at him and givin' the bloke bloody hell—beggin' yer pardon, miss. I didn't come back to his cell until she banged on the door for me to let her out."

"But how did his killer bring a knife into the jail?" I was still shaken, and it required effort to keep my voice even. "All packages and bags are searched before they're allowed to be brought in, aren't they? My briefcase is always inspected."

"That's right, miss. Only it ain't that big a knife. Could've been hidden anywhere—in a gent's pocket, or even under a lady's skirts—beggin' yer pardon, miss. We don't usually search visitors unless they look shifty like."

I looked at him disbelievingly and tried to shake off another attack of light-headedness. "You're telling me that inside an allegedly secure facility, Mr. Serkov was stabbed and you have no idea who did it?"

"Oh, but we do, miss," Cecil Vere informed me. "It could've only been one person. Lieutenant Ahern left Sergeant Jackson in charge this afternoon while he went to some meetin' or other. Jackson's already sent out men to find the Russki's sister—you know, that Madame Karpova. They're gonna arrest her for his murder."

Madame Karpova was brought into the jail not long after I'd spoken to Vere. Not surprisingly, she was extremely agitated, although whether this was because she'd lost her brother or because she'd been charged with his murder wasn't clear. The moment she set eyes on me, however, she seemed to quiet down, as if reassured by the sight of a friendly face. Then I realized it was more than just my face that had brought about the transformation; I represented a lifeline, someone to save her from the nightmare into which she'd been plunged. As they led her into the cell blocks, she cried out that I must defend her against these appalling accusations. In the end, I agreed to wait until she'd been settled into a cell, then promised to come back so that we might talk.

When Vere came to the jail's anteroom to lead me to Madame Karpova's cell about an hour later, I was shocked by how much his appearance had worsened in such a short time. In truth, the man looked wretched. His already-pale face had turned ashen, his features looked pinched and unusually sharp, and there was a heavy sheen of perspiration along his forehead and upper lip. Considering that he had held Serkov in such low esteem, I wondered why he seemed to be taking the Russian's death so to heart.

When I commented to him about this, Vere said, "He was a right sharper, that Serkov, make no mistake. And sure as hell—beggin' yer pardon, miss—he done the murders they tumbled him for. But I been thinkin', and I figure he shouldn't have got done in like that. It was just plain wrong. I knew that the minute I seen him lyin' there like that."

This was obviously not the time to be tactful; the situation was too dire. Taking hold of the jailer's sleeve, I forced him to stop walking and face me.

"Cecil, something tells me you know more about my client's death than you're admitting. Did you see the person who stabbed him? If you did, it's very foolish of you to protect him. One woman has already lost her life by not speaking up when she had the opportunity."

He bit his lip, and I noticed his left eye exhibited a severe tic. "I . . ." He hesitated, then shook his head. "No, Miss Woolson, I didn't see nothin'. It's just that—well, I feel like it's my fault is all. I shouldn'ta let it happen."

With that, he turned and, refusing to say another word, led me to Madame Karpova's cell. There, he fitted one of his many keys into the lock, gave it a scraping turn, and pulled open the door. To my surprise, Sergeant Jackson stepped out of the cell before I could enter.

"Are you Miss Woolson, Mrs. Karpova's attorney? Vere here told me you were a woman, but I—" He cleared his throat, seeming embarrassed. "If you don't mind, I'd like a brief word with you before you talk to your client."

"Yes, of course." I said, following the police officer a few yards away from the open cell door.

When we were out of Madame Karpova's hearing, the sergeant stopped. "I'm sorry, Miss Woolson, but I thought you should know that the evidence against Mrs. Karpova is pretty cut-and-dried. She killed her brother, no doubt about it. Vere tells me he was alive and talking to his sister when he let you out of the cell this afternoon. Five minutes after she left, Vere found him dead as a doornail. It's as simple as that."

"How can you be sure no one else visited his cell during that five minutes?"

"I asked Vere about that, and he claims he didn't let anyone else in. Besides, you and Serkov's sister were the only ones who ever came to see the fellow."

"Surely Mr. Vere can't be the only guard on duty."

"No, there's a second jailer who works the same shift. But he claims he didn't let anyone else in, either." Some of my dismay must have shown on my face, because the sergeant, who appeared to be a kind man, was regarding me with ill-disguised sympathy.

"I'm sorry to have distressed you, Miss Woolson. I just felt you should be forewarned of the situation."

"Thank you, Sergeant," I said, keeping my voice level. "Now, if you'd kindly allow me to confer with my client?"

The policeman turned and led me back to Madame Karpova's cell. Without a word, he unlocked the door so I might step inside, then silently departed.

The room in which Madame Karpova had been placed was located on the opposite side of the rectangular-shaped cell blocks maintained for male inmates. It was perhaps a little larger than the average cell, but equally chilly, and furnished with no more than the customary cot and single chair; no special concessions had been granted the woman because of her gender. As was usual, there was a barred window situated high on one wall, and a small barred opening in the door, through which guards could check on inmates as they performed their periodic rounds.

Madame Karpova sat straight-backed on her cot. She gave the outward appearance of being calm, but her pale face and overbright eyes betrayed her inner distress.

"Madame Karpova," I began, feeling profound sympathy for the woman. "I'm so very sorry about your brother."

She made a dismissive motion with her hand, as if brushing aside my condolences. When she spoke, her rich voice sounded hollow and tightly controlled. "Miss Woolson, do you still have the gold medallion I gave you to represent Dmitry?"

"Yes, I do, but—"

"Good," she said, breaking in. "Then you will please see about getting me out of this horrible place. I would prefer that you did so by this evening, as my daughter is by herself in our hotel room and will be worried. I have no wish for her to spend the night alone. Nor do I care to sleep on this—this so-called mattress. It is hardly thicker than a piece of cardboard, and is certainly infested with bugs."

She had not invited me to sit. However, I was so taken aback by this statement that I sank down, unasked, on the cell's solitary chair.

"Madame Karpova, first we must discuss what happened, and then decide what's best to be done about your—"

"Nonsense, there is nothing to discuss." Her voice did not falter, but I noticed that the hands she was clasping in her lap were trembling. "Please do not tarry, Miss Woolson. You must see to my release without delay."

Silently, I prayed for the words to make the poor woman understand her situation. "Madame Karpova," I began, "as much as I might wish to secure your release, I simply don't have the power. I attempted to explain this to you and your brother this afternoon. You're being held on a charge of capital murder, just as he was. It's extremely rare for bond to be set in such cases."

"But I am innocent!" she proclaimed, her voice growing more strident. "Why would I kill my brother? He and Yelena are all I have in this world."

As luck would have it, she had hardly finished speaking when the cell door clanged open and Yelena Karpova rushed into the cell. The girl's lovely face was as white as her lace collar, and her eyes welled with tears as she fell into her mother's arms.

"Hush, *moya malenkaya*," said Madame Karpova, comforting the girl in a surprisingly gentle voice. "*Vse budet khorosho.* Everything will be all right. But how did you get here? Did the police bring you?"

"*Nyet,*" the girl said between sobs. "Nicholas—Mr. Bramwell. In his carriage."

"Nicholas Bramwell brought you?" I asked in surprise.

"Yes, he is in front," the girl said. "Not let him in." She looked into her mother's dark eyes. "Mama, please, you come home now?"

Madame Karpova kissed her daughter on the forehead. "Hush, *moyo zolotse.* I will be home before you know it."

Yelena turned to me. "Dmitry—how he die?" she asked.

I looked at Madame Karpova, seeking her permission to describe the murder to her daughter. The woman closed her eyes, then gave a small nod of agreement.

"I'm afraid Mr. Serkov was stabbed to death this afternoon," I told the child. "The police claim your mother was the last person to see him alive." I hated being the cause of the wretchedness I saw on the poor girl's face. Her uncle was dead and her mother stood accused of his murder. In one afternoon, Yelena's entire life had been ripped apart. "I'm truly sorry to have to give you such tragic news about your uncle."

The girl suddenly pulled out of her mother's arms and rose to her feet. "He not uncle," she exclaimed, tears spilling out of her lovely brown eyes.

Madame Karpova's face drained of color. She tried to grab hold of her daughter's arm, but Yelena squirmed out of her reach. "Yelena," the woman pleaded. "Please, do not do this."

"Mama, *dostatochno,*" the girl cried. "No more lies. It is time for truth."

"But it will do no good, *dochka.* Don't you see that?"

The girl shook her head. Expelling a great sigh, she said, "No, truth better. No more lies."

Madame Karpova stared at her daughter as if she were seeing her for the first time. I thought I understood how she must feel. In the short time I had known the girl, she had appeared to be a frightened little mouse, reticent and exceedingly shy. She had never shown even a fraction of the emotion she had demonstrated here in the past few minutes. It was rather like witnessing a butterfly emerge from its cocoon, full of energy and eager to make its mark on the world.

Madame Karpova muttered something in Russian; then slowly her expression changed. The arrogant air she wore like a royal crown was replaced by a look of such profound pain, I felt as if I were seeing a different person altogether. With a little shock, I realized this was probably the first genuine emotion I'd ever seen on the woman's face. The rest had been an act, much like the one she'd put on for us at the Cliff House. Perhaps I was finally seeing the real Olga Karpova, the woman behind the impervious mask.

"All right, *mozo zolotse*," she told her daughter. "For your sake, I will tell our story, although I do not see how it will alter the situation." She looked at me. "We are not Russian royalty, Miss Woolson, but I see by your face that this admission does not come as a surprise."

"Actually, I did wonder about it," I admitted. "But please, go on. Yelena is right. It's best to tell the truth. Especially now."

"The truth, yes," she said with a dry little laugh. "Well, you may make what you wish of the truth, Miss Woolson, for I am certain it will help me not at all."

Giving her daughter's cheek a final pat, she said, "We are Rom, or, as many call us, Gypsies. Dmitry Serkov was not my brother. He was *lubovnik,* my lover. He was also a thief. In Russia, we lived on what I made telling fortunes, and whatever he could steal, or blackmail, from those who consulted me and foolishly confided too many of their secrets. Then, one night, Dmitry drank too much and killed a man with his bare hands. Regrettably, this was a person with much money and power, and we were forced to flee for our lives.

"For a long time, we moved from place to place, but when the authorities got too close, we had to leave the country. Gradually, we made our way through Poland and Germany until we reached London. By then, I had heard of the great Madame Blavatsky, and I attended one of her readings. I was much intrigued, for here I saw a way to use my psychic talents to greater advantage than ever before."

"Is that when you and Dmitry came up with the effects we saw performed at the Cliff House?" I asked.

She smiled sardonically. "People expect that sort of thing, so we gave it to them. But it was not all an act. Oh, no, much about it was real. It is true that I have been blessed with psychic powers. My mother was born with the gift, as was her mother before her."

"How long did you study under Madame Blavatsky in London?" I asked.

"For almost five years. I'm afraid I was not entirely truthful when I claimed to have left Russia only three years ago. I thought it best not to discuss the years we spent fleeing from the authorities." She smiled. "Under Madame Blavatsky's tutelage, I was able to perfect my abilities. The high priest Tizoc came to me for the first time, and through him I was able to communicate with those souls who have passed over to the other side."

Once again the woman expelled a long sigh. "There is little more to tell. I went on to join the Theosophical Society Madame Blavatsky formed when she moved to New York. Despite what that horrible Darien Moss claimed, I have helped many people to heal and to communicate with loved ones who have passed beyond the pale. I am proud of what I have accomplished."

She looked me full in the face. "I am aware of Dmitry's faults, Miss Woolson. But he was good to me. He . . ."

She paused, and I was surprised to see her eyes fill with tears. "When I was a young girl, Dmitry saved my honor as well as my life. He killed the men who tried to make me *robi,* Gypsy slave. For weeks, he made sure I had a roof over my head. He fed me and cared for me, nursed me back to health. I owe—I owed him everything."

"But you didn't marry him," I said when she again stopped speaking, this time to wipe at the tears that coursed freely down her face.

She shook her head, then lowered it without speaking. Yelena gave a little cry and rose from the floor to sit next to her mother on the cot. Gently, she placed a protective arm around the woman's shoulders.

"She not proud of what she do," the girl explained. "She and Dmitry—how you say?—make—no, arrange for her to marry rich merchant. Then after while, I come. They wait until I am one year, steal man's money, then leave. I do not see—not remember father."

"Madame Karpova?" I said when she showed no sign of responding to her daughter's disturbing revelations. "Is this what happened?"

She raised her tear-stained face. "Yes, that is what we did. It was a long time ago." Rather roughly, she wiped her face with a handkerchief, then made a conscious effort to pull herself together. "Now you know the truth, Miss Woolson. Does it change anything? No, I thought not. Except now you know why I would never murder Dmitry. Never!"

After promising the distraught woman that I would do what I could to help her, I gathered up my things and asked to be let out of the cell, so that mother and daughter might spend some time alone together.

Still uncharacteristically silent, Cecil Vere led me through the corridor of cells and out to the front of the jail, where I found Nicholas Bramwell pacing in the antechamber.

"Miss Woolson," he said, his face grave as he came to meet me. "How is Madame Karpova? Is it true that her brother was murdered this afternoon?"

"I'm afraid so, Mr. Bramwell." At his insistence, I went on to relate that afternoon's tragic events, including the reasons Madame Karpova had been arrested for Serkov's death. The only information I left out was the psychic's turbulent history in Russia, as well as her true relationship to the man we had accepted as her brother. Something that personal, I felt, should come directly from Yelena, or from Madame Karpova herself.

Leaving the young attorney to continue his vigil for Yelena, I prepared to depart, when I had a sudden impulse to speak to the guard at the front desk. Mr. Alston, after all, had the responsibility to authorize or reject all visitors to the facility.

"I wonder if you could give me some information?" I asked, approaching his station. I went on to request that he look through the ledger that every visitor to the jail was required to sign before entering the cell block. The time frame I gave him was two hours before to one half hour after Serkov was killed that afternoon.

Without much enthusiasm, Alston ran a broad finger down the list of that day's visitors. He identified several people I didn't know, along with Eddie Cooper, who had returned to the jail to visit his friend after he'd dropped me off at my office.

"I think that's it," the guard said. "Oh, wait a minute. There's one more. Some big shot came in just as Serkov's sister was leaving."

"Whom did he come to see?" I asked.

The guard scanned the list of names in the second column, where the visitors were supposed to name the inmate they had come to see. "That's strange. Whoever was at the desk earlier didn't write in the name of the prisoner the senator was here to visit."

"Senator?" I repeated. "Which senator?"

"Let's see," Alston said, running his finger back up the left-hand side of the page. "Says here his name was Woolson, Senator Frederick Woolson."

CHAPTER TWELVE

I went directly from the jail to Frederick's house, my mind whirling with questions and barely suppressed fear. What had my brother been doing at the jail? I kept asking myself. And at the same time Dmitry Serkov was being stabbed. Surely it was a coincidence. But taken with my client's baffling murder, it seemed one coincidence too many. What had Freddie become involved in? Was he in some kind of trouble? He was arrogant and critical and I had a hard time being in the same room with him. Still, he was my brother. And I loved him.

When I reached Frederick's house, I was told by Woodbury that he was out. When the butler offered to see if Henrietta was in (a mere formality, since Woodbury knew precisely who was at home at any given moment of the day or night), I thanked him and said I would call back later. I had no wish to speak to my sister-in-law until I'd contacted my brother. There was no love lost between Henrietta and myself, but I didn't want to worry her when there might be a simple explanation for her husband's actions. At least I prayed there would.

Samuel and I sat in the library that evening, drinking coffee and trying to make sense of the day's events. Mama and Papa had gone out for the evening with Celia and Charles, so we were able to speak in privacy. I told him I was worried about Frederick but that first I needed to discuss Serkov's bizarre murder.

"I know," Samuel said when I introduced the subject. "I met George at the gymnasium this afternoon, and he told me the Russian had been found stabbed to death in his cell. He also said his sister had been arrested for the murder."

"It turns out she wasn't his sister," I said, and went on to describe the story of Madame Karpova's life in Russia and how she had become a spiritualist.

"Madame Blavasky," he repeated when I mentioned Olga Karpova's mentor. "I've heard that name before. Oh, yes, she's a flamboyant spiritualist who claims to have been trained by the famous Scottish sorcerer Daniel Dunglas Home." He chuckled. "I understand she has a legion of followers, despite the fact that she's been exposed several times as a fraud."

"That's not much of an endorsement."

"I doubt that many of these so-called clairvoyants could pass careful scrutiny." He looked sharply at me, as if struck by a sudden thought. "Hold on a minute, Sarah. Don't tell me you intend to represent that woman?"

"As a matter of fact, I do," I told him, unhappy to detect a defensive tone in my voice. Frankly, I was growing weary of men passing judgment on whom I should and should not defend. I could not imagine Robert, or Samuel, or Papa, for that matter, expressing the same objections to their male colleagues. And it was easy enough to see by the dumbfounded expression on my brother's face what he thought of my decision. It came as an agreeable surprise, therefore, when he didn't deliver the lecture I was expecting.

Instead, he commented calmly enough, "All right, if Madame Karpova didn't murder Serkov, who did? Who else had access to his cell?"

"I don't know," I admitted unhappily. "But we only have Sergeant Jackson's word that no other visitors were admitted after Madame Karpova left."

"Why would Jackson lie about it? Do you think he's involved?"

"No, I don't have any reason to believe he is." I racked my brain, searching for some other explanation for how the Russian managed to get himself murdered inside a locked cell. "Serkov was disliked by everyone at the jail, prisoners and guards alike. What if a jailer let one of the inmates into Serkov's cell long enough to kill him?"

Even to me, this theory seemed far-fetched, and I could see Samuel suppressing a smile. "That's an interesting supposition. Do you have any particular guard in mind?"

"No," I said with a sigh. "I'm just grasping at straws, so you can wipe that silly grin off your face. It's frustrating to believe so strongly in someone's innocence and yet be powerless to prove that you're right."

I sipped my coffee, more than ready to talk of something else. "Did you have any luck tracing people's whereabouts the afternoon Mrs. Reade was killed?"

"Actually, all things considered, I think I did rather well," he said, going along with the abrupt change of subject. He pulled some notes from his pocket. "Let's start with Lieutenant Ahern. Supposedly, he was leading a group of men to the site of yet another one of Kearney's sandlot speeches." My brother was referring, of course, to the volatile labor leader Dennis Kearney, who several years ago had organized the Workingman's Party of California. "As usual, it seems Kearney was trying to incite a riot against the Chinese," Samuel went on.

I thought of the discussions I'd had with the powerful tong lord Li Ying on this very subject. He had made me realize all too vividly the prejudice the Chinese were forced to endure in San Francisco, especially from laborers competing against them for the same jobs. I hated the thought of Kearney once again stirring up long-brewing hatreds and resentments. People were bound to be injured, and very possibly killed.

I came out of these thoughts with a jolt. "Wait a minute, Samuel, did you say *supposedly?*"

"It took you long enough to catch that," he said, giving me that 'Pay attention, little sister; what I'm saying is important' look. "It means that in the process of trying to disperse over a thousand angry rioters, Ahern seems to have gone missing. At least no one recalls seeing him at the height of the fray."

"Who told you this?"

"I got it from George, secondhand, of course, since he was with you and the late Mrs. Reade in Washington Square at the time. He heard it from some of Ahern's men, who were disgruntled their lieutenant made himself scarce once the punches began flying."

He now had my complete attention. "Did anyone actually see him leave the area, or go off in the direction of Washington Square?"

"No, and before you get excited, I take it this kind of spineless behavior isn't that unusual for Ahern. According to George, he revels in any commendations that come his way, but he prefers that his men fight the actual battles while he's safely off the firing line."

"So, it proves nothing," I said, feeling a sense of deflation.

"I don't know that it proves, or disproves, anything. For now, it simply means Ahern is still on your list of suspects."

"All right," I said. "What about Senator Gaylord?"

"Gaylord was supposed to meet a couple of state congressmen for lunch that day, but he turned up an hour late. He told his colleagues his hansom got stalled by an overturned drummer's wagon on Clay Street."

"I don't suppose you were able to confirm that with his hackman, were you?" I asked hopefully.

"As a matter of fact, I was. The hansom driver claims the senator became impatient, paid his fare, and got out to walk, claiming he could make better time on foot."

"How far was he from Washington Square at that point?"

"That's what I wanted to know, so I checked it out." He consulted his notes. "Gaylord left the cab on Clay and Grant streets, which is approximately two-thirds of a mile from Washington Square, and a straight shot down Stockton Street. Even with lunchhour traffic, I managed to walk it in less than ten minutes. I'll be generous and give Gaylord fifteen minutes at the outside."

I did some mental calculations. "So, fifteen minutes to walk to Washington Square, a few minutes to change into his Serkov outfit, another ten minutes to kill Mrs. Reade, then change back into his regular clothes and walk to the restaurant. Where was he meeting the congressmen, by the way?"

"Giuseppe's on Pacific Avenue. I walked there from Washington Square in fifteen minutes. Add up the times and—"

"He could easily have murdered Theodora Reade and made it to the restaurant in an hour. So Senator Gaylord remains on the list. Dash it all, Samuel, I was hoping we'd be able to eliminate some of these people. What about Nicholas Bramwell? Can we at least rule him out?"

"Possibly. I used the excuse that we belonged to the same club to visit his house—he still lives with his parents, by the way. He wasn't home, but I did see his mother. I made up some story about his failing to show up for lunch with me the afternoon of Mrs. Reade's death, and his mother informed me he'd been ill with fever and ague that day and was confined to his bed."

"Would she be willing to swear to that?"

"Ah, therein lies the rub. Mrs. Bramwell admits she was at a charity affair most of the afternoon."

I threw up my hands in frustration. "So he could have evaded the servants, slipped from the house, murdered Mrs. Reade, and been back in his sickbed when his mother returned." I felt a sudden ache developing between my eyes. "And Dmitry Serkov?" I asked with resignation.

"According to the desk clerk at their hotel, the Russian went out in the morning and didn't return until late that afternoon. For what it's worth, he believes Madame Karpova and Yelena spent most of the day in their rooms."

He folded his notes and placed them back in his pocket. "That's about it. I didn't have time to check on the women. But I can't seriously imagine any of them garroting either of the victims."

"No, I can't, either. Well, so much for culling down our list of suspects."

He refilled our coffee cups, then leaned back in his chair and crossed his legs. "All right, little sister, enough about clairvoyants and murders. Tell me why you're worried about dear old Frederick."

Briefly, I told him what Ahern had said about Frederick watching his political dealings. When I'd finished, Samuel was staring at me in amused disbelief. "He said that about Frederick? *Our* Frederick?"

"I know, I had the same reaction. I spoke to Freddie about it that very night—actually *last* night. Good Lord! So much has happened since then that it seems ages ago. Anyway, he didn't appear particularly upset. In fact, he accused me of making the whole thing up just to annoy him."

Samuel smiled. "Quite honestly, Sarah, if I didn't know you better, I might think you'd made it up, too. The very idea of prim and proper Frederick getting himself involved in anything the slightest bit shady is ludicrous."

"I'm afraid there's more." I told him about finding Frederick's name on the visitors' list at city jail that afternoon. "I can't believe he had anything to do with Serkov's murder, but what could have prompted him to visit the jail in the first place? Taken with Ahern's remark about his dubious political dealings, I have to wonder what Freddie's gotten himself into. To be honest, I'm really worried. You know the old saying, Where there's smoke, there's fire."

"Actually, the correct quote is from John Lyly's *Euphues*: 'There can be no great smoke arise, but there must be some fire.' But I take your meaning."

"I can't believe he'd knowingly become involved in anything

illegal. But what if he thought what he was doing was perfectly honest and aboveboard?"

"Who knows," Samuel said. "Sadly, it wouldn't be the first time he's allowed ambition to stand in the way of common sense. I gather you plan to confront him about it."

"Yes, tomorrow. I'm going to try to catch him at his office downtown; then I'll go straight to the jail to see Madame Karpova."

"Busy day." His look was quizzical. "By the way, George tells me you went to his station today and looked over Moss's diary. What did you find?"

"Good Lord! I can't believe that totally slipped my mind." I brought out my little notebook, opening it to where I'd copied Moss's diary. The first page read:

Iɴqopuᴀᴛıoɴ qpou [н̄. Tʒε ɯκθ roλ ʒᴀɯ
ɴεɯ uıɯᴛpεɯɯ. Ɯεεɴ ᴛoreᴛʒεp ᴀᴛ Eλ λopᴀλo.
  Bλᴀcκ λorгλᴀɯɯ ɯıqε ʒᴀɯ ɯεcpeᴛ
λoфεp. [ᴀ̄ı ɯᴀɯ ᴛʒεu ᴛoreᴛʒεp ᴀᴛ Uгpпʒθɯ .
  Iɴqopuᴀᴛıoɴ qpou [г̄. Χᴀɴɯɯ ɯεεɴ ɯıᴛʒ
ɴεɯ гεɴᴛλεuᴀɴ qpıεɴλ ᴀᴛ Nᴀɴcθɯ . Ɯʒoxλλ
пхᴛ εɴλ ᴛo пoλıᴛıcᴀλ ᴀɯпıpᴀᴛıoɴɯ.
  Ɯʒεpε λıλ Nᴀпoλεoɴ ɯxλλεɴλθ couε xп
ɯıᴛʒ uoɴεθ qop ɴεɯ ʒoxɯε oɴ Pxɯɯıᴀɴ
ʒıλλн.

Samuel studied the page, then looked at me, baffled. "I'm not even sure what language this is written in. You don't suppose he made it up, do you? As a kind of code?"

"I don't think so. Some of the characters remind me of the Greek alphabet, and vaguely of Egyptian hieroglyphics. Yet it's different, too. I thought I'd show it to Mr. Ferrier at the public library tomorrow. Maybe he can make sense of it."

Samuel yawned. "You do have a full day. You'd better make an early night of it."

Naturally, that caused me to yawn, as well. Then, as I drew breath to ask him one last favor, he held up a hand and smiled.

"Yes, little sister, you don't even have to ask. First thing tomorrow morning I'll start looking into the background of every person who was present at that séance, including Darien Moss." He chuckled. "*Especially* Darien Moss. I can't wait to find out how he came to write his notes in those glorified hen scratches. It ought to make a great story."

San Francisco's first public library had opened just the year before, and was located on Bush Street, between Kearny and Dupont. The rented quarters were less commodious than one might have desired, but it was a decided improvement over having no library at all.

It was my opinion that the best thing about the new facility was its librarian, Mr. Alvis Ferrier, a small, fussy man with horn-rimmed spectacles perched upon his sharp beak of a nose. A Harvard graduate, Mr. Ferrier was extremely knowledgeable and persevering, almost to a fault. The more obtuse and difficult the inquiry, the more he poured through his books, his "friends," as he called them, until he came upon the desired information. I entered the library that morning, counting on the little man's seemingly inexhaustible curiosity to decipher Darien Moss's "hen scratches."

I was not disappointed. Almost immediately, Mr. Ferrier confirmed my guess that the notes had been written in a Semitic language. After thumbing through several of his 'friends,' he informed me with satisfaction that the text had been written in the Coptic language.

"Coptic is the common colloquial language of Egypt," he explained. "The Coptic alphabet is based on the Greek alphabet, but it contains extra letters for sounds that are not used in the former language. These are derived from the demotic script, which was used to write the Egyptian language."

Warming to the subject, he went on to narrate the history of the Coptic language, which dated back to the Hellenistic period, when Alexander the Great invaded Egypt in 322 B.C. After some ten minutes of this, I took advantage of a momentary break in this narrative to ask if the Coptic language was still used today.

"It is almost exclusively employed now by the Coptic Church," Mr. Ferrier said. "Although over the past decade, it has been experiencing something of a revival."

"Then would it be possible for you to translate this text for me?" I asked, showing him the rest of my notes.

I thought for a moment he was actually going to rub his hands together in glee. Nodding his small birdlike head, he said, "When would you require them back?"

"As soon as possible, Mr. Ferrier. I assure you it is a matter of the greatest urgency."

The eager gleam in his eyes reminded me of a child about to open his stocking on Christmas morning. "I shall give the matter my full attention," he promised. "Would it be possible for you to come back for it, say Monday morning? That will give me the weekend to work on the translations."

"Yes, that would suit me very well," I agreed, feeling the thrill of victory within my grasp. "I would appreciate it if you would keep these notes to yourself, however. They are of a very sensitive nature."

"Naturally, I will take no one into my confidence, Miss Woolson. You may set your mind at ease on that point."

I exited the library with a sense of elation. I cautioned myself not to get my expectations up too high, but it was impossible not to hope that the notes held a vital key to Moss's murder.

In the meantime, I had several more errands to run, starting with a trip to my brother Frederick's office on Market and Geary streets. Since his official headquarters were in Sacramento—California's state capital—the Market Street accommodation was mainly utilized as a home base, where he and his supporters—unbelievably, he actually had a sizable group of followers, who should have known better but apparently didn't—might plan election campaigns, entertain constituents, and meet with visiting dignitaries.

It did, however, have the advantage of being located in what many San Franciscans considered to be the heart of the city. My brother's front window boasted a view of Lotta's Fountain—a gift from the volatile actress, Lotta Crabtree, who had fallen in love with our fair city—the new Geary Street cable car line, and the fashionable and exceedingly plush Palace Hotel.

Unfortunately, it seemed that I had once again missed my brother. According to Mr. Whelan, who stood guard over Frederick's domain with a glib tongue and a steel grip—for anyone foolish enough to try to push past him—my brother had left the previous day for Sacramento. (Why Woodbury hadn't informed me of this the night before was anyone's guess!) Senator Woolson was not expected back until the following Monday. I was free to call then if I wished. What I wished, I thought as I took my leave of Mr. Whelan, was to speak to my brother *now*, not next Monday!

Since my Sutter Street office was only a few blocks away, I decided to walk instead of catching a horsecar. The morning was sunny and brisk, with no sign of the unseasonable fog that had plagued the city for the past several days. I took in a deep breath of fresh air and, despite the present difficulties which occupied my thoughts, felt a thrill of pleasure. It seemed as if autumn had finally arrived, and with it the warm, sun-drenched weeks San Franciscans looked forward to all year. Why was it, I wondered, that even our most dire problems seem more bearable when the sun is shining?

While I walked, an idea began forming in my mind. It might achieve nothing, but there was always the possibility I might find something I had originally overlooked. The thought cheered me, as coming up with a plan of action always did. As far as I was concerned, a well-ordered offense was always preferable to sitting back and allowing fate to buffet one helplessly about.

After a refreshing cup of coffee and mouth-watering apple

pandowdy with my downstairs neighbor, Mrs. Goodman, I ascended the stairs to my office and settled down to work on the Sechrest case. With Papa's permission, I had borrowed from his library several law books pertaining to divorce and child custody. Unfortunately, they were just as vague and ill-defined as those I had found at the courthouse. I decided that the state of California had much work to do if it were to reform and standardize these laws, particularly those affecting the children caught in the middle of their parents' battles.

I was jotting down notes on how we might best counter Luther Sechrest's accusations concerning my client's so-called drunkenness and erratic behavior, when there was a knock on the door and Robert peered in.

"Truce?" he asked, waving a white handkerchief at me. "I come in peace."

The last thing I intended to do was laugh at the irritating man, so naturally that was precisely what I proceeded to do. "You've got a nerve, Robert Campbell," I said, realizing I had pretty much ruined any chance of sounding annoyed. "Come in and sit down. Actually, I was thinking of sending you a note by messenger."

"Why?" He gave me a suspicious look. "I thought you weren't speaking to me."

"Professionally, I'm not. But this is personal—well, in a manner of speaking at least. I was wondering if you'd care to ride out to the Cliff House with me tomorrow afternoon. I'd like to refresh my memory about one or two details from the other night. For obvious reasons, I'd prefer to have a gentleman accompany me."

"What sort of details?"

"You needn't look so worried. Everything was so chaotic the night Moss was strangled, I'm afraid I might have missed something. Since you were also there, I thought you could help me note any discrepancies."

"Do you really expect to find anything, Sarah, or is this a desperate last attempt to prove Dmitry Serkov innocent of Moss's murder?" Before I could answer, he went on. "By the way, I was shocked to hear of his death yesterday, and that his sister had been arrested for his murder. I find the whole thing unbelievable."

"Actually, there's more to the story than appeared in the papers," I said. "But I'll tell you about it on the drive to Land's End. Will you accompany me?"

He hesitated, then nodded. "All right, I'll go. It's probably nothing but a wild-goose chase, but I agree that you shouldn't go there alone."

"Excellent. I think you'll find the experience far more pleasant on a clear evening than during a thunderstorm." Consulting the gold timepiece pinned to my shirtwaist, I realized it was growing late. I still intended to visit the jail before returning home for the day.

"Eddie and I will pick you up at your boardinghouse tomorrow afternoon at five," I told him, rising from my chair. "Perhaps we should plan on dining at the Cliff House, since it will be well after the dinner hour by the time we return to the city. I've heard that their food is actually quite decent."

I was reaching for my wrap, when Robert cleared his throat. "Sarah, wait. There's something I need to discuss with you. It's about the Sechrest case."

"Oh?" I sank back into my seat. I didn't like the tone of his voice. Nevertheless, I endeavored to keep my manner composed. "Has your client finally decided to behave responsibly and return the boys to their mother?"

"I'm afraid not." His naturally ruddy complexion had turned an even deeper shade of red, and his r's had become more pronounced, which only increased my unease. Whenever Robert was angry or nervous, his Scottish brogue always became more noticeable. "You're not going to like this, Sarah, but I thought you should know. In light of some unsavory news, Mr. Sechrest has reluctantly decided that he must alert the court to the fact that Mrs. Sechrest is an unfit mother."

"What!" I exclaimed. "That's preposterous."

"Sarah, for God's sake, calm down. Yelling at me isn't going to change my client's mind. Let's try to discuss this rationally."

"How can I possibly remain calm when Luther Sechrest is accusing my client of being an incompetent mother? Mrs. Sechrest was right. Her husband is a cad of the lowest order."

"Believe me, he's doing this in the best interests of his children."

"Of course he is," I replied scornfully. "On what possible grounds is he basing this outrageous allegation?"

Robert did not immediately answer. In fact, his expression clearly indicated that he sincerely wished he could avoid giving me any answer at all. For the first time, I truly understood what Alexandra Sechrest had meant when she told me at our first meeting that we must prepare ourselves for a bitter battle. Thanks to Luther Sechrest, it seemed that the battle had now been engaged.

"Oh, for heaven's sake, Robert, spit it out. Whatever Sechrest told you about his wife will certainly turn out to be false, so there's no reason for you to beat about the bush."

His face grew even redder, but finally, reluctantly, his blue-green eyes met mine. "He claims he can produce several witnesses who will testify that they saw Mrs. Sechrest—er, that is, they'll swear that she was carrying on an affair with the boys' tutor, Mr. Gideon Manning."

I fought to hide my shock. At all cost, I could not allow him to see my growing alarm. "This goes beyond outrageous. First, he accuses her of drinking, when he is, in fact, the drunkard. And now he has the effrontery to claim she carried on an illicit affair with her sons' tutor? Is there no end to the man's lies and treachery?"

"Sarah, I—"

"No, Robert," I said. "Don't sit there and try to defend the brute." I took in a deep breath, then went on in a more controlled tone, "Have you questioned Mr. Manning for yourself? Or the witnesses, for that matter?"

"Not yet. But I will."

"Good. Be sure to watch their eyes when they give you their answers. Luther Sechrest has some very unsavory men in his employ. I'm sure they wouldn't scruple to substantiate anything their employer asked of them."

"Don't you think you're being a bit overdramatic?"

"Believe me, I wish I were. I understand the court date has been set for a week from today."

"Yes, that's what I was told." His eyes searched my face. "What about our trip to the Cliff House? Do you still want me to go with you?"

"I won't lie to you," I told him, striving to keep my temper under control. "I find Mr. Sechrest's behavior unpardonably cruel. However, Joseph Shepard has assigned you to his case, and there is little you can do about it. I'll do my best to confine my anger to the courtroom. I just wish you could view the matter with a more open mind."

Getting to his feet, he said, "It's a tragic situation for everyone involved."

"Yes, it is," I agreed. "I'll see you at five o'clock tomorrow afternoon."

He nodded, then turned and, without another word, walked out the door.

During the horsecar ride to city jail, I made an effort to push my concern over Madame Karpova, and, of course, my brother Frederick, to the back of my mind. Instead, I contemplated Luther Sechrest and this nasty turn of events. Was it possible my client had deliberately deceived me? I'd specifically asked her if there was anything in her past that her husband might use against her in a custody battle. She had assured me there was nothing. Either her husband was truly the lying, despicable beast she had described or Alexandra had allowed her shame over some indiscretion to override honesty. Either way, with the divorce hearing only a week away, we would have to discuss the situation frankly as soon as possible.

All the tension of the previous day settled back upon me as I entered the jail. I wondered if any progress had been made in locating Serkov's killer, then realized with a sinking heart that the police probably hadn't even tried. As far as they were concerned, his murderer was already in custody. Why bother to look any further?

I found an agitated Paul Alston on duty at the front desk. Without stating a reason, he once again denied me admittance. Really, I was in no mood to go through this nonsense again.

"See here, Sergeant Alston," I began. "I have every right to see my client. I insist that you—"

The steel door leading to the cell blocks flew open and Sergeant Jackson came hurrying out. He was in such a rush that he seemed not to notice me standing at the desk.

"Sergeant Jackson?" I called out. "What's wrong? Has there been more trouble?"

"Oh, it's you, Miss Woolson," he said, belatedly recognizing me. He regarded me in some distress. "Yes, miss. I'm afraid it's Mrs. Karpova. She's—"

I did not wait to hear the rest, but pushed past him through the still-open door, all but running toward Olga Karpova's cell. When I arrived there, I found her cell door wide open. I hurried forward, only to stop short, horrified by the scene spread out before me like a grisly illustration from the pink pages of the *Police Gazette*.

It was Madame Karpova. She lay sprawled on the floor of her cell, eyes closed, face blue. A torn piece of white material was knotted tightly around her neck.

CHAPTER THIRTEEN

A uniformed officer knelt next to her body, his large square fingers fumbling to ease his penknife through the knots tied at her throat.

"She tried to kill herself," he said, glancing up at me, his broad face covered with perspiration. "Must have been feelin' guilty for killin' her brother. Still, she shouldn't oughta have done this."

I stood frozen inside the doorway, my breath suspended as I stared down at the silent form. "Is she—" I couldn't bring myself to say the word.

"Dead? No, miss, least ways not yet."

His words seemed to release me from my spell, and I hurried inside and crouched down on the opposite side of the medium. "Here, let me help, Officer . . ."

"Wolf, Miss, Jimmy Wolf." Obviously grateful to be relieved of the responsibility, the guard handed me the knife. It was then I noticed how young he was, probably no more than nineteen or twenty. And his hands were shaking badly. No wonder he'd had so much difficulty trying to cut through the material; he was probably afraid he'd gouge her neck in the process.

"How long has she been like this?" I asked, working my fingers between the twisted cloth and her throat in order to slice through the first knot.

"I don't know." His voice was unsteady. "Sergeant Jackson cut her down soon as he saw her hangin' from the window." He nodded toward the barred window above our heads. The remainder of the stained white material, obviously the sheet covering the thin cot mattress, was hanging from one of the bars. "He's gone to fetch the surgeon."

"Yes, I passed him as he was going out." As I spoke, I cut the final knot and pulled the sheet free from Olga Karpova's throat. The material appeared to have been hastily fastened, causing it to encircle her neck loosely. In all likelihood, I thought with a shiver, that was what saved her life. Instead of cutting off the air through her windpipe, the knot had lodged up against her throat. It was tight enough to render her unconscious, but not to end her life—at least not immediately.

I gently raised Madame Karpova's head and brought it to rest in my lap. Then I felt beneath her chin for a pulse. It took several frighteningly long moments before I detected a faint beat. But it was there. Thank God it was there!

The doctor arrived about ten minutes later, closely followed by Sergeant Jackson and Lieutenant Ahern, who silently stepped inside the cell and studied the scene.

He gave me a slight nod of acknowledgment as I moved aside to allow the surgeon access to his patient, then turned his attention to the sergeant. "When did it happen?"

"I found her about half an hour ago, sir," Jackson said. "She was barely alive when I cut her down."

Ahern shook his head. "Guilt, of course. Couldn't live with the fact that she'd killed her own brother. Sad, but it happens."

I opened my mouth to protest this rush to judgment, then realized this was neither the time nor the place. Besides, it would have done no good. Ahern had been convinced of Olga Karpova's guilt since Serkov's death. I was sure that finding her like this only served to strengthen this conviction.

We all watched as the physician examined Madame Karpova, confirming that she had escaped death primarily because she'd made a poor job of tying the knot around her neck. That and the fact that she'd been discovered so quickly. As it was, he was confidant she would make a full recovery. And no, despite my objections, he didn't think there was any need to take her to a hospital. However, he promised to leave medicine for her throat, as well as laudanum to help her sleep.

Lieutenant Ahern lingered behind after Jackson and Wolf carried the clairvoyant to the cot, then departed to attend to other duties. "Guilt does terrible things," he said, gravely regarding her prone and silent form.

"Yes, I'm sure it does," I replied noncommittally, unwilling to be drawn into an argument I had no hope of winning. I was also reluctant, for the moment, to correct his assumption that Serkov was Madame Karpova's brother. "If you don't mind, Lieutenant, I'd like to stay here with my client until she regains consciousness."

"Of course, Miss Woolson," he replied, agreeing more readily than I had expected. Or perhaps he was simply concerned what legal steps I might initiate if Madame Karpova died alone in her cell due to lack of proper medical supervision. Sometimes, I thought, it is a decided advantage having a father who is a superior court judge for the county of San Francisco. "Under the circumstances I think we can relax the rules a bit," he went on. "If you need anything, just call out for one of the jailers."

It was dark outside by the time Madame Karpova finally opened her eyes. Indeed, she had been unconscious for so long, I began to fear that the doctor's nonchalance about her condition might yet end up costing her life. Each passing minute had seemed like a lifetime as I'd sat watching her from the wooden chair.

"*Gde ya? O moya sheya,*" she said in a hoarse whisper, reverting to her native Russian. She looked around the dingy cell in growing panic. "*Gde ya?*" she repeated, her dark eyes dilated in fear.

I had no idea what she'd said, but I could guess. "It will be all right, Madame Karpova," I murmured soothingly, rushing to her side.

She turned her head to look at me, her frightened eyes gradually clearing as she recognized my face. "Miss Woolson?" Her voice was so low and raspy, I had to move my ear close to her mouth in order to catch the words.

"Yes, I'm right here."

"What happened?" she managed to ask.

"You've had an accident," I told her gently, not wishing to add to her alarm. "You were unconscious for a while. But you're going to be fine now."

She reached a hand to her neck, then looked at me in confusion. "My throat," she croaked, and closed her eyes in obvious pain. "Hurts. Can't swallow."

"Shh," I told her. "Don't try to talk. I have some water here and a little soup, although I'm afraid it's cold by now."

I helped her sit up, and she took several sips of water. She refused the soup, indicating without words that she felt a bit nauseous; then she lay back down upon the cot and closed her eyes. Although she was still very pale and her skin felt clammy to the touch, her color had vastly improved since she'd lain unconscious beneath the window.

She was still for so long that I thought she had fallen asleep. But when I started to get up to move back to the chair, she weakly reached for my arm.

"Please," she whispered. "What happened?"

I didn't know what to say. If I told her she'd been found hanging by the neck from the bars on her cell window, how would she react? Would she suffer a relapse? It troubled me that she seemed to have no recollection of the attempted suicide. Surely if she'd been desperate enough to do away with herself, she'd remember tearing the mattress cover into strips, twisting them together, and tying them around her neck. She had kicked away the chair, until she'd hung helplessly a foot or so off the floor. How could anyone forget such an experience? On the other hand, perhaps memory loss was a common side effect when one came so close to death.

"Tell me," she repeated in a faint whisper.

"Don't you remember anything?"

She closed her eyes for a moment, then slowly shook her head. "Ate lunch, then nothing."

"You don't remember removing the mattress cover from your cot?"

She looked at me blankly. "What?" She tried to raise her head, but the exertion proved too much, and she fell back down with a thin little cry. I wondered if the disgrace of trying to take her own life had pushed the ordeal out of her mind. If so, I thought it best if it stayed forgotten, at least until she was stronger.

"Don't upset yourself, Madame Karpova. We can discuss this later. Right now, you should try to get some sleep."

"Have to know!"

"Shh. I'll be back in the morning. We can talk about it then."

"Now!" Her voice, still very hoarse, was growing stronger, as was her grip on my arm. Despite her recent brush with death, her dominant personality was reasserting itself. I sighed. Obviously, she was going to be just as upset if I didn't tell her.

"Very well," I said. "A guard found you hanging from the bars of your window, your mattress sheet tied around your neck. Everyone assumes you attempted suicide."

This time, she managed to pull herself nearly upright, staring at me in disbelief and mounting anger. "No!"

Concerned that she would further harm her throat by this outburst, I reached for the bottle of laudanum the police surgeon had left. But before I could remove the stopper, she once again took hold of my arm, causing me to drop the spoon onto the floor.

"No suicide!" she repeated.

"Please, Madame Karpova, don't excite yourself. I realize this is hard to take in, but that's why your throat is so painful, and why it's difficult for you to speak."

Without taking her eyes off me, she ran trembling fingers along her neck. When they reached the spot directly below her chin, she stopped. "Ah, *bolit*! Hurts." She stared at me with wide eyes. "You are telling truth?"

"Yes, I am." Is it possible, I wondered, that she *didn't* attempt suicide? But what other explanation could there be for what happened? Unless—Could it be that someone else tied those strips of sheet around her neck? "Tell me, Madame Karpova, what's the last thing you remember?"

She thought for a moment, then said in a breathy croak, "Eat lunch. Then sleepy—lay down to rest."

I considered this, but it made no sense. Even if she'd fallen asleep, surely she would have instantly awakened if someone had pulled her off the bed and tied the sheeting around her neck.

"Are you a particularly sound sleeper, Madame Karpova?"

"No," she whispered. "Light. Hear every sound."

Stranger and stranger, I thought. No one could sleep through something like that. Yet if she was telling the truth about not attempting suicide, then someone had managed to pull off a very challenging maneuver. I was struck by a sudden idea. "What did you have for lunch?"

"Jailer call it stew. And bread."

"Were you given something to drink?" I asked, pressing her for more information.

She nodded painfully. "Coffee—strong coffee."

"And it was after eating and drinking your coffee that you became sleepy?"

Again she nodded, but this time she did not attempt to speak.

Good Lord, I thought. That must be why she has no memory of what happened. Whoever did this probably drugged the stew, or, more likely, her coffee. Then, when she was unconscious, they set the stage to make it appear as if she'd committed suicide. I said none of this aloud, of course, but she seemed to come to the same realization herself.

"Who do this to me?"

"That's what I intend to find out." I took one of her hands in my own. It was very cold and still trembling.

"Before they . . . try again?" she whispered.

I wouldn't have put it so bluntly, but I saw no reason at this point not to be equally frank. "Yes."

She started to say something else but was stopped by a sudden fit of coughing. Pouring some laudanum into a spoon, I carefully guided it into her mouth.

"Shh, don't try to talk. An officer has been sent to get your daughter," I continued. "She should be here soon. And I'm going to see about having one of the guards keep an eye on you during the night."

She clutched at my hand. "But can we trust—"

"I think we can trust Cecil Vere," I told her reassuringly. "I'm sure he'll do everything possible to see that you're safe."

I waited until Yelena arrived, accompanied by the officer who had fetched her from the hotel. The poor child was nearly hysterical to find her mother in such a condition. It required all of my efforts, and some little time, before I could convince the girl that her mother would be all right. When she'd finally calmed down, I left her sitting by her mother's bedside, while I went in search of Cecil Vere. I was frustrated to find no sign of the jailer. When I spoke to Sergeant Jackson, he said Vere hadn't shown up that afternoon for his regular shift, nor had he sent word to the jail explaining his absence.

He listened dubiously when I told him my concern about my client's safety. According to the sergeant, he'd seen this sort of thing too many times to believe it was anything but a suicide attempt. In the end, I had to be satisfied with his assurance that he would look in on Madame Karpova regularly during the night. Which was fine, I thought, as long as Sergeant Jackson didn't turn out to be the killer.

Just to be on the safe side, I found the young jailer, Jimmy Wolf, and he readily agreed to watch Madame Karpova, as well. Finally satisfied that I had done everything I could to safeguard my client for that night at least, I wearily left the jail and boarded a horsecar for home.

The following morning, I was back at city jail by nine o'clock. To my surprise, Yelena had arrived a few minutes earlier. With her was Nicholas Bramwell, who motioned me aside as I passed through the antechamber.

"Please, I'd like a word with you before you go inside," he said quietly.

"What is it?" I asked, following the young man away from the guard's desk.

His handsome face was filled with anger and concern.

"Yelena is extremely distraught," he began. "I can't believe her mother could be so cruel. If she dies, that poor girl will be left in a strange country, with no one to look after her. You don't think Madame Karpova will try anything that foolish again, do you?"

I studied his face. "Mr. Bramwell, I hope you'll forgive me for asking such a personal question, but just how serious is your friendship with Yelena Karpova?"

He regarded me with an expression of such boyish charm and sincerity, I could understand how this man might sweep any woman off her feet, much less a vulnerable young girl like Yelena.

"Actually, I'm very fond of her, Miss Woolson, and I'm not ashamed to admit it."

"But your mother—"

"Ah, yes, my mother." His face took on a pained look. "She's been determined for some time that I marry Miss Radburn."

"It seems that her determination has born fruit, since the two of you are engaged."

"I'm afraid that's no longer the case," he said, feigning a regret I felt certain he didn't feel. "Aldora—er, Miss Radburn, I mean—decided to call off our engagement. Yesterday, as a matter of fact."

"Because of Yelena?"

"I'm afraid so." He sighed; then, as if making up his mind, he said, "Look here, it's no use trying to pretend that I'm sorry about breaking it off. It was never my idea to get married so soon after school in the first place. Miss Radburn is a wonderful woman—she would make any man a fine wife. I just—well, I'm simply not ready to settle down yet."

"What about Yelena? Have you explained this to her?"

Now he looked sheepish. "Not exactly. She's aware that I like her very much, but I haven't led her to believe I want to get married. She's just seventeen, Miss Woolson, far too young to think of marriage."

"I quite agree with you." I looked him in the eye. "I would hate to see that girl hurt, by you or by any other man. For her sake, Mr. Bramwell, be very certain that she understands your feelings and isn't looking for a commitment you're not prepared to make."

The way he smiled at me made me feel like a spinster schoolteacher I'd had many years ago. She'd been a severe, if well-meaning, woman, who never hesitated to voice her opinion, even when it had not been asked of her.

"Believe me, Miss Woolson," he said, "the last thing I would ever want to do is hurt Yelena."

I was about to impart a final bit of advice, when the jailer impatiently called out from the door leading to the cell block that he couldn't wait for me all day. With a final warning look at the young man, I turned and started down the corridor to Madame Karpova's cell.

My visit with my client was necessarily short. I was mainly concerned with seeing how she had weathered the night, and ensuring that she was being afforded adequate medical care and personal protection. To my relief, she informed me that she was feeling considerably better and that a nice man named Sergeant Jackson, had checked on her all night along with a jailer she didn't know.

When Yelena assured me that, because of her mother's poor

health, she was being allowed extended visitation privileges for the next day or two, I felt it safe to leave. Secretly, I guessed that the increased leniency stemmed more from the hope that Yelena might prevent her mother from any more suicide attempts than from concern for my client's health. Since our goals in this instance happened to coincide, I was happy enough to overlook the motivation.

Before I left the station, I entrusted a note in a sealed envelope to the guard at the front desk, addressed to Cecil Vere. In it, I requested that he keep a close eye on Madame Karpova when he came on duty later that afternoon. I have to admit I was becoming a bit worried that he still hadn't sent word to the jail explaining his absence. The guard was of the opinion that Vere had simply tied one on the day before and had been too hungover to make it in to work.

"He'll show up this afternoon," he assured me. "Always does. Good man is our Vere."

Walking to the nearest omnibus line, I boarded a horse-drawn streetcar and set off to see Mrs. Sechrest at Annjenett Fowler's home for abused women. I was utilizing public transportation as much as possible these days, so that I might adequately reimburse Eddie Cooper for his increased duties as my hack driver. I truly was beginning to rely on Eddie, not only because he was so dependable but also because of his unfailing enthusiasm and eagerness to do whatever was necessary to help in my investigations. I was also discovering that the boy possessed a very keen eye, a great advantage in my line of work, especially in those parts of town where I felt less than comfortable.

If Alexandra had not confided the location of the safe house, I would never have located it. Of course, the primary function of a safe house is to provide a hideaway where the women's abusers cannot find them. In this regard, the property Annjenett had chosen was perfect, being indistinguishable from its neighbors on the respectable middle-class street. The tiny bit of garden to either side of the stairs was neatly tended, and of course there was no sign posted anywhere on the house to announce its true function.

My knock was answered by a pretty young maid dressed in a plain black dress covered by a starched white apron. A small white cap perched atop a head of lovely brown hair, which had been pulled back into a neat bun at the nape of her neck.

Curtsying but failing to open the door so much as an inch wider, she politely requested my name and the nature of my business. Presenting my card, I assured the young woman that I was a friend of Mrs. Fowler, and asked to see her mistress if she were in. The maid nodded, promised to see if Mrs. Fowler was receiving, then softly closed the door, leaving me standing outside. It was opened again in a matter of minutes, and with a cry of delight, I was pulled into the arms of my old friend and very first client, Annjenett Fowler.

"My dear, dear Sarah!" she exclaimed, giving me a kiss on the cheek. "What an absolute delight to see you again." She flung the door open and beckoned me inside. "Please, come in. I'm sorry you were kept waiting at the door, but it's our policy to admit no one until we can vouch for the person's identity and the purpose of the visit.

I couldn't help but smile at her radiant face. It was a far cry from that of the pale, frightened woman who had sought my help at the beginning of the Nob Hill murders. Ever since then, Joseph Shepard had continued to insist that I had stolen Annjenett from beneath his nose. Since he and his firm had been doing almost nothing at that time to help the poor widow—whose husband had been brutally murdered several weeks earlier—I'd felt not the slightest modicum of guilt for stepping in to remedy the situation.

"A most sensible precaution," I said, taking a seat in the comfortable yet simply furnished parlor.

After requesting that the maid notify Mrs. Sechrest of my arrival, Annjenett asked her to please bring us coffee. She then leaned forward in her chair and begged me to tell her everything that had happened since our last meeting, which had been several months ago at her wedding to the talented and extremely handsome young actor Peter Fowler.

I spent a pleasant five or ten minutes giving her a capsulized version of leaving Joseph Shepard's firm and setting up my own law practice. Without revealing attorney-client confidences, I went on to tell her about Mrs. Sechrest's divorce and the upcoming hearing.

Her pretty face grew solemn. "Oh dear, that is what Alexandra most feared. Although I think she has suspected all along that her husband would challenge her for custody of the children." She shivered. "He is a very nasty man, Sarah. You should have seen the bullies he sent to kidnap their sons. They knocked Alexandra to the ground, picked up the boys, and tossed them into a waiting carriage. It all happened so quickly, the poor woman had no time to call for help."

"How did Luther Sechrest discover your location?"

"He hasn't. At least I sincerely hope he hasn't. His men grabbed the boys several blocks from here when their mother took them shopping for new shoes."

"At the very least, it sounds as if they've narrowed it down to your neighborhood. I suppose you have a plan in place should they identify the actual house."

She gave a long sigh. "I've done what I can, of course. Unfortunately, I don't dare notify the police, since two policemen's wives have taken shelter here, both of them viciously beaten by our so-called guardians of the law." She looked over my shoulder with a broad smile. "Ah, Alexandra, there you are."

Mrs. Sechrest silently entered the room, her uncertain smile revealing she was not sure if my being there heralded good news or bad. I wished with all my heart it was the former.

"Mrs. Sechrest, how nice to see you," I said, rising from the sofa and reaching out to take her hand.

"Miss Woolson, do you have new information about my case?" Somewhat warily, she took the seat next to mine on the sofa.

Annjenett Fowler stood. "You'll excuse me, won't you? I have duties I must attend to. I'll leave you to discuss Alexandra's case in private.

"Thank you, Mrs. Fowler," Alexandra said to her benefactor. "That's kind of you. Truly, I don't know what I would have done without you."

"Don't be ridiculous," Annjenett said, looking embarrassed. "I'm just grateful I had the wherewithal to help you and the others. Sarah, I'd like to say good-bye to you before you leave."

With a parting smile, Annjenett swept from the room. Both Alexandra and I watched her depart, a splendid figure in a light blue day gown and practical walking shoes.

"Now then, Sarah," my client said, bracing herself. "You might as well tell me the latest news and get it over with."

I smiled, but I feared it fell short of the reassuring gesture I had intended. I was pleased to see that the bruises on her face—the result of her last encounter with Luther Sechrest—had faded. Unfortunately, it was all too evident from her solemn, worried eyes that the emotional bruises he had inflicted were as raw as ever.

"Yes, I do bring news, Mrs. Sechrest." I tried to keep my voice calm, in a mostly futile effort to allay her fears. "I'm afraid your husband is determined to put the matter of child custody before a judge. The hearing will be held next Friday. It will be necessary for you to be present."

Alexandra deflated before my eyes like a balloon that had been pricked with a pin. "I see," she said weakly.

Next came the most difficult part of our meeting. Taking a bracing breath, I said, "Mrs. Sechrest, I need you to be brutally honest with me. What is the nature of your relationship with Mr. Gideon Manning?"

"Gideon Manning?" she repeated, obviously taken aback. "You mean my sons' tutor?"

"Yes, that's the gentleman I'm referring to."

"But I don't understand." Her direct gaze showed no sign of comprehension. "Why are you asking such a question? What can Mr. Manning have to do with any of this?"

"I'm sorry," I said, wishing it had not fallen to me to deliver such distressing news. "I'm afraid there's no tactful way to put this. Your husband is accusing you of having an affair with Mr. Manning."

Alexandra looked at me as if I'd slapped her across the face. "What? Is he mad? How can he believe such a thing?"

"Quite frankly, I don't know if he actually does believe it. He's simply using it as grounds for having you declared an unfit mother."

This time, she looked at me in stunned silence, then managed to say in a very small voice, "But he can't do that. Can he?"

"Before I answer, I must repeat my earlier question. How would you characterize your relationship with Mr. Manning?"

I watched the color drain from her face. "Oh, dear Lord, I truly never expected Luther to stoop so low." Her eyes pleaded with me to understand. "Mr. Manning and I were friends, Miss Woolson, nothing else. I know it sounds, well, unusual to be friends with your children's tutor, but we found that we had much in common. Our love of poetry, for one thing, and of art, particularly the Impressionists. Luther cares little for these pursuits. His life revolves around his work and his clubs, and the friends he spends most of his evenings with. He never took me to the theater, or to a concert, or, indeed, to an art museum. It was so wonderful to find someone who shared my interests."

"Are you telling me you spent time alone with Mr. Manning?" I tried not to let her see my growing alarm.

"Yes, I suppose I am," she admitted. "But I promise you that nothing improper occurred between us. Nothing!"

"Do you know of anyone who could substantiate that claim in

court? Someone who might have come into the room when you and Mr. Manning were together? Perhaps one of the children, or the servants?"

She shook her head, by now thoroughly frightened. "No, I can't think of anyone. Oh, Miss Woolson, surely you don't think—"

I sighed. "Unless we can refute this charge, I fear Mr. Sechrest will use it to good advantage during the custody hearing. But we cannot allow ourselves to become pessimistic. We must direct our energy into fighting these allegations."

She immediately brightened. "Yes, that is exactly what we must do."

"All right, then," I said in a businesslike tone. "How long has Mr. Manning been tutoring your sons?"

"Let me see. About two years, I should say."

"And where do you and the tutor usually meet?"

"Sometimes in the library, where we would read poetry, especially poems by Lord Byron, Shelley, and, of course, Keats. In good weather, we occasionally took walks in a park not far from our home." She looked up at me from beneath long lashes. "Once or twice, we—we met in Mr. Manning's sitting room." She gave a small flinch as she admitted this, realizing, no doubt, how damaging it sounded.

"And during those times, you were alone with Mr. Manning?"

"Yes," she replied softly, again lowering her eyes.

"How often did you meet with him, Mrs. Sechrest?"

"Not often. Perhaps once a week, sometimes twice. My husband keeps Mr. Manning quite busy. In addition to his tutoring responsibilities, he performs clerical duties for Luther, including monitoring, filing, and answering his correspondence—at least his business communications."

"I see. So would it be correct to say that you and Mr. Manning often met in the evening?"

She nodded.

"And how long did these meetings generally last?"

She looked at me, her lovely face pale. "Are all these questions really necessary, Miss Woolson?"

"I'm afraid they are. If for no other reason than to make you aware of what you will be up against in the courtroom. You must be prepared to answer these, and far more personal questions, during the custody portion of the hearings."

"*More* personal?" she asked with a stricken look. "Can you—can you give me an example of what I may expect?"

"For one thing, you will be asked to describe your feelings for Mr. Manning, and whether you were ever intimate with him." I studied her face carefully as I added, "Will you be able to answer truthfully that you were never on those terms with him?"

"No!" She looked flustered, and her face flushed bright pink. "I mean yes, I will be able to swear that we were never . . . intimate. Do you think they will believe me?"

"I honestly don't know. It depends upon so many factors—the judge, your husband's testimony, how convincingly you come across to the judge. It's really impossible to guess."

"But you don't think I have much of a chance, do you? I can see it written on your face." She had a sudden thought. "What about Gideon—Mr. Manning, I mean? Will he be asked to testify? If he corroborates my story, Miss Woolson, won't that—"

"I'm afraid it will do little to help you," I replied truthfully, determined that the time for false reassurances had passed. "It is, after all, in his best interests to deny the allegations. He would be ruined as a tutor if it was even rumored that he'd been intimate with the lady of the house. The judge will take his motivations into consideration."

"Yes," she said as the full and terrible reality of my statement became clear to her. "Yes, I can see that he would."

"I doubt we shall encounter any difficulties proving that your husband abused you throughout most of your marriage. But can you think of anything he's done that is outside the law? Perhaps in his business dealings, or in his personal life?"

She looked startled. "You mean do I know if he's committed a crime?"

"Yes, that's exactly what I mean. If we can prove he's engaged in some sort of illegal activity, it would cast doubt on his integrity, which, in turn, might cause the court to question his allegations against you."

Her face lit with sudden hope, only to be dashed a moment later. "Knowing Luther, I wouldn't be surprised to learn that he has not always been completely honest in his business dealings. Unfortunately, there's no way I can prove it." She was silent for several moments, then went on. "I don't know if this will help, but Luther regularly spends a good deal more money than he earns."

I drew in a deep breath at this first sign of an Achilles' heel. "Has Mr. Sechrest ever mentioned where this extra money comes from?" I asked.

She shook her head, looking ever more dejected. "The few times I got up the courage to ask him, he always told me that what he did with his money was no concern of mine." She buried her face in her hands. "Oh, Miss Woolson, I know you're doing the best you can, but I cannot believe we have a hope of winning. I just don't know how I'll be able to go on living without my children."

I gave her arm a reassuring squeeze, realizing as I did that I could feel the bones beneath her skin. Dear Lord, I thought, she is becoming thinner by the day! I would have given anything to promise that we had a legitimate chance of reclaiming her children. How incredibly sad that the best I could offer was a pat on the arm.

"Believe me, Mrs. Sechrest," I said, meaning every word, "I promise to do everything humanly possible to fight these charges. After that," I added more quietly, "we shall have to place the matter in God's hands."

CHAPTER FOURTEEN

R obert was waiting outside his boardinghouse when Eddie and I arrived in the brougham at five o'clock that afternoon to pick him up. He was hardly inside the carriage when I broke the news of Madame Karpova's so-called suicide attempt the day before, then went on to recount her surprising revelations to me the afternoon she'd been arrested for Dmitry's murder.

"So, you see, the two were actually lovers," I concluded, "not brother and sister, as they claimed."

Robert was silent for a moment, presumably digesting this new information. At length, he said soberly, "I see. In some ways that makes the situation even more tragic. Madame Karpova and Serkov had been together a long time. She must be regretting it terribly by now."

I gave him a hard stare. "What do you mean, regretting it now?"

He looked honestly surprised. "Why, sorry she killed him, of course. What else would I mean? Once she had time to think about what she'd done, she couldn't live with the guilt."

"Good Lord, Robert! You sound just like Lieutenant Ahern. Why is it you both automatically assume she tried to kill herself?"

"Come on now, Sarah, don't be naïve. At the very least, it demonstrates guilt by association, both in Moss's and Mrs. Reade's murders. Serkov must have threatened to expose her complicity in the crimes, and she stabbed him before he could go ahead with his betrayal."

"You know my feelings on that subject," I said as the carriage dipped going over a large pothole.

"Blast it all, it's not a matter of knowing your feelings; you've made them perfectly clear. It's trying to understand them that's giving me a headache. This is the only explanation that makes any sense."

"To you, perhaps, but not to me. I was there yesterday; you were not. Madame Karpova did not attempt to kill herself. She looked completely bewildered when I told her what had happened. I'm convinced someone drugged her coffee at lunch. Then, when she was unconscious, they set the stage to make it look as if she'd committed suicide."

I sat waiting for a response. None was forthcoming. Yet every inch of Robert's stiff body proclaimed his contempt for this declaration of my client's innocence.

"Robert, didn't you hear me?" I demanded, holding on to the seat as Eddie took a corner too fast and we nearly collided with a fruit vendor. We could still hear the merchant's curses from a block away. "Someone tried to murder her! If I can't find a way to keep her safe in that place, then the next time the killer tries, he may succeed."

"Of course I heard you," he responded at last. "I'm sure half of San Francisco heard you. That doesn't mean I agree."

"You are so frustrating! The blinders you wear are just as dense as the ones on Eddie's horse. For heaven's sake, open your eyes. If Madame Karpova was seen to have taken her own life out of guilt for killing Dmitry, the case would be closed. Three murders tied up in one neat package."

"Naturally, they'd be closed. They would have caught the

killers—of all three victims!" He looked at me, thoroughly exasperated. "Damn it all, Sarah, why do you always have to make everything so blasted complicated? Just once I'd like you to admit that the simplest answer is usually the correct one. Serkov murdered Moss because he was about to expose their little dog and pony show. He killed Mrs. Reade because she witnessed this murder. When he threatened to implicate his lover, she stabbed him to death. Now, what could be simpler than that?"

I held my tongue. Everything Robert said made logical sense; I was hard-pressed to say why I found his logic so difficult to accept. Mama had often chided me for being stubborn. She was probably right. On the other hand, there are times when one has to listen to one's instincts. Mine told me that Dmitry Serkov did not murder Darien Moss or Theodora Reade. Madame Karpova might be a charlatan, but I did not believe she was a cold-blooded killer. Since I lacked even a shred of evidence to support these feelings, however, I preferred to spend the remainder of the bumpy ride in uncomfortable silence rather than in verbal sparring, which neither of us would win.

We arrived at our destination, to find it teeming with carriages. I had completely forgotten that Saturday evening was the busiest night of the week at the Cliff House. Yet, even if I'd remembered, I wouldn't have wanted to put the trip off for even one more day. We'd simply have to do the best we could despite the crowd.

On this evening, I was truly able to appreciate the Cliff House in all its considerable glory. There it was, perched spectacularly high upon the cliff, the Pacific Ocean crashing upon the boulders below. The Seal Rocks, which had loomed up as sea monsters the night of the séance, could now be clearly seen, a peculiar arch in the largest one giving it a very picturesque appearance.

I had already given Eddie his instructions. After dropping us off at the front entrance, he was to park the brougham, then somehow make his way into the kitchen. I hadn't taken into account how hectic it would be, but Eddie had met the cook the night of the séance, and he was a clever lad. I still hoped he might learn something new that the cook had failed, or forgotten, to tell the police.

As the boy descended from his perch to assist me out of the brougham, I noticed one of his Rollo books had fallen from the driver's seat onto the gravel.

He picked it up, then looked at me a bit sheepishly. "Thought I might have a chance to read some," he said rather unconvincingly, especially when I could clearly see the latest copy of the *Police Gazette* tucked into the seat padding. Catching the direction of my gaze, Eddie quickly jumped back onto the carriage seat and clicked his horse toward the stables.

Robert had been assigned the task of investigating the dining room, in particular the door that had been hidden that night behind the Japanese screen. If Serkov did sneak back into the room during the séance, he would have had to use this door. I had a good idea where it led, but it was always best to be sure.

"What am I supposed to be looking for?" Robert asked as we made our way to the main entrance.

"Anything that strikes you as suspicious or out of place, or just plain odd." I sighed. "I'm sorry I can't be more specific, Robert. To be honest, I really don't know what we're looking for. Anything that might shed some light on the case."

He gave me a strange look before reaching out to open the door. "You know that I consider this trip to be a wild-goose chase. And you are without a doubt the most annoying, obstinate, headstrong person I've ever met, male or female. Once you agree to defend someone, you simply will not give up until you've turned over every rock, examined every insect crawling beneath it, and followed every possible lead, no matter how slim or improbable."

His broad sunburned face broke into an unexpected grin, which actually made him look quite handsome, in a rugged, slightly skewed sort of way. It's a shame he doesn't unbend and smile like this more often, I thought. I was surprised to find myself quite enjoying the effect it had on his overall appearance.

Gruffly, he cleared his throat. "Don't take this as a blanket approval of your tactics, Sarah, but if I'm ever unfortunate enough to get in trouble with the law, I want you to represent me."

Before I could respond to this startling and totally out-of-the-blue compliment, he opened the door and was nudging me inside. I caught a quick glance of his face before he walked off toward the dining room. He was actually blushing!

I decided to commence my part of the investigation in the saloon. Naturally, this area now looked very different from the way it had on the evening of the séance. Every table was full of raucous men, all of them drinking alcohol and smoking cigarettes, cigars, or, in a few cases, pipes. The smoke hung over the room like a dense and exceedingly pungent fog, making it difficult to draw breath without falling into a fit of coughing.

I was not surprised to count fewer than a dozen women in the room, most of them gaudily dressed, their faces flushed, their demeanor a bit giggly from consuming too much champagne. All of the women displayed a great deal of cleavage, and a great many were smoking cigarettes or small cigars. I trust I am not a prude; normally, I would not fault a woman for indulging in a behavior that is usually reserved for a man. Mimicking a habit, however, that must surely be every bit as unhealthy for women as it is for men appears to me not only foolish but sadly lacking in good female judgment. Under any other circumstance, I would have been more than happy to escape the noise and putrid air. As it was, I vowed to make my inspection as brief, albeit thorough, as possible.

Since, as I had stated to Robert, I had no real idea what I was looking for, I decided to start my search with an open door located on the opposite side of the room. As I made my way around men standing at the bar or carrying drinks to their tables, I became conscious that a number of male eyes were focused on me. Some grinned fatuously, while others studied me with open curiosity.

One particularly inebriated man approached me, waving a shot glass of whiskey, and, leering rudely, invited me to join him for, as he put it, "a horn or two." As I was attempting to maneuver around him, I was surprised, and I'm not too proud to admit, relieved, to spy a familiar face in the crowded room. It was Nicholas Bramwell.

Ignoring the stares and a few crude comments directed at me, I made my way over to his table. Nicholas sat with three other young men, all of them well groomed, sporting neatly tied cravats and wearing fashionable suits. Four top hats sat perched neatly on a hat tree beside the table. As I reached the group, all four men politely rose to their feet.

"Miss Woolson," Bramwell said, giving me a welcoming smile. "How very nice to see you. Have you come to dine? I hear that the halibut was freshly caught this morning and has been prepared in a delicate wine sauce." He looked behind me, as if searching for my companion. "Surely you haven't come all the way out to Land's End by yourself?"

"No, Mr. Campbell escorted me." I indicated that the young men should resume their seats.

Nicholas Bramwell remained standing and proceeded to introduce his companions. Two of his friends had also passed the California Bar examination within the past few months, and one was planning a career as a surgeon.

I politely declined to join their party, or allow them to buy me a sherry, explaining that Robert would be wondering where I'd gone off to.

"It's quite busy on a Saturday night, isn't it?" I said, raising my voice so as to be heard over the din. "I didn't realize the Cliff House had become so popular."

"Oh, yes," said the young man studying medicine. "It's become all the rage, especially on the weekend. I'm sorry to say it has also become greatly admired by tourists."

One of the new California attorneys nodded his head in agreement. "Yes. So much so that it's worth one's life to get a decent table in the dining room. We put our names in almost half an hour ago, and we're still waiting to be seated."

The other new lawyer, whom I suspected had already had rather too much to drink, laughed and raised his glass. "But who's complaining?" He looked at me. "Are you sure we can't get you a sherry, Miss Woolson? Or perhaps you'd prefer some champagne, or a flip?" Once again he raised his glass, and everyone at the table laughed. "The Cliff House makes the best flips in town."

"Thank you, but no," I replied. Flips, made with beer, rum, and sugar, were very popular these days. I'd tried one once, just to see what the fuss was about, and found the drink entirely too sweet, and a great deal too strong, for my taste.

Preparing to resume my inspection of the door to the rear of the saloon, I said to Nicholas, "Before I leave, Mr. Bramwell, would you please tell me how Miss Karpova is getting on? She was still quite upset when I left her with her mother earlier this afternoon." I purposefully did not mention *where* I had left them, not wanting to call attention to the fact that Yelena's mother was in jail.

For some reason, Nicholas's three friends seemed to find this statement exceedingly funny.

"Oh, oh, Nikki boy," said the boy who had had too much to drink. "The lady is asking about your little sweetheart."

One of the other young men began making the most unpleasant kissing sounds with his lips, while the third said, "Yes, do tell us all about her, Nikki boy."

Nicholas Bramwell's face turned brick red—whether from anger or embarrassment, I wasn't sure—and he took hold of my arm. "Let's move away from these b'hoys, Miss Woolson. I believe we can find a bit more privacy over there."

As he led me off to a small table that had just been vacated, one of the men called out, "Nikki, when are you going to take your little girlfriend out to meet Nancy? She'd get a real kick out of it." This comment propelled the young men into fresh fits of laughter, causing customers at nearby tables to give envious looks, as if they thought they were missing out on great fun. Was the Nancy they were referring to one of young Mr. Bramwell's special friends? If so,

I failed to see why it had elicited so much hilarity. I was about to ask him to explain the joke, then decided it was none of my concern.

"You'll have to excuse my friends, Miss Woolson," Nicholas said as we took seats at the new table. "They can become a trifle boorish after they've had a few drinks."

"It appears that your companions don't approve of your friendship with Yelena Karpova," I said. "Is that because they think she's the reason your fiancée broke off your engagement?"

"No, that's not it," he said, looking embarrassed. "Yelena told me the truth about her life, you see. She said she wanted no more lies between us. I'm ashamed to admit it, but my companions ridicule Yelena because she's a Gypsy. They think I'm risking my political future by befriending a Russian peasant. Please, Miss Woolson," he said, hurrying on as I started to speak, "don't judge them too harshly. They behave like this only when they're drinking. Sober, they're really quite decent fellows."

"I'm sure they are," I said, not quite truthfully. By now, I am sure you know my feelings on this subject. I have little patience with those who judge other people on the basis of their gender or skin color. This was not the time, however, to debate the inevitably volatile issue of prejudice, although I fairly itched to do so.

"Please, Mr. Bramwell, do tell me how Yelena is coping with all that has happened to her family over the last week or so."

Before he could reply, I was jostled from behind by a man who was decidedly feeling no pain, as the saying goes. As the unsteady patron had managed to knock my hat askew, he stopped and apologized, nearly asphyxiating me with his sour breath in the process.

As the man continued his somewhat wobbly journey to the bar, Nicholas shook his head and gave me a cheerless smile. "I believe you were asking about Yelena. Actually, she's been considerably upset, which is understandable under the circumstances. She's so alone now, you see, and in a strange country. I've tried to be supportive, but I can hardly take the place of her own family, especially her mother."

"No, of course not. Where is she staying now? Surely not alone in the hotel."

He smiled. "One of her mother's clients has graciously taken Yelena into her home. The woman has a daughter about the same age, so that's provided Yelena with some comfort. At least I hope it has."

There was a loud shatter of glass from an adjoining table, and a young woman gave a little scream as some of her escort's beer spilled onto her gown.

During the ensuing laughter as the man attempted to mop off the woman's bodice with his handkerchief, I took out my notebook and pencil and requested Nicholas to give me the name and address of the residence where Yelena was staying, so that I might reach the child if need be.

The young man's face looked suddenly weary, and for the first time I noticed dark smudges beneath his eyes. I wondered if he cared more for Yelena than he was willing to admit. "I don't know what she'll do if Madame Karpova is found guilty of killing Serkov. Not a very likable man, as far as I could tell, but he seemed to be very fond of Yelena, and, of course, Madame Karpova. In some ways, I suppose you might say that he was the only father Yelena ever knew. Poor girl, she's going to miss him. And now with her mother in jail—I just don't know."

"I promise you I'm doing everything possible to ensure that Madame Karpova is proved innocent, Mr. Bramwell," I reassured him. "In fact, that's why Mr. Campbell and I have come here tonight."

He looked surprised. "You think there's something the police missed in their investigation? But it's been over a week since it happened. Surely any evidence that wasn't discovered then would be gone by now."

"Yes, that very well may be," I told him honestly. "But we're attempting to reexamine the events of that night through fresh eyes. If we're fortunate, perhaps we'll find something that was overlooked during our initial shock over Darien Moss's death." I regarded him levelly. "What about you, Mr. Bramwell? Thinking back to that night, is there anything you forgot, or neglected to tell the police? Perhaps something you've since remembered?"

He was silent for several minutes, and I was pleased to see that he was taking the question seriously. "It doesn't matter if it seems inconsequential," I urged. "The smallest detail, even one that seems totally unrelated to the crime, may turn out to be of vital importance."

Nicholas shook his head, then was forced to raise his voice as several men at the bar began a noisy argument. "I wish I could help you, Miss Woolson, truly I do. I'd do anything to prove Yelena's mother innocent of this awful charge. But I can think of nothing I haven't already told the police."

He closed his eyes, as if reliving that terrible evening in his mind. "What remains most vivid in my memory is the expression on Yelena's face when the lightning flashed—you know, after the candle blew out. She looked absolutely terrified. I don't know, perhaps it was a sixth sense warning her that something horrible was about to happen. She'd witnessed so many of her mother's séances, yet she seemed to know this one would be different in some ghastly way." He smiled sheepishly. "Perhaps she's inherited some of her mother's psychic abilities. I understand it runs in the family."

"Yes," I agreed doubtfully. "There's always that possibility."

I looked over and saw Robert standing at the main saloon door, which led in from the front hall. "I must go now," I said, getting to my feet. "But I want to thank you for being honest with me, and for the comfort and companionship you've offered Yelena. As long as she doesn't form the wrong idea about your intentions toward her, I think your support will prove to be very good for her indeed."

Nicholas also stood. "I only wish I could have been of more help, Miss Woolson. Madame Karpova and Yelena are very fortunate to have you on their side. I've never before known a woman attorney, but I must say I'm impressed with the success you've achieved over this past year. I think Yelena's mother is in very good hands."

Thanking the young man, I took a moment to walk to the back of the room and peek through the door I had originally sought to investigate. I'd expected it might lead to the dining room, but I was mistaken. Instead, it led to two washrooms, one for ladies and one for gentlemen. While these were conveniently placed, considering the amount of alcohol being consumed in the saloon, I was disappointed that they provided no new insights into our investigation.

I joined Robert, hoping that he'd had better luck, but it seemed he had not. Moving away from the cacophony coming from the saloon, he led me down the hall to the entrance to the dining room.

"You were right about the door behind the screen," he said. "It leads into the kitchen. The kitchen itself has four doors, the one I just mentioned, one leading into the hall outside the saloon, one that goes down into the larder, and one that leads outside. I don't see how any of this helps us, though, except to substantiate your theory that Serkov used the entrance behind the screen to sneak back into the dining room during the séance."

A feeling of deep frustration settled upon me. Until then, I hadn't realized just how much I'd been counting on our visit to the Cliff House to reveal something useful. Why had I allowed myself that absurd hope? I wondered. No one was likely to remember anything helpful so long after the fact.

I had not counted on Eddie Cooper. Robert and I were about to go looking for the lad, when I noticed his eager face peering out at us from behind the Japanese screen. Caring not one iota that he was most inappropriately dressed for a dining establishment of this caliber, he strutted across the room, seemingly oblivious to the curious stares of the diners.

"I got Cook to remember somethin', Miss Sarah," he proudly announced. "It ain't much, but like you always say, sometimes it's the little things what count the most."

"What is it, Eddie?" I asked, unable to hide my excitement. "What has he remembered?"

The boy was practically bursting with pride. Looking from Robert back to me, he paused a moment intending, I suspected, to increase the suspense.

"Come on, boy," Robert said impatiently. "Out with it."

Eddie beamed. "You remember that bloke what attacked the Russian girl the night that Moss feller was done in?"

"Yes," Robert and I replied simultaneously.

"What about him?" Robert asked.

"Well, Cook says he seen a feller runnin' full chisel through the kitchen and out the back door. Said he knocked over a basket of spuds and never so much as picked one of 'em up."

"Did he see his face, Eddie?" I asked.

The boy screwed up his face as he thought about this. "No, I don't think so. He did say the bloke moved pretty frisky, like he had a herd of buffalo on his tail."

Robert and I looked at each other, probably thinking the same thing. Without a description of the villain's face, the running figure could have been any man at the séance, including Dmitry Serkov, although it was difficult to imagine the unwieldy man moving that quickly.

"You've done very well, Eddie," I told the boy. "Better than either of us, as a matter of fact. But we'll need to talk to the cook ourselves. There are one or two questions I'd like to ask him."

Eddie looked doubtful. "He's pretty busy right now, Miss Sarah. He warn't too happy to talk to me, but I kinda got in his face, if you know what I mean. In fact, he used some words I don't think you'd approve of."

"No, I probably wouldn't have approved. The important thing, though, is that you found out something new about the case. That was a fine piece of investigating."

I turned and whispered something to Robert, who surprised

me by replying that he'd taken care of that matter upon our arrival at the restaurant.

"The maître'd told me it wouldn't be too long now," Robert added quietly.

"I imagine you're hungry, Eddie," I said. "How would you like to have dinner here tonight?"

The lad's eyes grew large as saucers. "Here? With you and Mr. Campbell? I ain't never eaten in a fancy place like this before." He appeared so excited, I was afraid for a moment he might actually reach out and kiss me. I was surprised when that thought led to my almost wishing he would. "That would be a real frolic, Miss Sarah!"

"I assume that means you'd like to stay," Robert said, trying not to smile at the boy's eager face.

"Yes, sir, I truly would."

We were seated less than fifteen minutes later at the table Robert had requested by the window. Without discussing the matter, Robert and I automatically made sure that Eddie was given the seat facing out over the water and Seal Rocks below. The evening light was fading, but it was still possible to see the waves breaking below the cliff, as well as spot one or two ships offshore. Since it was an unseasonably warm evening, several windows had been left open, so we could hear as well as smell the ocean and all its sea life below.

Unlike our last visit, when we were beset by the worst storm of the season, now dozens of sea lions, otters, and California seals frolicked upon the rocks. One stellar sea lion was so huge, he seemed to tower over the rest of the mammals, proudly raising up on his front flippers as if to proclaim his sovereignty over the herd. Despite the serious business that had brought us to the Cliff House, I couldn't remember when I'd enjoyed such a wonderful evening. It was heartwarming to watch Eddie's delight as the monster bull barked and roared and laboriously pulled himself over even the highest rocks.

Dinner was excellent. I had taken Nicholas Bramwell's suggestion and ordered the halibut, while Robert and Eddie had steak.
There was but one uncomfortable moment, when I realized we
were sitting not far from where our table had been situated for the
séance. I experienced a moment's disquiet as I once again imagined
Darien Moss's limp body slumped in his chair, his neck dripping
blood onto his immaculate brown jacket. Fortunately, this disturbing vision was fleeting, thanks to Eddie's animated chatter. Even
when he was at his most annoying, it was virtually impossible to remain depressed when in Eddie Cooper's company.

After dinner, we managed to speak to the cook during a brief
lull in his food preparation. Chewing on the stub of an unlit cigar,
and barking orders to everyone employed in his kitchen—his voice
nearly as loud as the bull sea lion's, I thought—he merely reiterated
what Eddie had already told us.

A man dressed in a long black cape, with a black hat pulled low
over his face, had come running hell-to-split through his kitchen
and out the back door into the storm. Yes, he'd knocked over a basket of potatoes, as well as a pitcher of milk lying on a counter.
"Made a right mess of the place, too," the cook informed us. And
no, he hadn't been able to get a good look at the bounder's face.

"Do you remember if he had a beard?" I asked.

He thought about this, then said he didn't think so. But the
bloke had run through his kitchen so fast, he didn't think he'd care
to swear to that in court.

When asked why he hadn't reported this to the police, the cook
insisted it wasn't his business to do the foxes' work for them. Having said that, he turned his back to us and promptly went back to
his work.

Since Serkov's death had sidetracked me from telling Robert
about the extra copy I had made of the notes from Moss's diary, I
had Eddie drive to my home first, before taking Robert on to his
boardinghouse. Instructing the boy to wait with the carriage,
Robert and I went inside.

The house was surprisingly quiet. I had just decided that every-one must have retired for the night, when I saw a light coming from the back parlor. There, I found Samuel talking quietly with his friend George Lewis in front of a welcoming fire. My brother seemed unusually subdued, as did the police sergeant.

"There you are," he said as Robert and I joined them. After the usual courtesies had been observed, Robert and I took seats on the sofa. Before returning to his own chair, Samuel quietly closed the parlor door, explaining that he didn't want to wake the entire house.

"What's wrong, Samuel?" I asked. "I can tell by your face that something's happened."

"I'm not sure what we have to report will even concern you, Sarah," he said. "George and I decided we'd let you be the judge. I asked him to stay so that he could tell you about it himself."

"George, what is it?" I asked the policeman, my heart beating faster despite my brother's reassurance.

"A man's been killed, Miss Sarah. Fact is, he was a guard at city jail," George said. "And I know you've spent a good deal of time there lately. His body was found on the waterfront this morning. He'd been beaten to death and his body was thrown into an old shed. I'm sure that's why it took so long to find him. The coroner says he's been dead since sometime Thursday night."

"George," I said, my voice tight with growing fear. "Who was it? You still haven't told us the guard's name."

"It was Vere, Miss Sarah. The dead man's name was Cecil Vere."

CHAPTER FIFTEEN

I stared at George for several long moments. This was a development I could not possibly have foreseen—one, in fact, I could hardly believe. That nice man, so in love with his Annie, so full of life. How could he be gone—just like that? I remembered Celia saying she sensed a great evil at work here. In less than two weeks, Darien Moss, Theodora Reade, and Dmitry Serkov had been killed, Madame Karpova had been attacked, and now Cecil Vere was dead. I shivered. Who could have guessed she'd come so close to the truth?

"Sarah, are you all right?" Robert asked. "You've gone pale as a ghost."

I started to tell him not to be ridiculous, that I was fine, then realized that actually I wasn't. Despite the fire crackling in the hearth, my hands were icy cold, and I was a bit light-headed. I had known Cecil Vere for only a few days, yet I'd come to like the man.

"I'm all right, Robert. There have just been too many deaths lately." I felt another chill and folded my arms across my bosom.

Silently, Samuel rose and stoked the fire, although the room temperature had nothing to do with my discomfort. I was loath to admit it, but deep inside I was truly frightened.

"Do the police know how it happened?" I asked George. "Was Vere drinking, or in a fight?"

"Likely enough he was drinking, but it seems he was mainly on the waterfront to gamble. Must of won, too, because he was robbed and—well, you know the rest."

"Gambling?" I repeated. "But he was planning to be married. Remember, Robert? He told us that he and his Annie were saving every penny so they could rent an apartment and settle down together."

"No, I don't remember," Robert said. "But I can't see that it makes much difference. A man may claim to be saving his money, but if he sees a chance to double his stake on a roll of the dice, he's going to take it." Despite these seemingly unsympathetic words, the Scot looked subdued. "Poor bugger. I admit I rather liked the fellow."

"Yes," I agreed softly. "George, do you know if anyone's notified Mr. Vere's fiancée of his death."

The policeman shook his head, causing his hair to fall across his wide forehead, which made him look ten years younger. "We didn't even know he had one, Miss Sarah. You say her name was Annie? I'll speak to some of the other guards at the jail and see if anyone knows her surname."

Samuel looked at me quizzically. "What's wrong, Sarah? You seem pretty upset over a man you hardly knew."

"I know, Samuel. It just strikes me as all wrong. Vere was working hard to save up for his life with Annie. It's hard to believe he'd chance squandering his earnings so frivolously."

"It happens all the time," Robert put in. "There are secret, and not so secret, gamblers in the best of families. Besides, I can't see how Vere's death has anything to do with Dmitry Serkov or your case."

"I wonder," I said thoughtfully.

"What's that supposed to mean?" Robert asked, his tone daring me to find some sinister meaning behind what appeared to be a tragic, if all too common, crime.

"It's the strange way Vere behaved after Serkov's murder," I explained. "He was noticeably shaken, far more than I would have expected, especially over a prisoner he openly disliked. He kept blaming himself, saying it shouldn't have happened. I wondered at the time if perhaps he'd seen Serkov's killer but was too afraid to say anything."

George looked at me with interest. "Did you ask him about it?"

I nodded. "After what happened to Mrs. Reade, I felt I had to say something. But he denied seeing anyone."

"Did you believe him?" Samuel asked.

"You know, I'm not entirely sure that I did." I tried to remember my last conversation with the jailer. So much had happened since that afternoon, it actually felt like weeks had passed, rather than just a few days. And, of course, I'd been considerably upset over Serkov's death at the time; I might well have missed a word or a nuance I might otherwise have caught.

Robert shifted on the sofa next to me. "I think it's unlikely Vere saw anything. He was probably just feeling guilty because he was off putting his feet up when he should have been paying attention to his charges."

"Yes, Mr. Campbell," George said, "no doubt you're right. Vere was questioned by Lieutenant Ahern, and even by the captain himself. He claimed it must have been the sister who did the Russian in. I know it seems like a coincidence, Miss Sarah, but I just don't see how it could be connected to your client's death."

"Or Madame Karpova's attack?" I asked, feeling myself decidedly outnumbered.

There was a murmur among the three men. None of them met my eyes, but I knew they all believed Madame Karpova had killed Serkov, then attempted suicide out of guilt. It was not difficult to read from their expressions that they thought I was grasping at straws in an effort to save my client.

A log fell in the fire, and while Samuel rose to prod it back into position, Robert went outside to tell Eddie he was free to take the horse and carriage back to the stables. He and George had decided they would share a cab when it came time to leave, so there was no sense leaving the poor boy sitting out in the cold.

When Robert returned, Samuel resumed his seat and asked me if I'd had any luck translating Darien Moss's notes.

Realizing that further speculation about Cecil Vere's death would be futile, I gave a brief account of my trip to the public library.

"Mr. Ferrier thinks Moss's notes may be written in Coptic, which is used almost exclusively now in the Coptic Church's religious ceremonies. He promised to have the translations ready for me by Monday morning. I'll see that you receive a copy, George."

George thanked me, then added, "You know if that Ferrier fellow does a good job with the pages you gave him, I think I'll ask him to try his hand at the whole diary."

"Good," I said, wishing the police had thought to do this sooner. Lieutenant Ahern had seemed so convinced he had the killer in custody, he didn't bother to look beyond Serkov for possible suspects.

"Tell us about your visit to the Cliff House today," Samuel said, looking from Robert to me. I gave my colleague the opportunity to answer, but he deferred to me, explaining that since I'd been blessed with such a fertile imagination, I'd make a better story of it.

Ignoring this not so subtle jab, I duly related our visit that evening to the Cliff House, along with what little new information we'd managed to glean from the cook.

"Since the cook didn't see the person's face, it probably won't do you much good, George" I concluded. "But it does reinforce Yelena's account of someone attacking her in her room."

"Oh, we never doubted that, Miss Sarah," George said. "We found blood on that wire you spotted under her bed. I'll grant you it wasn't much, but enough for us to be pretty certain it was the weapon used on her neck."

"So, what's the official police explanation for the attack?" I asked.

"The department is convinced that Serkov's intended victim was not Miss Karpova, but Mrs. Reade," George replied. "He must have thought she'd seen him murder Moss, and decided to silence her. Unaware that Mrs. Reade's room had been changed with Miss Karpova's, he hid there until the girl arrived to retire for the night. As soon as he discovered his mistake, he ran from the room. Waiting his chance, he strangled the old lady in Washington Square."

Once again, I resisted the urge to protest this assumption of the killer's identity, knowing it would be useless. Instead, I asked my brother if he'd learned anything new about Darien Moss, or any of the others present at the séance.

"As a matter of fact, I have," he replied, looking pleased with himself. He pulled out his notebook and thumbed through the pages. "I'll start with Darien Moss, or Daoud Moussa, the name he was born with. If you remember, Sarah, I told you I thought his father had been some kind of minister? Well, it turns out he was a priest in the Coptic Church. Unlike the Catholic Church, which requires its priests to be celibate, the Coptic Church strongly urges its priests to marry. It was a tradition in the Moussa family for the eldest son of each generation to join the clergy.

"That is, until Daoud Moussa came along. It seems he dutifully entered the seminary—which is where he must have become so proficient in the Coptic language—but left barely two years later. After working at one or two newspapers, he moved to California and changed his name to Darien Moss. You pretty much know the rest. He became a reporter for the first *Morning Chronicle* in 1868, then was hired by the *Informer* in 1873, where he commenced a lucrative career terrorizing businessmen, politicians, and, of course, the cream of San Francisco society. The slightest whiff of a scandal, and he was on it like a flea on a dog."

Samuel went on to report that the Aherns were second-generation Americans, and that over the past twenty years Frank Ahern had earned a commendable reputation with the police department. Despite, he added with a wink in my direction, the lieutenant's habit of leaving the more physical assignments to his minions.

He'd found little that was new on Senator Percival Gaylord, who had started as an attorney at the Thompson and Fox law firm here in the city and was currently serving his fourth term in the state senate. It was widely known that he'd set his cap on becoming the next California governor, and that his chances of achieving this goal were excellent.

According to Samuel, Philippa Bramwell was pretty much what she appeared to be, the vain, ambitious, domineering wife of Edgar Bramwell, owner of Bramwell and Sons Construction Company. She was mother to Lyle Bramwell, who worked in the family business, and his younger brother, Nicholas, who had recently passed his bar exam.

"Here's an interesting, if irrelevant, bit of minutiae," he went on with a chuckle. "It seems Philippa Bramwell was born Lotty Chance on a corn farm in Kansas City, Missouri, the eldest girl in a family of twelve children. As a respected member of San Francisco society, she undoubtedly prefers not to advertise her humble lineage. But I doubt she'd go so far as to commit murder in order to keep it quiet."

Even I had to smile at the notion of the haughty Philippa Bramwell growing up on a Missouri corn farm. But I agreed with my brother that this was an unlikely motive for murder.

"After you told me Olga Karpova's story," Samuel went on, breaking into my thoughts, "I was able to trace some of Serkov's criminal history in Russia. According to my sources, he was one very nasty character." He checked his notes. "Ah, yes, it seems that Madame Karpova did spend four or five years in London, honing her psychic abilities with Madame Blavatsky."

We spent the next hour going over more or less the same territory, including everyone's whereabouts during the time Mrs. Reade had been killed. Since my companions remained convinced that Serkov was the villain, this discussion, predictably, went nowhere.

By the time everyone left, I felt, and undoubtedly looked, exhausted, a statement my dear brother did not hesitate to confirm. It had been a long, trying day, and I feared the following week would be equally taxing—but one, I fervently prayed, that would include no new murders!

Monday morning, I would pick up Mr. Ferrier's translations of Moss's diary notes, after which I hoped to speak to my brother Frederick about what he had been doing at the jail when Dmitry Serkov was killed.

As soon as George could locate Cecil Vere's fiancée, Annie, I would call upon the poor woman to offer my condolences and to see if she could shed any light on Vere's tragic death. Then, of course, I would have to prepare for Madame Karpova's arraignment, scheduled for Tuesday morning. And in less than a week, the Sechrest divorce hearing would begin.

Wearily, I climbed the stairs to my room, changed into my nightdress, and crawled gratefully beneath my bedclothes. I had time to say a brief prayer for the repose of Cecil Vere's soul before falling into a deep sleep.

As planned, first thing Monday morning, I visited the public library, where I discovered, to my delight, that Mr. Ferrier had indeed finished translating Moss's diary notes.

"I had a bit of trouble identifying the exact interpretation for one or two of the words," he said apologetically. "But I'm confident I have the nouns correct, and the general meaning of each sentence has been preserved to the best of my ability."

After thanking the librarian for all of his time and effort, I took a horsecar to the Central station, where George Lewis and I poured over Ferrier's notes.

Below the Coptic sentences I'd copied from Moss's diary were the recently completed translations. The first page read:

Iнформатіон фром [н̅. Тⲅε ⳍⲕⲑ ⲅⲟλ ⳍⲁⳍ
ⲛεⲱ ⲙⲓⳍⲧⲣεⳍⳍ. Ⳍεεⲛ тоⲅεтⳍεⲣ ⲁт Ελ
λορⲁλⲟ.

Information from #8. Sky god has new mistress. Seen together at El Dorado.

Βλⲁⲥⲕ λⲟⲩⲅλⲁⳍⳍ ⲱⲓφε ⳍⲁⳍ ⳍεⲥⲣεт
λⲟφεⲣ. [a̅i̅ ⳍⲁⲱ тⳍεⲙ тоⲅεтⳍεⲣ ⲁт
Uⲩⲣⲡⳍⲑⳍ .

Black Douglas's wife has secret lover. #10 saw them together at Murphy's.

Iнформатіон фром [ⲅ̅. Ⳡⲁⲛⲩⳍ ⳍεεⲛ ⲱⲓтⳍ
ⲛεⲱ ⲅεⲛтλεⲙⲁⲛ φⲣⲓεⲛλ ⲁт Nⲁⲛⲥⲑⳍ . Ⳍⳍⲟⲩλλ
ⲡⲩт εⲛλ то ⲡολⲓтⲓⲥⲁλ ⲁⳍⲡⲓⲣⲁтⲓⲟⲛⳍ.

Information from #3. Janus seen with new gentleman friend at Nancy's. Should put end to political aspirations.

Ⳍⳍεⲣε λⲓλ Nⲁⲡολεⲟⲛ ⳍⲩλλεⲛλⲑ ⲥⲟⲙε ⲩⲡ
ⲱⲓтⳍ ⲙⲟⲛεⲑ φⲟⲣ ⲛεⲱ ⳍⲟⲩⳍε ⲟⲛ Рⲩⳍⳍⲓⲁⲛ
ꙄⲓλλH

Where did Napoleon suddenly come up with money for new house on Russian Hill?

"Even though Moss wrote everything in Coptic, he still used a code for the people he was investigating," I said in frustration. "Or perhaps these are just nicknames he assigned to each of them."

"He must have really worried about another reporter stealing his stories," George commented, looking equally disappointed. "Why don't we read through these again and see if any of the entries ring a bell."

We had been at our task for only a few minutes when a young uniformed officer knocked and entered the room.

"Sorry to interrupt, sir," the man said, "but Lieutenant Ahern wants to see you in his office." He hesitated, then added, "*Immediately* is the way he put it, sir."

"Yes, Osborn. Tell the lieutenant I'm on my way." After the

young man left, George regretfully folded up the copy I'd given him of Moss's notes. "Sorry, Miss Sarah. I was hoping we could go over these together. I'd appreciate it if you'd write down the name of the librarian who did these translations and where he can be reached. I'm going to ask him to transcribe the rest of Moss's diary." He gave a rueful smile. "I know we don't agree on this, but I honestly believe Serkov was our man. Still, I think it would be as well to know what else the reporter was working on."

"I'm glad to hear that, George. It's one thing we can both agree on." I jotted down Ferrier's particulars and handed them to George. "Before you go, I'd like to know if you've been able to locate Cecil Vere's fiancée?"

"Yes. In fact, I broke the news of Mr. Vere's death to her yesterday." I read genuine regret in his intelligent brown eyes. "She took it very hard. Not that I can blame the poor girl. You were right when you said they were counting on getting married. A very sad state of affairs." He pulled a piece of paper from a pocket and gave it to me. Upon it was written Annie's full name and address. "I'd better go now. Lieutenant Ahern gets into a real lather when we're late."

"Thank you, George. Don't worry, I'll see myself out."

"And you'll tell me if you come up with any more ideas about the notes?"

"Yes, of course. I'll let you know right away."

It was nearing lunchtime as I exited the station, yet I was disinclined to put off my next errand even long enough to eat. Since my failure to speak to Frederick the previous week, my imagination had conjured up all sorts of reasons why he'd visited city jail the afternoon of Dmitry Serkov's death—none of them good. I could not stop worrying about what my brother might have become involved in. I would get no rest until I had asked him to his face.

Too impatient for public transportation, I hailed the first hansom cab to come along, then gave the driver my brother's Nob Hill address. It was not a long journey, but midday traffic was heavy and it was half an hour before we pulled up at our destination.

As usual, the front door was answered by Woodbury, who somberly informed me that he would see if Senator Woolson was in. Going along with the charade, I allowed him to lead me into the front parlor, where I was forced to wait a quarter of an hour before my brother joined me. He swept into the parlor, a sour expression on his broad face, and, without sitting down, regarded me with displeasure.

"These unannounced visits of yours are growing tiresome, Sarah. What is it now? And please keep it brief. I've been out of town the past several days and have important business awaiting my attention."

"I'm sure you do, Freddie," I answered. "But the matter I wish to discuss must take precedence, I'm afraid. It's of the utmost importance."

"For the love of heaven, Sarah, what are you babbling on about?" he asked brusquely. "What can possibly be that important?"

I was far too worried to mince words. "Why did you visit city jail last Thursday afternoon?"

Frederick's eyes widened in surprise, and I watched the color drain from his face. Of all the subjects he might have expected me to broach, this one had obviously not entered his mind. Even as he attempted to mask his distress, I knew my question had hit a nerve.

"What makes you think I was at the jail?" he countered, bringing his voice, and his expression, under control. "And even if I was, what possible business is it of yours? I am growing exceedingly weary of your incessant meddling, Sarah. It is a most unattractive trait in a woman. You'll never find a man willing to marry you if you—"

"Frederick, this is serious!" I said, cutting him off. "Please, sit down. We have to talk." I realized that this attack on me was my brother's attempt to draw attention from himself. It was an old ploy he'd long used on his younger siblings, particularly his little sister. This time, I would not be sidetracked.

"Yes, you are quite right," he said, taking a seat in the armchair across from mine. "It is high time we had a serious discussion. I have been meaning to speak to Papa again concerning your marital prospects."

"Frederick, this is about you, not me. You may be in grave trouble, and I need an honest answer. What were you doing at the jail last Thursday? Whom did you go there to see? And don't bother to deny that you were there, because your name is entered in the visitor book—in *your* handwriting."

"You are hysterical, Sarah, completely out of control. I have repeatedly told Father that—"

"Listen to me!" I all but shouted at him. "Don't you realize that a murder was committed in the jail at the very same time you were there?"

His face turned very red and he sat straight and stiff in his chair. "How dare you march into my home without an invitation and insist I answer your outlandish, not to mention extremely rude, questions. I am a good deal older than you, Sarah, and I am a state senator. I will not stand for this disrespect. Certainly not when it comes from an ill-mannered, opinionated female who behaves as though she has no breeding. You may be my sister, but you are a disgrace to the family!"

"What is going on in here? Why are you yelling, Frederick? You are setting a bad example for the servants, not to mention your own son."

My brother and I turned, to find Henrietta regarding us from the doorway, her brittle face scowling with displeasure.

"Sarah and I are just having a little chat," he said with an unconvincing smile. "It doesn't concern you, my dear. I'm sure you have other matters to attend to in preparation for Senator and Mrs. Gaylord's dinner party Saturday night."

"Nonsense, Frederick." Henrietta entered the room but did not take a seat. "Sarah, I am surprised to see you here again so soon after your last visit," she said, not bothering to mask her dislike for me. "Now, what are the two of you arguing about? You are disturbing the entire household."

"My dear, I assure you it is nothing," he insisted in a voice that had become disgustingly obsequious.

Why was Frederick so desperate to exclude Henrietta from our conversation? I wondered. Could it be that she had no more idea than I did what business took him to the jail last Thursday afternoon? I felt a wave of dread at the possible implications.

"I have simply been giving my sister some advice about her prospects for contracting a suitable marriage," he added, somewhat lamely, I thought, since Henrietta was well aware of my views regarding matrimony.

"Don't be ridiculous," my sister-in-law said matter-of-factly. "Who would possibly wish to marry a woman who possesses absolutely no sense of fashion, who displays a vulgar interest in politics, and, worse of all, who insists on competing in a man's world?"

"Thank you, Henrietta," I told her dryly. "Now, if you would please allow Frederick and me a little privacy, perhaps we can finish our conversation and I can be on my way."

"As attractive as that sounds, Sarah, I would prefer to know what you have said to my husband that has caused him to lose his temper."

I heard the clock strike the hour in another part of the house as she gathered her skirts behind her and took a seat on the sofa. "Now, for the final time, I demand to be told what this is all about."

My gaze went to Frederick, wondering how he planned to extricate himself from his wife's inquisition. The flush had drained from his face, and his left eye was twitching, as it often did when he was under stress.

"Henrietta, my dear, you are making far too much of this," he protested. "We were simply discussing—"

There was a knock on the parlor door, causing him to break off in mid-sentence.

"Yes?" Henrietta called out irritably.

The door opened and Woodbury entered the room. His lined,

exceedingly proper face was creased with concern and disapproval, as if he were about to introduce a vagrant off the street.

"I am sorry to interrupt you, madam, sir, but several, ah, gentlemen are here to see Mr. Woolson. I informed them you were presently occupied, but they refuse to withdraw and come back later. It seems they are members of the, er, the police, sir." The butler noticeably cringed as he uttered these words.

Frederick and Henrietta both looked at Woodbury as if he had taken leave of his senses. I felt as if I'd been suddenly drenched with a pail of ice water. I stared at my brother in undisguised dread, panicked that my warning for him had been delivered too late after all. Dear Lord, was my worst fear being realized?

"The police?" Frederick repeated, as if this word were foreign to his vocabulary. "Whatever for?"

"I cannot say, sir," Woodbury replied, striving to regain his customary unruffled composure. "They declined to state their business."

"Well then, I suppose you had better show them in." He looked nervously at Henrietta, then at me, his expression hardening, as if I had personally brought this dishonor upon himself and his family.

Several minutes later, Woodbury ushered Lieutenant Ahern into the parlor. To my surprise, he was followed by George Lewis and a second uniformed officer. Ahern seemed equally taken aback to see me sitting there. George looked profoundly uncomfortable and avoided meeting my eyes.

The icy knot in my stomach grew into near panic. I was certain the police had come to interrogate my brother about Dmitry Serkov's murder. Someone else had gone through the jail's visitor log and discovered his presence at the jail that afternoon. Now Frederick would be forced to explain why he'd been there— whom he had gone to visit. I had to speak to my brother first, prepare him before he was grilled by Lieutenant Ahern. In this state of arrogant indignation, who knew what my brother might say, and live to regret?

"Lieutenant Ahern," I said, rising from my chair. "If you have come here to question my brother, I should—"

Ahern held up a hand to silence me. "Please remain seated, Miss Woolson. This business will not take long. We will interview your brother down at the station."

"Surely that's not necessary," I protested. "You can speak to him just as easily here in his own home. There's no need to cause unnecessary embarrassment."

George Lewis cleared his throat nervously, while Ahern fixed me with an angry glare. "I'll thank you to stay out of this, Miss Woolson. We have not come here to question your brother, but to arrest him."

Frederick gasped, his eyes opened wide in shock. He seemed to be trying to speak, but no sound issued from his mouth.

Henrietta leapt off the sofa, her bony face bright with anger. "That is preposterous! It is—it is an outrage!" Her voice was shrill with righteous fury.

"I apologize for distressing you, Mrs. Woolson," Ahern replied without looking at her. His eyes remained riveted on Frederick, as if expecting him to bolt at any moment.

"Lieutenant," I cried out. "My brother never even met Dmitry Serkov. Why would he wish to—" Catching the expression on George Lewis's face, I broke off. He gave the slightest shake of his head, as if trying to warn me of something.

Lieutenant Ahern was regarding me in bewilderment. "Serkov?" he said. "What in the name of Mary and Joseph does Dmitry Serkov have to do with this?"

I stared back at him, equally confused. "But you said—"

Once again, I could see George was trying to send me a message, this time with his eyes. I was far too upset to play this game of charades! "If it has nothing to do with Mr. Serkov, Lieutenant Ahern, then why are you here?"

"If you can control that bloody tongue of yours for one damn minute," Ahern shot at me angrily, "then you'll find out, won't you?"

George Lewis looked at me with profound regret as he reluctantly followed Ahern across the room to stand in front of my brother. Frederick remained stock-still, as if frozen in shock. Apparently, he was as unable to move as he was to speak. The second uniformed policeman remained stolidly in front of the parlor door, having obviously been instructed to block any ill-considered attempt by my brother to escape.

"Senator Frederick Woolson," said Ahern in a somber voice. "I arrest you on the charge of accepting illegal bribes from Mr. Edgar Bramwell, and other contractors—as yet unnamed—and delivering payoffs to various public officials involved in the construction of the new City Hall building. You are advised that anything you say will be duly noted and may be used against you in a court of law."

CHAPTER SIXTEEN

Not surprisingly, Frederick's arrest threw the entire family into a turmoil. Henrietta was in hysterics as they led her husband away in the police wagon, and the moment the van was out of sight, she turned on me in a fury. As the result of some convoluted reasoning, it appeared my sister-in-law held me responsible for this outrage, mainly, I gathered, because I associated with known murderers and other criminal riffraff. My scandalous behavior was dishonoring the entire Woolson family, she accused, and had now directly led to Frederick's ruin. How, she wailed, would they ever again be able to hold up their heads in polite society?

Although thankfully no one at home blamed me for my brother's arrest, the news was greeted with incredulity and shock. Upon hearing that her eldest son had been taken to jail, Mama, who had never been prone to vapors, turned very white and came dangerously close to collapsing. It required our combined efforts to urge her to take a sleeping draft and retire to her bed.

As soon as Mama fell into a deep sleep, my grim-faced father hired a hansom and commanded the driver to take him to city jail.

As a county superior court judge, he would undoubtedly use his influence to arrange for a speedy arraignment and reasonable bail or, ideally, convince the magistrate to release my brother on his own recognizance. Frederick's heretofore-blameless record, as well as his position as a state senator, would work in his favor, assuring the court that he was a reputable citizen who presented a negligible flight risk. Inevitably, though, whether he waited in his home or at the jail, he would be called upon to account for his actions.

Since there was little I could do to aid my brother, at least in the matter of his arraignment and bail, I forced myself to go on with my scheduled duties. Madame Karpova's own arraignment the following morning went as expected. After pleading not guilty to the charge of murdering Dmitry Serkov, she was ordered to be held over for trial. I had already advised my client that, because the crime was a capital offense, the judge would almost certainly refuse to set bail. Even forewarned, Madame Karpova did not accept the verdict with dignity, or indeed with any degree of self-possession. After unleashing a string of what I took to be Russian profanities, it required two bailiffs to usher her from the room.

Before they could lead her through the door, she cried out at the magistrate, "You will regret this injustice, sir. I, Madame Karpova, see all, and your fate grows ever more imminent. You will not live out the week."

Judge Mortimer Raleigh's face grew dark. "Are you threatening me, madam?" he demanded, his voice equally acerbic.

"I reveal only what I see," she replied sonorously, her voice projecting into every corner of the courtroom. "Be prepared. Before many more days pass, you will stand before your Maker."

Handling her more forcefully, the two bailiffs hurriedly pulled Madame Karpova out of the chamber. The judge stared after her. Despite his stern expression, his ruddy face appeared considerably paler.

W hat made you tell Judge Raleigh he'd be dead before the week is out?" I asked Madame Karpova when we were back in her cell. "That is not going to earn you any friends in court."

She shrugged her slender shoulders. "I did not like him, but what I said about his death is true. I, Madame Karpova, see these things, even when I have no wish to."

Despite my better judgment, I couldn't resist asking her how she did it.

"I know it in many ways. Sometimes, I simply sense it. More often, I see those who are about to die on their deathbeds, or in their coffins. A few times, I have observed a person surrounded by a bright light, and I know then they are about to cross over. It upsets most people to know they are near death, so I rarely tell them unless they ask."

"But you told Judge Raleigh because you didn't like him."

"He acts like he is God, sitting on his bench passing judgment on those he considers beneath him." She gave me a sidelong glance. "I wanted him to know that he is only human, no better than the rest of us."

Her expression suddenly changed. She no longer looked confident, as she invariably did when discussing her psychic powers. In its place, I saw anxiety reflected in her dark eyes, and I knew she was thinking of her daughter.

I spent the next half hour attempting to reassure her that Yelena was in good hands. I had paid a visit to the home where the girl was temporarily residing, so I was able to reassure her mother that she was receiving excellent care and comfort through this difficult time.

When I was finally able to take leave of my client, I did not immediately exit the jail. Instead, I sought out Sergeant Jackson and the young guard, Jimmy Wolf, who had become my allies since the attack on Madame Karpova. Both promised to continue looking out for her safety. After a good deal of persuasion, they agreed to let it be known throughout the jail that they were tasting her food before it was delivered to her cell. This last concession, I suspect, had been granted more to appease me than because they believed anyone would attempt to drug her meals. I cared little about their motivation, as long as they faithfully carried out my instructions.

Later, while riding on the omnibus, I examined the address George had given me for Cecil Vere's fiancée. It seemed that Annie Fitzgerald lived in a women's boardinghouse south of Market Street, or South of the Slot, as it was more commonly known. It was a respectable neighborhood, mainly comprised of young immigrants, typically employed in unskilled or semiskilled jobs.

Annie Fitzgerald was a small, thin young woman with brownish red hair tied back in a bun and light blue eyes that were puffy and red-rimmed from crying. She was dressed in a plain but neat brown dress with few frills. I judged her to be in her early twenties, and probably quite pretty when not suffering the pain of such a devastating loss.

Upon hearing that I'd been acquainted with her Cecil, Miss Fitzgerald readily invited me inside the simply furnished room that was her home. Directing me to take a seat in the more comfortable of the room's two chairs, she hurried to a small table containing a spirit lamp and the necessary accoutrements to brew tea.

"I was about to brew meself a cup," she said, carefully measuring out a rounded tablespoon of tea leaves. "It won't take but a minute."

When we were seated facing each other in our chairs, and sipping remarkably good tea, Annie Fitzgerald begged me to tell her everything I knew about her Cecil, including how we had met and when I had last seen him.

I explained that I was an attorney—eliciting the usual surprise and incredulity—then went on to relate how I had met Cecil while visiting one of my clients at the jail.

"He was invariably cheerful and polite," I said, helping myself to one of the home-baked cookies Annie had served on a clean but slightly chipped plate. "He spoke of you often, as well as your upcoming marriage. He was very much in love with you, Miss Fitzgerald."

She smiled even as tears formed in her eyes. "That was my Cecil, always goin' on about me and about our weddin'. Settlin' down and startin' a family was all he ever talked about, the silly ol' bear." Tears streamed down her face, but she seemed not to notice. "I still can't believe he's gone."

I was struck with sudden guilt, knowing I had handled this badly. I realized I should never have mentioned Vere's continual talk about his fiancée, or their plans to marry. Her wound was still too raw to discuss such intimate emotions, especially with a stranger. I had merely succeeded in causing the poor woman fresh pain. When would I ever learn to think before I spoke?

As if reading my thoughts, Annie said, "I'm sorry to break down like this, Miss Woolson. Can't seem to help it, no matter how hard I try. But I'm awful glad you told me what my Cecil said about how much he loved me an' all."

She rose from her seat to fetch a handkerchief from a bureau drawer. "His death"—she swallowed hard, fighting off fresh tears—"his death came just when everythin' was beginnin' to look so good fer us. He'd come into some money workin' extra shifts at the jail, and haulin' crates down at the docks on his day off." She managed a weak smile. "He was so excited. Said he figured it was enough money fer us to get married right away, instead of havin' to wait another year, like we'd planned. Then the next day—sweet Jesus, the very next day, he was gone!"

Tears spilled, unchecked, down her cheeks. Feeling helpless to comfort the poor woman, I said gently, "I'm so sorry, Miss Fitzgerald. I should never have bothered you at a time like this."

"No, Miss Woolson!" she exclaimed, raising her tear-stained face. "You were good to my Cecil. You comin' here like this—a lady like you carin' enough to come see me—that means more than I ken say."

She blew her nose into the neatly mended cloth, then met my eyes with unsettling directness. "I told you this 'cause I wanted you to know why I'll never believe that he was gamblin' the night he was killed. I swear, as God is my witness, he weren't no gambler. He used to say he worked too hard fer him to be handin' his money over to some card sharp." The glistening blue eyes bore into mine, as if begging me to believe her. "Whatever Cecil was doin' at the waterfront that night, Miss Woolson, it weren't to gamble!"

"I believe you, Annie. I don't think Cecil would have touched your savings, especially not to gamble."

I hesitated, not wishing to add to her distress. But the question had to be asked. "Annie, can you tell me if Cecil acted troubled or worried after Mr. Serkov was murdered at the jail last Thursday afternoon? Did he mention what happened?"

"He told me everythin' that went on down at that jail," she said with obvious pride. "Cecil didn't much like that Russki fellow. Said he complained about everythin' and caused trouble with the other prisoners. Still an' all, now you mention it, he did seem upset the day the bloke got hisself stabbed. Said he had to think things through before he could talk to me about it, which weren't usual."

She gave an unexpected smile. "He cheered up some when he told me about the extra money he'd come into, though. I don't know how he was able to save up so much cash, but that were my Cecil, always full of surprises." Tears once again began rolling down her wan cheeks. "That was the last time I ever seen him, Miss Woolson."

I waited patiently while she fought to regain control of her emotions. Sensing her embarrassment, I said, "Crying isn't a bad thing, Annie. It isn't good to keep all your grief bottled up inside. It won't bring back your Cecil, but it will allow the healing to begin."

"It's real kind of you to say that, Miss Woolson, but I don't know as I'll ever heal. Cecil was me life. I can't think how I'm gonna get along without him."

I leaned forward and patted her hand, the skin rough and reddened by years of hard labor. "I can't begin to understand your grief, Annie. But I know from others that, with time, the healing does begin. You'll never forget Cecil, nor should you. But eventually you'll find the strength to go on living without him. He would want you to do that, my dear."

She attempted another smile, then, giving a loud sniff, returned to the bureau and pulled another clean handkerchief from the drawer. "I know yer right, Miss Woolson, but it's just hard right now. I got a sister who's comin' in from Modesto tonight to stay with me fer a while. It'll do me no end of good havin' her here."

When I took my leave some minutes later, I was grateful to know that Annie would soon have her sister to help her bear the shock and grief. Still, the visit had drained me, and I broke down and hired a passing cab to take me to Annjenett Fowler's home for abused women.

During the ride, I reflected on what Annie had said about Cecil not being a gambler, an assertion which served to reinforce my own sense of the man. But what had really caught my attention was her statement that he'd recently earned enough extra money to move their wedding up a full year. I hadn't wanted to challenge the poor girl over the source of this sudden windfall, but it did cause me to wonder. That seemed a great deal of money to make in such a short time, especially when he had only one day off a week in order to pick up extra work. Could it have been payoff money to keep silent about Serkov's death? I wondered. If so, why had Vere been murdered? Did the real killer not trust Cecil to remain quiet about what he'd seen?

When my cab reached Annjenett's safe house, I was forced to put the matter aside, at least for the time being. The same young maid answered my ring, only this time she recognized me and I was shown directly to the parlor. Alexandra Sechrest joined me almost immediately, looking even more worried and drawn than the last time I'd visited.

We spent several minutes speaking of inconsequential matters, after which I inquired if she could give me Gideon Manning's address. "I must meet the man before the hearing," I explained. "There are several questions I wish to ask him."

A shadow crossed Alexandra Sechrest's lovely face. "I would prefer not to involve him in this, but I suppose that's impossible."

"I'm afraid it is." I placed little hope on the answer to my next question, but it was necessary to ask. "Please, Mrs. Sechrest, have you been able to think of anyone who might verify the platonic nature of your friendship with Mr. Manning?"

Alexandra Sechrest let her breath out slowly. "I've given it a great deal of consideration since our last meeting," she said at last. "Unfortunately, I cannot think of anyone who could swear to it in a court of law." She tilted up her chin in an unexpected gesture of defiance. "Unless someone never leaves your side, is with you every day and night for weeks on end, how could they possibly swear to such a thing?"

"They couldn't, of course."

She gave a dry little laugh. "The thing I find most absurd about my husband's accusation is that he has engaged in countless extramarital affairs. He no longer makes much of an effort to be discreet." The laugh turned into a half sob. "Yet no one takes the slightest interest in *his* infidelity. It is so terribly unjust!"

Not trusting myself to get started on a subject that rankled the very core of my being, I merely stated that I agreed and let it go at that—for the moment.

Alexandra was studying my face, as if trying to gauge my thoughts. All the while, she betrayed her nerves by twisting and untwisting the long, slender fingers that lay in her lap.

"Miss Woolson, I beg you to tell me the truth. What will happen to my sons if Luther convinces the judge that I'm an unfit mother?"

I considered how best to answer this question. I preferred that my client enter the courtroom on Friday feeling positive about her prospects. On the other hand, she would have to be prepared for the worse, which, at this juncture, appeared the most likely culmination of the case. In the end, I decided that only the truth would serve.

"I fear they'll be sent to live with their father," I said, forcing myself to go on even as I observed the anguish on her face. "Your husband has enlisted the services of a very competent attorney, who will seize upon any opportunity to win his case. You must realize, Mrs. Sechrest, that the most damaging accusation a man can make against his wife in a custody battle is that she is immoral. I can think of no court that would give such a woman custody of her children, especially two boys over the age of seven."

She sank back into her chair, appearing suddenly exhausted and drained of hope. Clearly, she had not allowed herself to truly contemplate the idea that she might permanently lose her sons.

"Dear Lord," she said in a very faint voice. "What are we to do?"

Now that Mrs. Sechrest was aware of the worst that could happen, it was time to rekindle at least a small flame of hope. I infused my voice with purpose and resolve.

"We will start by questioning Gideon Manning. Until this past week, he was in your husband's employ, whereas you've been out of the house for more than a month. We can only hope that he is privy to, or perhaps has overheard, some of your husband's plans. We must also learn what Mr. Manning will say if he is called upon to testify during the hearing."

"Surely Luther wouldn't call Gideon to testify on his behalf," she said, looking askance.

"No, but *we* certainly will. That's one of the reasons I must speak to him. It's important to determine what kind of witness he'll make on the stand." I drew out my notebook and began jotting down notes. "I must also visit your neighbor, the woman who took you in last week after Mr. Sechrest's attack. What was her name again?"

"Mrs. Jane Hardy," she said. "She is a widow."

"Yes, I'll make a point of speaking to her. Also, have you talked to your sister yet? You said she saw some of the bruises your husband inflicted."

"I've spoken to her, but she's reluctant to appear as a witness. She's concerned about our mother and the effect this will have on our family's reputation." She lowered her eyes. "There has never been a divorce in our family. Mama is of the opinion that I did not try hard enough to make it work. She's of the old school, which does not believe in airing one's dirty linen in public, no matter the provocation."

"I see," I said, although in truth I found it hard to countenance a mother who would prefer her daughter to remain in an abusive marriage rather than to lose face in the community. "The question is, Will your sister stand up for you despite her misgivings?"

"I think—well, at least I hope she will," she replied, looking uncertain. "I know she believes I should have my boys. And she and my mother have never cared much for Luther. Yes," she pronounced with more conviction. "I will ensure that she appears on my behalf."

We spent the next half hour going over our strategy for the divorce hearing, after which I caught a brougham to the address Alexandra had given me for her boys' former tutor. It was not Gideon Manning's residence, but his brother's house in the Mission District. Since Manning had been a live-in tutor at the Sechrest home for the past two years, Alexandra thought he might have gone there until he could find a place of his own.

I was in luck. A pretty young woman with thick brown hair braided about her head answered the door. She looked a bit fatigued as she attempted to balance a fidgety baby boy of about ten or eleven months on her right hip, but she still managed a broad smile. "Yes, miss? Can I help you?"

Giving her my name, I explained that I was representing Mrs. Sechrest in her divorce and would like to speak to Mr. Gideon Manning. After a moment's hesitation, and a curious look that traveled from my hat to my boots, she threw open the door and invited me inside.

It was a small house, simply furnished, but neat and clean. There was a homemade hooked rug in the hallway, and several pictures hanging on the walls looked to have been painted by a talented amateur. I could hear the sound of a slightly older child playing with a barking dog somewhere upstairs.

"I'm Loretta Manning," she told me. "Gideon is my husband's younger brother. He's been staying with us for the past week." She shifted the plump, wriggling baby to her other hip, then said, "I think Gideon is upstairs in his room. If you'll please wait in the parlor, I'll tell him he has a visitor."

Thanking her, I made my way into the room she had indicated. The parlor boasted a comfortable-looking sofa and several armchairs, a well-stocked bookcase, and a pianoforte located in the recess of a large bay window. The fireplace mantel contained a matched set of pewter candlesticks and several family photographs, including one of two small boys, the baby I had just seen and a boy of about three, probably the one I could hear running around upstairs. A mending basket lay on the floor beside one of the chairs, and a book had been left open, facedown, on an end table, as if the reader had been suddenly interrupted. It was a friendly, cozy room, one that the family actually used, rather than reserving it for the sole purpose of receiving guests.

I had been waiting only a few minutes when a tall, clean-shaven young man wearing dark-rimmed glasses and a rather inexpensive, although presentable, brown woolen suit joined me. He had a full head of sandy blond hair, an angular but pleasant face, and very penetrating dark brown eyes, which regarded me quizzically.

"Good afternoon, Miss Woolson, I am Gideon Manning," he said, coming over to shake my hand. "My sister-in-law mentioned that you're representing Mrs. Sechrest's interests in her divorce petition."

Returning the young man's handshake, I said, "Yes, Mr. Manning. That's why I've come to see you this afternoon. I apologize if the questions I must ask appear overly candid, but the circumstances leave me no choice."

The unemployed tutor regarded me seriously. "I understand, Miss Woolson. I wish to do everything I can to help Mrs. Sechrest."

"I'm relieved to hear that, Mr. Manning." I reached into my briefcase and pulled out my notebook. Obtaining his permission to jot down any pertinent facts concerning the case, I said, "Now then, I understand you were recently dismissed as tutor for Mrs. Sechrest's two young sons by her husband, Luther Sechrest."

The young man sank into the chair opposite me, his expression grim. "Yes, I was." Once again he studied me, as if trying to judge how much he might safely confide. At last, he seemed to make up his mind. "Has Mrs. Sechrest mentioned the reason for my dismissal?"

"Yes, actually she has," I said. "I understand Mr. Sechrest has accused you of carrying on an improper relationship with his wife."

"That's exactly what he inferred." His voice betrayed anger and a sense of injustice. "I assure you it's not true. Not one word of it! I cannot understand a man who would slander his wife in such a despicable manner, especially when he himself is so untrue to his marriage vows. Of course, for men, it's different," he added with a note of derision, unwittingly echoing Mrs. Sechrest's recent sentiments. "They're judged by an entirely different set of standards than their wives. Still, it's unforgivable to put those poor boys through such an ordeal."

"I quite agree, Mr. Manning. That's why I'm determined to do everything in my power to ensure that those children are returned to their mother, and that these slanderous allegations are proved to be completely without merit."

"I pray that you will succeed, Miss Woolson. Mrs. Sechrest is a loving, dedicated mother. Unfortunately, quite the opposite is true of her husband. During my two years service in their home, I observed little indication that Luther Sechrest cares one whit about those boys. He leaves the house before they're up in the morning and returns home long after they've been put to bed at night. I'm convinced he's merely using those children as weapons against his wife."

"Sadly, that's often the case in divorce actions," I said unhappily. "When one or both parents use their offspring as bargaining chips, or to achieve a power advantage over the other, it's the children who suffer." I glanced down at my notes, primarily to regain my composure. The welfare of children caught in the middle of a rancorous divorce contest was a cause I hoped one day to address.

A child's raucous laughter came from upstairs, followed by a dog barking in excitement.

Gideon Manning smiled affectionately. "My three-year-old nephew, Simon," he explained. "He and his dog, Muffin, can get carried away at times. Soon little Lenny will start to walk, and I shudder to think of the bedlam my brother and sister-in-law will be forced to endure."

His expression belied his words; he looked as if he were describing a slice of paradise, the life, perhaps, he envisioned for himself one day.

Almost regretfully, I went back to the task at hand. "Have you ever known Mr. Sechrest to use corporal punishment on his children?"

"No, I can't say that I have." His face grew hot with justifiable anger. "He seems to have reserved that particular hell for his wife. Have you seen her bruises, Miss Woolson? Only a cowardly brute would sink to such depths of depravity."

"What about his job, Mr. Manning?" I continued, not allowing myself to be sidetracked by yet another issue close to my heart. "I understand he's employed as foreman at the Leighton Mining Company?"

"That's his official title, but for all intents and purposes, he runs the company. Mr. Leighton is in his eighties now and has no children, so he depends on Sechrest to make all but the most important business decisions. There's talk that he may leave the plant to Luther when he dies, but that's mainly conjecture. I've never met Mr. Leighton personally."

"What does the company do?" I asked, honestly curious.

He smiled a little sadly. "Ironically, the boys asked me that very question several weeks before Mr. Sechrest terminated my services. They seem to have a very sketchy idea of their father's responsibilities at the plant." His eyes took on a distant look, as if he were reliving that lesson with the children, and perhaps others. Then, with a sigh, he explained. "Leighton Mining works with limestone shipped in from various West Coast quarries. Depending upon how it's processed, it has any number of uses, including the manufacture of paper, glass, soap, textiles, and concrete, to name just a few. Chiefly, though, it's used in construction. In fact, many train stations, banks, and office buildings here in the Bay Area are made primarily of limestone."

"How interesting," I said, realizing that my knowledge of this industry was more limited than I'd realized. "Mrs. Sechrest tells me that you provided services for her husband other than tutoring the children. Is that correct?"

He gave a wry chuckle. "Let me put it to you this way. Mr. Sechrest made certain I earned every cent of my salary. When I wasn't busy with the boys, I did his accounts, along with a good deal of his correspondence." He leaned forward in his chair. "Frankly, I think Mr. Sechrest is marginally illiterate. He can read at an elementary level, and do simple sums, but I suspect that's the extent of his abilities. Not that the man is stupid. Actually, he's exceedingly clever, if not exactly intellectual, if you take my meaning."

"Yes, I do," I said thoughtfully. "Given his limited education, how does he manage to run Mr. Leighton's company?"

"Evidently, Mr. Leighton employs an accountant who takes

care of the company's finances, and of course an attorney reads and approves all of the firm's contracts. And as I say, Sechrest is a clever man. He always makes certain to have someone on hand to help him if he runs into a problem, even if that person doesn't realize exactly how he's being used."

I phrased my next question carefully. "Did you ever come across anything that might be interpreted as . . . illegal?"

He looked surprised. "It's uncanny you should ask me that, Miss Woolson. Actually, it's a question I've often asked myself. Of course I was hardly privy to all of Mr. Sechrest's business affairs, but a few things struck me as strange."

"What sort of things?" I asked, allowing myself a faint ray of hope.

"Well, I'm almost certain he kept a second set of books. Mind you, I have no proof, although one day I did get a look at an open account book on Mr. Sechrest's desk. I was surprised, because, you see, the official account ledger was in my hand at the time. That and the way he hurried to cover up the book convinced me he was up to no good. I also wondered at the way Sechrest smirked whenever he mentioned the company books to his friends. They always laughed, as if he'd just told them a good joke."

"But you never actually saw anything incriminating on paper?" I asked, trying not to reveal my disappointment. If I were to have a chance of nullifying Sechrest's accusations against his wife, I'd have to bring more than hearsay or speculation into the courtroom.

He started to shake his head, then seemed to remember something. "Now that I think about it, he also dictated some rather strange letters to me."

"Oh? In what way were they strange?"

"They seemed to contain information about recent shipments. The problem was, they weren't addressed to any of the company's usual clients, although some went to very highly placed men. And the details were often sketchy. For instance, there was never a proper order number, nor a list of what products had been shipped.

And they were written cryptically, and not on the company letter-head."

"Did Mr. Sechrest retain copies of these letters?"

"I'm not sure if he kept them, but I always made a duplicate. He usually put them in the bottom drawer of his desk, which is locked, or in the wall safe in his study."

"A safe? Do you have any idea what he keeps there?"

"I'm afraid not. I wasn't even aware of its existence until I happened to enter the study one day when it was open. Naturally, I've never examined its contents."

I didn't say it aloud, but I would have given a pretty penny to see the contents of that safe. Unfortunately, no judge would issue a warrant to search a man's private safe just because his wife's attorney hoped to find ammunition to use against him in a divorce case.

"Oh, there's one more thing. Because I occasionally made entries into the account book, I had a fairly good idea what Sechrest earned managing Leighton Mining. I found it curious that he regularly spent well in excess of his salary."

I sat up straighter. "Mrs. Sechrest mentioned that, as well. Have you any idea how he earns so much extra money?"

"I have no idea." He gave a bitter laugh. "As I said, I wondered more than once about Mr. Sechrest's business ethics."

"Will you please do me a favor, Mr. Manning?"

"Yes, of course. I'll do anything to help Mrs. Sechrest."

"That's good of you. What I'd like is a list of all the people you remember writing to for Mr. Sechrest. Hopefully, they'll lead us closer to the source of this mysterious money Mr. Sechrest earned."

His eyes lit up with hope. "I never thought of that, Miss Woolson. I promise to get to work on it right away."

"Excellent." I handed him my business card so that he would know where to reach me, then put aside my notebook. "My last question is very important, Mr. Manning. In fact, it's central to Mrs. Sechrest's case. She mentioned that you and she occasionally spent time alone together, either in the house or taking long walks in the park."

His face flushed. "Yes, we did. We were pleased to discover that we shared a great many interests in common."

"So Mrs. Sechrest told me. The problem, of course, is finding witnesses willing to swear that an innocent friendship is all you shared."

He turned an even darker shade of red. "You're very blunt, Miss Woolson. I've stated that I am prepared to testify on Mrs. Sechrest's behalf."

"Which, in the end, will come down to your word against Mr. Sechrest's. I do not mean this as a slur on your profession, or your integrity, Mr. Manning; however, Luther Sechrest is not only the boys' father but their sole provider, as well as a prominent member of the community. That carries tremendous weight in a child-custody hearing."

"In other words, they'll believe him over me."

"Once again, I apologize for speaking so directly, but your actions with Mrs. Sechrest were exceedingly ill-advised. It is, as you pointed out, a double standard. However, the fact remains that even the hint of a scandal will almost certainly cost any woman the custody of her children."

"Then what are we to do? I swear we did nothing improper. Mrs. Sechrest is a wonderful mother, and a virtuous, lovely woman. The boys miss her horribly. It would be monstrously unfair if the court gave those children to her husband. He—he hardly knows they exist!"

"You're right, Mr. Manning," I replied, feeling the same sense of helplessness. "It would indeed be monstrously unfair."

CHAPTER SEVENTEEN

I t was nearly five o'clock by the time I arrived at my office from the Mission District. Wearily, I unlocked my door and, taking off my wrap, collapsed into the chair behind my desk. It had been a tiring day and, all in all, a frustrating one, as well. Frederick was in all probability still in jail, Madame Karpova had been denied bail and had been returned to her cell, and Cecil Vere's murder was being treated as a sad but all-too-common waterfront tragedy. To top it off, I could think of no way to prove Alexandra Sechrest innocent of the adultery charges her husband had leveled against her.

I had just rested my head back against the chair and closed my eyes when the sound of a man's voice almost caused me to jump out of my skin.

"So, you're finally back."

"Samuel!" I cried, spying his grinning face in the doorway to the back room. "Don't sneak up on me like that."

"Sorry, little sister," he said, placing a cup of hot tea in front of me. "But you shouldn't hand out keys to your office if you don't expect visitors."

"I expect visitors to announce themselves and not pop out at me like a jack-in-the-box." I placed both of my hands around the cup in an effort to warm them. "However, I do approve of visitors who serve me refreshments."

"Don't mention it." He sat in the chair across from my desk. "You look worn out. What have you been up to all day?"

"First, give me an update on Frederick. Has Papa been able to get him out of jail yet?"

Samuel's smile faded. "Unfortunately, no. Although he managed to have his arraignment hearing set for tomorrow afternoon."

"Good heavens! Two days and nights in jail. I wonder how Freddie's handling it?"

"Not well, according to Papa. He's proclaiming his outrage to anyone within hearing distance. And his innocence, of course." Despite his glib response, Samuel looked worried. "I'm afraid Father's got his work cut out for him."

He took a sip of his tea, then placed the cup in its saucer on the desk. "All right," he said, obviously trying to lighten the heavy mood that had settled upon us. "It's your turn, little sister. Tell me about your day."

Starting with Madame Karpova's hearing that morning, I went on to describe my visit with Annie Fitzgerald, and the stop I'd made to see Mrs. Sechrest at Annjenett Fowler's safe house.

"Gideon Manning seems like a nice young man," I said, completing my narrative with the Sechrest's ex-tutor. "Clearly he's in love with Alexandra, but I'm not sure he even realizes it yet."

"If the judge in the divorce hearing picks up on that, it isn't going to help your client."

"I know. Yet I have no choice but to call him as a witness. I believe Alexandra and Mr. Manning when they say they did nothing improper. I'm not sure either of them could tell a lie if their lives depended on it."

"So, as it stands, Mrs. Sechrest will most likely lose her children."

"I'm afraid so. Unless I can somehow pull a miracle out of my hat by Friday."

Samuel's reply was cut off by a knock on the door. Before either of us could answer, Eddie bounded into the room, closely followed by Robert.

"I was comin' for my readin' lesson when I met Mr. Campbell outside." The boy beamed at the sight of my brother. "How are ya, Mr. Samuel? Did you bring any more of them *Police Gazette*s with you? I'm learnin' an awful lot from 'em."

"Eddie, I thought we had an agreement," I said. "Once you finish your Rollo books, I'll let you read *Tom Sawyer*. It's far superior to that awful rag Samuel gives you."

Eddie did not appear convinced, but he wisely chose not to argue the point. While Samuel retired to the back room to brew more tea, Robert sank into the room's only other chair.

"Where have you been all day?" he asked. "I came by twice this afternoon, but no one was here."

Since I had no wish to discuss the Sechrest case with counsel for the opposition, I evaded his question by asking why he'd wanted to see me.

"I heard about your brother's arrest," he told me as Samuel reappeared carrying another cup of tea. "What makes the police think Frederick's involved in the mess over the new City Hall project?"

"That's what we'd like to know," Samuel said before I could answer. "Freddie has any number of faults, but taking bribes isn't one of them. I'm convinced he's been set up."

"By whom?" I asked. "And why? If you're right, they couldn't have found a more unlikely candidate."

"You and I know that," said Samuel. "But whoever's behind this obviously feels he can get away with it."

"Have you seen Frederick yet?" I asked my brother.

"For a few minutes earlier this afternoon. Papa was in and out of the jail most of the day. Fortunately, he isn't hearing a case in county supreme court until tomorrow afternoon, so he's made Frederick his number-one priority."

"I can't think of anyone I'd rather have on my side than your father," Robert said with genuine respect. "Oh, by the way, I also came by earlier to see if you'd picked up the Coptic translations."

The translations! In all the excitement, I'd completely forgotten about them. Opening my briefcase, I pulled out the notes Mr. Ferrier had given me the previous day and spread them out on my desk.

"The translation itself appears excellent," I said. "The problem is that all the names are written in code, so even in English, it's difficult to make out who Moss was referring to."

Ⲓⲛϥⲟⲣⲙⲁⲧⲓⲟⲛ ϥⲣⲟⲙ [ⲏ̄. Ⲧⲅⲉ ⲩⲕⲑ ⲅⲟⲗ ⲅⲁⲩ
ⲛⲉⲱ ⲙⲓⲩⲧⲣⲉⲩⲩ. Ⲩ̄ⲉⲉⲛ ⲧⲟⲅⲉⲧⲅⲉⲣ ⲁⲧ Ⲉⲗ Ⲗⲟⲣⲁⲗⲟ.

Information from #8. Sky god has new mistress. Seen together at El Dorado.

Ⲃⲗⲁⲥⲕ Ⲗⲟⲩⲅⲗⲁⲩⲩ ⲱⲓϥⲉ ⲅⲁⲩ ⲩⲉⲥⲣⲉⲧ
Ⲗⲟϥⲉⲣ. [ⲁ̄ⲓ ⲩⲁⲱ ⲧⲅⲉⲙ ⲧⲟⲅⲉⲧⲅⲉⲣ ⲁⲧ Ⲩⲣⲡⲅⲑⲩ.

Black Douglas's wife has secret lover. #10 saw them together at Murphy's.

Ⲓⲛϥⲟⲣⲙⲁⲧⲓⲟⲛ ϥⲣⲟⲙ [ⲅ̄. Ⲭⲁⲛⲩⲩ ⲩⲉⲉⲛ ⲱⲓⲧⲅ
ⲛⲉⲱ ⲅⲉⲛⲧⲗⲉⲙⲁⲛ ϥⲣⲓⲉⲛⲗ ⲁⲧ Ⲛⲁⲛⲥⲑⲩ. Ⲩ̄ⲅⲟⲩⲗⲗ
ⲡⲩⲧ ⲉⲛⲗ ⲧⲟ ⲡⲟⲗⲓⲧⲓⲥⲁⲗ ⲁⲩⲡⲓⲣⲁⲧⲓⲟⲛⲩ.

Information from #3. Janus seen with new gentleman friend at Nancy's. Should put end to political aspirations.

Ⲩ̄ⲅⲉⲣⲉ Ⲗⲓⲗ Ⲛⲁⲡⲟⲗⲉⲟⲛ ⲩⲩⲗⲗⲉⲛⲗⲑ ⲥⲟⲙⲉ ⲩⲡ
ⲱⲓⲧⲅ ⲙⲟⲛⲉⲑ ϥⲟⲣ ⲛⲉⲱ ⲅⲟⲩⲩⲉ ⲟⲛ Ⲣⲩⲩⲩⲓⲁⲛ Ⲥⲓⲗⲗⲏ

Where did Napoleon suddenly come up with money for new house on Russian Hill?

"I see what you mean," Robert said at length. "First, he writes in Coptic, then assigns everyone a nickname. I assume the numbers signify one of his spies."

"Of whom it seems he had many," Samuel put in dryly.

"Sky god, Black Douglas, Janus, and Napoleon?" Robert mused. "And ten to twelve more on the other pages. Where do we begin?"

"With sky god," I replied. "Although I haven't the vaguest idea whom that might refer to."

Eddie piped up from his seat on the windowsill. "Sky god? I know who that is. I read all about that sky god feller in the *Police Gazette*."

"The *Police Gazette*?" The three of us said in unison.

Robert gave the boy a sidelong look. "What in Sam Hill is he going on about?"

"Wait a minute, Mr. Campbell. I'll show you." Eddie thumbed quickly through the well-worn pages of his current copy of the *Police Gazette*—which by now he probably could have recited by heart—stopping when he came to a grizzly picture of a man holding a knife over a very gory body. "See, here it is." He squinted at the newsprint, then began reading aloud. "It says, 'Like Horus, the Egyp—Egyp—' "

"Egyptian," I said, helping him with the unfamiliar word.

"Yeah, that's it, Egyptian. 'Like Horus, the Egyptian sky god, Ruther—' "

"Rutherford," I prompted.

Eddie shook his head quizzically. "That's a dang funny name, ain't it? Beats all what some folks will name their kids. Anyway, it goes on, 'Like Horus, the Egyptian sky god, Rutherford Mills of Los Angles, Cali—California, slayed the man who murdered his father.' There," he declared proudly. "Told ya I'd read all about that sky god bloke."

"Eddie, that's wonderful!" I said in genuine amazement. Without thinking, I planted an impromptu kiss on the lad's forehead, causing his face to turn bright red. "I think you're onto something."

"Very good, my boy," Samuel seconded, much to Eddie's delight. With a wink, he handed Eddie the latest copy of the *Police Gazette*. Grinning broadly, Eddie accepted it as if he'd just been given a priceless jewel.

"Thanks, Mr. Samuel. See you tomorrow, Miss Sarah. Wish I

could stay and help you with them other fellers, but I gotta finish my fares for the day." Tucking the paper beneath his arm, he threw open the door and flew down the stairs.

I shook my head at my brother, but really, what could I have said? Even I had to admit that the boy's reading skills were improving at a remarkable pace, no little thanks to that disgusting tabloid.

To my chagrin, I realized the two men were regarding me with broad grins. "Now then," I said briskly, getting back to the task at hand. "Who could Horus refer to?"

"Hmmm," Samuel said, "there's Horus Duncan, who owns the bookstore on Gough Street, but since he's well over seventy, I doubt he's our man. Then there's Horus Belcher, the fishmonger. No, that can't be right, either."

"Wait a minute," Robert said, breaking in. "I'll wager Moss is referring to Horus Spellman, the banker. Although I can't think that his having a mistress would sell many newspaper copies. Now if Moss found a banker in this city who *didn't* have a mistress, that might rate a front-page headline!"

We spent the next hour going over the three and a half sheets of Coptic translations. Of course it was all guesswork, but I was fairly sure we were on the right track. After some discussion, we decided that Black Douglas very likely referred to Kendal Douglas, a member of the city's Board of Supervisors, and that Napoleon might be Fulton Bragg, the new fire chief. Bragg was a small, pushy, overbearing man who did, in fact, slightly resemble the fallen emperor. It was also rumored that he had political aspirations, which extended well beyond the fire department.

Oddly, as we went over the pages, I kept thinking there was something I was missing, some point about the case that I should remember. The harder I tried to focus on it, however, the more elusive it became. I finally decided to put it out of my mind, reasoning that it would come back to me when I least expected, as such things often do. Besides, I told myself, it probably wasn't that important—which, of course, turned out to be yet another of my famous last words!

We found ourselves stymied when we came to Janus, and someone Moss called "the Parrot." In the end, however, we'd identified with some degree of certainty the deputy mayor, two more bankers, a city council member, and the city assessor.

By far the most disturbing entry we found concerned Frederick and Bramwell's construction company. The notation implied that the two of them had arranged a series of kickbacks having to do with the new City Hall project.

After reading the item over a second time, Samuel gave a low whistle. "What in God's name has Frederick blundered into? Do you suppose Moss passed his suspicions on to the police before he died, or did Lieutenant Ahern figure it out on his own? That is, if there really is anything to figure out."

"How was this bribery scheme supposed to have worked?" asked Robert.

"The police maintain that Frederick colluded with Bramwell to overcharge the city for work that was never done, and for materials that were never used," Samuel explained. "He was supposedly paid handsomely for turning a blind eye to the fraud."

"Can they prove these allegations?" Robert asked.

"Ahern gave a statement earlier today claiming they can," Samuel replied. "For one thing, a number of unexplained checks have been deposited in Frederick's bank account over the past few weeks, money far in excess of what he earns as a state senator. Ahern also says he has witnesses who saw money exchange hands, with Frederick as the recipient."

"Good heavens!" I exclaimed, shocked that the evidence against Frederick was so extensive. "Why didn't you tell me this before?"

My brother shrugged. "What good would it have done? There's nothing you can do about it. Besides, you have more than enough to deal with at the moment."

"That may be, but you should know by now that I'd prefer to be told the truth than to be cosseted like a child." Much as I disliked Samuel playing the protective big brother, I realized this was not the time to fuss over injured pride. "I'm sorry, Samuel," I said in a calmer voice, then asked, "Do we know yet whom Frederick visited at the jail that afternoon?"

Soberly, Samuel nodded. "Here's where everything goes from bad to disastrous. According to Freddie, he went there to visit a man by the name of Joseph Vincenzo, who'd been arrested for drunkenness and creating a public disturbance." He paused and looked each of us in the eye. "The problem is, Vincenzo works as a wagoner for Bramwell Construction."

Robert and I stared at Samuel, shocked. When neither of us spoke, Samuel went on.

"Freddie maintains Vincenzo sent a friend to his Van Ness office, claiming he'd been arrested for a crime he didn't commit." His voice grew sardonic. "As one of Frederick's constituents, he wanted his senator to post bond for him."

"That's complete balderdash!" Robert exclaimed. "Who ever heard of asking a senator to bail you out of jail?"

"My thoughts exactly," Samuel agreed. "Freddie swears that all he did was talk to Vincenzo, put up bail, and leave. He insists the man gave him nothing, much less an envelope containing money."

"What about the bank deposits?" I asked.

Samuel held up both hands in a gesture of helplessness. "Frederick says he knows nothing whatsoever about them.

"And Vincenzo?" Robert asked. "What does he have to say about all this?"

Samuel looked weary, and suddenly older than his thirty years. I could see that he was considerably more worried about our elder brother than he was prepared to admit.

"He claims Frederick showed up to collect his latest bribe payment. According to him, they were supposed to meet at some park or other. But when Vincenzo got arrested for being drunk and disorderly, he sent a friend to tell Freddie to pick up his money at the jail instead."

"Very clever," I said. "By sending a messenger, he avoided leaving a paper trail. But wouldn't the guards have discovered the money when they booked Vincenzo into jail?"

"Not necessarily," Samuel replied. "When it comes to drunks and vagrants, I don't think they search too carefully. Mainly, they look for bottles and weapons, I should imagine."

Robert's expression was grim. "Has Edgar Bramwell been taken into custody along with your brother?"

"According to George, they arrested him early this morning."

I felt dreadful. Frederick and I rarely, if ever, saw eye to eye on any subject, yet he was my brother. It was painful to think of him sitting alone in a jail cell. The reputation he and Henrietta had worked so painstakingly to cultivate was unraveling faster than a snagged sweater.

"Do you think the judge will grant Frederick bail tomorrow?" I asked.

"I don't see why not." Samuel's lips drew together in a tight, humorless smile. "He's a state senator, the son of a judge, has a family, and owns a home on Nob Hill. Hardly a flight risk." He sighed. "Anyway, there's not much more we can do until Freddie decides to tell us the truth about Vincenzo."

With less enthusiasm than before, we turned our attention back to Mr. Ferrier's translations. The final page listed what we took to be bribe money paid to Darien Moss in order to prevent certain stories from appearing in his column. Although his blackmail victims were again referred to by their nicknames, the sums had not been disguised.

"Now I understand how Moss was able to afford a suite of rooms at the Baldwin Hotel," I said, my mind boggling at the amount of payoff he had collected over the past ten years.

Robert grunted in disgust. "And those who could not, or would not, pay could look forward to seeing their names blackened in Moss's newspaper."

"You've got to hand it to him," Samuel said. "Moss had it arranged so that no matter what happened, he couldn't lose."

"Until someone throttled him," I put in dryly.

"Someone? You mean Serkov, don't you?" Robert said. "We've been over this a hundred times. Serkov killed Moss and Mrs. Reade, and Madame Karpova killed Serkov. Now, once and for all, there's an end to it!"

"If that's true," I asked with deliberate calm, "then who murdered Cecil Vere? Madame Karpova can't have done it, since she was locked up in a jail cell."

Both men stared at me, but Robert was the first to speak. "Damn it all, Sarah, what makes you think Cecil Vere's death has anything to do with this? Vere was beaten to death after a night of drinking and gambling on the waterfront. I'm not saying it isn't tragic, but it happens all the time."

"What if he wasn't gambling?" I put in. "Or even drinking, for that matter? Suppose he went to the waterfront to meet someone, and that person killed him."

Robert rolled his eyes; Samuel regarded me speculatively. "You're basing that on what his fiancée told you today?"

Realizing I had not told Robert of my visit with Vere's fiancée, I described my conversation with Annie Fitzgerald.

"So, she swears Vere didn't gamble," Robert said, dismissing my story with a wave of his hand. "Be realistic, Sarah. How many men tell their wives or lady friends the truth when they go out at night? I feel genuinely sorry for the poor woman, but it just means she didn't know her fiancé as well as she thought she did."

"I'm convinced she was telling the truth," I argued, angry to hear a defensive tone in my voice. "The night he died, Cecil told her he'd earned a substantial amount of money working overtime and at odd jobs. Enough money, I might add, to move their wedding up by an entire year."

"Sarah thinks that's why Vere was murdered," Samuel put in. "Because he saw whoever killed Serkov."

"Not Madame Karpova, the *real* killer," I added, pleased to see that we finally had Robert's full attention. "Vere said he was making his usual rounds when it happened. But what if he was actually near Serkov's cell when the murderer struck?"

Robert looked skeptical. "Was Vere the sort of man who would allow an innocent woman to hang for a crime he knew someone else had committed?"

"If he were paid enough, he might," Samuel said, then had another thought. "What about Madame Karpova? If she really didn't attempt suicide, then who attacked her? And why?"

"That's what I'd like to know," I said. "If you accept that someone other than Olga Karpova killed Serkov, the answer is obvious: It was a deliberate setup. The killer frames Madame Karpova for Serkov's murder, then makes it appear she's taken her own life out of guilt and remorse. All the loose ends neatly tied up, and the real killer gets off scot-free."

"The only problem with that theory," Samuel said, "is that, other than Serkov, we have no likely candidates for the first two murders. Or have you been struck by a sudden brainstorm, little sister?"

Before I could answer, Robert stirred and spoke, almost as if he were thinking out loud. "If we rule out the women—and considering the way the victims were killed, I think we must—we're left with Senator Gaylord, Nicholas Bramwell, and Lieutenant Ahern."

"None of whom were at the jail the afternoon Dmitry Serkov was stabbed," I reluctantly admitted.

Robert smiled faintly. "Which points the finger of guilt directly back to Madame Karpova. Nothing else makes sense."

"We need to know more about Joseph Vincenzo," I said, ignoring

Robert. "Samuel, can you do a little digging and see if he has a police record, and how long he's worked for Bramwell's construction company?"

Samuel nodded. "I'd already planned on doing that."

I looked over my notes. "Oh, and if you happen to see George, will you ask him if Mr. Ferrier has had time to translate the rest of Moss's diary? It might be helpful to read the entire book, not just the few pages I copied."

At my brother's ready agreement, I said, "That's about it, then," and started picking up the papers scattered about my desk. "I don't know about you, but I'm more than ready to call it a day."

Since Samuel was going directly to the Bohemian Club and Robert to his lodgings, which were in the same general direction, they decided to share a hansom. I opted to catch an omnibus to Rincon Hill.

"Are you ready for the Sechrest hearing?" Robert asked as we followed Samuel down the stairs to the street.

It still angered me to think of Robert defending that bully Luther Sechrest, and I certainly had no desire to discuss the case with him beforehand. "You'll have to wait and find that out on Friday, won't you?"

He took my arm, halting my descent. "Sarah, can't you talk some sense into your client? So much embarrassment and pain could be avoided if Mrs. Sechrest would simply accept her husband's offer and return home. She should do it for her children's sake, if not for herself."

"Robert, listen to me. My client would dearly love to avoid dragging her boys through what is sure to be an ugly battle. But if she agrees to her husband's terms, they might end up with no mother at all. Luther Sechrest is a dangerous man, especially when he's drunk, which is nearly every night. The wounds he's inflicted upon his wife are real. I've seen them for myself. I cannot in all good conscience advise her to return to such a brute."

Two bright patches of color appeared in Robert's ruddy cheeks, and his back stiffened as he stood on the stair directly above my own. I was forced to bend my head back in a most uncomfortable fashion in order to meet his eyes.

"How can you be sure she didn't fake those bruises to gain sympathy?" he challenged. "An inability to tell the truth is one of the symptoms of her condition. You aren't doing the poor woman any favors by offering her ill-informed advice. Give in gracefully, and the family may yet be whole again."

A sound escaped my throat, half laugh and half a cry of frustration. "This is useless, Robert. Luther Sechrest must be a very persuasive man to take you in so completely. I honestly thought you were more discerning than that." Turning around, I continued down the stairs, calling over my shoulder, "As I said before, I'll see you in court."

Samuel started to say something to me at the foot of the stairs, then had second thoughts when he observed the tension between Robert and me. Instead, the two men silently started toward the nearest intersection, where they might more easily find an unengaged cab.

I was about to start the short walk to the horsecar line, when I saw my downstairs neighbor, Fanny Goodman, beckoning to me from the front door of her shop. Curious, I stepped inside.

"What is it, Mrs. Goodman?" I asked.

Without answering, she looked cautiously up and down the street, then shut the door and put up the SHOP CLOSED sign.

"Mrs. Goodman, what's wrong?" I asked when we reached the kitchen.

"Sit down, dear," she said, nodding toward the table. She went to the kettle and poured out two cups of tea, then sat down opposite me. Her face was unusually grave. "Sarah, I'm worried about you. I've been trying to catch you for the past two days, but you've hardly been in your office."

"I have two cases which require a great deal of my attention just now," I explained, curious that my neighbor should find this troubling. She was the one, after all, constantly predicting my professional success.

"Yes, and I'm delighted that your services are in such demand. But not at the cost of your well-being." She stared hard at me, and I felt a sudden stab of alarm. "Sarah, do you know of any reason why a man would spend the past two days standing across the street watching your office?"

It took a moment for her words to register. "What makes you think someone is watching my office?"

"Because I've been keeping an eye on him, of course. When you run a business, it's important to pay attention to that sort of thing. It wouldn't be the first time a hooligan has stood out there planning to rob my store."

"You say he's been there for two days?" It was chilling to think some stranger had been spying on me. Why should I suddenly be of such interest to anyone?

"What does he look like?"

"He's not someone I'll soon forget. He's tall and rail-thin. He wears a black hat pulled low over his face, so it's difficult to see his eyes clearly, but his skin is very pale. The hair that shows under his hat is white, and so is his mustache. Oh, and he's always dressed in black. He's a sinister-looking character, Sarah. Not someone you'd want to run into on a dark night, or even in broad daylight.

I searched my memory but couldn't place anyone of that description. Yet why would a perfect stranger watch my office?

"Every once in a while, he leaves," Fanny went on. "Probably to get something to eat. But he always comes back."

"I don't understand," I said in honest bewilderment. "It's not as if I keep any money or valuables in my office."

We spent some time in fruitless speculation, which, not surprisingly, got us nowhere. Fanny was convinced the man was somehow connected to one of my current cases, but I failed to see how. True, by agreeing to represent Madame Karpova and Alexandra Sechrest,

I'd made enemies. But in my profession, that was hardly unusual. Who could consider me such a threat?

"You'll be careful, dear, won't you?" Fanny asked, looking nervously up and down the street as I left her shop.

"Of course I will. Please, Mrs. Goodman, don't worry. I'll be in my office first thing tomorrow morning. I only have two more days to prepare for the Sechrest divorce hearing."

I set off in the direction of the nearest horsecar line, thinking, as I stepped off the curb to cross Sutter Street, that traffic was unusually light for this time of evening.

I had reached the middle of the street, when two things happened almost simultaneously: Mrs. Goodman screamed, and I heard—as well as felt on the unpaved street beneath my feet—the rumble of horse's hooves coming upon me at a dangerous clip. I looked up and saw the driver cracking his whip, urging his animal forward at an ever-faster speed. For one terrifying moment, the man's face loomed before me, his pale face and white mustache standing out starkly in the gaslight, his thin mouth set in grim determination.

There was no time to scream. Instinctively, I dove forward in a desperate effort to avoid the vehicle, which was nearly upon me. From what sounded like a great distance, I heard a horse's loud whinny, then a man's voice calling for the beast to stop. I managed to roll over onto my back in time to see the huge animal rear up above me like some monster out of one of Mary Shelley's tales of horror.

With a preternatural sense of calm, I watched the horse's front hooves begin their inevitable descent toward my head.

CHAPTER EIGHTEEN

To this day, I refuse to believe I fainted. Succumbing to fits of the vapors is an absurd practice, one, I'm sorry to say, that is all too often abused by members of my own sex. Honesty, however, compels me to admit that the next several minutes passed in a painful blur. I seem to remember hearing Mrs. Goodman scream yet again, then feeling strong hands grip my arms. With no clear idea how I had gotten there, I now seemed to be lying on the sidewalk.

The first thing I saw upon opening my eyes was my neighbor stripping off her apron and placing it on top of my head. Then she started to press down so hard, I felt a sharp stab of pain.

"I'm sorry to hurt you, Sarah, but we have to stop the bleeding," Fanny said, looking more worried than I'd ever seen her.

It was then that I noticed something hot and sticky running down my face. I reached up a hand, and my fingers came away dripping blood.

I started to ask why I was bleeding; then memories of the racing carriage and the rearing horse came flooding back.

"That driver," I said, finding it curiously difficult to speak. "He deliberately ran me down."

"Shh, dear," Fanny told me. "You have to hold still until Dr. Mallory gets here."

"No, I don't require a doctor." I attempted to raise myself up, then gave a another cry as the same sharp pain bolted through my head, forcing me back down again.

"The driver of that carriage was the man I was telling you about," Fanny told me. "He must have been waiting for you to cross the street."

"So that he could run me down." Even as I said the words, I found them hard to believe. "Why would he want to kill me?"

Taking hold of Fanny's arm, I once again tried to pull myself up, but she gently laid me back down. It was then I realized something soft had been placed under my head, and I saw a coatless man standing behind my neighbor. I must be lying on his jacket, I thought, and worried that between the sidewalk and my blood, the garment would certainly be ruined.

"You're a very fortunate young woman," the coatless man said in a shaky voice. "This woman risked her life pulling you out from beneath that horse. The crazy driver didn't even stop, just took off like the devil himself was after him."

"But who would want—" I began, but Fanny cut me off.

"Just lie still, dear."

In the end, I was obliged to endure the attentions of Dr. Mallory—whose practice was but two blocks away—while he cleaned the lesion and applied a bandage. His biggest fear, he said, was that I had suffered a concussion, and would need to be watched carefully over the next twelve hours.

After explaining that my brother was a doctor and that I felt quite well enough to ride home in a cab, he finally gave his consent for me to leave. It proved considerably harder to extricate myself from Mrs. Goodman's well-meaning clutches. However, when I promised to seek out my brother Charles the moment I arrived home, she finally relented and flagged down a brougham for my use.

My main concern upon returning home was that I'd be seen by my parents. Now that my head was clearing, I realized my gown was not only torn and dirty but badly splattered with blood from my head laceration, which was the sort of wound that always bleeds profusely. With Frederick in jail, Mama and Papa had enough on their minds without worrying about me.

As it happened, our butler, Edis, was the only one about when I slipped into the house. Those old eyes, which had observed so much over the years, registered shock when he took in my disheveled appearance. Assuring him that my condition was not as bad as it appeared, I made him promise not to inform my parents of my mishap. He could, however, ask Charles to visit my room as soon as he returned home.

I'd just changed into a robe when my brother knocked and entered my bedroom, closely followed by my worried-looking sister-in-law Celia. Briefly, I told them what had happened, taking care to portray the incident as nothing more than an accident. Charles examined my wound, then confirmed Dr. Mallory's diagnosis that I had very likely suffered a concussion and would require close observation throughout the night.

Which is exactly what he did—with annoying frequency. Every hour or two, he appeared to check my eyes by the light of a candle. During the long night, I slept little, kept awake by my brother, my headache, and theories about Moss's notes.

Despite the busy schedule I had planned for the day, by morning I was forced to admit I was unfit to rise from my bed. My head still ached, and I was unsteady when I stumbled to the lavatory. Naturally, all my plans to keep the incident from my parents had been for naught. Not only had I been betrayed by Edis, who'd appeared so troubled the following morning that Papa easily wheedled it out of him, but by Charles, who had enlisted my mother to care for me during the day.

"It will be good for Mother," he explained. "She needs to get her mind off Frederick and his arraignment this afternoon. You're not seriously injured, thank God, but she'll enjoy fussing over you." He went on to say he would leave some medicine to relieve my headache and would check on me again that afternoon when he made his house calls.

After promising to let Mrs. Goodman know I was on the mend, Charles sent Samuel up to see me before he left for the day. If I was forced to spend the day resting, I reasoned, I could at least pursue some of the ideas that had occurred to me during my restless night.

I thought it best not to share my speculations with Samuel until I could prove their validity, and as a result, he was bursting with curiosity at the selection of books I requested from Papa's library. As soon as Samuel was gone, I took a dose of Charles's pain medication, then settled down to work. I was hard at it when my mother came in carrying a breakfast tray. I felt a stab of guilt to see new worry lines on her face, undoubtedly put there by her eldest son and only daughter.

"Sarah, darling, how are you?" she said, placing the tray on an end table and coming over to examine my bandaged head. "I'm not sure I'll ever be able to forgive you for not telling me you were injured last night."

"I'm sorry, Mama," I said a bit feebly. "I didn't want to add to your troubles just now."

"Oh? And you don't think being treated as if I'm too old and feeble to help my child when she's hurt doesn't add considerably more to my troubles?"

Heat rose to my face as I recognized the truth in what she was saying. After all, I'd felt the same way when Samuel failed to tell me the full circumstances surrounding Frederick's arrest.

"You're right, Mama, I should have told you. Actually, I'm very happy to have you here now."

"I'm glad to hear it," she said, plumping my pillows and placing the tray across my lap. "There now, I want you to eat every bite of that porridge. Cook made it specially for you."

Pleased to discover I was hungry, I required no further encouragement. For the remainder of the day, Mama fussed over me like a happy mother hen, fetching, chatting, and bringing me one restorative dish after another from Cook's kitchen. Charles had been right: This was exactly what she needed to get her mind off Frederick and his arraignment hearing.

As for me, I continued to peruse Papa's books and study Mr. Ferrier's translations of Moss's diary. I drew yet another diagram depicting where everyone had sat during the Cliff House séance, then considered it for a long time. Gradually, certain facts began to emerge, if not yet entirely clear, cogent enough to let me know I was headed in the right direction.

The last thing I did before Mama took away my books and notes and informed me it was time to take a nap was to make a list of what remained for me to do before Friday's divorce hearing. When I finally closed my eyes and succumbed to sleep, I felt as though the fog was finally beginning to lift!

Despite the lingering remains of a dull headache, I awoke the next morning feeling refreshed and eager to carry out the plans I had formulated while lying in bed. It was a glorious morning, and not entirely due to the weather. To my family's profound relief, Frederick had been released from jail the previous evening. The presiding judge had denied the assistant district attorney's request for bail, allowing my brother out on his own recognizance. Such had been my mother's joy that she and Celia had departed first thing that morning to visit Frederick and assure themselves that he was truly well after his two-day confinement.

Not long afterward, I asked Samuel if I could share a ride downtown with him. There were a few rather sensitive questions I wished to ask him, and a hansom would provide the privacy I deemed necessary.

Staring at my hat, he somewhat reluctantly agreed. "If you're sure you feel up to it, of course. But where in the world did you find that hat?"

"I borrowed it from Mama," I explained. I'd chosen a large dark blue Gainsborough hat from the back of Mama's armoire. I'd settled on this particular style not because I cared for the design (which I didn't) but because it covered the entire top of my head, bandages and all. Above the wide brim, it was decorated with feathers and several enormous artificial flowers. It was far too friv-olous to be worn with my tailored brown suit, but needs must. At the moment, it was more important to hide my injury than to appear stylish.

While we rode, I asked my brother for more details about Frederick and his arraignment hearing the previous afternoon.

"All things considered, he looks well enough," Samuel told me. "More than anything, I think he's mortified by the whole experience. Heaven only knows how this will affect his career in the state senate. I do know it's going to be hard for him to show his face in public until he's been cleared of these ridiculous charges."

"Has he told anyone the real reason he went to see Vincenzo at the jail?" I asked, getting to the heart of what I wanted to know.

"Yes, he finally broke down and told Papa." He smiled wryly. "I gather Father didn't leave him much choice in the matter. Evidently, it's all to do with Rudolph Hardin."

"Hardin?" This was a surprise! "You mean Frederick's political rival? The one who's been leaking those awful stories to the newspapers?"

"That's the one." We were both jostled as our cab narrowly missed colliding with an omnibus that had careened recklessly around the corner. Samuel took a moment to resettle in his seat, then continued, "According to Freddie, Vincenzo sent a man to see him, claiming he was a good friend of Hardin's footman. If Freddie bailed him out of jail, he promised to pass on some information that could ruin Hardin."

"So that's why he didn't want to tell us," I said thoughtfully.

"Exactly. And, as it turns out, Vincenzo did give Frederick an envelope. Only Freddie swears that it contained some cock-and-bull story about Hardin buying up a string of bawdy houses along the Embarcadero and setting his sister Clara up as a madam in one of them."

"Good Lord! Did Frederick actually believe him?"

There was a loud cry out on the street, followed by a string of curses from our hackman. Our hansom made an abrupt turn to the right, which took us over several large potholes. Each bounce made my head feel as if it were being hit by a sledgehammer. Observing my discomfort, Samuel leaned his head out the window and shouted at our driver to slow down, but as far as I could tell, it did little good.

"Freddie says he didn't believe any of it," Samuel said at length. "Given half a chance, though, I suspect he would have been happy to use it against Hardin. Which would have been disastrous, considering that Hardin's sister Clara has been a Roman Catholic nun for the past fifteen years."

Despite my throbbing head, and the gravity of our brother's situation, I couldn't help laughing at the mental picture this invoked. "That rather proves our theory about Frederick being set up, doesn't it?"

A shadow crossed my brother's face. "Yes, and that's what worries me. Whoever is behind this has laid his plans very cleverly. Even if the charges can't be conclusively proved, the suspicion and innuendos will be more than enough to ruin Frederick politically, not to mention socially. I doubt that any law firm in town would hire him after this."

Suddenly, I felt tense and chilled inside. This kind of scandal would utterly destroy my eldest brother and his wife. It would also sully Papa's good name, which would be horribly unfair; Papa was the most ethical man I knew!

"Samuel, we have to find the person who initiated this smear campaign. The only way to save Freddie is to prove without any doubt that he's innocent of these charges."

Samuel gave me an ironic smile. "What do you think I've been trying to do since Frederick was arrested? Do you suppose I could just sit back and watch our entire family being thrown to the wolves, simply because our big brother is so damn gullible?" He sighed. "I'm sorry, Sarah. I shouldn't have said that. Freddie means well, I suppose. He just can't seem to see beyond his own self-importance."

I nodded. "He can be unbearably annoying at times. Still, we've got to find a way to get him out of this mess."

We'd just reached the city jail when I remembered to ask Samuel the question I'd placed uppermost on my list the day before.

His eyebrows rose in surprise. "You want to know what? How did you even hear about that place?" Laughing, he raised a hand to cut me off before I could explain. "Never mind, I haven't time to hear it now. But you have to promise to give me all the gruesome details later."

Still shaking his head in bemusement, he gave me the information I'd requested, then helped me out of the carriage and instructed the driver to take him on to the offices of the *San Francisco Examiner.*

Entering the jail, I was shown to Madame Karpova's cell by Sergeant Jackson, who updated me on my client's state of mind since her arraignment hearing two days earlier.

"She's been a real pest, asking for you over and over," he said. "Other than that, she's doing all right. I've been keeping a close eye on her, although I still can't believe anyone is out to hurt her."

Madame Karpova was beginning to show the strain of her incarceration. Her face was pale and pinched, her already volatile temper frayed. The moment I entered the cell, she commenced berating me for not visiting her the day before. She went on to complain about the dreadful food, the surly guards, the lumpy cot, the cold temperature, and the lack of adequate blankets. She was especially upset that everyone at the jail treated her like a criminal, when she was completely innocent of wrongdoing. When I was finally able to get in a word, I explained that I had been ill the day before and thus unable to journey outside my house.

To my considerable surprise, she closed her eyes, then blurted, "You were injured in an accident." Her black eyes studied my face. "You have a head wound, have you not? That is why you were unable to come to me yesterday."

I felt tiny goose bumps rise on my arms. "How did you know?"

"I, Madame Karpova, know these things," she proclaimed, as she had so many times before. This morning, however, she lacked much of her earlier arrogance, and I thought this illustrated the strain of her confinement far more than her litany of complaints. Still, what she'd said about my head was uncanny. I lifted a hand to my hat, thinking that perhaps it had slipped and revealed my bandages, but it had not. I would have liked to question her further about this strange insight, but unfortunately there was no time.

Pulling the chair closer to the cot, I told her I had an important matter to discuss. "It's vital that you're completely honest with me. Your life may well depend upon it."

She regarded me warily, then slowly nodded her agreement. "Very well, I will attempt to do so."

"Where did Dmitry go when he left your hotel all day?"

She looked startled. "Why do you ask such a thing? What possible difference does it make now that he is dead?"

"It might help me find his killer," I said. "Please, Madame Karpova, just answer the question,."

She sat very still on the edge of the cot, regarding me with slightly veiled eyes. "He would tell me only that he was going for a walk."

"Come now, Madame, the two of you were very close," I chided, not bothering to hide my incredulity. "You must have some idea where he went and what he was doing for all those hours. It can't hurt him now, and it might help solve his murder."

Still, she hesitated to speak. Why, I wondered, was the woman being so obstinate? I was about to take her to task, when she let out a long breath and said, "He followed people, Miss Woolson. I am not proud of it, but in hard times it put food on the table and a roof over our heads."

" 'Followed people'?" I repeated. "You mean in order to rob or blackmail them?"

She nodded. "I made him stop thieving when we left Russia, but some habits are difficult to change. Sometimes he would eavesdrop when I did private readings. If he heard something promising, he would follow the person to see what else he could discover."

"And who was he following here in San Francisco?"

"I do not know," she said. "No, truly, Miss Woolson, he wouldn't tell me. All I know is that he was watching two men, both of them prominent and possessing political power."

"But you don't know their names?" I urged in growing frustration.

"No. Dmitry would not tell me." I was watching her face, and I thought she was telling me the truth. "We spoke freely about everything, except that. But he gave me money every week," she continued, a note of pride in her deep voice. "He always ensured that Yelena and I were well cared for."

"Do you think Dmitry was counting on one of these men to get him out of jail?"

"Yes, I am sure he was. I tried to get him to tell me the mark's name, but he refused. All he would say was that the man was in a position to have him released."

"It seems he was also in a position to have Dmitry killed," I said, letting out my breath. "I fear we're up against a ruthless and very clever villain, Madame Karpova, a man who will stop at nothing to attain his goal."

"Which is what, Miss Woolson?" Her husky voice was raised in anger. "Why has he chosen to do these terrible things to us?" She rose from the cot in sudden agitation and began pacing back and forth across the cell. "My poor, foolish *lubovnik*. I warned him that he was playing with fire, but he would not stop. Now he has been taken him from me."

I was struck by a sudden thought. "Madame Karpova, you somehow knew that I'd been in an accident this past Tuesday. You even knew where I'd been injured. Why couldn't you foresee when Dmitry would be killed, and by whom?"

"You do not know how many times I have longed to possess the ability to foretell these things," she said unhappily. "Unfortunately, that which I can see in other's lives, I cannot see in my own. It is as if a heavy black curtain hangs before my eyes whenever I attempt to look into my own future, or that of my daughter. I sit here in my cell waiting for the madman to strike again. I am like the defenseless mouse who is dropped into the snake's cage, with nowhere to hide."

I regretted that I had no comforting words to offer. Clearly, the only way I could get my client out of this cell was to see that Dmitry's real murderer was arrested. In growing desperation, I begged her to try to remember the names of the two men Dmitry had been following here in San Francisco.

She was near tears, and I was no closer to identifying the men, when Yelena arrived half an hour later. Taking my leave of my client's cell, I sought out Sergeant Jackson to ensure he'd remain vigilant in seeing to my client's safety.

After that, I traveled by hansom cab to Annjenett's safe house. The next morning was Alexandra Sechrest's divorce hearing, and I wanted to reassure her and answer any questions she might have. I was relieved to hear that her mother and sister had arrived that afternoon from Sacramento, and were staying at a local hotel. Mrs. Jane Hardy, the neighbor who had taken her in the last time she'd been beaten by her husband, had also promised to be present.

Finally, I went to my office to gather up all the pertinent paperwork I would need for the hearing. As I was leaving some two hours later, my head once again pounding, Fanny Goodman invited me in for tea and a slice of apple pie still hot from the oven. I tried to tell her I must be getting home, but she refused to take no for an answer.

"Where in the world did you get that horrible hat?" she asked as I sat down at her kitchen table.

"It's an old hat of my mother's," I explained. "I chose it because it covers my bandages."

"Well, you can't wear a thing like that to court tomorrow morning," she said, motioning for me to take it off.

Dutifully, I handed it over, and she disappeared into her shop. A few minutes later, she bustled back carrying a dark gray velvet hat, subtly decorated with feathers and two or three small artificial flowers. It had a full crown, which would easily cover my bandages, but the brim was less extreme than the one on Mama's hat and turned up at a jaunty angle on one side.

"This is the latest style from Paris," Fanny said, fitting the hat expertly onto my head. She handed me a mirror. "There now, that's much better, don't you think?"

She was right. Even I had to admit that Fanny's hat was most becoming. "It's lovely, Mrs. Goodman," I told her, tilting my head this way and that to make sure the bandages were well hidden. "But I can't possibly afford it."

"Don't worry about that, dear. I'm simply lending it to you to wear to court tomorrow. You can return it to me on Monday morning."

In spite of my protests that I couldn't borrow anything so expensive, she carefully removed the hat from my head and placed it in a hatbox.

"Nonsense, of course you can. It does my heart good to see you dressed like the fine, lovely lady you are. With your face and figure, I swear you could outshine Lillie Langtry herself. Now, why haven't you started on that pie?"

In truth, I'd become so absorbed with hats—which was most unlike me—I'd forgotten all about eating. Picking up my fork, I cut into the delicious apple pastry. As usual, it was excellent. Regrettably, my injury and fatigue seemed to have robbed me of an appetite.

I looked up, to find Fanny studying me speculatively. "Your

head is aching, isn't it, Sarah? Too much work and too little food and rest. I think I can help with that, as well."

Leaving me to pick at my pie, she bustled over to one of her cupboards, took out several small tins, and placed some of their contents in a square of cheesecloth. She tied off the cloth and placed it in a pan of hot water to steep.

"My mother brought this recipe with her from West Virginia," she said, placing the pan and a fresh cup on the table. "Willow bark, chamomile, and peppermint leaf, with a touch of honey. It helps a headache every time."

I was pleasantly surprised to find that she was right; my head felt considerably better when I left her cozy kitchen for home, although whether it was due to the apple pie or the willow-bark tea, I'd probably never know. Fanny had also tucked a small package of the ingredients for the tea into the hatbox for me to use over the next few days.

It was as well that my head had ceased throbbing by the time I reached my home, since Papa greeted me with stunning news: That afternoon, in the course of a routine hearing for a boy caught shoplifting, Judge Mortimer Raleigh had keeled over on the bench, dead of an apparent heart attack.

"Wasn't he the presiding judge at Madame Karpova's arraignment a few days ago?" Papa asked. At my bewildered nod, he continued: "The courthouse has been buzzing about how she ranted at Raleigh, telling him he'd die before the week was out." He eyed me in obvious bemusement. "If I didn't know for a fact that your client was locked up in a jail cell, I'd say she'd found some way to kill off old Mortimer, using some kind of Gypsy herbs to make it appear as if it were his heart."

"I don't understand it, either, Papa," I said, still in a state of shock. "It's uncanny, but most of the time Madame Karpova is right. She prophesied that Judge Raleigh would be greeting his Maker before the week was out. Apparently, that's precisely what he's doing."

CHAPTER NINETEEN

Because I was due in court the following morning, I had no opportunity to speak to Madame Karpova about Judge Raleigh's death. Frankly, I wasn't sure what to make of it. If this had been her first prediction to come true, I could have attributed it to coincidence. But it was not her first. I had never been a believer in psychic phenomenon, but this gave me pause.

I'd spent a restless night, too keyed up over the impending divorce hearing to sleep. Toward morning, I'd finally dozed off for an hour or two, then awakened with another throbbing headache. After Charles changed my bandages, I brewed a cup of Fanny's willow-bark tea and set about preparing myself for court. My spirits lifted as the headache gradually receded. I wouldn't have hurt Charles's feelings for the world, but I was convinced Fanny's tea worked better, and faster, than my brother's headache powders. And with the day I had before me, I could only say a silent thanks to my neighbor's mother for bringing the remedy with her from West Virginia.

Fanny had also been correct about the hat she'd lent me. It not only worked well with my bandaged head but was the perfect accessory for the light gray plain-cut suit I planned to wear for the proceedings.

The Sechrest divorce hearing was scheduled to begin at nine o'clock. Arriving at the courthouse, I was pleased to see Alexandra's mother and sister waiting with her outside the main entrance. There was a strong family resemblance, perhaps intensified at the moment by the state of their nerves. All three looked as if they were on their way to the gallows, rather than entering a court of law.

Also standing with them was Alexandra's neighbor and friend Mrs. Jane Hardy. I had spoken to Alexandra's maid, but the woman stubbornly refused to step foot inside a courtroom. Nor did she care to become involved in a divorce, since she had been raised to believe the disintegration of a marriage was contrary to church law. I wasn't unduly concerned about this. I was fairly certain the judge would grant my client a divorce. Gaining custody of her children, however, would be an entirely different matter.

As I led the four women into the courtroom, it seemed strange to see Robert sitting at the respondent's table across the aisle. The one time we had appeared in court together, it had been as colleagues fighting to save an innocent, if eccentric, man from the gallows. Now we were adversaries in a case that would decide the fate of a mother and her two small boys. Judging by the look on his face, Robert felt as uncomfortable with the situation as I did. Upon our arrival, he nodded his head rather stiffly and bade me a staid good morning. I replied with equal formality.

I gathered that the man sitting next to Robert was Luther Sechrest. This was my first glimpse of Alexandra's husband, and I covertly studied him as I opened my briefcase and arranged my papers on the table. Although he was seated, I judged him to be of average height, and handsome enough, in a cocky sort of way. He had longish brown hair, combed back from his brow, and a neatly trimmed mustache. His eyes slanted slightly upward and were golden brown, reminding me of a wolf I had once seen in the zoo. I was sad to see that the look he gave his wife, who was seated next to me at the petitioner's table, was one of ownership, rather than love or sorrow that their marriage had come to this unhappy end.

Behind Robert and Mr. Sechrest sat a group of men, all well groomed and smartly dressed. Quietly, my client identified the Reverend Henderson, the pastor of their church; Mr. Leighton, the elderly owner of Leighton Mining; and three of Luther's employees, or "ruffians," as Alexandra had described them.

"I don't know how Luther convinced Reverend Henderson to testify on his behalf," she whispered, looking hurt. "We've always been on excellent terms. I can't imagine he would say anything derogatory about me."

"Does your husband contribute to the church?" I asked, hating my suspicions even as I sought to confirm them.

"Actually, Luther is one of the parish's most generous benefactors." Her eyes lit with sudden understanding. "Oh, Sarah, this is going to be much worse than I anticipated."

I patted her arm and tried to look optimistic. "Let's not get ahead of ourselves. In cases like this, you never know what might happen."

As we were speaking, Gideon Manning hurried into the courtroom. "I'm sorry to be late," he said softly, slipping in beside my other witnesses in the row directly behind our table. "I . . ." he paused, and his gaze flickered across the aisle to Luther and his cronies, most of whom were now staring in our direction. Robert, in particular, appeared interested in what we were whispering about. I saw him shake his head in answer to some question asked by his client; then I turned my back to him, the better to hear what Gideon had to say.

Leaning over the wood panel that divided us, Gideon Manning said in a soft, faltering voice, "I'm afraid I did something illegal. I was just so afraid Alexandra—er, Mrs. Sechrest—would lose custody of those boys, I had to try."

"What have you done?" I demanded, fear forming a knot in my stomach at the word *illegal*.

"I waited until Sechrest and his men left the house for court; then I sneaked inside." He held one hand against the side of his mouth so that those on the other side of the aisle could not make out his words. "I still had a spare key to the front door, you see."

Beside me, Mrs. Sechrest sucked in her breath. "You shouldn't have taken such a chance, Gideon. You might have been caught, or even arrested."

He smiled grimly. "Only the servants were home, and I know their routines well enough to keep out of sight. What I wanted was in Luther's office."

"And what was that?" I asked, wishing he would get to the point before the judge arrived to start the hearing.

"These," he said, pulling some letters just far enough out of his pocket so that they were visible to my client and me but not to the "enemy camp" across the aisle.

"Are those the letters you wrote for Mr. Sechrest?" I asked in growing excitement.

"Yes, at least the few I could find. These were in the locked drawer of his desk." I could tell by his sheepish expression that he had jimmied the lock to pull it open. "He either destroyed the rest or they're in his safe."

"To whom were they sent?" I asked.

Without answering, he spread out the half dozen letters so I could see the addressees' names. I didn't recognize the first few names, but the fourth letter brought me up short. It was addressed to Senator Percival Gaylord!

I took it from his hand and examined it carefully. On the surface, it appeared innocent enough, but upon reading it a second time, I detected a more sinister intent. It read:

Senator Gaylord,
Your order has been arranged and is being processed by a trustworthy man long in my employ. I will notify you when the order has been executed according to your instructions.

Your faithful servant,
Luther P. Sechrest

"This letter refers to an order," I whispered to Gideon. "What sort of business does Sechrest do with Senator Gaylord?"

Manning opened his mouth to answer but was cut off as the clerk of the court announced the arrival of Judge Phillips. Whatever he'd been about to say would have to wait until later.

The hearing went much as I'd expected. After I had suffered the by now customary stares and murmurs of those individuals who had never before seen a female attorney, Judge Phillips called upon my client to state her reasons for requesting a divorce. As planned, I asked Alexandra's mother and sister to bear witness to Luther's brutality toward his wife, as well as Alexandra's superior attributes as a mother. Although their testimony was hesitant and somewhat timid, I thought Judge Phillips seemed disposed to believe their sworn statements.

Beside me, Alexandra tensed and grabbed my hand when it was time for her mother and sister's cross-examination. I murmured encouraging words, but in truth I wasn't sure how they would bear up under rigorous questioning. I caught Robert's expression as he stood, and read honest regret at his having to subject these gentle-women to such an ordeal. I also read blame that I hadn't persuaded my client to accept her husband's offer, and thereby avoided all this grief.

Robert truly was a gifted courtroom attorney. He had once confided to me that this was his dream, the reason he had left Edinburgh and come to America. He'd said he'd known that, as long as he stayed in Scotland, he would always remain in the shadow of his father, who was one of Scotland's leading defense attorneys. Now it seemed that dream was coming true, albeit at my expense. He framed his queries so cleverly that Alexandra's mother and sister soon grew muddled and began to contradict their own testimony. Both women left the stand in tears, and my hand bore the marks of my client's fingernails where they had dug into my palm.

Next, I called my client's neighbor, Mrs. Jane Hardy, to the stand. To my intense relief, she made a far better witness than her predecessors, boldly describing Mrs. Sechrest's bruises and ill treatment at the hands of her drunken husband. Robert utilized all his considerable skills, but he was unable to shake one word of her testimony. As far as Mrs. Hardy was concerned, Mrs. Sechrest was a virtuous, loving wife and mother. The very idea that she might be a slave to the bottle was ludicrous.

After Gideon Manning had his turn describing the troubled marriage, I called a very nervous Alexandra Sechrest to the stand. As I led my client through her tearful testimony, I caught the judge glancing at Luther in ill-disguised censure. For the first time, I allowed myself to hope that he might award her the children after all.

My brief moment of optimism was quashed when it came time for the respondent to refute our case and Robert called Luther Sechrest as his first witness. Sechrest slowly rose to his feet, a faint smile on his lips and a swagger in his step as he approached the witness stand. His entire demeanor radiated an easy self-confidence and the assurance that he held all the trump cards needed to win the case.

After his witness was sworn in, Robert asked him to describe his twelve-year marriage to his wife, Alexandra. Sechrest testified that the first eight or nine years had been everything any man could hope for. His wife had been obedient, respectful, modest, and diligent in carrying out her household duties.

"When did you begin to notice a change in your wife's behavior?" Robert asked.

Luther went on to weave a complex and utterly false story about his wife's growing drinking problem, which he stated had begun in the last three or four years.

"And how did this affect her relationship with your two children?"

As Sechrest described horrific examples of a drunken, out-of-control mother, Alexandra cringed in her seat next to mine. "None of it is true," she whispered, obviously holding herself together by sheer force of will. "Luther is the one who behaved like a madman. How can he tell such terrible lies?"

When Sechrest proceeded to relate how on one occasion his wife had severely beaten her sons for committing some minor infraction, I'd had enough.

"Objection," I said, rising to my feet. "Unless Mr. Sechrest saw this with his own eyes, it is hearsay."

"Did you personally observe this incident?" asked the judge.

Luther gave a slight smile. "No, Your Honor. But I have witnesses who were present. They'll be happy to describe the unfortunate episode to the Court."

Which was nothing less than the truth. One by one, Robert called several of Sechrest's servants to the stand—along with his stable of thugs—all of them substantiating their employer's damning testimony. The coup de grâce, of course, was delivered when they accused my client and Gideon Manning of carrying on an adulterous affair under Luther Sechrest's roof. Although I did everything I could think of to countermand their testimony, I was unable to budge them from their well-orchestrated stories. I glanced at Luther Sechrest as the last of his cronies left the stand, and my anger flared as I observed the self-satisfied smile plastered upon his arrogant face.

I felt a terrible heaviness inside me as the Reverend Henderson took the stand to praise Luther Sechrest as an exemplary, God-fearing man, who was in every way a role model for the community. He went on to decry Mrs. Sechrest as an unfortunate soul lost in the sin of drunkenness and adultery. After Luther's elderly employer, Howard Leighton, got through extolling his manager's long years of faithful service, the judge had obviously changed his mind and was now regarding Alexandra as the villain in this marriage, not her poor, long-suffering husband.

"Divorce is an abysmal matter, Your Honor," Robert said in his summation. "No matter what circumstances lead a man and wife to lose the love they once shared, it can only be regarded as a tragedy, not only to them but to society as a whole. If we cannot sustain the sanctity of marriage, what hope have we of upholding the righteous ideals of our great nation?"

He looked sadly at Mrs. Sechrest. "Some people regard the addiction to alcohol as a vice, or, as Reverend Henderson opined, a sin. Personally, I consider it to be a sickness, one which cannot be controlled by a person so afflicted. I believe that to be true of Mrs. Luther Sechrest, who, when sober, appears to be a loving and dutiful wife and mother.

"No matter how virtuous her behavior in this abstemious state, however, it does not diminish the chaos the unfortunate woman creates when she succumbs to the bottle. Unnatural as it is to separate a mother from her children, we must put their well-being above all other considerations. It grieves me to advocate such an extreme measure, but for the sake of those innocent little boys, I beg the Court to award my client, Luther Sechrest, full and unlimited custody of his two minor sons. Thank you, Your Honor."

As he returned to his seat, Robert glanced briefly at me. His expression was somber and awash with regret. I could detect not the slightest sign of satisfaction, although surely he must have realized that he'd won.

The final decision, however heartbreaking, came as no surprise. Alexandra was granted her divorce, but her husband, Luther, was awarded sole custody of their two sons.

I was so absorbed with trying to comfort my client, who was by now frantic with grief, that I didn't notice the tall, seedy-looking man who entered the courtroom. An abrupt burst of laughter from the Sechrest camp, however, caused me to look in their direction, and I saw the late arrival whispering to Luther. The malevolent gleam in the man's eyes as he smiled disdainfully at Mrs. Sechrest caused me to ask Gideon if he knew the newcomer's identity.

"That's Joseph Vincenzo," he replied, pronouncing the name as if it were an expletive. "In my opinion, he's the worst brute of the bunch."

"Did you say *Joseph Vincenzo?*" I asked, staring at Gideon in disbelief. "But I thought he worked for Edgar Bramwell's construction company."

"I don't know where you heard that, Miss Woolson," Gideon said. "Vincenzo is Luther's right-hand man. He's been with him for years."

"Oh my God!" I said, my mind now truly spinning. Senator Gaylord and now Joseph Vincenzo! What did it mean? What was their relationship to Luther Sechrest? It was difficult to see how it all fit together. Unless—

Despite Alexandra's tears and the commotion going on around me in the courtroom, I sat perfectly still, trying to fit this latest revelation into the overall picture. If I was right, the plan had been bold and extremely risky. But what if they'd had no choice? Glancing at Luther Sechrest, I decided he would be just the sort of man to throw caution to the wind and put a perilous plan like this into action.

Without taking time to explain my suspicions, I asked Alexandra and Gideon to accompany me to my home. "Please, trust me," I entreated. "It's extremely important—to us all!"

While I pushed my papers back inside my briefcase, Alexandra asked her mother and sister to return to their hotel, where she would meet them later. They looked confused, and still somewhat shaky from their ordeal, but agreed to do as she suggested.

As my client, Gideon, and I were departing the courthouse, Robert caught up with us. "Sarah," he asked, a bit out of breath, "how is Mrs. Sechrest?"

I continued walking as I spoke. "I trust she'll be a great deal better after we've seen to some urgent business."

"What business?" he asked, continuing to follow. "Sarah, you've got that look on your face again. What are you up to?"

I turned then, my expression deliberately reproachful. "Why aren't you toddling back to Joseph Shepard so he can pat you on the head for a job well done? Today, you helped rob a devoted, innocent mother of her children. You should be very pleased with yourself."

"That's hardly fair," he protested as I turned and continued walking toward Eddie and his cab. I was grateful now that I'd thought to ask the boy to meet me at the courthouse after the hearing. It would save a great deal of time and bother.

"The case is over," Robert went on. "Mr. Sechrest gave his wife ample opportunity to save the marriage, but she chose not to accept."

Even though I made no reply, Robert was still at my heels as Eddie assisted me into the brougham, where Gideon and Alexandra were waiting. When Robert started to follow me inside, I stopped him, saying that after what my client had just been through, having her husband's lawyer in the same carriage would be like rubbing salt in the wound.

Reluctantly, he stood down as I instructed the lad to take us to my Rincon Hill home. Robert continued to watch us from the curb as Eddie clicked the reliable dappled gray into traffic.

I was relieved to find Papa at home when we entered the house some thirty minutes later. After I'd introduced my two companions—I'd warned Gideon not to mention the fact that he'd broken into Sechrest's house earlier—Papa invited us into the front parlor. Too edgy to accept our maid's offer of coffee or tea, I gave my father an abbreviated version of the divorce proceedings, then got straight to the point.

"We need a search warrant, Papa," I told my startled parent. "I know you can't give us one yourself because it might constitute a conflict of interest, but surely you know a judge who would issue one."

My father's eyes narrowed. "Why don't you start at the beginning and tell me why you suddenly feel a need to search someone's house."

"Not the entire house, just a safe inside the house."

"Whatever it is, Sarah, you have to demonstrate a serious reason to search a private residence."

Trying to control my impatience, I told him about Joseph Vincenzo working for Luther Sechrest, not Edgar Bramwell, as well as about the letters Manning had written to Senator Gaylord on Sechrest's behalf. I would have loved to have shown him the letters Gideon had taken from Sechrest's desk, but of course that would have meant admitting he'd entered the house illegally.

"Both Mr. Manning and Mrs. Sechrest claim that Luther Sechrest spends a good deal more money than he earns at Leighton Mining. And Gideon is convinced Sechrest keeps a second set of company account books."

As I'd hoped, we now had Papa's full attention. He spent the next several minutes peppering Alexandra and Gideon with questions, then turned back to me.

"Let me make sure I understand this, Sarah. You think Senator Gaylord and Luther Sechrest set up Frederick and Bramwell to take the blame for crimes they themselves committed."

"That's exactly what I think."

Papa shook his head. "To be honest, Sarah, I'm not certain you've established probable cause to justify a search warrant. On the other hand, it may be our best chance to save Frederick, and the Bramwells, of course." He looked from Alexandra to Gideon. "Are you both willing to swear to the statements you've made concerning Luther Sechrest."

After both responded in the affirmative, Papa went on: "And you're willing to sign an affidavit to that effect?"

Again, they both agreed. I watched Alexandra's eyes grow wider as the implications of this action sunk in.

"If Sarah is right and Luther has committed some sort of crime," she asked, looking intently at my father, "how will that affect the ruling about child custody?"

"It means, young lady," Papa answered, "that you will more

than likely get your sons back. Your husband can hardly raise those boys from a jail cell." He pulled on his coat, then cautioned, "But don't get your hopes up too soon, Mrs. Sechrest. First, we have to find evidence that a crime was committed, and, if it was, that Mr. Sechrest was involved." He motioned for Alexandra and Gideon to follow him. "You'll both have to come with me. Judge Aldwin will undoubtedly want to question you himself, and he will almost certainly require you to sign affidavits before he'll issue the warrant."

We were almost to the front door when it opened and my brother Samuel entered, followed closely by Robert.

"Look who I found drawing up in his cab," Samuel said, indicating Robert, who gave me a sheepish smile. Alexandra stiffened at the sight of her husband's attorney, and Gideon's look was frosty. "Well, well, what do we have going on in here?" my brother asked, sensing the sudden tension.

I performed hasty introductions, explaining that Robert had represented Mrs. Sechrest's husband in her suit for divorce, then asked Robert why he had come to my home.

Robert colored slightly as he looked at Alexandra. "I'm truly sorry for the way matters turned out for you, Mrs. Sechrest. Divorce is painful for everyone involved. I want you to know that I meant you no personal harm."

Alexandra's expression did not soften. Inclining her head to demonstrate that she had heard his apology—although not that she had accepted it—she silently followed Gideon and Papa out to Eddie's brougham.

"To answer your question, Sarah," Robert said after everyone had left the house but Samuel and me, "I came here to talk to you about the case."

"The case?" I asked, my attention so taken up with the search warrant, I wasn't really listening. "Oh, you mean the Sechrest divorce?"

"Yes, I—"

"Sorry, Robert, but I've no time for that now. We have pressing business to attend to." Turning to Samuel, I handed him a piece of paper with Luther Sechrest's name and address printed on it. "Samuel, would you please try to find George Lewis and meet us at this address? The police will have to conduct the actual search."

"What search?" both men asked. But I had already turned and was hurrying toward the waiting cab.

Ninety minutes later, we had our search warrant and were on our way in Eddie's brougham to Luther Sechrest's home. Upon my father's advice—and after promising Alexandra I would tell her what we found in the safe—Alexandra and Gideon had taken a separate cab to their respective destinations.

Samuel, Robert, Sergeant Lewis, and a uniformed patrolman were waiting for us in a police wagon parked down the street from the Sechrest home. When we explained why we had asked them to meet us, Robert was irate.

"Why didn't you tell me that was your plan?" he demanded. "As Mr. Sechrest's attorney, I can't allow you to go forward with this search."

"I'm afraid you have no choice, Robert," I told him. "We have a perfectly legal search warrant signed by a judge."

This did not mollify him. "Just because your client lost custody of her children does not give you the right to stoop to such a barefaced act of revenge."

"Calm down, Robert," I said. "Believe me, this is not about revenge. I'll explain everything as soon as we've taken care of the warrant."

He was still sputtering as Papa handed Sergeant Lewis the search warrant, which named him as the officer authorized to carry out the search. According to the laws of search and seizure, the document spelled out exactly what Lewis could look for in Sechrest's safe, as well as what he could legally remove from the premises. Armed with this paper, the two policemen approached the Sechrest residence.

While we waited for their return, I filled Robert in on what had prompted this action. "So you see why it was so vital to search the safe before Sechrest could destroy any incriminating evidence. Papa and I believe it was Sechrest and Senator Gaylord who set up my brother Frederick."

"According to Bramwell's records," Papa put in, "Joseph Vincenzo had been working for them less than three weeks. Sarah discovered only this afternoon that Vincenzo has been with Sechrest for years. Obviously, Gaylord and Sechrest planted Vincenzo at Bramwell's company in order to authenticate his bribery charges against Frederick."

Robert looked dazed. "Are you sure, Judge Woolson? Luther Sechrest seems such an honest, upstanding fellow."

"Yes, well appearances can be deceiving," I said dryly.

While we waited for their return, Eddie peppered me with questions: Was Sergeant Lewis going to arrest someone? Was there a dead body inside the house, maybe even stuffed in the safe? Did I suppose the bad guys had guns and did I think they'd try to shoot us all? Holding up his homemade cosh—which seemed even heavier now than it had the night of the Cliff House séance—he swore that if called upon, he was more than ready to help the coppers.

Sergeant Lewis and his junior officer were inside the Sechrest home for less than an hour, but for those of us waiting inside the brougham—especially with Eddie's nonstop jabbering!—it seemed a lifetime. Like the boy, I kept wondering what was happening inside the house. Was Luther proving difficult? Had he already destroyed the documents we needed to prove our case?

As it happened, the search went far more smoothly than it had in either Eddie's or my imagination. Luther Sechrest and his cronies were not at home, and the door had been answered by a maid. Opening the safe proved to be the thorniest problem the policemen faced, and that was solved once they'd convinced Luther's butler that it was in his best interests to show them where his master kept a copy of the combination.

To our delight, and relief, the safe held a treasure trove of incriminating evidence, more than enough to clear Frederick of having had any part in the scandal over the new City Hall building. Not only did Lewis find a second set of books for Leighton Mining Company—which, upon examination, revealed in detail the profits Luther had skimmed from his employer; they also found half a dozen letters written to Luther by Gaylord, spelling out the senator's role in the construction fraud.

"Why do you suppose Sechrest didn't destroy these letters?" asked Robert. "They point the finger of guilt directly at him."

"He may have kept them for insurance," Papa ventured. "If he were caught, Sechrest could bring all the bigwigs down with him." He gave a grim smile. "My guess, though, is that he was planning a bit of blackmail somewhere down the line."

"I'll be damned!"

We all looked at George Lewis, who was staring at one of the letters as if it had come from Beelzebub himself. Wordlessly, he handed it to Papa, who, in turn, held it out for the rest of us to read.

I stared at the paper. It was not until I'd read the addressee's name at least three times that I finally believed my eyes. For several long moments, no one spoke, obviously as dumbstruck as I was. Finally, I shook myself, feeling as if I were awakening from a bad dream.

"Good Lord in heaven," I said, my voice little more than a whisper. "It's addressed to Lieutenant Frank Ahern!"

CHAPTER TWENTY

S amuel read the letter aloud. Evidently, Luther Sechrest was advising Lieutenant Ahern that several tons of limestone would be delivered, free of charge, to the construction site of the Aherns' new house on Russian Hill. He went on to tell the lieutenant that he was also including a bill of sale—spurious, of course—should anyone question the shipment.

As damaging as this letter was, even more incriminating were the letters that had been sent from Ahern to Sechrest, detailing how much he expected to be paid for looking the other way while Sechrest and other contractors raked in money from the new City Hall project. Each letter ended with a reminder to destroy all correspondence between them. That warning must have given Sechrest a good laugh, I thought. Judging by the amount of mail George had recovered from the safe, Sechrest had kept every letter he'd received!

When he was finished reading, Samuel turned to me. "You know what this means, don't you, Sarah?"

"Yes," I replied numbly. "Frank Ahern is the 'Napoleon' Darien Moss referred to in his notes."

"I'm going to have to take these letters directly to the captain,"

George said. "He'll have to decide what's best to do about Lieutenant Ahern."

Papa left as soon as he could flag down an unoccupied cab, while George, Samuel, and the patrolman left minutes later, intent on delivering the contents of Sechrest's safe to Capt. Pete Gregory. I wasn't sure what would happen after that. Hopefully, Gregory would issue a warrant for Ahern's arrest, along with ones for Senator Gaylord, Luther Sechrest, and his motley band of associates. My focus remained squarely fixed on clearing Frederick's name, and seeing that Alexandra regained custody of her boys.

After the search of the safe, I felt we were well on our way to accomplishing these first two objectives. Unfortunately, I wasn't nearly as confident I could do the same for Madame Karpova. Despite recent developments, the circumstances surrounding Dmitry Serkov's murder remained murky. I strongly suspected it was somehow connected to the City Hall scandal; I just wasn't sure how.

For reasons best known to himself, Robert insisted on accompanying me to the city jail in Eddie's brougham. We had not been long in traffic when he awkwardly cleared his throat.

"I feel I owe you an apology," he said a bit gruffly. Since it was rare indeed to hear my colleague admit he was wrong, I sat quietly, waiting for him to go on. "You were right about Luther Sechrest," he continued after several moments. "Only a coward and a bully would brutalize a woman as he did. He completely took me in."

"As he did his pastor and his employer," I replied. Now that Robert had expressed repentance for having sided with that dreadful man, I was surprised to feel the need to lessen his discomfiture. "You were in good company, Robert. And you didn't see his wife's bruises firsthand as I did."

"Humph" was his only reply, and I knew he saw through my less than subtle attempt to diminish his guilt.

We were both silent for a time as Eddie threaded his dappled gray through the heavy late-afternoon traffic, jostling Robert and me from one side of the seat to the other in the process.

I started to speculate aloud about whom Dmitry Serkov might have been blackmailing, when Eddie swerved the brougham so sharply, I slid hard against the left-side door. As I gathered my wits, and my borrowed hat, back into some semblance of order, I happened to look outside at the people and shops we were passing. My breath caught in my throat.

"That's him!" I cried out, banging my fist against the roof to catch Eddie's attention. "Robert, tell Eddie to stop the carriage."

For once, Robert did as I asked without demanding an explanation, and the moment the brougham was reined up, I was out the door. Tripping over my skirts, I started running toward the man I'd just spied leaving the Bush Street Saloon.

"Wait!" I called out to him. "I want to speak to you."

The man turned and blinked at me, as if his eyes had not yet adjusted to the bright daylight outside the saloon. Then he seemed to place me, and his watery eyes opened wide with alarm. Whipping around, he started running down the street.

"Sarah!" Robert yelled from behind me. "What's gotten into you?"

I didn't stop to answer, just hitched up my skirts to a decidedly immodest position just below my knees, elated to have so much more freedom of movement. Paying no attention to angry and scandalized passersby, I slowly gained on my prey, who was weaving a bit, undoubtedly as the result of the whiskey he'd imbibed.

By the time Robert caught up with me, the man had just collided with an outdoor vegetable display, which caused him to tumble onto the sidewalk.

"Damn it, Sarah," Robert said breathlessly. "Who in hell are we chasing?"

Without lessening my pace, and keeping a firm hold of my skirts, I pointed my chin toward my intoxicated prey. "Him!" I managed to say, my own breath coming in shallow gasps.

Ahead of us, the man scrambled to his feet. Panicked to see that Robert and I were almost upon him, he dashed out into the street, directly in front of an oncoming carriage. The driver swore, and did everything he could to stop, but it was too late. Veering his cabriolet sharply to the left, the driver managed to avoid a head-on collision, instead clipping my quarry on the side, probably saving his life, but causing him to fall within inches of the carriage wheels.

Before I could catch my breath, Robert raced by me and, lifting the unconscious man by the shoulders, pulled him over to the curb. While traffic sorted itself out with loud profanities mingled with looks of concern, I stared down at the fellow I'd been chasing. His pale face, white hair, and bushy white mustache were unmistakable. In a dramatic display of poetic justice, the villain who had tried to run me down in his carriage only days earlier had suffered the same fate he had tried so diligently to inflict on me!

R ather more abruptly than necessary, Eddie pulled up in front of the city jail. A second later, he came flying out of the driver's seat to open the carriage door. Eyes wide, he stared at our prisoner, who had by now regained consciousness.

"Has he confessed yet?" the boy asked. "I still got my cosh. If you or Mr. Campbell need help makin' the bloke talk, just give a yell and I'll get him to chatter like a magpie."

"Thank you, Eddie," I replied, allowing him to help me out of the carriage. "But I don't think your cosh will be needed. You can, however, help Mr. Campbell get this fellow inside the station."

The lad required no further prompting. Eagerly, he climbed inside the carriage and pushed on the man's back as Robert pulled him out the door. Because we'd bound our prisoner's hands behind his back with strips torn from my petticoat, he moved awkwardly. And not surprisingly, he kept dragging his feet, not at all eager to enter the jail.

I was pleased to see that Sgt. Paul Alston was on duty at the front desk. Since he knew who I was, I hoped there'd be less difficulty turning the fellow over. As it turned out, our captive was no stranger to city jail. In fact, Sergeant Alston regarded him with open disdain.

"So you just couldn't stay away, huh, Whitey?" Alston said. "What is it this time—robbery, assault, breaking and entering, or just being an all-around jackass?"

"It was an accident, Sergeant, I swear," Whitey protested, squirming unsuccessfully to free himself from Robert's and Eddie's grip.

"Of course it was," Alston said, his voice heavy with sarcasm. "Miss Woolson, Mr. . . ."

"Campbell," Robert answered. "Robert Campbell."

"Well, Mr. Campbell, Miss Woolson, let me introduce you to Harry Gazo, better known to his friends here at the jail as 'Whitey' Gazo. Now then, why don't you tell me how you came to meet up with this ornery plug-ugly."

I explained the attempt on my life and assured Sergeant Alston I had a witness who had seen both the attack and Whitey watching my office for two days beforehand."

"Still say it was an accident, Whitey?" Alston asked, filling out an arrest form. "Looks like this time you were caught red-handed. Attempted murder is a serious charge, b'hoy. It'll go a lot easier for you if you own up to it now, instead of making us pull it out of you one piece at a time."

Whitey looked around helplessly. Finding no sympathetic faces, he glumly admitted, "All right, I done it. But it warn't my idea to go after the lady. Some big bug paid me to watch her office. Then when she come out, I was to run her over."

"Just what 'big bug' was that?" Robert asked, his voice tight as he held the hoodlum by the scruff of his neck.

"Dunno his name," Whitey whined. "I met him in Shakey's Saloon. Bought me a few bald-face whiskeys and asked if I wanted to make some easy money."

"And naturally you said yes," Alston put in dryly.

Staring up at Robert, who looked as though he'd love nothing better than to tear the thug apart with his bare hands, he reluctantly nodded.

Sergeant Alston had just called the young jailer, Jimmy Wolf, to process the prisoner before locking him in a cell, when Lieutenant Ahern entered the jail. He looked taken aback to see me, and clearly stunned at the sight of Whitey Gazo being led toward the cell blocks.

Spotting the plainclothes police lieutenant, Whitey cried out, "That's him! That there's the sharper what paid me to run down this lady. You outta be pinchin' him, not me."

Robert and I stared at Whitey in shock. "Lieutenant Ahern?" I said to the hooligan. "Are you sure this is the man who paid you to . . . to kill me?"

"It surely is, miss," Whitey confirmed. "He paid me a double eagle to flatten you out." Obviously, the offer of a twenty-dollar gold piece had been too good to turn down.

For a split second, I read panic in Ahern's eyes, but it was gone in a flash. He gave the desk sergeant an easy smile, dismissing the accusation as too preposterous to bother disputing. "The man's obviously inebriated, Alston. Lock him up in the drunk tank until he sleeps it off."

Lieutenant Ahern was so preoccupied dealing with Whitey Gazo, he seemed not to hear Samuel, George Lewis, and Capt. Pete Gregory enter the station behind him. With them were two patrolmen.

Pete Gregory wasn't a particularly big man, but he carried himself with so much authority and confidence that he appeared much larger than his actual size. His dark brown hair was turning gray, while his mustache was nearly white, as were his bushy eyebrows. His sharp, intelligent eyes took in the situation before he was halfway into the lobby.

"Not so fast, Sergeant Alston," he said. "I want to question that man before he's placed in a cell."

At the sound of Gregory's voice, Ahern spun around, blanching to see his captain standing behind him. He watched openmouthed, as Gregory nodded to George Lewis and the two men approached him.

"Lieutenant Ahern," Captain Gregory said in a sober voice. "I arrest you for accepting bribes from Leighton Mining Company, and other contractors—as yet unnamed—involved in the construction of the new City Hall building. You are advised that anything you say will be duly noted and may be used against you in a court of law."

"Lord Almighty," Eddie murmured, staring at the two police officers. "They've gone and tumbled the lieutenant."

"What!" Ahern exclaimed. He was grinning foolishly at his superior officer, as if the latter had just told a joke he didn't quite understand. "What's going on, Pete?"

Captain Gregory regarded his lieutenant for several moments, his strong round face expressing a deep personal sadness. "We came through the ranks together, Frank," he said at last, his voice heavy with regret. "I've known you for over twenty years. You were the best of the best. What happened to you? When did things start going wrong?"

Ahern gave a nervous laugh, as if he couldn't yet accept what was happening to him. "You're making a terrible mistake, Pete. I've spent my whole career fighting bribery and corruption in this city. How can you even suggest that I might be part of it?"

Captain Gregory silently removed Ahern's letters to Luther Sechrest from his breast pocket. "We have it in writing, Frank," Gregory said unhappily. "I would never have believed it if I hadn't seen the evidence for myself."

Ahern's sharp blue eyes darted nervously about the room. Looking for a means of escape? I wondered. If so, there was none. The only way out of the jailhouse lobby was either through the front entrance, which was guarded by the two patrolmen, or through the door leading to the cell blocks, where Jimmy Wolf and his prisoner still stood, intrigued by the unfolding drama.

"Come on, Pete," Ahern said with a conspiratorial smile. "Those letters have to be forgeries. You know as well as I do that good cops make enemies. Somebody's trying to set me up."

Gregory shook his head. "I know your handwriting as well as I know my own, Frank. You wrote these letters all right; it's no good saying you didn't."

At the captain's nod, George stepped forward, holding a set of handcuffs. But before he could get close enough to slip them onto Ahern's wrists, the lieutenant spun around, darted past Whitey and Jimmy Wolfe, and ran through the door to the cell blocks.

"Get him!" Captain Gregory shouted, and he, Samuel, and the rest of the policemen sped after Ahern. While the desk sergeant was busy grabbing hold of Whitey, I ran through the door behind them, Eddie hot on my heels.

"Sarah, wait!"

I could hear the sound of Robert's feet pounding after me, but I didn't stop. When I turned the last corner leading to Madame Karpova's cell, my heart leapt to my throat.

Captain Gregory and the four officers were standing stock-still in the middle of the passageway, their backs to me. Several yards farther down the corridor, I saw a pile of weapons lying scattered on the floor, as if they'd been kicked there. Behind the policemen stood Samuel, Yelena Karpova, and Nicholas Bramwell. As I moved quietly closer, Yelena turned her head for a moment, and I saw that her face was ashen, her eyes wide with terror.

It was only when I came even with the two of them that I saw the cause of Yelena's alarm. Just inside my client's cell, Lieutenant Ahern had pinned Madame Karpova in a chokehold around the neck. His free hand held a pistol pressed against her temple. Her face was a blotchy red; the lieutenant was holding her so tightly, it was obviously cutting off her air.

"Don't move, any of you!" Ahern commanded nervously.

"You don't want to do this, Lieutenant Ahern," I said, keeping my voice nonconfrontational. "This woman has done nothing to harm you."

The Irishman's face blazed red. "Oh? You don't think so? Well, let me set you straight, Miss Know-It-All. If this meddling charlatan hadn't come to San Francisco, claiming she could see into the future and talk to the dead, my wife wouldn't have gone to her blabbing all our private affairs. And that scheming, no-good Serkov wouldn't have eavesdropped and then followed me all over town in order to ferret out even more secrets that were none of his damn business."

"That's how he discovered you were taking bribes to turn a blind eye to the new City Hall project, wasn't it?" I said. "Then, when he was arrested, he promised not to tell anyone about the scam if you'd get him released from jail."

"The bastard!" Ahern spat. "Moss was bad enough, but that idiot Serkov expected me to perform miracles. How the hell was I supposed to get him out of here without everyone knowing something was going on?"

"So you had to shut him up," Captain Gregory put in.

I heard Yelena give a little sob at this, and her mother's eyes went very wide, first in surprise, then in fury.

"How could I have killed him, Pete?" Ahern protested. "I was at a meeting with you and the mayor that day, remember?"

"Yes, but Cecil Vere was here—while you were making certain you had an airtight alibi." The words were out of my mouth before I even realized they were there. It was as if a fog had suddenly lifted, and I began to see the jailor's peculiar behavior after Serkov's death in an entirely new light. "Cecil wasn't upset because he'd failed to protect a prisoner, or because he recognized Serkov's killer," I continued, wondering why I hadn't realized this sooner. "He was wretched because he *was* Serkov's killer."

"So what if he did kill the Russki?" Ahern said, fixing me with a murderous glare. "That doesn't mean I had anything to do with it."

"You had everything to do with it, Lieutenant." I forced myself to look at Ahern's face and not the gun he held to Madame Karpova's head. "You paid Cecil to stab Serkov. And he accepted because he was in love and needed the money to get married. But almost immediately, he was racked by guilt. You must have panicked, afraid he'd confess his crime, along with your role in it. In the end, you had to silence him, too."

"It's not my fault that chirky simpleton suddenly developed a conscience," Ahern spat out. "Blubbering on about how wrong he'd been to take the Russian's life. He didn't leave me any choice but to get rid of him."

My mind was racing, piecing details together as I went along, not entirely sure they fit, but blurting them out anyway. I was terrified of what Ahern might do to my client if I pushed him too far, but I could read in Olga's dark eyes that she wanted me to take the risk. She knew as well as I did that we wouldn't get another chance. And either way, her life hung in the balance.

Saying a silent prayer, I pressed on. "My guess is that you offered to pay Cecil to hang Madame Karpova, so it would appear as if she'd committed suicide out of guilt for killing Serkov. But Vere refused, didn't he? And in the end, you were forced to do it yourself. You drugged her food, then because you were nervous one of the jailers might catch you in the act, you botched the job, and she survived."

"If you don't shut that cussed trap of yours, you're going to have a dead woman as a client," Ahern shouted. I was alarmed to see the gun against Madame Karpova's temple begin to tremble. "Move out of my way—all of you!" he demanded. "If anyone tries to stop me, I swear I'll shoot her."

Sergeant Lewis hesitated, then moved aside, followed by Jimmy Wolf and the two uniformed officers. Captain Gregory stood firmly in place, refusing to retreat.

"You haven't a chance of getting away, Frank," he told his lieutenant. "Why don't you do the smart thing and let Mrs. Karpova go? Then we can sit down, you and me, and talk this over. Just like the old days."

"Sorry, Pete, but the time for talking is over. Now move!" The pupils of Ahern's eyes had become pinpricks, and they darted nervously around, as if he expected someone to jump him at any minute. Keeping his arm tightly clamped around Madame Karpova's neck, he pushed her forward. "Last chance, Pete," he threatened when the captain still wouldn't budge.

I sucked in a gulp of air as I saw his finger tighten on the trigger. Gregory must have seen it, too, because he finally stepped back a few feet, clearing the way for Ahern and his hostage to pass. Never taking his eyes off us, Ahern began backing up the corridor. At the end of the hall, he'd be able to turn and escape out the back of the jail.

I felt someone stir behind me, and glimpsed Eddie heading in the direction of the lobby. I tried to grab him, but he was too quick. I could only pray that Ahern wouldn't notice him. Still, I wondered fearfully, What in the world was the boy up to?

In front of me, Captain Gregory, Lewis, Jimmy Wolf, and the two patrolmen started to move toward Ahern. Seeing this, the lieutenant raised his gun and fired a shot. I heard Jimmy Wolf cry out, then drop heavily to the floor.

George Lewis gave a loud curse and, against Captain Gregory's orders, started running toward Ahern. He had gone only a couple of yards when Ahern again raised his pistol, aiming it at Lewis's heart.

Then the most peculiar thing happened. Just as Ahern was about to pull the trigger, he suddenly grunted and released his grip on his hostage. Staggering forward a step or two, he fell facedown onto the floor. The gun discharged, but thankfully the bullet lodged harmlessly in the ceiling.

Directly behind Ahern's prone body stood Eddie Cooper, a huge grin on his narrow little face as he stared down at his victim. His homemade cosh still rested in his hand, at the ready in case he might need to use it again. I realized now why he'd slipped away and run toward the jail lobby. He must have circled

around the men's cell blocks in order to come up on the lieutenant from the rear.

Good Lord! And to think I'd told the boy his cosh wouldn't be
needed. From now on, I vowed, I never wanted to see Eddie without it!

Jimmy Wolf had been taken by stretcher to the nearest hospital,
while Madame Karpova had been removed to a room, where
she, too, was being examined by a doctor. The rest of us, still shaken
by the ordeal, watched numbly while Sergeant Lewis handcuffed
his former lieutenant, who had regained consciousness and was fixing us all with baleful glares.

As soon as Lewis hauled Ahern to his feet, Captain Gregory approached his old friend. "Frank Ahern," he began, "in addition to
the earlier charges made against you, I'm arresting you for the murders of Dmitry Serkov, Cecil Vere, Darien Moss, and Mrs. Theodora
Reade. You are advised that anything you say will be duly noted
and may be used—"

"Oh, but he didn't kill Moss and Mrs. Reade," I said, breaking in.

Annoyed, Captain Gregory turned to me. "Oh, really. And just
who are you, miss?"

"I'm Sarah Woolson—Madame Karpova's attorney."

"Oh, yes, I remember hearing she had some woman representing her, but I thought it was a joke. Now what are you going on
about? Ahern just admitted Moss was blackmailing him. And we
know he had to get rid of Mrs. Reade because she was a witness to
the murder."

"You have the motives correct, Captain," I said. "But I'm afraid
you have the wrong villain. Lieutenant Ahern paid Cecil Vere to
stab Dmitry Serkov, and then he killed Cecil to keep him from
talking. And of course he attempted to strangle my client in her jail

cell. But he had nothing to do with the Cliff House murder, nor that of Theodora Reade."

Captain Gregory was clearly losing his patience. "Then who the hell did kill Moss and Reade?"

"Actually, the murderer is right here," I said. "Perhaps he'd prefer to tell you what happened. After all, it was his secret he was trying to protect." I turned to the new attorney. "Do you want to tell them, Nicholas?"

Yelena started, then looked up at the young man with frightened eyes. "Nicholas, what is she saying?"

"Nothing, darling," he told her, not taking his eyes off me. "She's talking nonsense."

"I only wish I were," I replied sadly. "Unfortunately, Nicholas, you were responsible for strangling Darien Moss the night of the séance."

"But why?" Robert demanded before Captain Gregory could gather his wits to speak.

"Because Moss had learned something about Nicholas which would have ruined him, and very likely devastated his entire family, as well. Certainly, if it became known, it would have prevented him from ever practicing law in this city, much less running for public office."

All eyes were on Nicholas, whose face had drained of color. "Why are you telling these lies, Miss Woolson?"

I looked at the young man, so tall and handsome, sharp intelligence gleaming in his dark hazel eyes. What a tragedy, I thought, to possess all this talent, only to have his life cut short by the gallows. I sighed. "You know I'm speaking the truth, Nicholas."

"That's ridiculous," he protested. "Why would I kill Moss? I have no ties to my father's construction firm. I've certainly had nothing to do with the new City Hall project."

"Oh, Nicholas," I said wearily. "What Moss learned about you had nothing to do with the new City Hall enterprise and you know it."

"Well then, what did Moss have on him?" Captain Gregory demanded impatiently.

"Wouldn't you rather be the one to tell him?" I asked, but the young man merely glared at me and remained silent. "Very well, then, I suppose I must." I turned to the captain. "I'm afraid Darien Moss discovered that Nicholas has a——" I cleared my throat. Normally, I would never have divulged such a sensitive and personal secret. I strongly believe that some matters are best kept private, and Lord help me, this was certainly one of those times. Yet in the interest of justice, I knew I must go on. "Shall we say, ah, that he has a preference for the company of other young men?"

"He what?" Captain Gregory said, looking confused.

"Sarah!" Robert blurted, his face red with embarrassment. "You're not accusing Mr. Bramwell of being, er, a sodomite."

"Lordy, the bloke's a Mary?" said Eddie, clearly astonished. "Sure don't look like any I've ever seen."

"Nicholas," Yelena asked in a small voice. "This is true?"

"No, of course not." His face was flushed and damp with nervous perspiration.

"How did you come to that remarkable, and extremely unlikely, conclusion?" Captain Gregory cynically demanded.

"For several reasons," I replied. "To begin with, Darien Moss referred to him as 'Janus' that night at the Cliff House. I had totally forgotten about it in all the excitement. When I did remember, I looked the name up in one of my father's books and found that it referred to the Roman god Janus."

"Janus," Robert said thoughtfully. "Wait a minute. Isn't he the god known as the guardian of portals? He's always shown as having two heads, one in front, the other in back."

I nodded. "It was Darien Moss's none-too-subtle reference to Nicholas's two natures, the persona he displayed in public, and his true nature, which he had to guard at all cost."

"You based all this on the fact that Moss called him Janus?" Gregory asked skeptically.

"No, Captain," I said, "There's more. When Robert and I went back to the Cliff House a week or so later, we met Nicholas and some of his friends in the saloon. When Yelena's name came up, Nicholas's friends teased him about their relationship. Among other things, they wanted to know if he'd taken her to meet Nancy yet. There was something about their goading that bothered me. It was obvious they shared some sort of private joke. When I asked my brother Samuel about it, he told me that Nancy's is a popular saloon frequented by gentlemen with, ah, the same tastes as Nicholas's."

"So that's why you were asking me all those bizarre questions," Samuel put in. "I couldn't imagine what—"

Captain Gregory interrupted somewhat testily. "Wait a minute. Even if Bramwell is a—well, what you said, Miss Woolson, that doesn't necessarily make him a murderer."

"No, but the fact that he described Yelena's face when the lightning struck during the séance does. He told me she wore an expression of horror, an expression, I might add, he couldn't possibly have seen from where he was sitting. Only someone on Moss's side of the table could have observed her face at that particular moment. And, of course, that's exactly where Nicholas was standing, behind Moss, whom he had just garroted with the balalaika wire."

"This is ludicrous!" Nicholas exclaimed. "I tell you I had no reason to kill Darien Moss. If I had the—the attributes you described, I hardly would have asked Aldora Radburn to marry me."

"Did you ask her, Nicholas?" I inquired. "Or did your mother push you into it as a means of furthering your career? You went along with the match, intending, no doubt, to continue your own pursuits even after the marriage. Then you began to realize how domineering and forceful Miss Radburn is—perhaps too much like your own mother for comfort. Aldora would likely be the sort of wife to watch her husband's every move, choose his friends, his clothes, even approve his clubs. You saw your plan of carrying on with your private life fading with each passing day. You must have panicked as the wedding loomed closer. Somehow, you had to find a way out of the marriage."

Yelena's face had grown pale. She looked up at Nicholas, her large dark eyes intense. "This is true? This is why you take me out, say you love me? So to break off marriage with other woman?"

"I—" If he was about to protest his innocence, something in her face made him change his mind. "It's true that I'm very fond of you, Yelena," he said, hedging.

"Fond," she spat out. "Fond is not same as love. You tell me fiancée break off wedding because you tell her it is me you love. But you not love me. You love no woman!" Her beautiful eyes filled with tears. "You use me. You want out of marriage, so you use stupid little Russian girl to scare off fiancée."

"Yelena, please," the young man pleaded. "You don't know what you're saying."

She looked up at him through her tears. "Oh, yes, I know. I wonder why you no hold me like other men. No kiss, no hug. I think this strange. But I love you. I tell myself it is because I am so young and when we marry it will change."

Yelena was weeping now, but when Nicholas tried to put his arm around her, she pushed him away. "*Dostatochno!* I even lie for you!" she managed to say between sobs. "At séance, I see you out of seat when lightning strike. I see you rush around table. But I lie when policeman ask what I see. I tell him I see nothing."

"Yelena, please!" Nicholas pleaded, his nervous eyes going to Captain Gregory.

"Miss Karpova," Captain Gregory said. "Do you mean to tell me you actually saw Nicholas Bramwell out of his seat when Darien Moss was killed?"

She nodded. "On other side of table. Then he run back fast to seat." She looked up at Nicholas, who was now perspiring profusely. "At time I think maybe he kill evil man, but I not care because reporter says bad things about Mama. Better he be dead."

"That's enough!" Nicholas shouted. "Don't you see what you're doing to me, Yelena? You said yourself that Moss was evil. They should be thanking me for getting rid of him. He didn't care what he did to people. All he cared about was selling newspapers."

"So you admit you killed Moss?" Captain Gregory said.

"I don't think of it as murder!" There was a wild gleam in his eyes now, like that of a hunted animal who's been cornered and has no place to run. "Darien Moss deserved to die. You must see that. He was a monster! He wanted me to pay him a small fortune to keep my secret—money I had no hope of raising. It would have destroyed me, and killed my mother. He left me no way out."

"Except murder," Robert said, regarding the young man with disdain.

"What about Mrs. Reade?" I asked softly. "Did she also deserve to die?"

A flicker of guilt crossed Bramwell's handsome face. "I didn't want to kill her, but she'd seen me strangle Moss. The only reason she didn't tell the police was that she couldn't believe her own eyes. She was my godmother; she'd known me since I was a baby."

"So, you dressed up as Dmitry Serkov, got out of your supposed sickbed, went to Washington Square, and strangled your own god-mother," I said in a flat voice. "When I first realized you were the killer, I felt genuine sympathy for the impossible situation Darien Moss had placed you in. Now, the only compassion I feel is for your victims, not only Moss and Mrs. Reade but Dmitry Serkov, whom you were willing to see hang for your crimes."

"Serkov." He said the name as if it were of no consequence. "He was nothing but a common criminal. Even you admitted that, Yelena. He had nothing to contribute to society. But my life was just starting. It's like Mother said: I could be governor, maybe even president one day."

Yelena's eyes blazed at him. "Dmitry was thief, yes. But he was only father I know. He take care of me, of Mama. He was not evil. Not like you."

"But don't you see?" Nicholas said, his eyes welling with tears. "I had no choice. Moss would have ruined everything my mother and I had worked so hard to achieve. I couldn't let that happen. You must see that!"

Captain Gregory made a slight motion with his head, and George Lewis walked over to Nicholas Bramwell, quietly cuffing his hands behind his back. Tears streaming down his face, the young lawyer made no attempt to escape the manacles.

All I could read in those striking hazel eyes was the humiliation of defeat. Not guilt or sorrow that he had killed two human beings, but sorrow that he'd been caught. I also read self-pity there. Yes, I thought sadly, a great deal of self-pity.

CHAPTER TWENTY-ONE

To Eddie Cooper's considerable delight, Samuel wrote an article about the boy's skill and bravery in single-handedly bringing down an armed murderer at the city jail. The story made the front page of the *Chronicle,* and included a picture of a beaming Eddie brandishing his beloved cosh. Of course there was no living with the lad for days after the article came out. I suspect he seriously depleted his wages buying up every edition of the paper he could find and handing copies out to anyone who could read.

Lieutenant Ahern and Nicholas Bramwell were arraigned and were being held without bail. Having them safely behind bars did not bring back any of their victims, of course, but I daresay I was not the only one in the city who was sleeping better at night.

Philippa Bramwell took the arrest of her younger son very badly. Naturally, she hired the best defense attorney in San Francisco, and quickly become persona non grata at the jail because of her constant complaints that they were treating her son as if he were a common criminal. To his credit, Edgar Bramwell managed to strike a balance between standing by his son and at the same time holding him accountable for his actions.

Personally, I felt sorry for Cecil Vere's fiancée, Annie Fitzgerald, as well as for the Ahern family. I have always found it unfair that when a family member breaks the law and is placed behind bars, innocent relatives are forever forced to bear that individual's shame and dishonor.

Loyal to the end, Annie Fitzgerald flatly refused to believe that her Cecil could be a murderer, and no one, including Capt. Pete Gregory, could convince her otherwise. I went to visit her shortly after Ahern's arrest, and it was Annie's considered opinion that the lieutenant had blamed the Russki's death on her Cecil in order to save his own neck from the noose. She argued this so vehemently, I wisely decided not to dispute the issue.

As for Nora Ahern, the last I heard was that she eventually planned to move back to the Midwest, where she'd been born and raised and where her family still resided. Perhaps there she would find the loving support she needed to live out the remainder of her life in peace.

On a happier note, shortly after Luther Sechrest's arrest, Alexandra was awarded sole custody of her two boys. Luther was also required by the court to make full financial restitution to Leighton Mining Company and the city of San Francisco for money he'd stolen over the past ten years. Since the Sechrest home would most likely have to be sold to help pay these debts, Alexandra accepted an invitation from her neighbor, Mrs. Jane Hardy, to move in with her until matters were settled. Both women began volunteering their time at Annjenett Fowler's safe house. Along with Annjenett, they were dedicated to bringing the ignominy of spousal abuse out of the bedroom and into community awareness, efforts I whole-heartedly applauded and supported.

The day before Madame Karpova and her daughter, Yelena, were scheduled to leave for Los Angeles, my sister-in-law Celia shyly asked me to accompany her to see the psychic. I think she feared I might consider her foolish, but I assured her that the one thing I had learned over the past month was to keep an open mind.

I couldn't begin to explain Olga Karpova's uncanny predictions, and I'd finally decided that Hamlet was correct when he observed, "There are more things in heaven and earth, Horatio, than are dreamt of in your philosophy."

When we arrived at the Karpova's hotel rooms, we found them a beehive of activity. Two large trunks stood open, filled to near capacity with clothes, shoes, hats, undergarments, and various paraphernalia I presumed were used during the clairvoyant's séances and other performances. While Celia had her private reading with Madame Karpova, I spent a pleasant hour chatting with Yelena as she completed her packing.

Although Nicholas Bramwell's name was not mentioned, I could tell from the girl's downcast eyes and quiet demeanor that she continued to mourn for the dashing, handsome young attorney. Despite his eventual betrayal, Nicholas had provided a strong shoulder to cry on after Dmitry Serkov's death and her mother's arrest. And he'd offered Yelena a world she could only dream of, a world she frequently glimpsed through Madame Karpova's work, but one she'd never expected to be part of.

"Will you continue to tour with your mother?" I asked. "Or do you have other plans in mind?"

Yelena smiled very faintly. "I would like to be teacher. But must make English good. Someday maybe I go to school. Be clever, brave woman like you."

I felt blood rush to my face, pleased and a little embarrassed by such a sincere and heartfelt compliment. "My dear, that would be wonderful. If there is anything I can do to help further your dream, you have only to ask." I opened my reticule and handed her one of my business cards. "You can reach me at this address."

The girl's smile became much brighter, as if she had at last found a new focus for her life. "Thank you, Miss Woolson. I keep card safe. Maybe see you again."

I took one of her dainty hands and gave it a little squeeze. "I hope so, Yelena. I would like that very much."

Celia had come out of Madame Karpova's room fairly glowing with happiness, and she insisted on treating us to a hansom cab for our journey home.

Our carriage had barely left the curb, when she could contain herself no longer. "I saw Sophie, Sarah! I'm convinced Madame Karpova was able to bring her to me." She flushed and looked embarrassed. "I know I sound naïve, and I probably am. But, oh, Sarah, I could actually feel her in my arms."

Sudden tears welled up in her eyes. "Oh, no, not again," she groaned, taking a lace handkerchief from her reticule. "These days, I seem to cry over the least little thing."

"I would hardly call holding your lost child a small thing, Celia," I said, putting my arm around her slender shoulders.

"I don't know how she does it, but Madame Karpova told me things no one else could possibly know. She also insists the new baby will be a boy, and that he'll be healthy and smart, and have a tiny mole on his back, right below his left arm." She sniffed and wiped at the tears rolling down her cheeks. "I feel so silly even talking about it."

"There's no need to feel foolish, Celia. Since meeting Madame Karpova, I've had ample opportunity to wonder about her abilities. The truth is, her predictions are more often right than wrong."

A small frown line appeared between Celia's lovely blue eyes. "Do you think she realized Mr. Serkov was using her readings to blackmail people?"

"She says she didn't know, but . . ." I thought back to my last conversation with Madame Karpova after she was released from jail. When I'd questioned her about Dmitry's habit of eavesdropping at her readings, she swore she'd forbidden him to do it anymore after they'd made their way to London from Russia. "I can't help but wonder if a leopard can so easily change its spots."

"So you believe she condoned his actions and perhaps even

aided him to rob people?" she asked, looking shaken by the idea. "Now that I've met her, I can't imagine her doing anything so despicable. She seems so sensitive, and genuine, and caring."

I gave a soft laugh. "Perhaps she truly is all those things. We'll never really know, will we?" I thought of Madame Karpova's hard life in Russia, her struggle to survive, her love and loyalty to the man who had saved her from a fate very probably worse than death. No, I thought, it is not up to me to judge.

"The only thing I can say for certain, Celia, is, whether she's the real thing or a talented charlatan, Madame Karpova is an amazing woman."

I am delighted to report that earnings from my first two cases as an independent attorney have ensured the solvency of my law office for at least another six months. Robert insists that still qualifies as living from hand to mouth, but I consider it a triumph.

As does my downstairs neighbor, Fanny Goodman, who surprised me with a small but most enjoyable victory party in her millinery shop. Robert, my brother Samuel, and, of course, Eddie were invited, as well as half a dozen adjoining shopkeepers. With a mouthwatering display of homemade pies, cakes, brown Betty, peanut brittle, taffy, and fudge, as well as apple cider, hot chocolate, tea, and coffee to drink, the celebration was judged by all to be an unqualified success!

After most of the guests had departed, including my brother Samuel, I was delighted to receive a letter by afternoon post from Pierce Godfrey. Because of my mother's continued determination to see me settled down with a husband and children, I had asked Pierce to send his letters to my business address, instead of my home. Unfortunately, Robert happened to spy the sender's name on the envelope as I was hastily placing it, unopened, inside my skirt pocket.

"Don't tell me you're actually corresponding with that pirate," he said with a frown. "Where is he anyway?"

"Hong Kong," I replied. "And you know very well that he's a respectable businessman. I told you Pierce was sailing to Hong Kong to open another shipping office, which, by the way, is already showing a profit."

"Good for him," he commented dryly. "I hope he stays there."

I ignored his snide remark. "Actually, he said in his last letter that he planned to be home for the Christmas holidays." For some reason I could not fathom, Robert had taken a profound dislike to Pierce, whom I'd first met during my involvement in the Russian Hill murders. It seemed all the more inexplicable, given that Pierce invariably treated Robert with the utmost civility. "It will be nice to see him again."

He made a face. "I can't wait."

"Oh, really, Robert. Enough is enough! Just what do you have against Pierce Godfrey?"

"Let me see. Where shall I begin? He's cocky and brash and pushy—" He stopped, seemingly having run out of words to describe Pierce's shortcomings.

"Cocky, brash, and pushy," I repeated. "That describes at least half the male population of San Francisco. In fact, those are the very qualities that enabled our city to grow into such a thriving metropolis. I'm sure he would not take that as a—"

We both turned as the door to Fanny's shop flew open and my brother Charles burst into the room.

"It's a boy!" he all but shouted. "He's big and healthy and beautiful and Celia is tired, but they're both doing just fine," he went on without stopping for a breath. "Oh, I almost forgot. Celia wanted me to tell you that the baby has a small mole on his back, just beneath his left arm." His expression turned quizzical. "Although I have no idea why a mole should be important."

I smiled at my brother. "Let's just say that the mole signifies that your new son is going to grow up to be clever and handsome, just like his daddy."

"You base all that on a mole?" Charles looked first at Robert, who seemed just as confused as he was, then back to me. "Sarah, is this some sort of joke?"

"If it is," I told him, "it's a very pleasant one, don't you agree?"

Taking Robert by the arm, I started toward Fanny's kitchen, where she and Eddie were seeing to the last of the dirty dishes.

"Let's help our hostess finish cleaning up, Robert. Then I want to go home and be introduced to my newest nephew."